CAT FLAP

By

Ian Jarvis

Paperback ISBN 978-1-78705-041-9
ePub ISBN 978-1-78705-042-6
PDF ISBN 978-1-78705-043-3

Published in the UK by MX Publishing
335 Princess Park Manor, Royal Drive,
London, N11 3GX
www.mxpublishing.co.uk

Cover design by Brian Belanger

Chapter 1

The Yorkshire Wolds must have hired the wrong publicist. That was Lisa Mirren's private theory. Compared to the Yorkshire Dales and the North York Moors, few tourists have heard of these chalk hills to the east of the county. Unlike the other two celebrated regions, they were never awarded National Park status or classed as an *Area of Outstanding Natural Beauty*. If landscapes were in any way sentient, Lisa decided, the Wolds would definitely feel like the poor relation. The forlorn member of the trio, reminiscent of that other Kennedy brother – JFK, Bobby, and the Chappaquiddick one who never shone politically or got to sleep with Marilyn Monroe. Since her medical career brought her to York, Lisa had fallen in love with the Dales and moors, but she found this gentler terrain almost as beautiful.

The bright sun had little effect upon the temperature – a glacial cold, more suited to a Siberian night than a Saturday afternoon in the English countryside. Standing on a footpath beside a stream, Lisa peered into the hawthorn thicket on the opposite side of the shallow water. Deep inside, one of the five roosting owls blinked drowsily as it watched the girl.

'That's right.' Lisa's excited whisper clouded on the frigid air as she adjusted her camera tripod. 'Just keep looking this way.'

Long-eared owls gather at traditional sites during the winter and she'd discovered this secluded roost on an Internet birdwatching forum. Birdwatching and wildlife photography are mistakenly regarded as masculine pursuits, television and old movies collaborating to typecast any female who strays into the domain as a tweed-clad eccentric. Lisa's striking looks instantly demolished the frumpy stereotype.

'Now don't move.' She brushed a lock of fair hair from the camera viewfinder and fired off two shots. 'Good boy.'

With only seven shopping days remaining before Christmas, most people would be spending their weekend buying gifts in city stores. Lugging camera equipment around the frozen Wolds wasn't on the festive priority list of the average thirty-year-old girl, but Lisa was far from average. Tugging up the collar of her combat jacket against the chill, she turned from the bushes and raised her binoculars to scan the meadows and clumps of woodland beyond the water.

Rippled and undulating like an unmade bed, the landscape rolled away towards the east coast, crisscrossed with drystone walls and the dark skeletons of hedgerows. This was the last place to need a makeover, but the midday sun transformed the frosted panorama into a glitter-dusted Christmas card. Lisa remembered the James Herriot books she'd loved as a child, and the tales of the country vet visiting such places to tend to livestock.

Why hadn't she studied veterinary medicine instead of biochemistry? How wonderful it must be to work somewhere like this instead of her York dermatology lab.

Completing her binocular sweep, the young doctor returned her gaze to the hawthorns and smiled wistfully at a sudden recollection of last Christmas. The candlelit dinner where her ex-fiancé gave the binoculars as a gift didn't seem like a year ago, yet their summer break-up felt so distant. *Time screws with the memory,* she contemplated sadly, *and all things come to an end.*

Lisa sighed and focussed on the roosting owls again as crows exploded raucously from the tops of nearby ash trees. They sat erect, eyes wide and ear tufts raised in alarm. *Excellent!* This was better than the dazed expression owls normally wore during the day. She stooped to the camera, but it didn't show much–just a tail as the last bird bolted, and darkness as someone blocked the lens.

'Huh?'

'Well, Lisa, I can certainly see the attraction of ornithology. Fresh air and beautiful, isolated spots such as this.' Her visitor stepped around the tripod, squinting up at the sun. 'Ah, this amazing sunshine. I honestly can't remember it looking and feeling so good.'

'But I never heard…' A breeze wafted Lisa's face and, despite the warm jacket, her spine frosted over in gooseflesh. 'What are *you* doing here?' She laughed nervously. 'You sneaked up like a cat.

Where did you come from?'

'I always liked you, Lisa. I realise how clichéd it must sound, but this really is nothing personal.'

'What the hell...' A hand shot out, tearing open Lisa's collar and snapping the binocular strap. They fell to the ground as the girl pulled back. 'Those cost a fortune.'

Arterial blood splattered the camera and sprayed the frozen grass. As last words went, Lisa Mirren's killer had heard better examples.

* * * *

Chapter 2

The small city of York was named *Eboracum* by the Romans, but the Vikings christened it *Jorvik,* if indeed Pagans could christen *anything.* The Norse longships were an everyday sight on York's River Ouse before 1066 and little has changed topographically since their reign. The principal thoroughfares of Fossgate, Coppergate, Ousegate, Spurriergate and Gillygate still follow the same winding routes and bear the same Viking names. Elizabethan city walls encircle the centre with fortified barbican towers punctuating their two-mile run like miniature castles, Bootham, Micklegate, Walmgate, and Monk being the largest of these thirteenth-century gateways. John Watson knew quite a bit about this. Not because the boring history of his birthplace interested the teenager in any way, but because his new employer was constantly rambling on about how wonderful and fascinating it all was.

'Oh, come *on.*' The words were whispered through chattering teeth. Watson peered through a dripping camera, his numb hands protecting the lens as he focused on a van by a garage. 'Turn this way again.'

The teenager stood a short way south of the Micklegate barbican, at the end of Saxon Street. A row of honey-coloured houses, the Victorian terrace was built just below the city wall and its grassy embankment. Watson had found a hiding place with a good view of the rear garages, and sleet pelted the ramparts above him, soaking into his jeans and jacket as he sheltered behind shrubbery. Thrills, diversity, adventure – he recalled the various expectations when he answered the jobcentre advert for Bernard Quist's consultant detective agency, but he never anticipated this.

A lean, black youth of nineteen, friends often mentioned Watson's cheeky smile–an insolent smirk, his schoolteachers used to say–but there was no sign of it this Monday morning. The teachers also said: *extremely clever but doesn't try, intelligent and quick-witted but lacks discipline,* and quite frequently in his final year: *I see the smart-mouthed bastard is absent again.*

'Just a couple more shots,' he muttered, zooming in on an overweight man by the van. 'Let's finish this so I can get to a nice warm office.'

With his beer-belly and broken nose, Ronnie Garbutt was hardly photogenic, but Watson's picture of him loading the vehicle with plaster was the tenth taken in the past few minutes. Garbutt wasn't a plasterer; he was a council cleaner. None of his colleagues had actually seen his work-related accident, but it must have been a bad slip. He was supposedly incapable of any manual labour, yet he'd tossed five weighty sacks into the van and never shown a flicker of pain.

Wind whisked an accumulation of sleet from the wall above Watson, half of which landed on the back of his head.

'*Brilliant,*' he hissed. 'How wonderful.'

Yes, his employer loved these historic fortifications, but Watson guessed Bernard Quist had never had to stand beneath them in this kind of weather. The private investigator, or *consultant detective*, as Quist insisted upon being called, had a huge admiration for the ancient city of York, often referring to it as a *splendid medieval jewel*. Watson lived in an area that wasn't *too* splendid and was never mentioned by the Yorkshire tourist board – the Grimpen housing estate. He'd worked as Quist's assistant for the past three weeks and for the most part he'd enjoyed it. The detective work was varied, but hardly exciting, the assignments revolving around gathering divorce evidence, serving papers and tedious surveillance. Watson had grown up on a diet of private eye movies and television shows where the detectives had thrilling adventures that never seemed to involve being bored or piss-wet through.

'That'll do it,' he murmured to himself, lowering his camera as Garbutt vanished inside the garage. Stepping back behind the bushes, he ran a hand through his short black hair and shook off the icy drips. 'Those pictures should be enough.'

Hearing footsteps on the wet pavement to his rear, Watson

moved aside, but instead of passing by, the approaching man marched straight up to him. The glowering face and overalls looked familiar and the youth stiffened, his stomach lurching as realisation dawned–he'd been helping Garbutt yesterday when the first batch of pictures were taken. Watson was five-feet-ten, but the furious character looming above him was six inches taller.

'Nice camera.' The man's growl was reminiscent of a bear with laryngitis. 'What's the idea of photographing my brother? Are you snooping for the council?'

Watson's eyes flickered over the psychotic glare and pumped-up physique. He'd always hated confrontation and aggression. *I'm a lover, not a fighter* was his cheery claim, although past girlfriends would dispute this.

'Your brother?' He cleared his throat. 'No, mate, I was photographing the house with the blue door.' His shaking finger pointed away from Garbutt's. 'I'm an estate agent and we're selling number…'

'What kind of idiot do you think I am?' The man grabbed his canvas jacket and yanked the teenager up onto tiptoes. 'Taking photos of our Ron working on the side when he's supposed to be sick, are you? Give me that camera, you little twat.'

Quickly handing it over, Watson watched fearfully as the casing was opened.

'I'm keeping this.' Garbutt's brother held up the memory chip. 'If I see you again, I'm going to ram this camera up your arse. Do you understand?'

'I understand.' Watson eyed the zoom lens. 'Yeah, absolutely.'

In retrospect, the tedious aspects of his job didn't seem so bad after all. They didn't leave you with rearranged features, your teeth on the floor, or the local hospital being faced with an embarrassing extraction operation.

* * * *

Chapter 3

Revving cars crawled by Patel's newsagent on Fishergate, a morning fanfare of York Minster bells joining with dashboard radio jingles to rouse the yawning commuters. Watson jumped down from a bus outside the shop, called in to buy a newspaper, and watched for a gap in the traffic as he sheltered from the sleet beneath Patel's awning. The twenty-fifth was only a week away and tinsel twinkled with Christmas lights in the window.

'Horrible, isn't it?' squawked a texting girl to his right. Sucking on a cigarette, she stooped to a pushchair, showering her ugly infant in ash as she wiped its dribbling nose. 'Bleedin' horrible.'

Watson sought a diplomatic response, before realising she didn't mean the child, but the *Yorkshire Post* headlines on the shopkeeper's advertising board.

LEEDS UNITED GOAL DISALLOWED, and MURDERED GIRL NAMED.

'Oh, I see.' He turned back to the traffic. 'Yeah, it's certainly horrible.'

'They should hang the bastards.'

Hoping she wasn't referring to the footballers, he spotted a path through the slow-moving vehicles and darted across the road.

Devoid of medieval architecture, this end of Fishergate wasn't the most picturesque part of the city, but office rental was cheaper than the historical centre within the walls. Baker Avenue ran off this main street, with the Brightshield Glazing showroom on the corner and two separate firms above: Bernard Quist's detective agency and Ted Duggan's debt collection company. Watson ducked in from the weather and snatched a letter and postcard from the mail basket.

'Well, look who we have here.'

The teenager knew the gruff voice and cringed to see the biggest of Duggan's collectors descending the stairs. Kevin Selden appeared to have been quarried rather than born. Most people saw the swastika tattoo on the shaven skull and formed an instant dislike, but if they only took the trouble to get to know the man, they'd really loathe him. Moving aside, the teenager dropped his head to avoid eye-contact, meeting instead the baleful gaze of something equally terrifying on the end of Selden's leash. Rottweilers often have macho names – Rambo, Tyson, Conan – and this monster answered to *Klansman*.

'They say it's bad luck to pass people on stairs,' snarled Selden.

'Er, right.' Watson tried squeezing by, but a tattooed arm blocked the way.

'*Very* bad luck if Klansman's hungry.' The skinhead relished these chance meetings. 'What's wrong? In a hurry?'

'Actually, I *am* a bit late.' Watson stiffened as a rumble sounded in the dog's throat.

'Listen, he can smell black meat.' Selden's smile widened, his piggy eyes twinkling. 'When those jaws lock on, you need a crowbar to get him off. Do you want to find out how it feels?'

'Thanks, but no.' Watson had read somewhere that bullies acted this way due to being abused as children. He really hoped this was true here.

'So how's the detective business going? Private detectives? Hah! Some oddball and a wimpy little darkie. Who the hell would hire you two losers?' Selden laughed, his sloping forehead wrinkling. Shaven heads suit some people, but this resembled a medical school cadaver. 'Well, you probably have murders to solve, so I'd better not keep you, eh? See you later.'

Bolting up the stairs as the sniggering thug moved aside, Watson flung open Bernard Quist's door and vanished inside with a relieved sigh.

The agency was small. The only furniture here in the outer office was a desk, vacant due to Quist using an answerphone instead of a receptionist. The machine never demanded a rise, arrived late, or rang in sick; the advantages were numerous, but Watson would have preferred a sexy blonde seated there. He went through into the main office, his mouth falling open to see Quist sitting on his desk with legs tightly folded beneath him.

'There you are at last.' The consultant detective spoke in a clipped English accent. Glancing over the file he was reading, he drew on a cigarette. 'Do we have the photographs?'

'Er, what are you doing, Guv?'

'Yoga.' Quist turned a page. 'I practise every day before you arrive. Don't worry; I'm fully aware that you find me eccentric. Do we have the photographs?'

'Eccentric?' The teenager grinned. 'You're a total weirdo.'

Bernard Quist's own teenage years were a distant memory; a slender man, he stood six-feet tall and looked to be late-forties. Thick, dark hair, tawny eyes and arched eyebrows provided an aristocratic appearance, but his most prominent feature sat in the middle of his face. An academic might have described the nose as *aquiline*, but Watson–with a more limited vocabulary and far less tact–called it *huge* and often pictured his employer perched beside marabou storks.

The youth dumped the camera on the desk. He didn't think Quist would find nose jokes amusing but, in their three weeks together, he'd never seen the detective laugh at anything; the closest he came to smiling being a lopsided mouth-corner movement. The dourness was reflected in his dress, the cord jacket, brown trousers and fawn shirt looking pretty drab next to his assistant's bright trainers, yellow sweatshirt and blue jeans.

'I'm soaked.' Watson draped his blouson over a chair. 'How long are you going to be sitting like that? It's putting me on edge.'

'Deal with it.' Quist winced as the teenager rubbed his curly hair dry on the office curtains. 'Photographs?' he repeated, puffing cigarette smoke. 'Do we have the evidence?'

'Don't ask.'

'I *am* asking.'

'I nearly got beat up by Garbutt's brother.' Watson leant his wiry frame against a radiator. 'He stole the memory chip out of your camera.'

'I must say, you've taken to this work like a duck to pole-vaulting. Let's try something simpler, shall we? There's a hi-fi on the windowsill by the kettle. If you switch them both on, we can have music with the coffee you're about to make.'

'Talking of getting threatened…' Watson checked the CD and tutted. It was *Peer Gynt* by Greg someone or other. 'I bumped into Ted Duggan's pet psychopath out there again.'

'Kevin Selden? That must have been pleasant.'

'It's impossible to look at the twat without thinking of burning crosses and nutters wearing bedsheets. He doesn't exactly get on with good-looking black guys like me.' Watson clicked on the tiny hi-fi and pulled a sour face. 'Don't you have anything apart from this classical crap?'

'There are a couple of Bob Dylan albums in the desk.'

'Oh, whoopee!'

Watson gazed around the room as *Morning Mood* began to play. Shelves of directories and books lined one magnolia-painted wall and a filing cabinet stood opposite. Only one of the drawers held files, the emptiness echoing the fact that Quist had been working here for just six weeks. He spooned coffee into the mugs. As usual, it was decaffeinated and the milk was soya.

'This is the job of a detective's assistant, is it?' he muttered. 'Making coffee? What you need is a secretary.'

Quist snapped the file shut. 'The answerphone suffices. Unfortunately it's incapable of making drinks.' He uncrossed his legs and stood up. 'Perhaps I should send the answerphone to photograph fraudsters too. It couldn't do much worse.'

Watson sneered at the sarcasm. 'Will yesterday's pictures be enough evidence to show the medical board that he lied about his accident?'

'I suppose they'll have to be.'

'Why didn't *you* stop off at Garbutt's on your way to the office?'

'His house is on your morning bus route.'

'Ah, right, and you were too busy rushing in to sit on the desk like Buddha?'

'I came in early to finish the report. They need it before Christmas and the sooner I post it, the sooner we get paid.'

'Post? Oh yeah.' The youth pulled the *Yorkshire Post* along with the card and envelope from his jacket. 'Here's this morning's mail and a newspaper from Patel's.'

Quist flopped into the leather chair behind the desk. 'Mmmh, a doctor from York.' He drew on his cigarette and skimmed over the front page. 'The police have released details of the birdwatcher who was murdered on Saturday. A biochemist named Lisa Mirren, killed near the village of Lamberley in the Wolds. Looking at this photograph, she was a very attractive young lady.'

'Yeah, I saw the picture. I noticed in the shop that it's made headlines in all the national papers.'

'Good Lord! According to this, her throat was torn out.'

'That's right.' Watson brought over the coffee and sat on the edge of the desk. 'Nasty, eh?'

'Quite an understatement. The police are warning that the man they're seeking is dangerous, presumably in case the public haven't already guessed.'

'The tabloids are calling it the *Vale of Death*.'

'I've no doubt,' said Quist, sourly. 'The killer will soon have an enigmatic name too; *Yorkshire Butcher,* or *Wolds Slasher.*' He blew cigarette smoke. 'I assume *Rippers, Doctor Deaths* and *Black Panthers* sell papers, but I shudder to think what the grieving relatives must think.'

'Aren't there laws on smoking in the workplace?' Watson wafted a hand. *At least it was a cigarette. Quist also enjoyed cigars, and there was a ludicrous-looking calabash pipe somewhere in the desk.* 'Do you know I inhale twenty percent of that shit?'

'With today's prices, you must owe me a fortune. Here, you can open our mail.' Quist passed him the letter and picked up the Inverness-postmarked card.

'I bet that's from your pal Larry in Scotland.'

'Astounding deduction.' Quist smiled thinly at the picture of the stag, as though it were a private joke, then turned the card. 'Mmh, Larry spent the past week in the Cairngorm Mountains.'

'Winter up there? *Lovely*!' Watson opened the envelope. 'Oh, here we go again, Guv. It's another reminder asking when you want your double glazing fitted? Isn't it time you told them you're not interested?'

'I've already tried that.' Quist had recently made eye-contact with a salesman from the Brightshield showroom downstairs and mentioned the cold. The man had naturally taken this to mean: *Please replace my windows and relieve me of several thousand pounds*. He finished reading the postcard. 'Larry's calling to see me on his way back from Scotland. That should be sometime today.'

'Your pal wanted a holiday after his move to Oxford and he chose Scotland in December?' Watson heard the familiar tinkle of the detective's ring finger tapping against the coffee mug, something he often did when deep in thought. The ancient signet ring bore the worn initials: RQ. 'He had a Scottish break in October. Not big on variety, is he?'

'I'm going to miss Larry.' Quist sipped his drink and turned to the window as distant wailing grew louder. 'It'll be so different without him here in York.'

'Police sirens,' said Watson, peering out to see patrol cars hurtling past below. 'Something's happening somewhere, Guv.'

'Yes, deduction comes naturally to you,' said Quist. 'We'll make a consultant detective of you yet.'

* * * *

Chapter 4

The police cars that sped by Quist's office had been parked near the Holgate Road railway bridge for three hours when Inspector Katie Bradstreet pulled up behind them. St. Paul's Church stood on her left and a saturated Constable performed pavement sentry duty by a cordon of blue-and-white tape. Buttoning her coat, Katie glowered at the weather as she clambered out; the sleet had turned into freezing rain which beat a dreary tattoo on her short fair hair.

The Inspector nodded a moody greeting to a young man who appeared from the churchyard, although if anyone had a right to moodiness it was Tariq Aslam. Dark curls lay plastered to the Sergeant's head, and his green windcheater looked as if it had spent the day in a pond. The label claimed it was *windproof, waterproof* and *made in China*. Aslam had found only the latter to be true.

'So we have another body?' said Katie. Attractive and slender, she was ten years older than her thirty-year-old Sergeant. She gestured to the plastic evidence pouch he carried containing a red handbag. 'That doesn't match your shoes. I'm assuming it belongs to the victim?'

'Diane Woodall is her name,' said Aslam. He led his superior through the church gate and helped her negotiate the waist-high fence onto the railway banking. 'She's down on the tracks. The Scenes of Crime Officer has finished, so we don't need forensic suits.'

'Speaking of forensics, I've seen the SOCO report on Lisa Mirren and it isn't good. Apart from cat hairs on the body, they found no alien DNA whatsoever at the Wolds crime scene...'

'*Nothing*?' Aslam shook his head. 'Lisa must have struggled with her killer, so how could they tear her throat without leaving trace evidence behind?'

'I wish I knew.' Katie pushed through the leafless bushes and descended the slope beneath the bridge. 'I interviewed Lisa's colleagues this morning, but they didn't give me anything useful. She had no enemies and no boyfriends that they're aware of.'

'Do we know anything yet about the fiancé that Lisa broke up with?'

'The Avon police are checking him out. Did you make any progress in Lamberley before the Superintendent pulled you away?'

'Yes. Ralph Copley owns Black Leys Farm on the outskirts of Lamberley village. He found a Range Rover abandoned in one of his outbuildings. Turns out it was stolen from York on Saturday morning. I have a SOCO working on it.'

'A promising lead at last. The police divers have finished searching that shallow river and there's still no sign of Lisa's binoculars.'

'So there's a good chance the killer has them.'

'Yes, but it's a little odd, wouldn't you say? Our victim went photographing birds, someone killed her and took the binoculars, but left a fortune in camera gear. Then again, this isn't a thief, as such. Muggers don't prowl the countryside and they wouldn't kill to steal; certainly not in such a hideous fashion. I'd say we were looking for a lunatic, or someone who went there intending to murder Lisa. I want to speak to those seven motorcyclists again. I know they were in the village pub when the murder took place, but they may have seen something.' Katie's expression grew darker as she reached the tracks and saw the white tent erected over the closest of the four lines. 'This is Diane Woodall, you say?'

'Yes.' Aslam opened the flap of the shelter. 'Twenty-eight years old.'

'Good God!' whispered Katie. Diane lay face-down on the line. Chest-down was more accurate, for her neck terminated in a grisly scarlet mess. 'I assume a train did this?'

Aslam nodded. 'The seven-fifteen commuter this morning. These two lines are still closed, but the far two are moving slowly now under caution.' He left the tent and gestured to a huddle of police further down the track. 'Her head is over here.'

'Morning, Ma'am,' said Katie's Detective Constable. Turning from the forensic team, the ginger-haired Martin Gregson tugged aside a tarpaulin for the approaching officers. 'The train bounced it along and it isn't pretty.'

Katie had to agree. Diane Woodall stared up from the gravel, one eye hanging from its socket and her nose spread across lacerated cheeks.

'Life is definitely extinct, Katie,' said an elderly bearded man, pushing through the wet congregation. 'I think I've established the cause of death.'

'Decapitation?' sighed Katie.

'Good Heavens! Have you had medical training?' Jay Mortimer's humour had developed over the years to combat the horrors of his pathologist job. 'Yes, almost certainly decapitation; it usually does the trick.'

'I take it the blood has been washed away?' asked Katie.

'Ah, you've noticed the rain.' Mortimer rustled his saturated anorak. 'Yes, I'm afraid this weather is perfect for destroying evidence.'

'We have a statement from the train driver,' said Aslam. 'He looked up from his controls and there she was, lying in front of him. There are no signs of struggle or foul play and all the footprints belong to Diane.'

Constable Gregson opened his notebook. 'Her address on Southmoor Road is just around the corner from Holgate Bridge. This is the closest stretch of line where she could...'

'Suicide,' said Katie. 'So why was our team called to this when we're on the Lisa Mirren investigation?'

'This was in her purse.' Aslam passed her an evidence-bagged payslip.

'Ebor Pharmaceuticals?' said the Inspector, raising an eyebrow. 'Ah!'

'Diane was a researcher at Lisa Mirren's lab,' said the Sergeant. 'I thought you'd been told. That's why the Super' called me away from Lamberley.'

'I see.' Katie frowned contemplatively at the bag he carried. 'I wonder why she brought that? Who takes their handbag when they go to commit suicide?'

* * * *

Chapter 5

By mid-afternoon the band of dismal weather had left Yorkshire, but gunmetal rainclouds were still unloading themselves three-hundred miles to the south in Devon. Despite the downpour, Rex Grant wore expensive mirrored sunglasses as he sat in his car at Lympstone Commando on the Exe estuary. He gripped the wheel tightly, unconsciously digging nails into the leather as he waited by the gatehouse for the exit barrier to be raised.

Twenty-five-years-old, Rex had always been popular with certain types of beautiful female and this wasn't entirely due to his wealth. Blue eyes, short black hair and a toned physique placed him in the young Tom Cruise division when it came to looks and sex appeal, but his current expression was suicidal and the sunglasses concealed the redness of weeping. Fighting back a sob, he glanced in the mirror at the Royal Marines Training Centre behind him. Lympstone Commando had been the focus of his dreams for the past ten months, but he now wished he'd never heard of the place.

The first day of the Potential Officer's Course–the gruelling selection process that has to be completed before the Admiralty will consider a commission–hadn't gone entirely to plan. Press-ups, pull-ups and sit-ups had filled the morning and, following a bolted meal, Rex had been sprinted back onto the fitness field for the assault course and regurgitation. No, the first day wasn't at all what he'd imagined, especially the interview he'd just had with the recruitment officer.

A Corporal appeared from the gatehouse and ran an envious eye over Grant's black F50. Ferraris are normally red, but excessive wealth liberates people from the confines of normality and REX 1G resembled a bulimic Batmobile. Rex had never been conventional, but friends had noticed new eccentricities over recent months. Black clothing had taken over his designer wardrobe, although the outlets he frequented never used the word *black*. Just as the car paint was *Nero Daytona*, his leather jackets were *Midnight Panther*, his jeans *Ebony Graphite*, shoes and trainers *November Sable,* and sweaters *Evening*

Charcoal.

The Corporal smirked as he raised the barrier; the new clothes coupled with the Armani shades, gave Rex the bizarre appearance of a Sicilian hitman. Word of his being here had travelled around camp and the soldier recognised him; the Ferrari was a bit of a giveaway. Thanks to his family wealth and the company he kept, Rex enjoyed a certain amount of celebrity status. He was occasionally photographed leaving clubs with other pointless celebrities: ex-girlfriends of footballers, and models who slept with people and sold their stories to tabloids.

'Sorry to hear they turned you down, mate,' said the Corporal, trying not to laugh. 'Still, with that all-in-black look, you can always get a job as a ninja or something.'

Rex groped for a witty reply and came up with a surly 'Fuck off!' before accelerating out onto Exmouth Road. 'This can't be happening to me,' he groaned. He'd been trying his brother's telephone number every few minutes and thumbed the redial on his mobile. 'I don't believe this.'

'Hi, this is Raoul Grant,' announced the voice mail. 'I'm sorry I'm not in...'

'Where the hell is he?' Rex tossed the phone onto the passenger seat and thought again about his predicament. *Those idiots had kicked him off the selection course. He'd been rejected*! What were the words that imbecilic Captain used?

From the macho ramblings on your application and the observations of my officers, it appears you're living some Walter Mitty secret agent fantasy. Far too imaginative and not the sort of material we're seeking.

'I can't believe this.' Heading north for Exeter, Rex lit a cigarette and gave a bitter laugh. 'Walter Mitty? What was he talking about?'

This was a nightmare. What was he going to tell all those friends who wished him good luck at his party two days ago? He stifled another rising sob. Even his father would have expected him to last longer than this. After all the arguments over him joining the Marines, he could imagine what the old man would say when he heard the news. Thankfully, his parents were in America until Christmas Eve, but the twenty-fourth was less than a week away. *What the hell was he going to do*?

He snatched the phone and scrolled the contacts to a Marlborough number.

'Grant Homes.' The girl's polished tone spoke of expensive handbags and older, married boyfriends. 'How can I help?'

'I'm trying to reach Raoul.'

'I'm afraid Mister Grant isn't here at...'

'If I wanted that, I'd ring his mobile again. It's switched off. Where is he? This is his brother and it's important.'

'Mister Grant has been at the police station in Bath for most of the afternoon.'

'Police station? What time will he be back?'

'He's going straight from there to a Mister Mirren's house. I understand he recently lost his daughter. It was quite tragic.'

'Lisa Mirren is *dead*?' gasped Rex. 'Er, right. Look, if you see him, just tell him to call me, okay? Tell him to ring Rex.'

He thumbed off the phone. *Good God! His brother's ex-fiancé was dead*? The shock and disbelief lasted for almost five seconds before Rex sank back into his miserable abyss of self-pity.

* * * *

Chapter 6

Katie Bradstreet had spent most of her morning interviewing Lisa Mirren's colleagues at Ebor Pharmaceuticals and hadn't expected to return so quickly. A modern two-storey building, flanked by similar looking offices and companies, the York laboratory complex stood behind a conifer screen on Jefferson Road on the eastern outskirts of York. The detective Inspector sat at a table, watching the rain stream down the cafeteria windows, as her Sergeant spoke to a middle-aged man in a blue suit and two female doctors sitting opposite. The Minster rose beyond the conifers like some huge ethereal wedding cake. The largest Gothic cathedral in Europe, there were few places in the city where it wasn't possible to see the spectacular twin western towers soaring two-hundred feet above the rooftops.

'So basically,' said Tariq Aslam, 'you don't know of any reason why your colleague would take her own life?'

The more striking of the girls ran a hand through her long dark hair and tutted, her manner suggesting she'd answered enough questions. She checked the clock and rolled her eyes; this would make her late.

Will Gillette shook his head. Huge spectacles gave the slender research director the appearance of a startled owl. 'I'm sure Di would have come to me if anything at work was troubling her. She seemed happy and had no problems at home that I'm aware of.' He gestured to the doctor who'd tutted. 'Would you agree, Becca?'

Both girls were in their late twenties and wore white laboratory coats over blouses and jeans. Their identity badges read Amy Clarkson and Becca Travis.

'I've been here a year,' said Becca. 'I knew Di better than Amy, but God knows why she'd kill herself.'

'You were interviewed this morning,' said Aslam. 'You told my superior here that you both worked with Lisa Mirren. It now turns out that Diane Woodall was part of your team too.'

'You don't suppose there's a connection between Di's suicide and Lisa's murder?' asked Gillette.

Katie turned from the windows. 'We haven't ruled that out,' she said. 'Why didn't you mention this earlier? With one of your team dead, didn't you think it worth telling us that another was missing?'

'She wasn't missing.' Gillette shrugged. 'This is Di's week off.'

'Really?' The Inspector glared. 'She's certainly missing now, isn't she?'

'I still can't believe it,' said Becca, excitedly. 'Four of us worked together in South Lab. Within three days, two are dead. It's so deliciously creepy. I can't wait to tell everyone at the wine bar.'

Katie regarded her dourly. 'What exactly did Lisa and Diane do here? I know it's a medical lab, but what...'

'It's a dermatological research laboratory,' said Gillette.

Amy cleared her throat. 'When patents expire, we buy creams and lotions and develop them into better, safer products,' she explained. 'Pharmaceutical and beauty products; anything to do with the skin and eyes.'

Katie nodded. 'What was Diane working on prior to her death?'

'Two wrinkle creams and a moisturiser,' said Gillette.

'And the Solstice...' began Amy.

'I'll give you a list,' broke in the director. 'Mascaras, lipsticks, creams–it's all pretty mundane stuff.'

'I noticed earlier that you have no animals here,' said Katie.

'No, we don't conduct testing,' said Amy. 'Everything is sent to test centres.'

'Places with security to keep out the animal-rights lunatics,' added Becca.

'My ex would say they have a point,' said Katie, snorting. 'He's a Friend of the Earth.' She left out that he'd also been a good friend of his female gym instructor.

'Ah.' Gillette looked up as a red-haired girl in a turtleneck sweater and pencil skirt arrived at the table. 'Miss Patterson?'

'Sorry, Doctor.' The secretary smiled. 'You have a phone call. Shall I say you're busy? Er, the gentleman claimed it was important.'

'Take your call.' Katie climbed to her feet. 'We have everything we need for now. One last thing–Diane's gold bracelet.'

'That tacky Indian thing?' Becca pulled a face. 'Her name is etched on it in Sanskrit. What about it?'

'It's missing. Perhaps she lent it to someone here?'

'I wouldn't think so,' said Amy. 'She wore it everywhere.'

'Mmh, that's what her father told us.' Katie followed Aslam into the corridor and ran an eye over his red-haired secretary. 'Miss Patterson, wasn't it? I presume someone interviewed you earlier about Lisa Mirren? Did you know Diane Woodall?'

The secretary shrugged apologetically. 'I didn't know either of them; I only started this week.'

'Nicole is a temp,' explained Gillette, leading the way into the lobby. 'My usual assistant is sick.' He studied her through his huge glasses. 'Speaking of which, young lady, you look rather pale.'

'A cold.' Nicole coughed into her fist. 'It must be this weather.'

'You don't say.' Katie scowled at the rain through the glass doors and turned to the director. 'Have you informed the owner of the company about all this yet?'

Gillette gave an uncomfortable smile. 'Doctor Stapleton has been skiing in Canada for the past week...'

'And seems to be temporarily out of contact. Yes, you said this morning.' She pushed open the door. 'Goodbye for now then. We'll be in touch.'

'Doctor...' began Nicole.

Ignoring her, the director watched the police leave, then rushed to his office and lifted the phone.

'Ah, at last, Will. Being kept waiting is a new experience for me. The report was due last night, as you know.'

Gillette had been expecting this, but stifled a whimper. The voice on the line was purring and cold; the exotic accent difficult to pin down.

'Er, the police were here, Mister Silva.' He turned white, a trip to the bathroom suddenly seeming like a good idea. 'Two researchers are dead. One was murdered...'

'You put in progress reports to Stapleton, and Stapleton puts in reports to me. I'd say that was straightforward, but perhaps I'm mistaken?'

'Are you aware that Stapleton has vanished?' Gillette's voice quavered. 'I've been ringing the house and mobile, but there's no reply.'

'Seeing as I haven't received a report, perhaps you'd care to furnish one now?'

'Well... there hasn't been much progress and what with this, er disappearance...' The director gulped as the line went dead, his shaky hand replacing the receiver. 'Jesus! What am I doing?' he croaked. 'What the hell am I doing?'

* * * *

Once the main route from York to Scotland, the A19 runs north from the barbican gate of Bootham and changes its name to Shipton Road as it passes through the suburb of Clifton. A peaceful cul-de-sac of Victorian architecture and mature trees, Minster Avenue ran off this busy thoroughfare and Katie Bradstreet stood with Aslam and Gregson in one of the dark gardens. Stately developments like this began emerging after the seventeenth century, when York flexed its muscles and pushed outwards beyond the confines of its walls and fortifications. The movement was initiated by the aristocrats and wealthy merchants, who were offended by the ubiquitous stench of plague, dead bodies and shit.

'Very nice,' said Gregson, noticing his police colleague's interest in the cycle parked by the house. 'Is it American?'

'Yes, a Harley Davidson,' said Aslam. The Sergeant noticed an inflatable sex doll on top of the lawn Christmas tree, as Katie rang the bell. 'It's an Electra Glide.'

A girl opened the door. A very attractive girl, thought Aslam, smiling at the denim-clad legs, her shoulder-length blonde hair, and the glimpse of breasts before she closed her shirt.

'Oh, hello again,' she said. 'What can I do for you?' She looked the trio over with vivid green eyes and smiled mischievously. 'Are you carol singing?'

'Not tonight.' Katie showed her warrant card. 'We'd like to speak to Peter Hatton again.'

'Ah!' She folded her arms and leant on the jamb. 'You mean Creeper. No one calls him Peter.'

A naked creature loomed behind her, a cross between a long-haired Rocky Marciano and an actual pile of rocks. 'What's the problem, Fran?' he grunted. 'What do these twats want?'

'They want to see you again,' said Fran.

The monster snarled. 'I thought I could smell filth.'

Katie held up her identification on the chance Creeper could read. 'As you know, we're investigating the death near Lamberley,' she said. 'Seven motorcyclists, including you two, were in the village that afternoon.'

'Your memory can't be up to much, Sweetheart,' snorted Creeper. 'We've already been interviewed, and I reckon you must have spoken to the pub landlord?'

'Yeah,' said Gregson. 'But the thing is...'

'So he must've confirmed what we said and told you what time we went in his pub and what time we left. That means we're in the clear. End of story.'

Fran shrugged apologetically as Creeper shoved her down the passage.

'Mister Hatton,' said Gregson. 'We have to speak to you again to eliminate...'

The naked man spat on the stoop and slammed the door.

'Well...' Katie sighed and stepped back as Aslam hammered on the woodwork. 'I can see this is going to be fun.'

* * * *

Chapter 7

Like many lounge pianists, Craig Sinclair played even the slowest melody at half-speed and was well into his latest piece before anyone in the cocktail bar recognised *White Christmas*. The song fills people with festive warmth, but it was doing very little tonight for the drunk by the window. Nearby tables eyed Rex Grant warily. Slumped on a couch in his sunglasses and jet-black attire, he resembled a jewel thief from a corny movie.

'Merry Christmas,' he slurred, attempting to bring the pianist into focus. Swigging back another scotch, Rex pushed the shades up his nose to hide the redness and wondered whether to try calling his brother again. 'What's the point?' he muttered. He was sick of hearing the answerphone and Raoul's mobile was still switched off. This hotel in Bath was close to Raoul's Wiltshire home and he'd ring again in the morning. 'He doesn't care. No one cares.'

Staring miserably out of the window, he spotted a billboard advertisement down the street. '*Brilliant*!' he groaned.

The *Grant Homes* logo was all he needed to end the day; a little reminder of the joys awaiting him once his father Lionel returned from his American trip.

Lionel and Rupert Grant built their first housing estate in Cheltenham and soon had developments outside many southern towns. Rupert had no children and it was assumed that Lionel's sons Rex and Raoul would eventually head the company. Assumed by everyone except Rex, who enjoyed his huge allowance, but not the idea of running a building firm with his brother.

Rex had prolonged Cambridge as long as possible, blowing his cash on drink and girls, regularly appearing in tabloids with minor celebrities, and fuelling his vivid imagination with martial arts and executive wargames, the sort that supposedly build managerial skills. His plan had been to continue the playboy life, drinking, shagging, and shooting salesmen with paint, until one evening six months ago when everything changed. Destinies are shaped by bizarre events–

spiders in caves, falling apples, guys getting nailed to crosses–and with Rex it was a documentary about the eighties.

Britain had been in a dire state in 1980, with strikes, terrorists, and Thatcher becoming Prime Minister, her arrival delighting the population in the same way that a ferret delights a rabbit warren. A tonic was needed and it arrived when soldiers stormed the Arab-held Iranian embassy in London. The hostage liberation took minutes, but the legend would last decades. Along with stately homes, a Royal family and a colossal national debt, the proud British realised they also had the Special Air Service, one of the world's deadliest fighting forces.

Even if the SAS had been cocaine-snorting celebrities with weird sexual tastes, the tabloids couldn't have screwed more mileage from them. Over the months they were turned into superheroes. *These faceless supermen can silently kill with their hands in a hundred ways. Each is trained to surgeon standards and appendectomies are performed on one another in the field without anaesthetic. Surviving on worms and seawater, they're dropped from fifty miles up wearing nine-hundred kilos of hi-tech equipment. on landing, they run sixty miles and...*

Some people, like Rex, believed it all. This was the sensational life he was born for and, the moment the documentary ended, he adjusted the bulge in his jeans and made up his mind. The family building company could go screw itself, because the armed forces were about to get a debonair new Captain.

Choosing the right service had been the first step. The RAF and the Navy seldom abseiled through windows waving guns, which narrowed the field to the SAS and the Royal Marines. A call to the careers office narrowed it further still. The SAS only recruited from within the forces, which meant serving with some boring regiment before getting down to the real action in a sexy black outfit. This was no good to a man whose heart was set on tossing grenades into terrorist strongholds by Christmas, but there was no way around it.

Applications were completed and the Marines offered him a

place on their Potential Officer Course. Rex knew exactly what they were looking for: someone cool and dashing, who could leap through windows, throw knives and shoot from the hip. Training for the course was arduous–diving about on Hampstead Heath and watching Hollywood action movies–but quick-draws with the paintball gun hadn't felt right, and he'd bought something more realistic from an Asian gentleman in a pub toilet. The Walther PPK lay hidden in the Ferrari at the moment, but he normally carried it in the rear waistband of his jeans. Casually allowing the butt to be glimpsed in wine bars drew satisfying gasps from the type of women he dated.

Rex's father had exploded on hearing his plans, but eventually agreed that if Rex could make it as a military officer, then he'd accept his choice, otherwise he'd begin helping his brother at Grant Homes and finally start to earn his allowance. Rex had thrown a party to celebrate his new life on Saturday, before motoring to Lympstone the following day filled with exhilaration. It was now seven-thirty on Monday and the elation was long gone. *How could things go so wrong in one short day?* Failed candidates could return after twelve months to try again, but the maximum age was twenty-five and next year Rex would be too old.

'Merry Christmas!' he grunted, listening to the James Bond tune. *Where was the 007 music coming from?* Rex scanned the room drunkenly, then realised it was his mobile ringtone. 'Hello,' he slurred. 'You're through to a complete failure.'

'Are you okay.' Raoul Grant sounded worried. 'I've just found dozens of missed calls. What's happened? Are you at Lympstone?'

'Lympstone?' Rex laughed manically. 'The bastards said I was living in a fantasy. They said I wasn't the material they were looking for.'

'I might have known. What the hell did I say to you?'

'I don't know. What the hell *did* you say to me?'

His brother sighed bitterly. 'All that nonsense with the black clothes and wearing sunglasses all the time.'

'I had to get into the part.' Rex adjusted the shades. 'Lots of people apply, but they don't take just *any* arsehole. You have to make an impression on the selection staff and look the part of a special forces officer.'

'Yeah, well you obviously made an impression. For God's sake, you never listen to anyone, do you?' Raoul hesitated. 'Do you know about Lisa? Have you heard what's happened?'

'Some girl at your office told me.' Rex let out a sob. 'I'm exactly what they need and I've been training for months. How could they turn me down?'

'I don't need this right now,' snapped Raoul. 'I'll speak to you tomorrow when you're sober. God knows, I need a drink myself. I'll meet you in the village pub at noon. Pull yourself together and get some sleep.'

The line went dead, the lounge pianist's laborious music filling the silence.

'Yeah, goodnight,' muttered Rex. He shook his head and wished he hadn't as blurred walls rotated and his stomach lurched. 'He doesn't care. No one cares.'

* * * *

Chapter 8

Bernard Quist wore a dark, calf-length leather coat over his jacket. Sitar music and a fruity curry aroma drifted from Patel's shop behind him as he sheltered beneath the awning and flicked through the evening edition of the *Yorkshire Post* in the window light. He was aware of how the Wolds murder victim had died from the morning paper, but frowned apprehensively as he read it again. There are many ways to dispose of people, but not being the most ingenious of souls, killers usually resort to strangling, stabbing, or beating the poor sods to death. Tearing someone's throat out by hand was a real novelty.

'I wonder...' mumbled the consultant detective. He shook his head. *No, forget it*! This wasn't his problem. Whoever the unfortunate girl was, it was no concern of his.

A woman entered the shop and gave him a smile, which he returned. Despite the prominent nose, Quist was an attractive middle-aged man. Some girls had claimed the nose looked distinguished and made him stand out, and he suspected his new assistant would agree. Knowing Watson's humour, he'd certainly say it *stood out*. Quist had an inexplicable charisma which often drew females to him, although it had been some time since he'd had a real relationship. Relationships were difficult.

He returned to the newspaper front page. According to the report, the murder victim Lisa Mirren was single and had moved to York from Wiltshire to work as a chemist at Ebor Pharmaceuticals, a dermatological laboratory here. *Why did this murder intrigue him so much?* Taking a deep breath and folding his newspaper, he looked across the street at the city walls rising behind the pubs and shops. He knew why. It was the way in which this girl had been killed.

Illuminated by spotlights and looming high above their embankments, the limestone ramparts of York were the most complete medieval fortifications in Britain. Most people would find it impossible to believe that, back in the eighteen-hundreds, they were scheduled to be torn down to solve the perceived problem of horse-drawn congestion. Quist wondered what those Victorians would think of the traffic today. The artist Will Etty led the preservation campaign and had the stone-flagged path constructed alongside the top of the walls which allowed people to navigate the circuit and enjoy their beauty. The detective had completed the walk countless times to marvel at the city views. He turned at the sound of approaching footsteps, his thoughts of architectural grandeur instantly vanishing.

Selden from the debt collection agency walked past with his bullock-like Rottweiler, smirking at Quist and spitting on the pavement as he passed the newsagent's door. Knowing this skinhead would rather drink bleach than frequent a shop owned by Asians, the detective made a shrewd guess that Selden's agency didn't bother with Equality & Diversity training for its staff. He noticed how the man had developed the insolent swagger peculiar to people with large muscles and small IQs. His dog had a similar gait, but at least Klansman could blame it on selective breeding.

Stowing the newspaper in his leather overcoat, Quist hurried through the rain to his old Volkswagen Beetle with its canvas roof.

'Mister Quist?' enquired a lisping voice. 'Bernard Quist?'

He turned from the car to see a stranger approaching.

'I'm Carl Dreyer of Brightshield Glazing.' The man held out his hand. 'I'm manager of the central Yorkshire office in Leeds.' An aura of smarmy crookedness is common to many salesmen, but this creature had been practising. 'I control the York branch below your agency.'

Quist eyed the slender moustache, designer suit and Omega watch, then reached for the clammy hand. Shaking felt like sexual foreplay with a haddock.

'As you know, we're replacing your office windows.' Dreyer steered him back under the awning, his green eyes and grinning teeth sparkling in the shop lights. 'The good news is we have several Christmas offers and if we glaze your home at the same time...'

'I'm afraid you're misinformed,' broke in Quist. 'I don't need any windows.'

'We pay your VAT and if you sign tonight...'

'My house is double-glazed.' Quist gave a lopsided grin. 'And the office is fine. You mean to tell me you came from Leeds to see me?'

'But you spoke to John Wynn in our branch here.'

'A misunderstanding; I don't want any. Look it's raining and...'

'I wonder if I could explain?' Dreyer gazed into his eyes. 'It's delicate and I shouldn't be telling you, but John was recently treated for paranoiac depression. The treatment wasn't entirely successful and any rejection could push him over the edge.'

Quist peered back incredulously.

'If you rescind your agreement, John could easily do something silly.' The sales manager slid out an order form. 'I know you don't want a suicide on your conscience, so if you just sign and give him the sale he needs...'

'I'm sorry, but it sounds like your salesman should be back in medical care. Now if you'll excuse me?'

It didn't work. Dreyer moved aside, his jaw falling as Quist climbed into the blue Beetle and drove away. *It didn't work - but that was impossible! How the hell could it not work?*

* * * *

Kevin Selden opened the door of his Subaru car, allowing his dog to clamber onto the mess of Right Wing booklets and baseball bats on the back seat. The debt collector always carried a bat when visiting clients, but rarely used it; his forehead was much harder. Ted Duggan's debt company used a simple system; so simple, even Selden understood it. The more he battered from clients, the more he earned, and after a satisfying afternoon spent terrorising York, the skinhead was ready for a well-earned gallon at the Stormtrooper.

Selden's brother Barry opened the Stormtrooper public house in May, dressing his Aryan barmaids in SS uniforms and decorating throughout with Third Reich memorabilia. It had quickly become popular with a certain clientele. The Acomb residents resented a Nazi theme pub on their doorstep and had tried everything to get the place closed, so far only managing to get the swastika flags removed from outside. Barry argued that this was against his human rights, and that the protests were anti-German and therefore racist. Politically correct councillors had been feebly debating the point for three months. Kevin Selden hoped to retire from the rat race one day and run a similar pub himself. The rat race wouldn't miss him; most people who met Selden concluded he'd already retired from the human race.

The Rottweiler stiffened and growled in the back seat, glaring at a black car that had pulled up behind Selden's Subaru. The debt collector scowled as the driver's window sank.

'Excuse me,' purred a voice. 'Kevin Selden?'

'Why?' he grunted. 'You lookin' for trouble?'

Klansman whimpered and began to tremble.

'Oh, I don't think so.' Lisa Mirren's murderer leant out. 'I wonder if we could have a chat?'

'A chat, eh?' A leer wrinkled the swastika on Selden's brow. 'I don't see why not.'

* * * *

'It didn't work?' Frederick Tayman, the head of Brightshield Glazing in Liverpool, hissed down the telephone. 'What do you mean, it didn't work?'

'I can't explain, Sir.' Carl Dreyer sat in his car outside the York office. Sweat streamed down the Leeds manager's face as he pressed the mobile to his ear. 'He just pushed past and drove away.'

'Don't be ridiculous. How could he?'

'I er... don't know.'

Six seconds of icy silence followed. 'I take it this is the first time you've failed?'

'Of course, Sir.'

'Dreyer, I really don't need this; you know the kind of pressure I'm under at the moment. What was his name again?'

'Bernard Quist. He's a private investigator with an office above our York showroom.'

'And his home address?'

'I don't know yet. I've been checking, but no one seems to know much about him. I intend to follow him, find out who he is and...'

'Find out what you want,' snarled Tayman. 'But find out why you failed.'

* * * *

Chapter 9

Bernard Quist burst from the undergrowth and sprinted down an incline, dodging trees, to where a wide stream weaved through the wooded valley. Rich scents of wet earth and vegetation hung on the still air and a tawny owl called eerily overhead. The shard of crescent moon supplied little illumination, but Quist possessed excellent night-vision. Anyone else stupid enough to run through a wood in these conditions would have ended up in hospital with their face resembling an inept boxer.

Springing over the water and up the opposite banking, he leapt the fence into the meadow beyond where sheep scurried in a woolly turmoil of frantic bleating. The detective paused, lightly panting, to gaze meditatively at York some five miles to the east. The Minster rose above the rooftops, basked in a golden glow of floodlights, and a distant church bell tolled forlornly. Over the years, Quist had moved around, living quietly in many towns, but York was definitely one of his better choices. This ancient city had been his home for the past two years and he was still entranced by its enigmatic beauty. York rivalled most European capitals for bygone splendour, and every twist and turn in the medieval streets brought him face-to-face with antiquity: a Tudor inn, a Viking wall, a half-timbered Elizabethan building, or a Roman turret. A stroll through York was a stroll through the pages of history.

His thoughts turned once again to the way in which the Wolds girl had died. *Her throat had been torn out.* Quist pictured the horror, narrowing his eyes warily. Shaking himself, he jumped a wall and covered the last six-hundred yards to his isolated house. *No, just forget about it*! The murder had nothing whatsoever to do with him.

Briar Cottage on the outskirts of Askham Richard village was straight from an Enid Blyton story - the sort of thing seen on the lids of biscuit tins. Roses cascaded over a porch, a small orchard spread from the wisteria-covered gable, and a walled garden stretched into the rear meadow. Quist cleared the ivy-clad brickwork and leapt down onto the lawn beyond. He landed on all-fours and stiffened, his senses telling him he wasn't alone.

A chuckle sounded in the darkness. 'Still keeping yourself in shape, I see?'

'Larry?' The detective gasped his relief. 'For a moment...'

'You take your time on your runs. The taxi dropped me here ages ago.' The old man rose from the garden bench. 'I'd give you a hug,' he laughed, 'only...' He gestured to his friend's appearance.

'I see what you mean.' Quist shook himself, showering the grass with sweat. 'Come on in and make yourself at home while I change.'

* * * *

'Your postcard arrived this morning,' shouted Quist. 'Have you eaten?'

Taking an ice bucket from the kitchen freezer, he tightened his dressing gown and returned to the lounge. Paintings and bric-a-brac filled the room, a grandfather clock ticked in the corner and logs crackled in the grate of a black-leaded range.

'I ate on the train,' said Larry Reynolds, turning from studying a bookcase, one of the many antiques in the old cottage. 'In any case, you're still on the vegan diet. Still doing yoga too, I expect?'

'I remember when you were the same - plain food and yoga every day.'

'Fortunately I don't need to bother anymore.'

Quist smiled. It was probably just as well, because it was hard to picture this old, white-haired gentleman standing on his head in yoga meditation. He ran his eyes over the frail frame beneath the tweed jacket. It was hard enough picturing him climbing stairs.

'Impressive collection.' Larry stroked his snowy moustache and fingered a leather spine in the bookcase. Most of the volumes were devoted to anthropology, history and mythology. 'I see there are a few of yours here. I read this one again recently.' He slid out a book on the Egyptian city of Amarna.

'A knowledge of history is essential for an antique dealer,' said Quist. 'But, to be honest, I can't see my old writings being of much help to you. My controversial theories on why Amarna was abandoned and lost beneath the desert for over a thousand years.'

'Controversial,' agreed Larry, 'but we both know you were correct.' He moved to a painting below the open staircase. 'Is that a real Turner? I haven't seen it in here before.'

'It's just a print I picked up. If you're silly enough to hang the genuine article on your wall, people ask questions.'

'I remember when you had some *really* nice stuff.' The old man smiled at his friend. 'You donated everything to public collections, didn't you? No regrets?'

'Possessions don't amount to much.'

'By the way, we're not very festive, are we?' Larry looked around. 'You don't have a Christmas tree or anything.'

'It's a long time since I celebrated Christmas.' The detective took a deep breath. 'Anyway, did you enjoy your Scottish break?'

'Enjoy it? I certainly *needed* it after all the upheaval with the move and the sale of the business.'

'I hear your old shop reopens in two weeks. It'll be a bookshop.'

'Yet another bookshop in York.' Larry laughed. 'Just what you need.'

'I'll miss Reynolds Antiques on Micklegate.'

'Well... you know how it is.'

'Will you still be calling yourself Reynolds in Oxford?'

'Yes. Come to think of it, isn't it about time *you* had a name change?'

'Not for a few more years.' Quist examined his signet ring, then opened a cupboard and brought out a bottle of Askaig malt and a cedar box of cigars.

'Now you're talking.' Larry's moustache twitched enthusiastically. He took a cigar and clipped the cap with a guillotine from the box. 'Cohiba – excellent!'

'Your postcard didn't say, but I presume you're not travelling to Oxford tonight?' Quist dropped ice into two glasses and poured the whisky.

'No, tomorrow on the three o'clock train. I wanted to see you, Bernie. With the move and everything I never really got the chance to say goodbye properly. I've known you so long, it seemed the right thing to do.'

'Hardly goodbye.' Quist sniffed a cigar and snipped the end. 'We've lived further apart than York and Oxford before.'

Larry opened his mouth to speak and decided against it.

'Are you booked into a hotel?'

'No, I thought you might have a spare bed.'

'I have.' Quist lit the cigars and handed him a glass. 'So it won't matter if you have too many of these.'

Puffing on the Cohiba, Larry slipped off his jacket and removed his spectacles from misted brown eyes. 'I'll miss you, Bernie,' he mumbled.

'You seem to have smoke in your eye.' Smiling affectionately, Quist led him to the Chesterfield couch, stabbed the log fire with a poker and sprawled in the glow of the crackling flames. 'Come on,' he prompted. 'Tell me again. Where are these new places you've bought?'

'The antique shop is in Oxford city centre and the house is in Wolvercote. You'll have to see them when I get settled in. York was good, but it was time for a change.' Larry looked around. Shadows danced between the ceiling beams like ghosts in a disco. 'This is a lovely place, Bernie. How long have you been here? Two years? A few more and you'll have to move again. It's a pity.'

Quist fell quiet and inspected the ice in his drink.

'I'm tired of it all.' Larry ran a hand through his hair. 'You wouldn't believe *how* tired. Perhaps I've spent too long amongst antiques.'

'There's not much we can do about it.' Quist sipped his whisky and eyed the furniture. Aromatic Cuban smoke mingled with the scents of old leather and wood. 'And there's nothing wrong with antiques.'

'What if we *could* do something about it? What if...' Larry hesitated, studying his friend. 'Oh, I'm talking nonsense. We're like a couple of antiques ourselves. Just look at you. You used to have a sublime sense of humour; it was one of the things I liked best about you. These days you hardly laugh, and you've no friends.'

'Probably a stage I'm going through. Sometimes you get a little jaded with everything as time passes.'

'And *passes*.'

'Apart from you, how *can* I have friends?' Quist blew a cloud of smoke. 'The closest thing to a friend is the young assistant I employed three weeks ago. You met him at the office just before you moved south.'

'Yes, your private detective office. I was surprised when you started the business, but then I realised detective work is ideal for you. I know what that insatiable curiosity of yours is like.'

'I prefer *consultant detective*. Yes, it's just what I need. I'm enjoying it and it keeps my mind occupied.'

'But why did you employ this kid?'

'I don't know really.' Quist drew thoughtfully on the cigar. 'Maybe I'm tired of being alone. It's different having someone... *normal* around and Watson is as normal as it gets. He has a sprig of mistletoe ready to attach to his belt buckle and he can't wait for all the Christmas parties next week.'

Larry laughed. 'That's my point. Having people around has always been a problem.'

'Watson is far cleverer than he realises, but he's young and down-to-earth and hardly likely to notice anything... unusual.'

'Well, like I said, remember your curiosity. You'll just have to watch it doesn't get you into trouble again.'

'No fear of that. I only take on small stuff - divorces and suchlike. Nothing that would get me noticed.' Quist held up his glass. 'To your new life in Oxford, Larry. Merry Christmas.'

'Merry Christmas, Bernie. Many more of them.'

'Yes, *many* more.' Quist gave a hollow chuckle. 'There, I do laugh sometimes.'

Larry sipped his whisky. 'Speaking of news and detectives, I read something in Scotland about that murder on Saturday - the female birdwatcher. She had her throat torn out, didn't she?'

'Apparently so.'

'It wasn't too far from York, was it? I was wondering...' The old man gulped his drink. 'Do you have any ideas on the matter?'

'No,' lied Quist. He poured more whisky. 'I haven't thought about it.'

* * * *

Chapter 10

Raoul Grant lived in Musgrave, the pretty village being central for the Grant housing offices in Reading, Marlborough and Salisbury. Life in the hamlet wasn't so much tranquil as tranquillized. Nothing much happened, and if the place had been a patient on life-support, its relatives would probably have asked for the machine to be turned off.

Rex pulled into the car park of the Rathbone Inn and parked his Ferrari beside several huge 4x4 vehicles, proof that some were actually used in the countryside and not driven exclusively by city folk for school runs and the gym. A khaki Landrover stood near the rear entrance, echoing Wiltshire's large military presence, and Rex stared at it the way a father might stare at his daughter's number scrawled on a lavatory wall. His own military career had ended before it had even begun and he knew he had to accept it. Pondering, he took the Walther pistol from the glove compartment and hid it in his rear waistband before locking the car. The special forces dream might be over, but at least the 9mm comfort blanket made him feel exciting and a little happier as he trudged moodily across the gravel.

The dark passages and wood-panelled rooms of the inn hadn't changed since the civil war and oak beams were everywhere, crossing walls and supporting rafters. Mostly they were hidden in shadow at forehead height and, with the sunglasses, the place was a death-trap to Rex. Several couples were attacking lunch-hour meals in the taproom, a few green-welly types propped up the bar, and the two occupants of the army Landrover stood near the door. Rex glared enviously at their camouflage jackets and, pulling down his black sweater to ensure the gun was hidden, he walked over to where Raoul sat at the counter.

His elder brother ran a cold eye over the black leather jacket and jeans. The men looked similar and both had dark hair, although Raoul's grew longer and a well-tailored grey suit covered his plumpness. The age gap between them was nine years, but the mental age gap was much wider.

'Hello there,' said Raoul. 'What are you drinking?'

'Bitter,' muttered Rex, gesturing to the pumps. 'I don't imagine they serve battery acid.'

'Are you okay?'

'How would *you* feel if your world had just fallen apart?'

'And how do you suppose I feel right now?'

'Oh yeah, sorry.' Rex grimaced. 'Lisa Mirren.'

'Her father's in a bad way.' Raoul paid for two pints. 'He rang me on Sunday with the news and then the police were in touch. I was interviewed yesterday.'

'Why did they want to see *you*? You broke up around the time she took that York laboratory job.'

'The engagement was over, but we stayed friends.' Raoul glanced around the room. 'I wonder if you'd do me a favour?' Take off those glasses, would you? You look idiotic in this dim light.'

'They're for my hay fever.'

'It's winter. It was bad enough at your party in that club on Saturday, with you falling over everything. I don't want a repetition in my local.'

Rex grudgingly slid them into his jacket.

'Thank you.' Raoul carried the drinks to a table by the crackling fire. 'I gave the police a statement for what it was worth. They're questioning everyone who knew her.'

'It's murder then?'

'*What*? Haven't you seen the news?'

'The Royal Marines kept me kind of busy.'

'It was horrific. Her throat...' Raoul rubbed his eyes, voice trembling. 'It was torn out. According to the police, someone with enormous strength ripped it out by hand.'

'Christ!' Rex sat beside him. 'Where was this?'

'The Yorkshire Wolds, over towards Uncle Rupert's place.'

'What was she doing there? Birdwatching, I suppose?'

Raoul nodded. 'She was photographing owls outside a village called Lamberley when it happened.'

43

'Birdwatching in December? I thought owls hibernated?' Rex shook his head. 'Do the police know who did it?'

'They've no idea.'

'Well you're no suspect. You were at my party Saturday afternoon.'

'Apparently the killer took her binoculars; the ones I gave her last Christmas.'

Rex clicked open a silver Zippo lighter, the flame set high to give a macho blaze. He examined the engraved Marines crest and sighed loudly.

'Yes.' Raoul gazed into the fire. 'It's terrible, isn't it?'

'You can say that again. I'd staked everything on the Marines. What the hell do I do now?'

'I meant the murder.'

'Everything was planned. The SAS only recruit from other regiments. I was going to complete the officer training in the Marines and then transfer.'

'Into the SAS? Just like that, eh?'

'Well, not straight away, obviously; probably next summer.' He fired up the commando lighter again. 'Or maybe the SBS - they're like the SAS, but with cool underwater stuff.'

Raoul stared quietly. His younger brother and reality seemed to go together like Elvis and salad. 'But they kicked you out, did they?'

'Yeah. God knows what father will say.'

'He'll say he's sick of your wild dreams and, when he returns, you'll do as he says or he'll stop your allowance. He rang from New York this morning and I told him what happened.'

'I can't believe it,' stammered Rex, on the edge of tears. 'I had my whole life planned–an incredible life in the SAS–and now this. After Christmas, I'll be running a housing company.'

'You'll sit on the board with me and work in planning to begin with...'

'It's so unfair!'

'It's real life, Rex, and you don't think it's unfair to spend the money, do you? Grant Homes paid for your place in Hampstead and the Ferrari. Dad gave you a chance, but this is the thing with you - you get something into your head and just go for it, no matter how unrealistic or stupid.'

'A commission in the Marines isn't stupid.'

'I'm talking about this SAS thing and your bizarre perception of the special forces. All that nonsensical training you put yourself through to get into the role. That ludicrous image you cultivated: wearing black all the time and those stupid sunglasses. Why are you still dressing like that, for God's sake?'

'It feels good,' muttered Rex. He ran a hand through his short hair. 'I don't know; I'm kind of used to it.'

'You threw a party to celebrate becoming an officer and you hadn't even been accepted. It was just a three-day trial to weed out the...' Raoul paused and cleared his throat. 'You just don't seem to think the same way as everyone else. Look, I realise how lousy you must be feeling, but it's over. You really have to grow up a little now and begin acting like...' he groped for the correct words, '*normal* people.'

'Everyone came to the party and I can't face them. I was kicked off the course after six hours. How can I tell anyone that?' Rex slumped over the table. 'I just need time to come to terms with it.'

'*Jesus!*' Raoul dropped his voice to a hissed whisper. 'Is that a fucking gun in your jeans?'

Rex tugged down his sweater. 'What about it?'

'What *about* it? What the fuck do you think you're doing with an illegal handgun? Is that thing loaded?' Wide-eyed and ashen, he looked again at the black clothing. 'I imagine it makes you feel like a special forces secret agent...'

'It makes me feel *better*, okay?'

'Er, right.' Raoul coughed nervously. 'You know, what with your depression and er, everything, I think it might be best if you stayed with someone, rather than moping around your flat.'

'Oh, I don't know. Wiltshire isn't the best place to...'

'I don't mean here; I'm not the best company right now. Uncle Rupert and Marika didn't make it to your party. When did you last see them? A few days with a country eccentric might do you good.'

'Be serious.' Rex laughed dryly. 'You know how easily I get bored. I need excitement and something to take my mind off this mess, not relaxation. I need to keep my brain active and nothing ever happens in the wilds of Yorkshire.'

'Apart from murders,' snapped Rex. 'If you want to keep what little brain you have active, why not solve *that* for the police? God knows, someone should. I'll be honest, you also need specialist counselling. Not for this, but your entire state of mind.'

Rex paused, eyes narrowing in deliberation. 'Where was she killed? Where exactly?'

'I was being sarcastic. I didn't actually mean you should solve the murder.'

'Oh, come on. I doubt I could *solve* it. But you're right. If I'm up there visiting Rupert, I might just take a look around and see if I can find out anything. Do you remember Merlot?'

'Merlot? What the hell are you talking about?'

'The topless model I dated last August. She loved whodunits, not that she ever understood them. I took her on a couple of those hotel murder weekends and I was pretty good; a bit of a natural, they said. I unmasked the killer both times.'

'I don't believe this.' Raoul watched incredulously as Rex downed his drink and walked to the bar for a refill. 'My God! I really do not believe this.'

* * * *

Chapter 11

The lunch period allocated to the researchers was ending, and management and office personnel were taking their places in the refectory at Ebor Pharmaceuticals.

'Do we have to?' said Amy Clarkson, finishing her coffee.

'Yes.' Becca Travis pulled on her lab coat. 'We work on something for two months and suddenly everything disappears. I want to know why!'

'Why don't you see Doctor Keating?' Amy nodded to an elderly woman who had just entered. 'She ought to know.'

'She may be Assistant Research Director,' said Becca, 'but Margaret has no idea. I asked her yesterday and Will hasn't told her a thing.'

'After Lisa and Di, this seems so petty.' The young doctor pushed open the canteen door. 'Why not leave it? I don't know if it was the new work routine or Will's behaviour, but those projects never felt right.'

'He hasn't been himself for weeks,' said Becca. 'Most of the time he seems edgy. Did you notice him yesterday after the police had been?'

The corridor from the refectory ran along the rear of the labs to the busy main lobby where Lynn Chandler manned her reception desk. Another passage, decorated with paintings and cacti, led to the administrative lobby with its leather suite, copiers and shredder.

'Okay.' Amy brushed back her short blonde hair. 'Let's get it over with.'

Becca knocked and opened the research director's door.

'Yes, twenty in total.' Will Gillette spoke into the phone, but waved the girls in. He sat in a grey suit with his back to the windows, sunlight streaming onto his desk where papers and files were scattered around the computer. 'Yes, inform Delon that I'm cancelling the consignments. Yes, thank you. Goodbye.'

Amy glanced at the files as she sat at the desk, noticing

Merlax on one and *Grandier Haematology*. The pale blue sheet was an invoice for something named *Porphyrene*.

'Okay.' Replacing the phone and clicking off the computer, Gillette slid the paperwork into a drawer. 'What can I do for you two?'

'What exactly is happening?' Becca gave a condescending smile. 'We've been on our projects for two months. Batches were prepared on Thursday as normal and we were supposed to start new ones today.'

'Yes,' agreed Amy. 'Then we arrived yesterday to find everything gone.'

'We're now working on a lipstick range,' added Becca. 'I didn't get a chance to ask, what with the police. Doctor Keating didn't know and...'

'Of course,' chuckled Gillette. 'I cleared out South Lab over the weekend. Stapleton cancelled your two projects.'

'I see.' Becca frowned. 'Could we ask why?'

'The usual reason, finance. You weren't making any progress.'

'Perhaps it was the experimental retinols.' Amy chose her words. 'I know you insisted on them and I bow to experience, but I was never happy with…'

'We were losing money.' Gillette sat forward. 'And if we're talking *happiness*, I wasn't very happy with *you* yesterday. Despite the sensitive background of those projects, you almost mentioned them to the police.'

'They're conducting a murder inquiry' Amy laughed. 'They don't care about our research. It's best to give them all the information we can.'

'Relevant information, yes, but our work had nothing to do with Di's suicide or Lisa's murder. I must say, I assumed you were more discreet. We *did* discuss the need for discretion at the outset.'

'Well, yes.' Amy sighed. 'I suppose you're right.'

Gillette adjusted his huge spectacles. 'Anyway, is there

anything further?'

'No.' Becca climbed to her feet. 'I like to know what's going on, that's all. Sorry to have bothered you, Will.'

'Don't be silly; my office is always open.' He stood up politely. 'I'd have called to explain the cancellation, only I've been busy with the police.'

'Of course.' Becca opened the door. 'Thanks anyway. Bye.'

'Bye,' echoed Amy, slipping into the lobby.

Becca waited until the office was closed. 'Can you believe that? He did it *himself*? The Research Director claims he went in South Lab and cleaned it out himself.'

'Come on.' Amy laughed quietly as they set off towards reception. 'Before we turn into conspiracy nuts.'

Reaching the turn in the passage, Amy looked back to see Gillette at the shredder with the files from his desk. She watched curiously as the blue invoice from the Grandier Laboratories vanished into the buzzing slot.

* * * *

Chapter 12

Quist sprawled in the leather chair behind his office desk, sipping contemplatively at a coffee as Larry read through a divorce file with Watson. With his spectacles, snowy hair and moustache, the elderly man reminded the teenager of Geppetto, Quist's large nose doing little to detract from the Pinocchio impression.

'I see,' said Larry. 'Lumsden here is typical of your cases?'

'Oh absolutely,' said Watson. 'We only get the cream assignments.' He perched on the edge of the desk eating fish and chips from a newspaper, and leant over to pull a photograph from the file. 'You'll notice his wife's got a bruised eye. She deserved it apparently. She questions him when he comes home stinking of perfume and he's decided he's better off without all that.'

'Sounds like a real beauty,' said Larry.

'Yeah, try to imagine a tapeworm with permed hair. We start on his divorce tomorrow; another case to rival the Ronnie Garbutt thrill-fest. Hey, Guv, I wonder who's going to be running around taking the photos?'

Quist paused in tinkling his ring finger on the mug to deliver a sarcastic look.

'Aren't we better waiting until after Christmas?' asked Watson. 'I can't believe you don't celebrate it. You should come out to the pubs with me on Christmas Eve. I'll teach you the Macarena dance.'

'I'd pay money to watch that,' said Larry. 'The job's not *too* exciting then?'

Watson laughed. 'You'd get more excitement watching crown green bowling. In the three weeks I've been here, we've had two divorces and some council cleaner fiddling his sick board by claiming he'd fallen at work.'

'You have the finesse of a Turkish rat catcher,' said Quist, watching as the youth crammed chips into his mouth. 'As to the job, we also serve documents on people.'

'*I* serve the documents,' snorted Watson. He climbed to his feet as a knock sounded at the door. 'You sit in the car smoking.' Wiping his greasy hands, he headed through reception, opened the door and froze.

'Hello,' said Kevin Selden. The skinhead wore a T shirt, jeans and boots, and the huge Rottweiler stood growling at his side. 'I wonder if you could help me, mate? I'd like to see that bloke you work for.'

Watson's jaw fell. His first thought was that the debt collector had damaged his face in an accident, but Selden was smiling politely. He'd also called a black guy *mate*. This was like a priest calling a nun *honey*.

'Er, sure. Come on through.' Watson glanced at the fangs and glowering eyes as Klansman waddled into reception. Creatures like this could solve the stray dog problem overnight. Existing strays would be eaten, and if people bought their child a dog like this for Christmas, they wouldn't dare kick it out after the holiday. He opened the office door. 'Er, a visitor, Guv.'

The Rottweiler began snarling, its hackles rising.

'Sorry about this,' grunted Selden. 'He doesn't seem to like you and your pal.'

Watson raised his eyebrows. It was hard to imagine it liking anyone, apart from in the gastronomic sense.

'Good dog.' Quist reached out to tussle Klansman's neck. The monster sniffed and began wagging its stumpy tail. 'Yes, there's a good doggy.' A tongue flopped out to lick his hand; it seemed to be actual affection, rather than tasting. 'Yes, nice doggy. Sit!' Amazingly enough, it did. He turned to the shocked owner. 'Now, what can we do for you?'

The skinhead shook himself. 'I've got a personal problem.' Sitting down, he glared at Larry. 'Personal and private.'

'Don't worry about me.' Larry rose to leave, as most sensible people did whenever Selden entered. 'I'm on the three o'clock train.'

'I'll see you out,' said Quist. 'If you'll excuse me a moment?'

'Cheerio then.' Watson held open the door. 'Have a great Christmas and good luck with your new shop in Oxford.' Slurping came from the desk and he turned to see the dog eating his dinner.

'Bye.' Larry grinned at the youth, pulled on his tweed jacket, and followed the detective into the reception. 'Enjoy your meal.'

'Business is booming,' whispered Quist. 'Another potential client.' He smiled warmly and opened the corridor door. 'I'm really glad you called on your way home. That long chat last night was just like the old days.'

'Yes it was.' Larry picked up his suitcase. 'You must come to Oxford after Christmas. We'll have to arrange something.'

'You can count on it.' He clasped the old man's hand and shook firmly. 'Look after yourself down there.'

'I will.' Larry checked his watch. 'Ah well. Goodbye, Bernie.' He hesitated, his brown eyes filling up, then dropping the case, he embraced Quist.

'Go on, you silly old fool.' The detective hugged him, chuckling. 'You'll miss your train.'

'Yes, we can't have that.' Larry paused again, then nodded slowly. 'Goodbye.'

Quist watched his friend disappear down the stairwell and returned to the office. The skinhead sat picking a scab from his knuckle and waited until he'd flopped back into the chair behind the desk.

'Sorry about that.' Quist sipped his coffee, his gaze running over Selden's muscles; any sports judge meeting this character would definitely demand a urine test for steroids. 'A personal problem, I believe you said?'

'It's the coppers.' Selden fed the knuckle scab to Klansman. 'They're saying my bird topped herself.'

'Oh, dear! Er, your *bird*?'

'Diane Woodall. We were getting engaged.'

An ideal motive for suicide, decided Watson.

'I'm sorry to hear that.' Quist gestured to the *Yorkshire Post* on the windowsill. 'I recall her name and the unfortunate incident. I read about it this morning.'

'I've read it too,' said Selden, scowling. 'It happened on the railway near the train museum. The cops say she lay on the line while a train chopped her head off. That's a load of shit.'

Nodding grimly, the detective sat back in the chair. 'You believe the police are being hasty in their suicide assumption?'

'That's right,' said Selden. 'Diane wasn't the sort to take her own life. We were very much in love and she had everything to live for. There has to be more to it.'

Watson couldn't believe what he was hearing.

Quist spoke tactfully. 'I imagine that after an awful episode such as this, many relatives feel the way you do...'

'I'd like to employ you to uncover the truth,' broke in Selden. 'It's suicide as far as the police are concerned, but you could investigate privately. You could visit the railway and talk to the people at Ebor Pharmaceuticals. You could find out what really happened.'

The eloquence left Watson with the odd impression that he was reciting something memorised.

'Ebor Pharmaceuticals?' echoed Quist.

'The laboratory where she worked,' said Selden. 'She was a doctor there.'

'Was she indeed?' Curiosity twinkled in the detective's eyes, but common sense took over. 'I'll be honest with you, this isn't the type of work we take on. This sort of investigation is definitely police business. They have far better resources and...'

'What?' Selden's complexion drained. 'You're saying you won't help?'

Quist regarded him thoughtfully. 'No, I didn't say that.'

'I need you to investigate this. You could visit the railway and talk to the people at Ebor Pharmaceuticals...'

'Yes, so you just said.' Quist raised an inquisitive eyebrow. 'I'll tell you what, why don't you leave it with me for a while and I'll give you a decision.'

'Er, thanks, mate.' Selden hesitated, seemingly unsure of what to do next. 'Er, yes, okay.' He stood up and jerked the dog's chain. 'Come on, Klansman.'

Quist watched as the huge man saw himself out. 'Odd,' he purred, staring at the closed door. 'That repetition of words was bizarre and he was completely lost for a moment there. Did you see his expression when he realised I wasn't interested? He almost turned white, and I noticed fear in his eyes - genuine fear.'

'His bloody dog scoffed my dinner,' said Watson. 'I noticed *that*.'

Quist lit a cigarette. 'What did you deduce?'

'I deduced I'll be starving by five.'

'He didn't offer a contact number and never batted an eyelid when I told him to wait for my decision. That's way out of character. Tell a Neanderthal like Selden that you need time to think things over, and he'd use a few profanities and employ someone else.'

'He's sub-human, Guv. They're unpredictable.'

'What on earth would a doctor be doing with a brainless thug like that?' Quist drew slowly on the cigarette. 'Ebor Pharmaceuticals,' he murmured.

'Joking aside, you're right. Then again, it's hard to believe he'd come here asking for our help at all. Not after the stuff he's always saying to me.'

'*Very* hard to believe. How are you getting home tonight?'

'The Aston Martin, same as always, or maybe the bus. Why?'

'I'll give you a lift. We can drive by this railway track and take a quick look around.'

'You're not seriously considering this?' Watson laughed. 'I thought you were just getting rid of him when you asked for time to think.'

'I found his behaviour intriguing. You know what killed the proverbial cat?'

'Usually the proverbial busy main road.'

'Curiosity, which is something of a flaw in my make-up. Plus, the alternative to looking into Selden's problem is Mister Lumsden's exciting divorce case.'

'Come on, Guv. It's obviously suicide. Anyone shagging that would top themselves sooner or later.'

Quist frowned reflectively, his ring idly tinkling the coffee mug. 'Ebor Pharmaceuticals,' he repeated quietly.

Don't get involved. Common sense screamed out and Larry's cautionary advice from the previous evening echoed in his head - *make sure your insatiable curiosity doesn't get you into trouble, Bernie.* Eyes twinkling, he silenced the warnings, his ring-finger tapping faster. There was no harm in having just a quick look at the railway.

* * * *

Chapter 13

St Basil's infant school stood halfway along Bruce Rise in the eastern suburb of Heworth, a street of pretty sandstone houses and hanging baskets. Becca Travis found a space for her MG in the line of parked cars near the school gates and snatched her bag. She was already late, her inconsiderate parents were staying at Aunt June's in Scarborough, and preparing her own dinner would make her later still. Paul McCartney was having a *Wonderful Christmas Time* on the radio until she killed the engine and jumped out, fuming with irritation.

The young doctor flounced towards what passed for a home, eyeing the terraced houses with contempt. Becca had grown up in this street, but after escaping to Durham University, she'd never expected to return. Her flat was sold after meeting Adam North. *He* was to blame for this - Adam the solicitor, with his childish pride and prehistoric attitude to sex. She'd fallen for his salary, moved in with him, and all was fine until he checked her phone. Knowing how besotted Adam was, Becca had neglected to mention her other lovers. This in itself would probably have ended the relationship, but finding her system of performance points and seeing his own mediocre score hadn't helped. Thanks to Adam kicking her out, she was temporarily staying with her parents and, so far, she'd hated every minute.

What a tale she had for her pals tonight. Becca adored being the centre of attention and, as the wine bar crowd would have gleaned little about Saturday's murder from the media, they'd be begging for her juicy inside stories of decapitation and torn windpipes.

The girl shivered at a sudden wave of fear, St Basil's school fuelling the sensation. She glanced at the classrooms beyond the wall to her right and quickened her pace. There was something so spooky about a school at night – a building, normally so raucous with boisterous life, standing in darkness, still and as silent as the grave. Becca let out a short tense laugh. Her friends were right; she *did* have a vivid imagination.

Imagination had little to do with the footsteps approaching

from behind. Drawing level with the boiler room gate, she turned to find a familiar face.

'Shit!' The doctor giggled nervously. 'You scared the hell out of me.'

'Sorry about that, Becca.'

'You can't be too careful. Do you know about Lisa's murder? Er, what are you doing here anyway?'

'I know all about the murder.' A hand flashed out, clamping over Becca's mouth, and the girl was slammed against the school gate. 'Such a tragedy. I was fond of her.'

A metallic tinkle sounded behind the doctor as a broken padlock hit the floor. The gate squeaked open and Becca realised she was being dragged to the boiler house. She struggled and whimpered as the hand squeezed, crumbling a fortune in dental crowns.

'You'll be pleased to know,' said Lisa Mirren's killer, 'that I'm rather fond of *you* too.'

* * * *

Chapter 14

Matthew Strand cruised by the gleaming high-rise buildings of Salford Quays, his metallic grey Lamborghini looking more suited to gliding through outer space than driving in Manchester traffic. This vast waterfront area lay at the end of the Ship Canal, to the west of the city centre, and Strand recalled the wartime Luftwaffe attacks on the industries here. Those German airmen wouldn't recognise the place today. Then again, neither would the English pilots.

The docks and factories closed in the eighties. Some of the old buildings were refurbished, but the majority were flattened and replaced by huge futuristic structures and sculpture-filled water promenades. Strand looked around at the fountains gushing in colonnades and the neon-lit plazas surrounded by upmarket hotels and restaurants. Theatres, cinemas and sporting stadiums rubbed shoulders with nightclubs, malls and film studios. Salford Quays was the first and largest of Britain's urban regeneration programmes and the sparkling result was quite something.

Strand headed further along the waterfront to the four renovated warehouses on Raven's Wharf. Parking on the street between the looming office buildings, he locked the car, straightened his Armani suit and smiled at his reflection in the black glass. The dark green eyes and trim beard would have once earned good money in Hollywood playing villains in swashbuckler movies. The lean face was handsome, but the angular features hinted at a callousness which he regularly emphasised with a sneer.

Waves slapped at the dock as Strand walked across the business park to the largest of the warehouses, home to one of the many private companies trading on Salford Quays. Five stories high, the windows in the first three floors were bricked up, whilst the black armoured glazing of the upper stories presented outsiders with a reflection. Lawns surrounded three sides, the front pathway providing access to the glass entrance porch, whilst a quay allowed vehicles to the rear loading doors. A giant chromium cube stood on the grass and bore a central design of three letters over the company name, one S above and two interlocking below, like a radiation trefoil.

SILVER SECURITY SYSTEMS

The technical labs here specialised in state-of-the-art bugs and miniature cameras, surveillance, alarm, and protection systems. Strand checked his watch–the type with a price which most would consider a good annual wage–and pressed the porch call button, gazing into the lobby through the armoured glass of the inner doors. A marble desk stood by an elevator and Henry Moore statues reclined beneath chic paintings. The staff had finished at their usual time of five-thirty, but this building was never empty; the owner lived on the premises, along with several other individuals.

Two large men appeared in reception, one of them punching numbers into an electronic door keypad. Strand gave a derisive whistle of respect, amazed that these broken-nosed giants in black suits could tie their own laces, let alone operate a coded entry system. Not only did Sangster and Browning have problems in the looks department, their faces resembling angling bait, but neither was famed for a scalpel-sharp mind.

'Name?' said Browning.

'I'm the Committee Vice-President, you imbecile,' said Strand. 'I know you take security seriously, but are you actually asking *me* for my name?'

'You're expected, Sir.' Sangster accompanied their visitor across the lobby. 'You can go straight up.'

Strand stepped into the elevator, pressed *penthouse* and eyed the tinted mirrors on either side. If this X-ray system detected any indication of a weapon, he'd be dead before the door closed. The lift opened onto the fifth floor corridor, where a further three members of the protection squad stood waiting. Fisher, Hinds and Galeen, as unattractive and dense as the monsters downstairs, were never far from their master.

Galeen, the head of security, unlocked the penthouse and disappeared inside, leaving Strand to stare warily at the device suspended from the ceiling as he waited. Mechanised watchdogs like this monitored all private corridors and were unseen by the staff and public. The robo-sentry, thankfully dormant, looked like a futuristic CCTV camera, but had little to do with filming shoplifters. The compact units were equipped with heat sensors, motion trackers and miniature machine guns. When these were operational not even a speeding cat could make it along this passage.

Galeen reappeared. 'The President will see you now, Sir,' he said, stepping back as Strand pushed brusquely past. 'You'll find him in the upper section.'

Strand entered the largest room of the penthouse. Designed on two levels, a circular fire pit stood centrally in this lowest section, with gas jets erupting from broken stone and a cat statue towering over it. Eight feet tall and carved from basalt rock, the polished black surface of the Egyptian antique was lit by the dancing flames. Vegetation was everywhere. Vines covered the walls around the windows and tropical bushes and rockeries turned corners into jungle. The initial reaction of most visitors was to assume they'd mistakenly entered the roof garden. Sneering at the lily pond, Strand mounted the rock steps. He had difficulty in concealing contempt, but here it was inadvisable.

Strand had never been up to this higher level on previous visits, but saw it was a control centre with computers and screens connected to the countless cameras around the building. Three doors led off, possibly to bedrooms, but the fourth steel door with its coded keypad was another matter. SSS sold many of their specialised products to foreign clients and, like the robo-sentries, this express escape elevator was the ideal Christmas gift for dictators–the sort of people who might have unexpected guests waving guns and shouting about revolution.

A slender figure in an indigo suit, Lucius Silva stood with his back to the room, his gaze fixed on the rectangular pit at his feet. *He's got a hole in the floor*, puzzled Strand. *What's he looking at down there?* Walking closer, he silently groaned in disbelief.

'Kali and Shiva,' said Silva. 'They're quite beautiful, don't you think, Matthew?'

'Well...' Strand peered at the two king cobras curled in the gravel five feet below. 'I suppose it depends on your taste in pets.'

'I suppose so. I had a small dog about forty minutes ago.' Silva motioned to the hole. 'It was an interesting tug-of-war.'

At six feet-four, the old man loomed three inches above Strand and unlike many aged men, he never stooped. White hair, pale green eyes and a lined face placed him around seventy.

'You wanted to see me before the meeting?' said Strand.

'I did. I understand you have something for me?'

'Tayman's report.' Strand slid a folded file from his inside pocket. 'Everything is here and, loathe as I am to admit it, he was right to be concerned about Sharp. The places and times are all recorded.'

'Did you enjoy yourself?' Silva opened the folder. 'You were taking a vacation?'

'Oh, yes. It was okay.' Strand reached for a cigarette, reconsidered and adjusted his tie. The President of SSS didn't like people smoking. Ordinarily Strand wouldn't give a damn, but here he made exceptions.

Silva skimmed through the papers. 'Who did you go with?'

'No one. Why do you ask?'

There was no answer. Strand already stood four feet away, but shuffled further. Something emanated from the old man: icy vibrations that left people with a desire to stand a long way away. Preferably, another room.

'Very good.' Silva closed the file. 'We'll discuss this at tonight's meeting.'

'With respect, the winter meeting is only four days away. Couldn't this have waited until then?'

'*This* could wait.' The President fixed Strand with a frigid gaze, the green eyes reminiscent of glacial crevasses. 'But we have another problem – something in York that needs attending to by

Thursday.'

'York?' Strand raised an eyebrow.

'I'll explain in the conference chamber.' Silva turned back to the cobras. 'Merry Christmas, Matthew.'

* * * *

Chapter 15

'What could we possibly find that the cops haven't already found?' Watson munched a cheeseburger and followed Quist along the railway line. He brought out his mobile and read the messages. 'It's pitch black. You can't see a thing.'

'Then it might help if you looked too,' drawled Quist. 'Instead of constantly playing with that phone.'

'Why don't you get the torch from the car?'

'Torchlight would attract attention, just like the screen on that thing. Put it away. We're trespassing on railway property.'

'It's too dark to see what we're trespassing on.' He lifted a trainer and grimaced. 'Or *in.*'

Quist held up a hand. 'How many fingers?'

'Fourteen?'

'Close enough. The light from Holgate Bridge up there is adequate and I have exceptional night vision.'

'Oh great! Hey, what's the matter now?'

'That car.' Frowning thoughtfully, Quist pointed to the right of the bridge. The sapphire-blue vehicle stood beneath a streetlamp. 'It's still there.'

'Cool, it looks like a Maserati. What about it?'

'It arrived as we climbed down the embankment and I don't think anyone got out. The windows are so darkly tinted, it's impossible to see if it's empty or not.'

'Don't go paranoid on me, Guv. Surely you don't think we're being followed by someone in a Maserati?'

'You're right.' Quist shrugged and turned back to the tracks. 'It's hardly likely.'

Carl Dreyer would have disagreed. The Leeds Brightshield Glazing manager watched quietly from the car.

'What if a train comes?' asked Watson, glancing over his shoulder.

'I'll hear it and we'll move.' The detective walked up and

down the line, occasionally lifting his overcoat and squatting to examine the gravel. 'My hearing is on a par with my night vision.'

'Whooo! *Mister Super-Senses.* You should be in the X-Men.' Trudging behind, Watson checked the time on his phone. 'Mum will have the dinner ready soon. She thought I was coming straight home.'

'I bought that junk food to stop you complaining.'

'The cops have computers, you know? CSI and forensic labs and stuff.'

'Yes, I'm fully aware of their technological resources. Are you looking?'

'Yeah, though all I've seen so far is mud. How do you know this is the right place? She might have died over there. There might be loads of clues over...'

'If you check the tracks, you'll notice this particular section of line has recently been cleaned. There's a faint scent of bleach and you can see where the police footprints are concentrated and where poles supported a forensic shelter. It's elementary; you only have to use your eyes.' Quist lit a cigarette. 'You moan about our boring work and here's something different - someone asking us to investigate an unexplained suicide - and you're *still* bored.'

'I'm a teenager. We're always bored.'

The detective shook his head and laughed.

Watson's eyes widened. This was the most open display of amusement he'd seen from Quist. 'I suppose it's Selden,' he said, grinning. 'I'm a little pissed off to be helping a scumbag like that. Besides which, I thought we were winding down for Christmas, and if the cops are satisfied this Diane Woodall is a suicide, is it really worth investigating?'

'We're *not* investigating.' Sitting on the railway embankment, Quist drew on his cigarette. 'We're merely pandering to my curiosity. This girl worked at the same laboratory as the doctor who was murdered in the Wolds. It probably means nothing, but Selden's frightened attitude intrigued me. That and a... well, a feeling I had.'

'Talking of feelings, I'm starving.'

'You've just eaten a cheeseburger.'

'I'm a growing lad. My stomach knows mum has the dinner ready for six-fifteen. We have routines around her work.'

'What does she do?'

'Fish fingers and chips on Tuesday.'

'Actually, I meant for a living?'

'Oh... she's er, self-employed.' Watson busied himself with the mobile again.

Quist didn't pursue it. From the obvious embarrassment, *self-employed* might involve internet contact sites and gentlemen callers. 'Any new messages in the last two minutes?' he quizzed sardonically. 'What on earth do you do all day on that damned thing?'

'It's Facebook and all sorts of stuff. Everyone's got a mobile these days. Everyone except *you*. No computer, no mobile, an old Beetle car. Not exactly Mister Twenty-first Century, are you?'

'Hello!' The detective's eyes fastened on a twinkle by his assistant's foot and he picked up a tiny badge. It was a simple design - a skull with *Harley Davidson* beneath. He examined the open clasp and passed it to Watson. 'Take a look at this.'

'Nice.' Watson handed it back. 'What's it doing here?'

'The bent fastener indicates it was lost accidentally.' Quist puffed on his cigarette. 'It could have belonged to Diane Woodall, but from what I've read of this doctor, I doubt it. As for the police, even plain-clothes officers aren't in the habit of sporting motorcycle logos.'

'Weird,' said Watson. 'If this was here yesterday, why didn't the cops find it and bag it as possible evidence?'

'Exactly.' Quist watched curiously as the Maserati pulled away from the bridge. 'I told Selden to wait. I think we'll look into this matter a little further before giving him an answer.'

* * * *

Chapter 16

Matthew Strand sat in a conference room beside Lucius Silva, waiting for the Committee President to finish reading paperwork and begin the meeting. The windowless chamber lay on the fourth floor of Silver Security Systems on Salford Quays, and Strand gazed at the Egyptian statue by the door. Identical to the black stone antique in the private quarters above, the huge sitting cat was illuminated by spotlights.

Strand hated these gatherings, with their tense atmosphere and sycophantic obeisance. The table was circular, but it was clear that Silva sat at the head. The white-haired President wore a suit of grey silk, but preferred the Committee in sombre attire and the 21 dark-suited men surrounding him would never dare to disappoint.

An Edinburgh restaurateur sat on Strand's right, next to the owner of several Lancashire funeral parlours. The man behind the *Mister Quarry* boutique chain sat across, beside the proprietor of various northern nightspots and Polanski of *Polanski Computing*. To his left sat Doctor Jordan Zucco, the owner of Sunnyvale. The psychiatrist described his Lancashire institution as an oasis for the mentally incapacitated, which sounded agreeable, but didn't prepare for the axe-killers and other criminally insane held there. Sunnyvale was definitely not the place to stick granny when she became forgetful. The other Committee members, including the President himself, were all successful multi-millionaires in their own field, although Lucius Silva exuded something different. Something that left mouths dry and palms clammy.

Just look at the bastard, thought Strand, sourly. *He ought to have a white cat on his knee.* It was an unlikely scenario. Small dogs frequently came into Silva's possession, but never for long; about as long as it takes to be swallowed by a snake.

Oozing all the charm of a gangrenous wound, a Liverpool member sat beside Silva. In Strand's opinion, this was someone who should have been thrown to the cobras long ago. With his puffy face and bald head, Frederick Tayman, the owner of Brightshield Glazing, didn't have much going in the looks department and suffered from a nasty twitch. As Committee Executive, he was directly beneath Strand the Vice-President, and did little to conceal his promotion ambitions. Promotion would only occur if Strand died or made a stupid mistake, but in *this* cartel, it amounted to the same thing. Customers assumed Brightshield's *Steadfast and Immovable* motto related to their windows, but after hours of brain-destroying patter, they realised it referred to the salesman's refusal to leave without a sale. Whenever a salesman failed, the area manager paid a visit and, with their unique methods, the sale was guaranteed.

At least that had always *been* the case. Tayman sat pondering his Leeds manager's call from York, then realising he was being studied by Strand, he gave the Vice-President a sarcastic grin. Strand turned away as Silva closed the file.

'Well...' The President's rich foreign accent cut the silence. 'With our quarterly meeting this Friday, no doubt you'll be wondering why I called you tonight?'

Heads nodded, enough to confirm interest, but not enough to make it seem they were pushing for answers.

'We have a situation in York. Stapleton has been heading a project for me and forwarding twice-weekly progress reports. Twice weekly, that was, until Sunday. It seems the doctor has vanished.'

'As you all know,' said a tense voice, 'Stapleton owns a dermatology research company in York.'

All heads turned to Peel from Sheffield, a dark-haired man with a guilty expression. Despite his apparent youth, Peel was head of a successful insurance company. He was also Committee controller for Yorkshire.

'Yes,' said Tayman, turning to Silva. 'You ordered Stapleton and I to begin our projects at the autumn meeting. My glass filtration project is almost complete.'

Ignoring him, Silva handed a newspaper to Strand. 'Pass this around and please note the headline story.'

Strand glanced through the text and handed it on.

'I wouldn't worry too much about this disappearance,' said Tayman. 'I can't imagine how far the eye-droplet experiments have progressed, but chemical work will soon be redundant thanks to my success with the glass.'

'Who completes first is not an issue,' said Silva. 'Our friend has vanished at the same time as this murder and apparent suicide.'

'This could be coincidental.' Strand shrugged. 'You think there might be a connection, Sir? That Stapleton is responsible?'

'The murder victim and suicide both worked at the York laboratory, and as you read the reports, I suggest you note how both girls died. I haven't heard from Stapleton since Sunday. Yesterday I spoke to Peel and then to the laboratory research director. Doctor Gillette is the only one there who knows the truth about the project, but he knows nothing of this vanishing act and the deaths. If my suspicions are correct, I'm sure you can see how serious this is.'

'I could be wrong...' Tayman leered at Strand. 'But wasn't it *you* who introduced Stapleton to us? We're supposed to vouch for our introductions.'

'I'm not to blame.' Strand's tone would have made a Dalek sound friendly.

'It was long ago,' confirmed Silva, turning to Peel the Yorkshire controller. 'So can *you* shed any light on this?'

Peel coughed uneasily. 'Like I told you on the phone, Sir, the last time I saw Stapleton was at November's area meeting. I didn't know about this until you called.'

'You *are* the doctor's controller.'

'Yes,' he stammered. 'But I didn't...'

'That's enough.' Silva turned to the computer specialist, Polanski. 'Break into the Home Office police files and find out what the authorities have on these dead women. I need to know everything they're withholding from the media.'

'I don't like this,' said Polanski. 'We haven't had anyone turn rogue for years.'

'Stapleton will be found before the Elite are jeopardised,' said Silva. 'A security team will be sent to...'

'I could go,' said Strand.

Tayman gave a mocking laugh. 'The Vice-President offering to clear up this mess himself? An odd request, isn't it?'

Strand glared across the table. If looks could kill, the executive would have needed to be shovelled into buckets.

Silva shook his head. 'The problem is in Peel's area and as Tayman points out, this is hardly a task for you.'

'As he *also* pointed out,' said Strand, 'I made the introduction and I feel somewhat responsible. I know how Stapleton works. We've vacationed on occasions and...'

'Yes,' said Silva. 'That's why I enquired yesterday whether you went alone on your recent trip.'

Strand nodded. 'We need this clearing up fast and I can guarantee results.'

'The Mirren girl died on Saturday. That will certainly need clearing up by Thursday at the latest.'

'I'll leave tomorrow and deal with that problem first.'

'Even if my fears are incorrect, Stapleton was ordered to report twice weekly.' Silva thoughtfully inspected his immaculate nails. 'Failure to report once is serious. Twice is inexcusable.'

Orders and rules, reflected Strand, bitterly. *Well, not for much longer.*

'Very well, Matthew,' said Silva. 'You're in control of this.'

'Thank you, Sir. Stapleton will be here to answer to you at Friday's meeting.'

'You're going to York to rectify this.' Silva smiled, but the green eyes remained cold. 'That doesn't include bringing the doctor back alive.'

* * * *

Chapter 17

A rugged wilderness of storm-blasted heather and Jurassic rock, the North York Moors lie within a vast triangle formed by the Cleveland Hills, the Wolds and the North Sea. Stars encrusted the crisp night sky as Rex Grant sped across the desolate terrain, leaving the market town of Pickering and following signs for the fishing port of Whitby. It had snowed here, but the majority had melted, leaving only patches behind shaded stone outcrops and walls. Rex turned off the road near Lockton, heading west and descending into a wooded vale. The dark lane twisted alarmingly, but the Ferrari didn't drop below sixty until the turn-off outside Sedgefield village. The private road terminated at a pair of gates, and braking by the gatehouse, Rex pressed the horn and read the sign.

SEDGEFIELD GRANGE. STRICTLY PRIVATE
ULTIMATE FORCE USED ON POACHERS

Uncle Rupert hated poachers, but with the expensive game on his estate this was understandable. It was his loathing of the entire lower classes that amazed Rex. Rupert believed the unemployed should be used on the land; not as farm labour, but ploughed in as fertiliser. This afternoon Raoul had described the man as *eccentric,* but this was a little mild.

The electronic gates swung wide and the Ferrari drove into the parkland beyond. The headlights illuminated four swans on a lake, and as they were still alive, Rex could only assume that his uncle hadn't seen them. Rupert was a fanatical hunter, his passion for blood sports having begun in public school. He'd been champion fag-whipper for three years and had trophies for sissy-beating and boy-roasting.

Rex skirted a copse and the Grange appeared. The Yorkshire mansion was late sixteenth century, but extensions and features had been sympathetically added over the years, Rupert's swimming pool and outdoor hot-tub being the latest contributions. Skidding to a halt by the front steps, he reached onto the passenger seat for his bag and looked again at the front-page photograph of Lisa Mirren on the newspaper beside it. He'd bought this to read up on her murder, and he studied her face under the courtesy light. Lisa was certainly attractive and he remembered, uncomfortably, the time he'd once flirted with her behind Raoul's back. The guilt was unnecessary, as nothing came of it. For some odd reason, she genuinely seemed to prefer his brother. Rex shook his head; if he lived to a hundred he'd never understand women.

Climbing out, he mounted the steps and rang the bell. *Was looking into Lisa's death a good idea or as stupid and ill-advised as Raoul had made out*? His frown melted into a grin - *of course it was a good idea.* The police were baffled and he'd been brilliant on those 'murder mystery' hotel breaks. A bit of exciting amateur detective work would help him forget the Marines fiasco, take his mind off the impending meeting with his father, and hopefully keep him occupied until Christmas.

An elderly butler answered. 'Mister Rex. How nice to see you again.'

'Evening Barrymore.' Rex stepped into the hall. A fifteen-foot Christmas tree stood at the bottom of the staircase, its lights twinkling. 'Is my uncle about?'

'He's in the study, Sir. Mister Rupert has just arrived home. He's been shooting in the west wood.'

'Really?' Rex peered over his shades in the direction indicated, a view similar to looking down a coalmine at midnight. 'It's been pitch-black for the past hour.'

'He has a night-sight, Sir. He often returns with a brace of owl. Oh, by the way, I understand congratulations are in order.'

'Sorry?'

'Your exciting new career. I imagine you can't wait to begin your training?'

Cringing, Rex hurried across the hall and into the study. Lounging on a leather couch in a dressing gown, Rupert Grant flicked through a copy of *Horse and Hound.* He was fatter than Rex remembered; a sort of fat Oliver Hardy.

'Evening, Uncle,' said Rex. 'Merry Christmas.'

'Good Lord! How are you?' Rupert hauled himself up, hugged the young man and headed for the drinks cabinet. 'Nice to see you again, Rex. After your call from Raoul's place, we didn't expect you until tomorrow.'

'That was the plan, but I came straight here instead of going home. I had a bag in the car.' The bag had been taken to the Commando training centre and never unpacked.

'Good show.' Rupert took out a Cognac decanter. 'You've picked a fine time to visit. We can do some shooting and we have the hunt ball here on Thursday.'

Rex loved guns, but had never understood the attraction of shooting half-tame pheasants that were driven overhead. He wasn't keen on fox hunting either, unlike Rupert who lived for the chase. With the weight problem, his uncle found horse riding too strenuous, but an open-top Bentley provided the solution and the car was now a well-known sight on the moors as it crashed through hedgerows behind yelping hounds.

'You'll have to count me out of the shooting,' said Rex. Hopefully his stay would be filled with exciting detective work instead. 'I'm going over towards York tomorrow.'

'Shame!' Rupert poured two drinks. 'A few swans have turned up on the lake. I'm popping down with some bread and a shotgun tomorrow.'

Rex raised his eyebrows, but wasn't unduly surprised. This was a man who fired live rabbits from clay pigeon traps.

'Your father's in the States until Christmas, isn't he?' asked Rupert. 'Has he said how the American deal is going?'

'I'm not sure; I tend to keep out of all that.' He'd have preferred keeping out of it for the rest of his life. 'So how's married life treating you?'

'Marika is wonderful. I should have found myself a wife ages ago. There's only so much you can demand from servants before they go moaning to the authorities.'

72

Rex smiled. Rupert wasn't the most attractive of men but, there again, penniless Romanian girls like Marika weren't the most choosey of brides.

'But never mind me. What about you?'

'Me?' Rex laughed. 'I'm too young to get married.'

'No.' Rupert threw an arm over his shoulders. 'Sorry I missed your party. Come on, tell me all about the Marines. When do you begin your officer training?'

* * * *

Chapter 18

The Committee meeting in Manchester was drawing to a close.

'Anything further before we end?' Strand's gaze drifted around the conference room table. 'Okay then...'

'As a matter of fact, there is.' Silva reclined in his chair, his voice so smooth it could have been spread cold onto freshly-baked bread. 'I'm rather displeased with one of you.'

An aura of dread filled the chamber.

'Mister Sharp. Reports place you at a Glasgow railway station last Tuesday.'

'Er, yes,' said Sharp. The chubby restaurateur turned ashen. 'Glasgow Central.' Denial was useless; Silva had spies and his information service outclassed women in village post offices. Tayman was the worst informer and Sharp had noticed his piggy green eyes watching him recently.

'Glasgow Central,' echoed Silva, opening the file before him. 'Attempting to procure young ladies.'

'Sir,' stammered Sharp. 'If I may...'

'I presume Matthew sanctioned this, for you certainly didn't obtain *my* permission.'

Strand shook his head, smiling sombrely at the mounting tension.

'I tried,' said Sharp. 'My mobile didn't work and there was a line fault that night...'

'But despite being unable to obtain consent, you went anyway. There are procedures, as well you know.'

'Yes, Sir, but nothing happened.'

'You're an Elite area controller and relied upon to set an example. I assume this is easy enough for you to understand?'

'Nothing happened. I didn't find anyone, and if I had, I'd have got in touch with you first. You know that.'

'It wasn't a homeless teenager you spoke to, was it? Two girls

74

disappeared that evening. Not homeless unknowns, but people who will be missed. Office workers with friends and families–Sarah Aldridge and Lorraine Peters. You were seen speaking to the latter.' Silva took two enlarged passport shots from his file. 'Their photographs are in the Scottish newspapers.'

'I had nothing to do with this,' said Sharp. 'It wasn't me.'

Silva slid one of the pictures across the table. 'You're saying you didn't speak to this woman, Lorraine Peters?'

'Well... maybe.' A sweat droplet trickled down Sharp's cheek. 'I spoke to lots of people...'

'Coincidental though, that you were actually at this station. That you possibly spoke to one of these girls on the night she vanished.'

'I know how this looks, but I swear...'

'No need.' Silva held up a hand. 'If you say you had no part in this, I believe you. I have to ask, as I'm sure you realise. I must be certain of my people.'

'Of course.' The relief on Sharp's face would have sold any laxative. 'Thank you for...' The words dried as he noticed the President's eyes.

'The next time,' hissed Silva, 'you will follow Elite procedures.'

Strand cleared his throat. 'Anything further, Sir?'

'We're finished.' The President gestured to the door as the breeze from twenty relieved sighs almost blew the photos from the table. 'I'll see you all at our Winter Solstice meeting on Friday.'

The Committee hurried past the large cat statue and into the corridor, heart rates decelerating. Silva, Strand and Tayman were the last to leave the room, the latter pressing the elevator call and convulsing with a nervous twitch.

'Oh dear,' sympathised Strand. 'I'm sure that unfortunate condition of yours is growing worse, Freddie.'

'Don't be ridiculous,' snarled Tayman. 'How can it?'

Grinning at the exchange, Sharp took the opportunity to wipe the cold sweat from his face, then froze as the lift opened to reveal four large bodyguards. Strand had half-expected this and grimly backed away with the rest of the Committee. The most trusted of the Presidential security team, Hinds, Browning, Sangster and Fisher looked as if they'd been built in a Terminator factory, but their intellect was also on par with a robot. Hinds and Sangster seized Jordan Zucco, slammed him into the wall and forced an arm up his back.

'That's the wrong one,' hissed Silva.

'Sorry, Sir.' Sangster released the groaning doctor and grabbed Sharp.

Strand moved aside to let them pass and glanced at Fisher and Browning's compact weapons - Uzi machine pistols with silencers. Sharp noticed the guns too and whimpered as he was dragged down the corridor and through a door. The room was empty; just brick walls and a polythene-covered floor.

'Please,' sobbed Sharp, seeing the plastic sheet. 'I meant to tell you, but I couldn't get through that night. I was too scared later.' The man was thrown against the far wall. 'Listen to me,' he begged, scrambling to his knees on the polythene. 'It was just *one* girl, the one called Peters. I burnt her. I swear I never even saw the other.'

Silva signalled to the guards.

'Wait...'

The harsh splutter of silencers terminated the scream. Sharp kicked and writhed, blood splatters and flesh chunks bursting from his twisting torso. A hot cordite stench filled the room, the horrified Committee watching as the machine pistols were emptied into the scarlet carcass and fresh magazines snapped into place. Several seconds passed before Strand broke the silence.

'Excuse me.' Pushing between Browning and Fisher, he walked across the polythene, taking care not to step in the expanding pool; steaming blood and offal wouldn't do Italian leather any favours. Sharp lay spread-eagled, rib cage and stomach pulverised and tattered intestines covering the floor. The Vice President licked his dry lips, suppressing his mounting fury with deep breaths. *This lunacy would soon be over, and the sooner the better.* Regaining his humour and feigning a concerned frown, he turned to the chalk-faced audience. 'Is there a doctor in the house?'

Only Doctor Zucco responded, but the laugh sounded as genuine as a Thai Rolex.

'Clear that mess up,' said Silva. He turned to the twitching Tayman. 'Ring Oldman and inform him of Sharp's resignation from the Committee. Explain that he's replacing him. By the way... Peel?'

Conjecture or subconscious movement, Peel couldn't decide which, but a space had formed around him - a space that had little to do with body odour, but plenty to do with the unhindered passage of bullets. The Yorkshire Controller whimpered.

'Not today,' said Silva, guessing his thoughts. 'But if any more of your people contravene the rules like Doctor Stapleton, your removal will make this look like something from a children's lullaby.' He turned to Strand. 'Tell me, Matthew, who are you taking with you to York?'

'Taking with me?' said Strand. 'I didn't intend...'

'Take these gentlemen.' Silva motioned to the four deadpan guards and smiled at their smoking weapons. 'I insist.'

* * * *

Chapter 19

A herd of cattle watched from the meadow above Lamberley as Quist's soft-top Volkswagen passed by on the lane towards the narrow river. Iron-dark clouds hung low over the tarnished chrome water and ground frozen hard as steel. Nature was evidently in a metallic mood this Wednesday morning.

'Just look at this.' Watson nodded to the vale ahead. 'Talk about shitholes.'

'The Yorkshire Wolds?' The detective changed gear on the descent. 'I take it this bleak winter beauty does nothing for you?'

'It depresses me.'

'Ah.' Quist braked as the terrain levelled. 'Just out of interest, what sort of place *would* you class as beautiful?'

'Dunno.' Watson shrugged. 'Las Vegas.'

'The world's most ostentatious monument to gaudiness and excess.' He parked on the frosty verge by a gate. 'Yes, that sounds about right.'

'Don't get me wrong, Guv. Yorkshire's brilliant.' The youth clambered from the car. 'I'm just not into the crap historic stuff, or the boring countryside bits. Anyway, where the hell are we?'

'Lamberley is about a mile away.' Quist looked around. 'The village of Wetwang is a couple of miles to the south...'

'Yeah, that's what I thought.' Watson zipped up his jacket. 'The middle of bleedin' nowhere.'

Police tape across the gate still denied access to the meadow beyond, and the frozen grass down to the river had been trampled flat by forensic vehicles and constabulary boots. Quist ducked under the tape, lifted his leather overcoat and climbed the gate. Winter thrushes spilled chattering from the trees overhead.

'Are we allowed to do that?' Watson nodded to the sign on the wall. 'With your amazing powers of observation, I thought you might have spotted the notice saying: *Police - Keep Out.*'

'The place is deserted.' Quist headed for the hawthorn thicket by the water. 'We'll be fine.'

'Fine, unless we get hypothermia.' The teenager followed, scanning the surrounding hillsides and woods. 'It's freezing.'

'Invigorating is the word.' Quist had to secretly agree; cold like this was normally associated with penguins, igloos, and summer holidays on the British coast. 'You don't think it's pleasant to escape the city on such a bracing day?'

'Oh, absolutely.' Watson blew warmth into his hands. He could think of pleasanter things, involving lager and televised sport.

'Just look at the wonderful chalk landscape. Where's your soul?'

'Maybe it disappears in weather like this. My balls certainly have. You could have looked at this place on *Google Earth*, you know?'

Slowly pacing beside the shallow river, Quist stooped to inspect the path. 'Mmh! Camera tripod indentations and vague scuffle marks. What do we deduce from that?'

'The blood has been cleared up, but this is the spot where it happened?'

'Correct.' He stroked his nose thoughtfully. 'Strange that Lisa Mirren's binoculars were taken, but not her camera equipment.'

'Yeah, whatever,' said Watson. 'I still can't understand what we're doing here. Selden asks you to look into his bird's suicide and you come to the place where Saturday's murder happened. You obviously think the two are connected?'

'Both girls worked for Ebor Pharmaceuticals and died within forty hours of each other.'

'You've never heard of coincidences?'

'I've learnt never to dismiss them.' Quist knelt in the grass to check a nondescript mark. The secret longing to come here had been with him from the moment he read of how Lisa Mirren died. The Diane Woodall connection provided a good excuse. 'I don't expect to find anything, but I wanted to see this place.' Still kneeling, he leant on his hands and gazed at the nearby hedgerows from the strange press-up position. 'See it and get the *feel* of it.'

'Right.' Watson eyed him curiously, frowning as Quist lowered his head. *Was he sniffing the grass? No, surely not.* 'There was me thinking that trudging around a freezing field was a waste of time.'

Quist climbed to his feet. 'I notice you dressed appropriately for rural fields.'

'What's that supposed to mean?' Watson looked down at the red jacket, fluorescent trainers and yellow sweatshirt. 'I'm a bit too gaudy?'

'You'd appear gaudy in a Mardi Gras.'

'What did you expect me to wear?'

'I didn't expect you to dress like an explosion in a paint factory...' Quist stiffened, and gaping incredulously, stooped to pick up a tiny object. 'Oh, come *on*. This is ridiculous.' The badge was chrome with *Harley* engraved in crimson. He turned it over, half-expecting to find *clue* etched on the reverse. 'I really don't believe this.'

'You can say that again.' Watson laughed. 'Two deaths and the cops have missed a badge at both sites. How crap is that?'

'What on earth is *this* doing here?' Quist stroked his nose. 'A police search would pick up contact lenses, fingernails and needles in proverbial haystacks. There's no way this would be missed. First that strange talk with Selden and his behaviour, and then these badges. What the hell is going on?'

'Selden doesn't know we're here, Guv, or that we went to the railway last night. He's probably hired someone else by now.'

'Something tells me that won't be the case.'

'We were supposed to be starting that divorce case today. If Selden hires another firm, he won't be paying you.'

'Forget the divorce. I think we'll pursue this a little more.' Quist fingered the badge, common sense and danger screaming in his head. *Leave it! Don't get involved any further!* 'This is very intriguing.'

'Oh well,' said Watson. 'So long as *I'm* getting paid, who cares? If you reckon there's a connection between the dead girls, why don't we see the people at the lab where they worked?'

'Yes, we're going to Ebor Pharmaceuticals,' said Quist. 'But first I want to ask a few questions in Lamberley.'

* * * *

To call Lamberley a village would be lying. With its small church and huddle of limestone cottages by the river, even *hamlet* was an exaggeration. Quist parked his Beetle in the cobbled yard of the Hound inn and strolled about the car park inspecting the ground.

'What are you looking for now?' asked Watson.

Drawing on his cigarette, the detective ignored him and stooped to examine a cobblestone.

'Those fags will kill you, you know?'

'Don't bet on that.' Quist stood up, snuffed the cigarette underfoot and headed for the inn.

The rear door opened into a hallway with a taproom and lounge leading off. Quist chose the lounge, where a log fire bathed the flagged floor and rafters in a cheerful glow. From their appearance the customers appeared to be farm workers. Six were drinking at the counter, three pushed dominoes around a table, and a flat-capped villager, somewhere between eighty and deceased, sat by the fire.

Solid and bald, with red cheeks that belonged on a baboon's backside, the archetypal rural landlord appeared behind the bar. 'Afternoon,' he said. 'What'll you be having?'

Quist tugged off the overcoat and straightened his cord jacket. Theakstons was the guest beer. The flagship of this Yorkshire brewery went by the name of Old Peculiar. A brew with a gravity of some daft figure, a few pints left one experiencing similar floating sensations to the ones surgical patients describe when they leave their bodies and look down at the operating table from the ceiling.

He pointed to the hand pump. 'Two pints please.'

'And a bag of beef crisps,' added Watson.

Hearing the words, a collie trotted up, growled at Quist and backed away. Watson bent to stroke it, noticed the curling lips and decided it would be wiser to stroke a bear trap. The dog began barking.

'Pack it in you silly bugger,' bellowed the landlord. 'Or you'll get my boot up your arse.'

'Thanks.' Paying for the drinks, Quist lowered his voice. 'I imagine you're growing tired of this by now, but I'd like to ask a few questions about the girl who was killed near here.'

'Oh right.' The landlord ran a sceptical eye over the mismatched pair. 'You certainly don't look like police, so I take it you're reporters.'

'Neither. This is a private investigation.'

'Wow! A private eye?'

'Consultant detective. I wonder if you could help?'

'I thought the police would be sorting this out.'

'So did they,' agreed Watson, through a mouthful of crisps.

'We're investigating a case which overlaps with your local tragedy.' Quist sipped his beer. 'According to the newspapers, Doctor Mirren left her vehicle in your car park that day, but didn't call in the pub.'

'Ah!' Watson crunched his crisps. 'That's why you were looking around out there.'

To be truthful, Quist was amazed not to have found another motorcycle badge in the yard.

'That's right,' said the landlord. 'She left her car here around ten-thirty and followed the footpath. It runs east along the little river for about a mile.'

Quist nodded. 'To the hawthorn thicket with the owl roost.'

'Yes, where she was killed at noon. There isn't much I can tell you that you haven't read in the papers. Everyone here has been interviewed and the police have all the facts.'

'How about hearsay and rumour?' asked Quist. 'What ideas do your regulars have about the death?'

'Village gossip? That's important, is it?'

'Useful information can sometimes be found in the wildest theories.'

'No, the murder is the main topic, as you can imagine, but no one seems to know anything.'

'Any strangers in the area over the weekend?'

'Strangers? I should say so.' The landlord gave a humourless laugh. 'We had seven hell's angels in here on Saturday and they don't come stranger than that. A violent-looking bunch with a gorgeous blonde girl.'

'Bloody hell, Guv.' Watson nudged him hard. 'Harley Davidsons.' He looked around, eyes narrowing as a black Ferrari screeched by the window and turned into the car park.

'Indeed,' agreed Quist. 'Do you know where they were from?'

'No idea,' said the landlord. 'Leeds or Hull probably.'

'Satan's Heralds,' called out the old man by the fire. He'd either been listening or was quite insane.

'Yes, that's what they called themselves.' The landlord nodded. 'It was on their jackets.'

Tapping the beer glass with his ring, Quist raised an eyebrow.

'You can forget whatever you're thinking.' He glanced over his shoulder as the car park door opened. 'Their visit was a coincidence. All seven of them were in here when she died and the police seem satisfied they had nothing to do with the murder. Hang on, I'll just serve this chap in the other side.'

'How about that?' Watson gestured across the counter to the black-garbed man in the next room. 'Tom Cruise.'

A couple of locals were eyeing the newcomer suspiciously. It wasn't every day they got twelve grand's worth of designer leather jacket in the taproom, or the lounge. They didn't get many in the entire county.

'Get your autograph book ready.' Quist watched the man talking with the landlord, the latter pointing in their direction. 'I think we're about to meet him.'

The door opened and Rex Grant walked in. If looking cool

ever became a competitive event, mused Watson, here was a guy who'd need a wheelbarrow to carry his trophies. His jacket, Armani jeans and sweater were black, and his shades were Gucci. What degree of coolness the hidden Walther PPK in his waistband would have scored with the teenager was anyone's guess. Strolling casually towards them, Rex trashed the image by tripping over the growling collie and falling on his face.

'Oops!' Quist reached down to help. 'Are you alright?'

'No problem,' spluttered Rex, jumping up. 'I just mentioned Lisa Mirren to the landlord and he tells me you're asking about her too. Apparently you're some private eye investigating her death?'

'Consultant detective. And no, we aren't investigating. We were just passing through and asking a few questions. I'm Bernard Quist and this is my assistant, Watson.'

'Er... right.' Rex peered rudely at his large aquiline nose. 'I'd like a chat with you. Grant's the name. Rex Grant.'

Eyeing the designer labels on the trainers and jeans, Watson whistled to see the diver's wristwatch. It was accurate down to a thousand metres, a staggering technological achievement matched only by the staggering price. Rex, however, like most folk who could afford one, hadn't been deeper than three feet.

'Are you *the* Rex Grant?' asked Watson.

Rex frowned. '*The?*'

'Well, that's a Rolex, and the Ferrari out there is yours too. You've got to be *the* someone or other.' The youth grinned at Quist. 'How's that for elementary deduction?'

Quist nodded. 'As I've said before, we'll make a consultant detective of you yet.'

'Captain Grant, actually.' Rex straightened the sunglasses. 'SAS.'

* * * *

Chapter 20

Katie Bradstreet climbed from her Saab by St Basil's school and grimaced at the fleet of police vehicles. Even a probationer fresh from training college would know that the forensic team working on the cordoned sports car signified something a little more serious than a stolen satnav. The next time the owner of this MG took to the road, it would be in something much slower with room in the rear for a lengthy box. The Inspector smiled gloomily as Gregson appeared from the playground.

'Better prepare yourself, Ma'am,' sighed the Constable. It's Becca Travis.'

'Doctor Travis?' Katie's mouth fell open. '*Another* member of the research team at Ebor Pharmaceuticals has been murdered? Please tell me we have something here to work with.'

'I wish I could. We're doing a door-to-door on the residents, but there are no witnesses.' Gregson led her to the school boiler house. 'Forensics have finished and, er, the Superintendent is in there.'

'Is he indeed.' With the lack of progress, Katie knew that Superintendent Lynch wouldn't be in the jolliest of moods. She stooped under the gate cordon. 'I understand forensics have finished with the Range Rover found near Lamberley?'

'Yeah. It was stolen from the owner's house on Higham Road early on Saturday morning – an accountant named Nesbitt. They've found alien prints and DNA, but they don't match anything on our files.'

'Damn! Speaking of alien DNA, the lab can't identify the cat hairs found on Lisa Mirren's body. Apparently, they're closely related to leopard or lion.'

'What?' Gregson frowned. 'How the hell did she get those on her?'

'I've no idea. The team are checking her associates to see if any are connected with zoos, taxidermy, or the animal trade.' Katie opened the boiler house, salivating at the aroma of roast pork.

Forensic staff were busy around the furnaces and Tariq Aslam knelt examining a mangled padlock. It lay in two pieces, resembling a toy after ten minutes with a hyperactive child. 'Good God!' She looked over the Sergeant's shoulder. 'What did they use to get that off?'

'The SOCO isn't sure.' Aslam climbed to his feet. 'There's another broken open like this that came from the street gate.'

'Some wrench, perhaps?' The roast meat smell was making Katie hungry.

'Well...' Aslam laughed uneasily. 'From the indentations and the way the metal's compressed and torn, the SOCO says it looks as if someone ripped them off by hand.'

Gregson raised an eyebrow. 'Someone's been eating their spinach. It happened last night around five-thirty.'

'Who discovered the body?' Katie looked around as her Superintendent, an overweight man in a raincoat, appeared from behind the furnaces. 'And where is it?'

'Ashley Cooper, the janitor found her.' Superintendent Lynch beckoned Katie over. 'It was Cooper's morning off. He came across the forced padlocks when he checked the boilers at noon. Then he found these.'

The barbecue aroma was finally explained; two legs protruded from a furnace open door, blue stilettos still on the feet. The thighs ended in black stumps, the flesh a charred mess of flaked skin and melted nylon.

'My God!' whispered Katie. '*This* is Becca Travis? How can we know that for certain?'

'There's a unique tattoo on the left ankle,' said Aslam. 'Her father identified a digital photo. She lived with her parents just past the school. They stayed in Scarborough last night, so she wasn't reported missing until this morning. Her father says she should have arrived home around five-thirty last night and the lab claims she left at five.'

'I'm guessing,' said Aslam, 'but I'd say someone who knew Becca's routine was waiting.'

'I don't want guesses,' snapped Lynch. 'I want facts and results. And, so far, results are as rare as suspects. The police in Bath have faxed Raoul Grant's statement; Mirren's ex-fiancé is clean. I understand our motorcyclist friends are also in the clear now?'

'Lisa Mirren died at noon,' said Katie. 'The bikers arrived in Lamberley before eleven and were in the pub until two. The landlord and villagers confirm that. We really need to find the driver of that stolen Range Rover.'

Aslam nodded. 'I have a team searching for Becca's bag, but so far…'

'Bag?' echoed Katie.

'It's vanished,' said Lynch. 'An Italian shoulder bag. Same blue colour as the shoes.'

'It could be in the furnace.'

'The ashes are being taken for analysis,' said Aslam. 'If it's there, the lab will find metallic evidence. Her colleagues are certain she had it when she left, so if it isn't burnt and we don't find it in the area…'

'Her killer probably has it,' broke in Lynch. 'We know some psychopaths keep trophies. First Lisa's binoculars, then Diane's bracelet, and now this bag.'

'Right,' said Katie. 'We're heading over to Ebor Pharmaceuticals and I want to speak to the elusive owner. Gillette said Stapleton was skiing in Canada, but I want verification. Get on to the airlines and immigration offices.' She turned as Jay Mortimer appeared.

'Afternoon, Katie.' The pathologist waved to the furnace. 'I've made an initial examination and life is extinct. I can't tell you very much yet, except she had an expensive taste in shoes.'

'Becca Travis worked in South Lab,' said Katie. 'The same department as the other two girls. Two could have been coincidence, but not three.'

'You're including Diane Woodall in these murders, of course?' said Mortimer.

'Yes, I read your report.' The Inspector nodded. 'Diane's death looked like suicide, but after your post mortem and now *this* - yes, she was definitely the second murder victim.'

'Sounds like you have a serial killer,' said the pathologist, grinning. 'One with a weird fetish for dermatologists.'

* * * *

Chapter 21

By two-fifteen, only five customers remained in the Hound: two men at the bar and the three strangers at a table by the window. Quist sipped beer and studied the pictures that Watson was scrolling through on Rex's phone. Rex had opened the photograph album on his brother's social media page. He sat opposite, drinking a vodka martini and idly playing with his Zippo lighter, flipping open the casing and snapping it shut.

'Didn't mind the cold, did she?' said Watson, crunching crisps. He arrived at a picture of a young couple on moorland with an ocean background. 'Where's that dump?'

'The Isle of Fetlar,' said Quist.

'Yeah, sure,' laughed Watson. 'Obviously.'

Rex dropped the lighter. 'How could you possibly know that?'

'What?' Watson scrutinised the seascape. 'You mean he's right?'

The detective sighed. 'Lisa was a birdwatcher and she has binoculars in this shot, so we know that's why she's there. The terrain is definitely in the Northern Isles and that lighthouse in the distance looks familiar; I've visited the Shetlands myself. Also we know of her passion for owls. If she visited the Shetlands she'd hope to see snowy owls and the only place where there's a chance of that is Fetlar.'

'Er... right.' Rex adjusted his shades. 'Yes, it's Fetlar. That's Raoul, my brother.'

'Lisa's ex-fiancé.' Quist passed the phone back. 'An attractive couple, I must say.' He shuddered as Rex flicked open his Zippo and the nine-inch flame flared.

'Nice!' Watson tried the lighter, chuckling at the blaze and examining the engraved silver case. 'Shouldn't this crest be a dagger with wings?'

'If it was *my* regiment, sure.' Rex cleared his throat. 'That's the Marine's crest. A guy I rescued gave me this.'

'Whoo! What do you reckon to that, Guv?'

'Amazing!' Quist had watched emulsion dry with more enthusiasm.

'So is he right?' quizzed Watson. 'Were they birdwatching?'

'Er, yes.' Rex frowned warily at the detective. 'He was right about the owls too. Snowy owls were Lisa's favourites. They're deadly, but magnificent. So mysterious floating over the ice. So ferocious at the kill. We're talking about nature's ultimate silent killing machine; probably the closest thing in the animal kingdom to the SAS.'

Quist's mouth fell open.

'Want one, Guv?' Watson held out his beef crisps.

'No thanks. I keep an eye on my shape.'

'Owls, eh?' The youth chomped his snack. 'I've never seen one.'

'You should be in my job.' Rex pulled a face. 'After two weeks of undercover work in the Iraqi jungles, you'd be sick of the sight of them.'

'Perhaps we could return to the matter in hand?' said Quist.

'Yes, you've been pretty quiet.' Rex beamed. 'Thinking my proposal over, eh?'

'Yeah.' Watson gave the detective's shoulder an excited slap. 'Is this a brilliant idea or what?'

Quist regarded him with disbelief. This was certainly Raoul Grant's brother, the heir to Grant Homes, of that there was no doubt; he recalled various tabloid pictures with minor celebrities. But what the hell was this all-in-black SAS nonsense? Had the young man suffered some sort of mental breakdown?

'Er, on the contrary,' said Quist, 'I think joining forces, as you suggest, might be unwise. In private investigations, discretion and subtlety are imperative and I think it might be best if you left this to us.'

'Don't be silly,' said Rex. 'Three heads are better than two. I'm here asking questions about Lisa's murder and you're investigating some suicide. The two are connected, so we should work together on this. We could really help each other out.'

'Yeah, come on, Guv,' enthused Watson. 'Three heads *are* better and we can't go wrong with the Captain around. Talk about coincidences? We come here and meet up with the brother of Lisa's fiancé and, wow, he turns out to be SAS. It'll be like having James Bond helping us.'

'Er...' Quist hesitated. 007 was exactly who he *didn't* want helping. Three heads were fine, except when one wore shades indoors and saw itself as the *ultimate silent killing machine.* 'It's unlikely we'll be meeting Doctor No. This is a discreet suicide investigation, remember.'

'But your suicide is connected to Lisa's murder,' pointed out Rex. 'That's why you're in Lamberley.'

'It may be,' admitted Quist. 'But the girls working together could be coincidence.'

Watson laughed. 'But you said never to ignore coincidences.'

'Alright, something tells me they probably *are* connected, but it would be best if you left this to us, Rex. If you give me your number I'll let you know if...'

'I have an obligation,' said Rex. 'I made a promise to Raoul.'

'Yes, I'm sorry to hear about your brother's distress, and how he begged you to find out the truth behind this, but...'

'Like I say, I've an obligation. So what have we unearthed so far?'

'Not much,' said Watson. 'But with someone like you around, things should speed up.'

Quist closed his eyes. *This bizarre character wasn't going to be dissuaded. He'd have to find some way of ditching him, but it didn't look like it would be happening today.*

'So what's the next stage?' asked Rex. 'Where are we going next?'

'Jefferson Road in York,' said Watson. 'The lab where they both worked.'

'Just what *I* was about to suggest.' Rex nodded eagerly and knocked back his martini. 'Come on then, let's see what we can find out.'

'Yes, let's.' Quist tugged on his leather overcoat and strode to the door. 'Thank you, Watson.'

'Don't mention it.' The teenager followed with Rex. 'So you're here on leave, you say?'

'Sick leave.' He slapped his thigh. 'I took a bullet in the leg a couple of weeks ago. A bit painful, but it only tore through muscle. There's no real damage.'

'Where were you shot? Afghanistan? Iraq? Brixton?'

Rex smiled thinly. 'If I told you that, I'd have to kill you. People say that for a laugh these days, but I'm not joking.'

'Really?' Watson's face lit up. 'Phwoarr! Brilliant!'

* * * *

A Friesian herd huddled in a corner and watched the white car on the opposite side of their meadow. Cattle are perceived as stupid, but they possess enormous curiosity and if something stays motionless, they invariably stroll over to inspect it. Strangely enough, they hadn't been within a hundred yards of the BMW with the black windows and, from the terrified look in their eyes, they weren't likely to.

The car had been parked on the hill above Lamberley for ninety minutes, a Haydn concerto drifting through the open window. From this vantage point, the driver could see the Hound public house, but a Maserati by the church held his attention too. It arrived after the blue Beetle and, like the BMW, it was obviously waiting. Like the BMW it also had darkly-tinted windows.

Binoculars were quickly raised as figures left the inn. The middle-aged man in the overcoat looked irate as he stormed to the Volkswagen followed by a black youth, but the observer was more interested in the Ferrari owner. He noted the number and watched curiously as the black-garbed man threw himself into a press-up position to check the chassis for bombs. Switching off the music, the BMW driver adjusted the hi-fi tuner, his engine bursting into life as the cars in the valley pulled away. The binoculars were lifted again as the Maserati set off.

'Just as I thought,' he murmured. 'You *are* tailing them.' He took the number. 'I'm afraid that won't do at all.'

* * * *

Chapter 22

Watson watched the black F50 vanish around the bend ahead in a cloud of spray. 'I don't know what your problem is with him helping,' he said. 'I thought he'd be useful.'

'Really?' Shooting his assistant a withering look, Quist turned onto Jefferson Road in York and checked the mirror. The Maserati and white BMW, both of which had been behind for the past few miles, were still there. 'I think you'll find your cool new SAS friend will be as useful as a pack of hounds to a lame fox.'

'You didn't mention the Harley badges or those bikers the landlord told us about. What's the idea of keeping it to yourself?'

'Trust me, alright?'

Looking into Diane Woodall's suicide was probably a mistake, Quist realised that, but it was no longer possible to walk away from this. The badges had obviously been left there for him to discover, but why and by whom? His curiosity had been aroused by Selden's behaviour, but someone planting items at murder scenes was too intriguing to ignore. The priority was to investigate discreetly, without any police interaction. Avoiding contact with the authorities and blending into the background with his nondescript appearance had become second nature over the years. Rex Grant was the last person he needed around – an imbecile from the celebrity gossip columns who drove a Ferrari and wore sunglasses in the rain.

The F50 brake lights blazed in the distance ahead.

'Fantastic!' Watson licked his lips. 'All my life I've dreamed of driving a car like that.'

'It has a top speed of over two-hundred. I don't know if you're aware, but the British limit is seventy.'

'So you prefer this heap, and the worry of the pilot light blowing out?' The teenager patted the tinny dashboard. 'In every television detective show the hero drives a fast motor and has exciting chases.'

'What a shame I don't meet the standards of your fictional

94

detectives.'

'Well, you're quite like Miss Marple.' Watson watched the Ferrari turn off the road into the grounds of a two-storey complex. 'Hullo! That's the place, huh?'

'Yes, Ebor Pharmaceuticals.' Following the Ferrari onto the car park, Quist checked the mirror as the Maserati and BMW continued past. Three empty police cars stood near the front doors.

Watson watched wide-eyed as Rex twisted the wheel skidding the car to a sideways halt in a cloud of spray. 'Mmmh! Bit of a twat, don't you reckon?'

Quist had to disagree; Grant was far more than a *bit*. Grant was a twat who deserved to be on the cover of *The Observer's Book of Twats*.

'Nice motor,' enthused Watson, climbing out into the rain and walking around the black F50. 'They did a limited run of these, didn't they? What sort of speed will she do?'

Rex grinned. 'I've had two-hundred out of her in Germany.'

'I've always been into prestige motors.' Watson's gaze moved lovingly over the air intakes and rear spoiler. 'Er, any chance of a go in it?'

'A go?' echoed Rex.

Quist winced. Giving his assistant a *go* in an F50 would be like giving a shotgun with strawberry-flavoured barrels to a manic-depressive.

'A drive,' said Watson. 'Just a little drive around a car park, like this one, maybe?'

Rex laughed. 'About the same chance as me leaving a nightclub without a model on my arm.'

'If you're quite ready,' sighed Quist. He needed Grant here like a sleepwalker needed a cliff. 'We need to go about this tactfully. The last thing we want is to get involved with the police investigation in there.'

Watson chuckled. 'Not a wanted man, are you, Guv?'

Quist gave a lopsided smile and turned to Rex. 'When you say you're looking into Lisa Mirren's murder, how exactly are you intending to go about that? What sort of questions were you thinking of asking at the laboratory?'

'Well, er...' Rex nodded thoughtfully. 'Relevant, searching questions.'

'Ah!' The detective rubbed his eyes. 'Did Lisa have any cousins?'

'I've no idea. Why?'

'The staff here won't speak to strangers, but they will to Lisa's family. She has a cousin now - a geologist working in France. They were quite close and he's just arrived home with two friends.'

'Really?' Rex looked blank. 'I've never heard of this guy.'

'It's *you*.' Quist headed for the doors. 'Introduce yourself and then leave the talking to me. Come along, Mister Mirren, let's see what we can discover.'

They discovered impatient reps waiting in the lobby with sales and delivery people. Office and lab staff milled about, and a young black girl in a yellow mini dress fumed quietly behind reception.

'Merry Christmas.' Adjusting his shades, Rex leant over her desk. 'Who's in charge?'

'A good question,' said Lynn Chandler. 'One that I've heard several times today. Are you talking about our director, Doctor Gillette, or Superintendent Lynch?'

'Well, we don't want the cops, so I suppose we'd like to see Doctor Gillette.'

The receptionist smiled weakly. 'Then you'd better find yourself a place in the queue. It's not exactly business as usual, as you can probably see.'

'What's going on?' Quist looked around. 'We saw the police cars outside.'

'I'm not allowed to say, but everything is on hold while they interview the staff and take statements.'

'Oh dear,' said Quist. 'This gentleman is Doctor Mirren's

cousin. It wouldn't take long.'

'Lisa's cousin? Oh, I really am so sorry. Wasn't that just terrible?' Lynn glanced at the door to their left as Gillette entered the lobby with his secretary. 'You're in luck.' She raised her voice. 'Doctor, I wonder if you could spare a moment? There's someone to see you.'

The director turned as Amy Clarkson appeared from the corridor behind him.

'Will,' stammered Amy. 'About my overtime - I want to take it now, if possible?'

'Certainly,' said Gillette. 'But are you sure you're alright?' He slipped an arm around her shoulders. 'This has been a shock for you – a shock for us all. Why don't you go to the refectory and...'

'I'm fine,' said Amy, glumly. 'But now the police have finished with me I just want to get home and think about their proposal.'

'Your car's in the garage, isn't it?'

'I pick it up tomorrow. That's another reason why I need to leave early. I'm on the bus and it's raining.'

'I'll give you a lift,' said Gillette's secretary. 'But they haven't interviewed me yet. I don't know how long I'll be.'

Amy shook her head. 'Thanks, Nicole, but you could be ages. They're concentrating first on the staff who worked with Becca. I still can't believe she's dead.'

Watson nudged Quist. 'Another one?' he whispered.

'Goodnight then.' Gillette patted Amy's back. 'Please try not to dwell too much on all this. Make sure you look after yourself.'

Quist watched the girl leave and reached a decision. The longer they asked questions in here, the more chance there was of being noticed by the police, especially with Grant around.

Gillette turned to the waiting trio. 'Now, gentlemen...' He looked them over, taking in their odd appearance, especially Rex's shades dripping with rainwater. 'Er, how can I help?'

Rex opened his mouth.

'Are you aware that Christmas is a pagan festival?' said Quist, motioning to the twinkling lobby tree. 'Celebrating makes Jehovah very upset.'

The director studied him vacantly through his wide spectacles.

'We're in the area speaking to people about the coming apocalypse.' Quist assumed a Stepford Wife expression. 'Tell me, how often do you read your bible?'

'Fuck off, you half-wit,' snarled Gillette, his tone suggesting he hadn't perused the scriptures for some time.

Nicole Patterson watched curiously as the director stormed away and the taller of the strangers ushered his friends from the lobby.

'What the hell was that?' gasped Rex. 'You said...'

Quist ran to the car. 'I changed my mind.'

'Changed it?' Watson eyed him inquisitively. 'Sounded like you'd bleedin' lost it.'

'Will you get a move on before that girl disappears,' hissed Quist. 'With the police sniffing around, it'll be easier to speak to her than the staff in there.'

'Good thinking,' conceded Rex.

'You want to help, don't you?' Quist looked him up and down. 'Here's something you should excel at.'

* * * *

The Jefferson Road bus stop stood fifty yards from Ebor Pharmaceuticals at the entrance to an industrial estate. A Perspex shelter had been erected next to it, but local youths had obviously taken exception to this and the mangled roof lay in nearby shrubbery. Five people waited in the rain: three workmen, an elderly woman and Amy Clarkson. The doctor wore a saturated mackintosh and viewed the umbrella beside her enviously.

'Come on,' chuckled the old lady. 'Get yourself under here. It's a terrible day.'

Amy didn't argue. 'Yes, it certainly...' She paused as a black Ferrari skidded to a halt in the water-filled gutter and drenched the queue. 'What the hell...'

The window sank. 'Hi.' Rex winked at Amy over his shades. 'Fancy a drink?'

'What?'

'A drink in a pub. Soft lights, soft music... me.'

'Piss off,' snapped Amy, shaking her dripping coat.

Rex gaped in astonishment. *Was she blind or just stupid? Hadn't she noticed the car? More to the point, hadn't she noticed the good-looking guy behind the wheel?*

Something rang a bell in the back of Amy's mind, something about a black Ferrari and an imbecile, but she'd no idea what. Taking a deep breath, she leant down to the window. 'I saw you in the lobby back there with two other guys. Who are you and what the hell do you want?'

'It's your lucky day.' Rex patted the passenger seat. 'I'm offering you a drink and a lift home in style. Now who could refuse an offer like that?'

'*I* could.'

'I'm not bothered about a drink, luv,' said the lady with the umbrella. 'But I'll have a lift.'

'Oh, I get it,' said Rex. 'You're worried, right? The thing is, I have to talk to you and...'

'I don't get into cars with strange men. Talk all you want, but make it fast. My bus is due any second.'

'Okay, calm down. I should have shown you this straight away.' He held up his phone with a photo of Raoul and Lisa Mirren. 'This is my brother with his fiancé, Lisa. You knew her, didn't you?'

'Yes, I worked with her.' *Of course! That was it. Lisa had mentioned Raoul's strange brother.* 'What's this about?'

'Raoul asked me to investigate her death and I'd like to ask you a few questions. You might be able to help. Quist knows a pub on this side of town and thought it would be a good place to chat.'

'Quist?'

'A private eye who's helping me; you saw him in the lobby. So what do you say?'

'Maybe, but some other time.' Amy handed back the phone. 'Yes, Lisa mentioned you, but it's been a really bad day and I just want to go home.'

'You're still suspicious?' He removed the shades. 'Rex Grant's the name. I mean, honestly, do I look like a murderer or a loony?'

She smiled faintly. 'You don't look like a murderer. Investigating Lisa's death? What are you? Police or a private eye like your friend?'

'Hardly.' He stuck an arm through the window. 'Captain Grant, SAS.'

'Wow!' She shook hands. 'Lisa never mentioned *that*.'

'Naturally. Raoul will have told her not to.'

Ice water splattered down Amy's neck as the bus appeared in the distance. A Ferrari, a cheerful pub and the company of a Tom Cruise look-alike from the SAS were beginning to sound inviting. She checked to ensure a red Audi was parked down the road.

'Okay. I suppose you're safe enough.' She opened the door. 'It's Amy, by the way.'

'What is?'

'Er, my name.'

Rex pressed the accelerator, treating the bus queue to a second drenching, and Gregson in the Audi pulled out of the lab entrance to follow. The white BMW in the industrial estate started up too and the driver began to chuckle.

* * * *

100

Chapter 23

This *real* detective work was turning out to be much better than those murder mystery weekends in hotels, decided Rex. Already, he'd met a genuine private eye and taken a blonde doctor for a drink. He and Amy sat on one side of the pub table with Quist and Watson facing. A lovely wood-panelled tavern, with sagging beams and bulls-eye windows, the Golden Fleece was busy this Wednesday afternoon.

'This is the most haunted pub in York,' said Watson, looking at the Christmas tree beside them. 'What do you reckon to that, Guv?'

'Is that so?' said Quist, running an eye over the doctor opposite. 'I like inns with history, atmosphere and character, and the Fleece positively oozes all three.'

'So what's this about?' sighed Amy. Her wet raincoat hung over a radiator and she sat in a sweater and jeans. 'Rex was telling me about Lisa being his brother's fiancé and how he promised to look into this while he's on leave, but how are you involved? Murder is hardly private eye work, is it?'

'Consultant detective,' corrected Quist.

'There's a difference?' asked Rex.

'Not that you'd notice,' said Watson.

'Make yourself useful.' Quist passed the teenager a banknote. 'You know what everyone wants and I'm sure you can find the bar.'

'I don't understand what you're doing here either, Rex,' added Amy. She ran her eyes over his black clothing and sunglasses. 'I know your brother is upset and thinks you might be able to help, but surely the police will sort this out?'

'Yes.' He sat back and crossed his legs. 'But they'll catch Lisa's killer a lot faster with us working independently alongside them.'

Quist rolled his eyes. 'We met Rex in Lamberley, but it isn't Lisa's death I've been asked to investigate; it's Diane Woodall's.'

'Who's employing you?' asked Amy.

'No one as yet. I haven't decided whether to take the case, but

I still have to respect the client's confidentiality.'

'We think Lisa's murder and Diane are connected.' Rex winked conspiratorially at Amy over his shades. 'That's why he was in Lamberley and why we joined forces.'

The detective bit his tongue.

'You're probably right,' confessed Amy. 'It'll be in the papers tomorrow so I can tell you. With this latest death, the police no longer believe Di was a suicide.'

'Here we go.' Watson set down a tray of glasses and crisps. 'Merry Christmas.' He picked up the lager and passed Amy the white wine. Rex took the vodka martini, and Quist the beer.

'I hope this was made how I specified?' said Rex. 'Shaken, not stirred.'

'Ah!' Quist patted the pile of crisps. 'Watson seems to have treated himself to a snack with my money. Would you care for a bar meal, Doctor Clarkson? I've eaten here before. They have a good range of vegetarian dishes.'

'Vegetarian,' snorted Watson. 'Don't you ever eat proper food? Something that's frolicked with its mum in a meadow.'

'I'm not hungry.' Amy shook her head. 'And as I've said, I don't see how I can help. I don't know anything, and anything I *do* know I've already told to the police.'

'We overheard something about this latest death when we called at the lab,' said Quist, softly. 'Was it a friend?'

'Becca Travis.' The girl sipped her wine. 'Becca wasn't really my type, but I knew her pretty well. I knew all three of them. It's so hard to believe they're gone.'

'I'm very sorry.'

'Are you a secretary there?' quizzed Rex.

'She's a doctor,' said Quist, testily.

He peered curiously. 'Is that right?'

'Probably not the sort you're thinking of,' admitted Amy. 'A doctor of biochemistry, not someone who hands out pills.'

'Mmmmh!' Watson grinned. 'Obviously not as blonde as you

look.'

Amy dipped into Watson's crisps and smiled. It was difficult to dislike these three and she was beginning to appreciate this strange invitation.

Rex watched her munching with interest, having seldom seen girls eat. The models he dated usually picked at their food, before visiting the toilet to attend to their coke habit and surreptitiously regurgitate whatever had been swallowed. He was surprisingly attracted to this fair-haired girl - surprisingly, because in the clubs he frequented, he'd never have noticed her. Doctor Clarkson, in her non-designer sweater and jeans, wasn't exactly supermodel material. She was pretty rather than beautiful, and intellect had never ranked highly with him. On the Grant checklist of female assets, where a tight little arse was number three and long legs number five, brains limped in at number twelve.

'So what biochemistry work do you do at the lab?' he asked.

'Dermatological research,' said Amy. 'We develop pharmaceutical and beauty products for the skin and eyes. Lisa, Di and Becca worked with me in the same department.'

Rex paused, glass to lips. 'How many others?'

'No one, and that's the creepy part. I'm the last surviving member of South Lab.'

Watson choked on crisps. 'I take it you've slapped in a transfer?'

'What are you working on at the moment?' asked Quist.

'Everyday products. Wrinkle creams, mascaras, moisturizing lotions and... well, that's about it.'

'And...'

'Two unfinished projects.' Amy debated if she could trust them. 'Have you heard of Solstice, the sunscreen?'

'One of the first super-sunscreens,' said Rex. 'It's been around a while.'

Quist was impressed. Apparently Grant's head wasn't entirely empty: he knew something about sunbathing.

'That's the one,' said Amy. 'We purchase existing products to develop when their patents expire.' She leant forward. 'Complaints have been emerging from people experiencing burns and moles after using the original Solstice in hot countries.'

'I can guess why.' Quist smiled grimly. 'Solar radiation is increasing.'

'Right. We discovered the first ozone hole over Antarctica decades ago, but air pollution has damaged the atmosphere and more holes are appearing. Ultra-violet has increased ten percent in the past decade and every one percent rise leads to a two percent rise in melanomas and carcinomas.'

'Come again?' said Watson.

'Skin cancers. So far the situation isn't serious and everything has been hushed up, but the super-sunscreens, Solstice included, are becoming useless, even dangerous for sensitive individuals.'

'What exactly is a super-sunscreen?' enquired Quist.

'They were designed to remove holiday hassle,' said Rex.

Amy nodded. 'Active pigments absorb into the subcutaneous layer and biologically bind to the keratin - the skin itself. The barrier doesn't wash off like normal sun filters when bathing or swimming, so you simply apply them and forget them for up to forty-eight hours.'

'I see,' said Quist. 'But they were developed before the ozone damage and now need upgrading?'

'A much higher blocking factor is needed for fair skin,' confirmed Amy. 'And eye droplet protection too. That was our other unfinished project: a liquid solution to shield eyes from ultra-violet.'

'You say it's being hushed up?' Watson looked bemused. 'Why?'

'You can't allow people to become scared of the sun,' said Quist. 'Airlines, summer-wear industries and countless other firms would crumple overnight. Thousands would be redundant in this country alone.'

'On bright days no one would dare leave for work,' agreed Amy. 'That's why the lab director wants our work kept quiet.'

'This won't go any further,' Quist assured her.

'Fortunately the danger was discovered in time and many labs are working on protection.'

'I'm pleased to hear it.' Quist sipped his beer. 'Anyway, this superior Solstice and the eye droplets were the last products you worked on?'

'Yes. The moisturizer, mascaras and creams were completed, but those two were terminated. We weren't making any progress.'

'And nothing odd has happened recently at your company?'

'Apart from a string of murders,' said Watson.

'Not *really...*'

'That sounds like: *apart from,*' said Quist.

'It's nothing worth mentioning, but there were a couple of things. The new system in our department, for example. Will, the director, introduced it when we started on the eye droplets and bought the Solstice patent.'

'Doctor Gillette?' Quist nodded. 'We met him briefly.'

'Yeah, he doesn't read the bible,' said Watson.

Amy smiled. 'No one was allowed to work on the cream or eye drops as a whole. Each researcher worked on different solutions which were blended and finished by Will himself. I worked with the base bonding emulsions. Lisa, Becca and Di worked on various blocking agents, and then Will would take our work for completion in his private lab. We never saw the end product. Not even Doctor Keating had access to the completed batches and she's the assistant director. Secondly, it sounds stupid, but the chemicals weren't right. I suppose they must have been, but it didn't seem like it at the time.'

'How do you mean?' asked Rex.

'It's hard to say. I realise the new Solstice was specialised, but do you know anything about the spectrum?'

The trio nodded, but only Quist looked convincing.

'White light from the sun is made up of seven colours. The blue end of the spectrum contains ultra-violet that damages skin DNA and gives a tan. Blocking agents would need to absorb and filter this blue light, perhaps using paba-para amino-benzoic acid and titanium dioxide.'

'Yes, that's right,' said Rex, nodding astutely.

'What are you getting at?' questioned Quist.

'Well we seemed to be producing something that screened radiation from the red end of the spectrum. Becca worked on eight experimental retinols that were useless in stopping UV, but they all blocked red light.'

'Intriguing.' Quist stroked his large nose. 'Although you never saw the finished products, what effect did they have?'

'Everything is sent away for testing, but they can't have been much good. As I said, the projects were terminated due to lack of progress.'

'Okay,' said Watson. 'Now we know what Amy does for a living, how about getting back to the detective stuff? Instead of chemistry crap, what about those badges?'

Rex looked puzzled. 'What on earth do badgers have to do with this?'

Quist ignored him. 'Yes, Amy, what do you know about Harley Davidsons? Do you know of any motorcyclists who work or call at the lab? Especially anyone who rides a Harley?'

'There's no one that I know of.'

'I've been thinking...' broke in Rex. 'If you and this Gillette are the only ones left from your research team...'

'I know,' sighed Amy. 'It's scary, but the police want me to continue with my routines over the next few days. Undercover people are being posted at the lab, a policewoman is at my house and unmarked cars are following me. There's one right outside now. Believe me, if it hadn't been for that, I'd never have been stupid enough to come here with you.'

'They think the murderer will go after you next?' Watson whistled and peered through the window. 'How do you feel about being used as bait?'

'They've assured me I'll be fine.' She grinned nervously.

'Suspicious characters will be snatched before anything happens. Anyway, if they catch the killer, it'll be worth it. I suppose I was half hoping that Rex might have had something to do with this when I accepted his offer - to get it all over with quickly.'

'About that Harley Davidson,' said Quist. 'Can you recall if Lisa, Becca, or Diane ever mentioned a motorcyclist?'

'I don't think so.' Amy shook her head. 'No one called her Diane, by the way. She was Di to everyone who knew her.'

'That's weird, Guv,' murmured Watson. 'Selden called her Diane when he tried to hire you, and he's her fiancé.'

'Nice going with the confidentiality,' growled Quist. 'You're about as discreet as a wrecking ball.'

'Whoops! Strange though, eh?'

'Here's something stranger,' said Amy. 'She didn't have a fiancé.'

Quist stiffened. 'Are you sure?'

'Seventeen stone bloke,' said Watson. 'Tattoos, shaven head, and the IQ of an onion bhaji.'

'Pretty sure.' Amy nodded. 'Di was gay.'

* * * *

Due to the shortage of York Rastafarians and the police backlash against anyone harassing ethnic students, Selden and his cronies occasionally filled a van with lager and baseball bats and travelled along the A64 for a night out in Milverton, an area of Leeds that makes Harlem look like Shangri La. Although the authorities deny the existence of no-go areas, no sane officers patrol this Leeds borough and police vehicles never enter without riot gear.

The skinhead didn't seem worried as he strode alone along Milverton's main street in his swastika shirt. Turning onto an avenue of four-storey houses, he homed in on a loud Bob Marley drumbeat and arrived at his destination with minutes to spare. *Four-thirty he'd been told, but a little either way wouldn't matter.*

The tenement looked too dilapidated to be occupied, but it was home to an illegal club run by the more unsavoury elements of the community, where drink, drugs and girls could be purchased. Selden knew of several of these dives and had always intended to petrol bomb them one day. The cops didn't seem bothered. They were too busy making easier arrests on kids smoking weed in their student flats – somewhere else that Selden believed should be petrol bombed.

The skinhead kicked open the door. 'Move!' he grunted, pushing past three passage guards. One dropped his machete in disbelief. 'Why don't you piss off back to Africa and eat watermelon?'

Thirty black faces glared as Selden barged through the lounge to where the hi-fi blasted reggae. A giant with dreadlocks sat beside it, cutting cocaine with a knife. He cursed as the debt collector knocked him aside, spilling the tray.

'Right!' Switching off the music and turning to his audience, Selden shouted what were, understandably, to be his final words. 'Listen to me, you heroin-pushing bastards - this is a citizen's arrest.'

* * * *

'*I'm out, so leave a message. And don't get any ideas about robbing an empty flat. There's a dog here that'll rip your fuckin' arms off.*'

'No one home.' Quist passed Watson's mobile back across the pub table. 'It's a rather eloquent answerphone message.'

'So why would Selden say he was her fiancé and ask us to investigate?' Watson shook his head. 'It doesn't make any sense.'

'I have no idea.' Quist's signet ring tinkled thoughtfully against his glass. 'This is getting ridiculous!'

'Just give me five minutes with this guy.' Rex cracked his knuckles. 'I'll soon get us some answers.'

'Normally I loathe violence.' Quist stroked his nose to conceal a smirk. 'Although I'll be glad of your military fighting skills tonight.'

'You're going to let him kick the shit out of Selden?' Watson beamed. 'Can I watch?'

'I'm not talking about Selden. The chances are we'll be

needing his talents at our next port of call.'

'Next port of call? You mean you're not dropping this?' Watson looked baffled. 'If Selden spouted a pack of lies, it's a dead cert he isn't intending to pay you. What he thought about us was never a secret, so this is probably his warped idea of a joke.'

'Believe me, Watson, there's more to this than the stupid prank of some dumb thug. I need to know what's going on.'

'So where *are* we going next?'

'You'll soon see.' Quist gave Amy one of his lopsided smiles. 'Thank you, Amy. The talk was enlightening.'

'I suppose I should thank *you*.' The doctor finished her drink. 'I felt terrible after hearing about Becca and then the thought of being watched by the police. The company has done me good. I still don't think looking into this will help the police, but I wish I could have been more useful.'

'So what now?' Rex winked over his shades. 'Do you have any plans tonight?'

'Yes, a bath, a bottle of wine and a TV. The policewoman nanny will be arriving at my place soon to babysit.'

Quist picked up his coat. 'Come along then. We'll get you home safely. Leave the Ferrari here for now and we'll use my car. The Volkswagen has four seats.'

'Thanks.' Amy laughed as Rex pulled back her chair. 'Good thing I'm not a feminist.'

'I don't mind feminists,' he admitted. 'Providing they know their place.'

* * * *

Parked across the street, Constable Gregson sat watching the Golden Fleece from his Audi. Rain performed a drumbeat on the car roof and he switched on the wipers as Quist, Watson and Rex emerged with Amy. A Maserati started up several yards behind, and further away, a fourth vehicle pulled out to follow.

'Incredible!' The BMW driver chuckled into his mobile. 'It's like a convoy.'

'I shouldn't laugh yet,' warned the voice on the phone. 'I've checked the registrations you gave me. The Ferrari belongs to Rex Grant, the son of the building magnate Lionel Grant.'

'Grant Homes? What's he doing here? How about the Maserati?'

'The Maserati is the problem; it's Carl Dreyer. He's the Leeds manager for Brightshield Glazing - one of Tayman's men.'

'Ah!' The white BMW accelerated towards Ouse Bridge, keeping the cars in sight. 'I think I understand. Brightshield have a York sales office below Quist. He's probably been trying to sell him windows.'

'Mmmh, and Tayman wants to know how his sales technique failed? That's possible, but we can't have him watching them. It'll jeopardise everything.'

'Don't worry.' The BMW driver chuckled again. 'Leave the Dreyer problem to me.'

* * * *

Chapter 24

The Pennines are known as the Backbone of England–rugged hills of heather moorland and surly, damp sheep, that separate Lancashire in the west from Yorkshire in the east. The M62 motorway was constructed across this forbidding landscape in the early seventies, bisecting Northern Britain and connecting Manchester with Hull. The highest motorway in the country, the road rises to 1221 feet as it crosses the Rishworth and Saddleworth moors. In the right conditions, this wilderness can be starkly beautiful, but on winter days like this, it resembled Tolkien's land of Mordor.

The cab windows in the Mercedes van were fitted with black glass, which allowed the occupants to see out, but no one to see in. This was fortunate, as the opposite way around would have been awkward for Fisher the driver. He cruised along the M62 at eighty, with Browning beside him and Sangster, Hinds and Strand lounging in the luxuriously-upholstered rear. Despite the winter rain. all five wore sunglasses, which coupled with the black suits, gave the men the appearance of CIA operatives.

'Watch the speedometer,' said Strand.

The van drifted across the hard shoulder.

'I'll rephrase that.' He grabbed the driver's head, jerking it upright. 'Watch the road, but keep your speed below seventy - okay?'

'Okay, Sir,' said Fisher.

'Good.' Strand sat back. 'We don't want to attract motorway police.'

Strand stared out at the rain, his thoughts on the previous day's meeting. Disembowelled by bullets probably wasn't the way in which Sharp wished to depart this world, but it was preferable to some deaths he'd seen. Creasey from Aberdeen was the last society member to break Silva's rules. The furnace they threw him into had been turned down low and his demise had taken an awfully long time. Strand had smoked an entire cigarette before the scratching on the metal door stopped. It was typical of Silva to have the latest Elite execution performed theatrically before the Committee - as if they needed such warnings. If all went to plan, such deaths and the dark days of terror would be soon be over.

Browning turned. 'Good news with the weather, Sir.'

'Mmmh?' Strand realised the bodyguard had been listening to the radio. 'What is it?'

'Fog and possibly snow predicted for tomorrow in Yorkshire.'

'Excellent!' said Strand. 'We don't get enough fog these days. You can't beat a spot of pleasant weather on a field trip like this.'

* * * *

Driving rain soaked into the broad shoulders of Sangster's suit. The huge bodyguard kicked a broken padlock out of sight beneath shrubbery, swung open Stapleton's wrought iron gates and stepped back into the shadows of the high wall. Fisher killed the van lights and turned off the York cul-de-sac into the dark driveway. Sensor-activated floodlights kicked in, bathing the modern mansion and its pseudo-Georgian frontage in illumination.

'That's better.' Fisher pulled up by the porch. 'Now we can see to break in.'

'Yes.' Strand took a remote control from the glove compartment. 'Although, as those lights are there to warn of intruders, I think it might be a good idea to get rid of them, don't you?'

Dropping the window, he aimed at a tree where he knew some of the secreted motion sensors to be. The lights died, and adjusting settings, he pointed and pressed again. Stapleton's alarm and surveillance systems were supplied by Silver Security Systems and foolproof, unless you had a nullifier which could switch off the central defence computer.

'There. Now it's safe.'

Climbing from the van, Strand glanced around, ensuring trees concealed the nocturnal visitors from neighbouring houses. Bishopthorpe was one of the most exclusive suburbs of York and the Linden Mount residents would watch out for suspicious activity.

'It looks empty,' said Hinds, peering at the windows with

their closed curtains as Sangster returned from the gates. 'There are no lights showing in...'

'What the fuck do you think you're doing?' Strand turned to see Browning reaching for the porch doorbell. 'Get away from there, you lunatic. Come here, all of you.'

Browning joined the others in a semi-circle. 'I thought...'

'Listen,' snarled Strand. 'Now would be a good time to clarify things before your stupidity causes any problems. In Manchester you belong to the President and wield a certain amount of power. Here in the field it's different. Silva placed me in charge and you were ordered to obey. You'll do everything I say and nothing more, is that fully understood?'

The quartet blinked as the words sank in. Silva had hand-picked his private security squad from the muscle-bound, criminal dregs of run-down gymnasiums–psychopathic bodybuilders, violent boxers, and vicious heavies from protection rackets. They obeyed the President without question, but their cerebral skills could be likened to the lovemaking skills of pandas.

'I still think we should have set off sooner,' said Sangster. 'The President said he wanted this clearing up as soon as possible.'

'Don't worry about that,' said Strand. 'Follow me. I want to look around the back.' Moving cautiously to the house corner, he led them through the bushes to a terraced rear patio. 'The lounge is empty.' He cupped his hands against the French doors, where the curtains weren't fully drawn. 'Right, we're going to search the place.'

'What are we looking for?' asked Hinds.

'Anything to explain this vanishing act or tell us where Stapleton is. With the alarm neutralised, we can use the front door and...' Strand froze as a crash split the silent darkness. He slowly closed his eyes.

'No need to go back round.' Fisher clumsily disentangled his foot from the shattered glass door. 'We can get in here.'

* * * *

Chapter 25

Quist turned his Beetle off Micklegate and into a quiet backwater of Victorian houses. The terraces were arranged in neat rows beneath the grassy embankment of the city walls, with well-maintained gardens and mature trees. Amy lived three rows in from the battlements on Appleton Terrace

'So there was no reason why Diane would take her life?' said Quist. 'She didn't know about Lisa's murder, did she?'

'None of us knew until Monday when the police arrived at the lab.' Amy shrugged sadly. 'No one there can believe Di killed herself. She was the happiest girl you could imagine.'

'This really is a strange business,' murmured Quist.

'Not as strange as some weirdo claiming to be her fiancé,' said Amy.

'Yes, we'll be chatting with Selden about that tomorrow morning.'

'I'll be interested to hear what he says.' The doctor pointed halfway along the terrace to a smartly-painted house with wisteria. 'This is it - the white door.'

Quist brought the Volkswagen to a halt. 'I know this is asking a lot, but is there any way I could see the research for your recent products or learn where they were sent for testing? It could be important.'

'Important?' She looked puzzled. 'You mean to these murders?'

'I'm not sure. I just have a peculiar nagging feeling.'

'Not really. The Solstice and eye droplets were confidential and even mundane data isn't left around. Will keeps all the formulas, testing destinations and results on computer.'

'Wise man.' Watson eyed Quist. 'All practical folk use computers.'

'In that case,' angled Quist, 'I er, wonder if it's possible to access the computer?'

'If it was, do you think I'd tell someone I hardly knew?' Amy grinned. 'It's only my career and pension on the line. Besides, it's a personal office terminal that isn't hooked into the internet like the company computer. Hacking is impossible.'

'I admit it was a ridiculous request.' Quist smiled. 'Anyway, thanks again, Amy. It was nice meeting you.'

'And you.' She laughed as Rex leapt into the rain to help her out. 'You have my number. Let me know what your skinhead friend has to say for himself. Goodnight, Bernard.'

'You say an armed policewoman is staying?' Rex watched as she searched the mackintosh for her key. 'Will you be okay until she arrives?'

'I'll be fine.' Amy checked the time. 'WPC Farnon will be here any time now.'

'I could spend the night too, if you wanted. If it would help you sleep better.'

'I'll be fine.' Amy laughed again. 'I'll be seeing you, Rex.'

'Talking of seeing people...' He looked over his rain-spattered shades. 'It might be a good idea to get together again to discuss this situation. I mean if...'

'If you're saying you'd like to take me out, the answer's yes, if you take off those ludicrous sunglasses.'

He stuffed them into his pocket.

'Thank you.' She kissed his cheek. 'Ring me.'

'Yeah.' Rex watched her slip into the house, waiting until she waved from the window before climbing back into the Beetle. 'I'll do that.'

Twenty yards down the street, Gregson watched them pull away and settled down for the night behind the steering wheel.

'Nice kiss,' sighed Rex. 'The girl's crazy about me, but who could blame her?'

Watson turned to see if this was a joke and realised it wasn't. 'Will she be okay, Guv?'

'Don't worry,' said Quist. 'An unmarked police car has pulled

115

up. I wouldn't have left her otherwise.'

'That red Audi? How can you tell it's a cop?'

'It tailed us from the Golden Fleece and it was by the doors with the police vehicles at the lab earlier. The tax is in a Police Personnel holder.'

'You noticed that? You don't miss much, do you?'

'Not much.' Quist glanced in the mirror, but didn't mention the Maserati headlights.

Chapter 26

Will Gillette pressed his spine against the lounge patio door, his terrified eyes flickering over his unexpected house guests: four vicious-looking giants and a smaller bearded character leaning casually against the fireplace.

'Fulford seems to be a pleasant area of York.' Drawing slowly on a cigarette, Strand ran a lazy finger over the ornate mantelpiece clock, his green eyes unblinking and almost reptilian. He gazed around the Victorian-styled room. 'I can see why you chose to live here.'

The research director gave a tense smile, his eyes darting back to the bodyguards.

'Big boys, aren't they?' said Strand. 'They're Elite, as I'm sure you've guessed, and not the nicest members of the Elite either. Browning here was part of a white supremacy movement before Silva recruited him for his personal security squad.'

Gillette's face drained to a horrible grey, a sickly colour normally only seen in nursing home porridge. Patches of cold sweat bloomed on his shirt.

Strand gestured to the monster on his right. 'Sangster was a boxer, but beat two men to death in the ring. Quite a few *outside* the ring too. Yes, they're *very* big boys, but provided you assist me, Will, I don't see any reason for them to worry you.'

The doctor swallowed uncomfortably. His heart hammered and the pounding of blood in his ears almost drowned out the rain on the patio doors.

'So no one at the lab has seen anything of our friend since Thursday?'

'That's right.' Gillette cleared his throat. 'Stapleton called at the lab that night for a progress report and to make sure the latest batches had gone for testing.'

Strand blew a smoke ring. 'And there was a phone call?'

'Just one - Friday evening. I was ordered to clean out South

117

Lab and destroy all traces of the Solstice and the eye droplets. Also to cancel the French consignments, and erase the data...'

'Which you've done?'

'Yes. That was the last I heard. I've tried ringing the house, but...'

'What's Solstice?' enquired Hinds, his mind about twelve seconds slow.

'Shut up,' snapped Strand. 'No questions.'

'Silva rang me,' stammered Gillette. 'Apparently Thursday's report never reached him. I don't think he was pleased.'

'How astute. No he isn't pleased and that's why we're here to rectify matters. Tell me, Will, where are the authorities keeping Lisa Mirren's corpse?'

'Oh God!' The grey complexion drained to white. 'The autopsy was at the York Hospital. The coroner won't have released the body, so I imagine it's in the mortuary there.'

'Thank you.' Strand headed for the door, snapping his fingers for the security team to follow. 'If you need to contact us, we'll be at Stapleton's house.'

'Yes, yes...' *They were leaving – thank God!* Gillette's heart slowed as his visitors filed through the hall. 'Of course.'

'Are we going to the hospital now?' asked Fisher.

Strand peered curiously. 'Is that your concept of *no questions*?' He turned back to Gillette. 'One final thing. Have you had any strangers at the lab enquiring about the dead girls? Any unusual callers?'

'Apart from the police, no one. Er, well, three men called briefly today, but I never spoke to them. My receptionist told me later that one claimed to be Lisa Mirren's cousin.'

'Really?' Strand smiled evilly. 'Describe them to me, Will.'

* * * *

Chapter 27

'This consultant detective lark obviously pays well,' said Rex, sarcastically. He inspected the basic interior of the Beetle. 'Talk about cramped? This is worse than the mini-subs we use in the SAS.'

'Wow!' Watson gasped. 'What do you reckon to that, Guv?'

'Amazing!' drawled Quist. He turned off the Acomb road and into a pub car park. 'Here we are.'

Rex read the neon sign. 'The Squinting Ferret?'

The brewery believed *Slugs and Lettuces, Coughing Cats*, and other such jolly monikers attracted custom, and from the transport outside, the Squinting Ferret obviously enticed one particular clientele.

'Great!' Watson eyed the rows of motorcycles as he climbed from the car. 'I suppose you want to go in here because of the badges you found? Even though the Lamberley landlord said those bikers had nothing to do with the murder.'

'Bikers?' Rex looked bemused.

'Bikers,' said Quist, showing him the Harley badges. 'Someone either believes they were involved or wants *us* to believe that. That's why they left these for us to conveniently find.'

'What?' Watson's mouth fell open. 'You think they were planted?'

'Well of course they were,' said Quist. 'The police would have found them otherwise.'

'But they might have been dropped accidentally by someone who went there after the police left.'

'Watch!' Quist flicked up the darker one and let it fall at his feet. 'Each time I toss this up, it falls facedown. The convex face is heavier, like bread falling butter-side down. But as you can see the face is shiny and the reverse is matt black.'

'So...'

'So had it fallen accidentally, we'd have found it facedown. Someone left it shiny face up to ensure we didn't miss it. Someone wants us involved in this and I want to know who and why. Selden has no fiancé. I doubt he even knew Diane Woodall, so why would he come to the office wanting us to look into her suicide? I need to know what's going on here.'

'Planted clues?' Rex brightened. 'Hey this is starting to sound good. So why are we here?'

'Satan's Heralds.' Watson cringed. 'A bunch of bikers calling themselves that were in Lamberley on the day of the murder.'

'Correct,' said Quist. 'Whoever planted the badges wants us to believe they were present at both the murder and suicide. This pub is the sort of place where we'll learn who they are and where to find them.'

'Oh what fun!' said Watson. 'Bikers aren't renowned for their love of us handsome, dark-skinned types, Guv; it's their redneck genes. Anything could happen in there.'

'But we have Captain Grant with us,' pointed out Quist. 'I told you his combat skills could prove useful.'

'Er, yeah.' Rex swallowed dryly. 'No worries.'

Watson recognised the racket as Quist opened the pub door - *That Babe's Gonna Break Ya Spine*, by a group named Coronary. He enjoyed loud music, but this was like being lobotomised with a pneumatic drill. The heaving lounge was as inviting as a bidet full of rattraps, the hairy customers falling into two groups: the moody types seen in spaghetti westerns, and the sword-waving characters that swing from pirate ships. As Watson had suspected, the Squinting Ferret was one of those places where the lights can go out fairly quickly and you wake surrounded by hospital curtains. Rex realised it too and removed his shades before someone decided to do it for him.

'It'll be hard asking questions here,' yelled Watson, above the din. 'And asking for the jukebox to be turned down in places like this is a lynching offence.' He glanced pointedly at Rex. 'Pretty much like ordering a vodka martini.'

'Might be best if we return when it's quieter,' shouted Rex.

'Yeah,' agreed Watson. 'Like when it's shut.'

Quist noticed a door by the counter and led them through the crowd into a games room with a lower decibel level. Five glaring bikers sprawled on seats and drank from bottles, two played at the pool table, and a girl leant by the door, eyeing the strangers the way cats eye fledgling sparrows. The largest pool player bent over the table preparing his shot. Rex watched him warily. The last time he'd seen anything like this, it had been co-piloting Han Solo's ship in *Star Wars*. Quist spotted the skull design on his jacket with *York Cannibals* underneath.

He cleared his throat. 'Excuse our intrusion, but perhaps you could help. We're looking for a group of cyclists known as Satan's Heralds.'

'Fuck off!' grunted the biker, without turning, 'before I kill you.'

'Thank you,' said Watson and Rex together. They grabbed the detective's arms and pulled him towards the door.

'Nice one, Eddie,' cackled the girl.

'Really,' tutted Quist, shaking free. He plucked the ball from the table as Eddie's cue jabbed out and connected with thin air. 'That wasn't very nice.'

Every mouth in the room fell open.

Eddie rose slowly and turned. 'Don't bother, lads.' He waved away two large friends who were moving forward. 'I could use the exercise and this is a nose that'll be hard to miss.'

'Ah, I have your attention.' Quist watched Rex and Watson flatten themselves against the wall. 'As I was saying, have you heard of Satan's Heralds?'

'Have you heard of *this*?' Eddie swung a high-speed fist.

It wasn't speedy enough. His target ducked, and in the brief moment of realisation, the biker had taken four hard punches. Eddie's pool opponent flew across wielding a cue and snapped it across the detective's cheek. Watson winced at the gash and squeezed closer to the wall as Quist caught his assailant's head and slammed it into the table. The man folded, showering the floor in teeth, and Quist twisted to face two more bikers armed with jagged bottles. Eddie nursed his flattened nose as Quist booted the nearest in the plumbing, and throwing a pool ball, cracked the second between the eyes.

'What was the question again?' stammered Eddie.

'Satan's Heralds.' Quist turned back to him as the last attacker sank to the floor. 'Do you know them?'

'Er, yeah, that's Creeper's chapter.'

'And where would I find them?'

'They're a York bunch. Most nights you'll get some of them drinking at the Crown in Clifton. I've heard they're holding an all-day party tomorrow at Creeper's place on Minster Avenue. The whole lot will be there.'

Watson and Rex, who had been edging along the wall, slipped out.

'Thanks.' Quist turned to follow. 'You've been most helpful.'

'No problem.' The biker wiped his bloody mouth and turned to the groaning men on the floor. 'Good puncher, that bloke.'

Out in the car park, Watson couldn't agree more. 'Nice work, Guv.' He trembled with relief. 'For a while there I thought we were dead. I honestly can't believe what I just saw. You were amazing.'

'Yes, not too bad.' Rex jumped in the Beetle and lit a shaky cigarette. 'I was going to step in, but it was over so fast and you seemed okay. I have to be careful in violent situations.'

'In case you get hurt?' sniggered Watson.

'In case I forget to hold back and accidentally kill someone.'

'Oh right.' The youth inspected Quist's face as the Beetle pulled out onto the road. 'How's the cut?'

'What cut?' He wiped his cheek and dry blood fell away from unbroken skin.

Watson shrugged at his mistake; the blood obviously belonged to one of the bikers.

'I'll take you back for your car, Rex,' said Quist. 'Where are you staying?'

'Over on the North York Moors. I'll give you the number.

Hey, speaking of which, you never asked for the number of the house where this party is being held.'

'It's a biker's party.' Quist smiled. 'Believe me, we won't need a number.'

* * * *

Dreyer watched the Beetle leave the Squinting Ferret from his parking spot on the dark backstreet opposite. He reached for the ignition as a knock sounded on the Maserati window. 'What the hell do you want?' he snapped, lowering the black glass.

'Mister Dreyer?'

'Do I know you?' He noticed the stranger's BMW a short way down the road. 'What is this?'

'I believe you sell double-glazing? I need my windows replacing.'

'Are you serious?' Dreyer glanced at the departing Beetle. 'Go away. I don't have time for this.'

'No, you don't!' A hand fastened on his throat, wrenching him through the open window and slamming him onto the Maserati bonnet. 'You don't have time for anything.'

A scorching explosion of pain in Dreyer's abdomen was followed by a wet splatter. He clawed at the fingers clamping his neck and gazed incredulously at his own steaming intestines running down the windscreen. *That's something you don't see every day*, he mused. The philosophical thought ended abruptly as his windpipe and carotid arteries parted company with his spine.

* * * *

Chapter 28

Adrian Pitt had never set eyes upon Doctor Stapleton, even though the pair had lived next door to each other on Linden Mount for six years. Springer walked Rommel along this suburban cul-de-sac each evening and he'd seen the blue Porsche with its mirrored windows many times, but never the reclusive scientist who drove it.

'Hurry up.' Shuffling in the rain, the solicitor tugged at the Doberman's leash. Rommel's leg quivered as he urinated over their neighbour's gates. 'Wait until we reach the field.'

Nipping the flow, Rommel set off, then stopped dead, bringing Pitt to a halt again. He sniffed at the new gate padlock and curled his lip.

'What's the matter?'

The dog hesitated and trotted on before stopping at the shrubbery by the gatepost. He stuck his head beneath the evergreen foliage and snarled at the broken lock that had been removed and now lay hidden in the grass.

'What is it? A hedgehog?'

Rommel began barking. The dog was always drawn to the gates of this particular house on his evening walks, but although he often growled, he'd never carried on like this before.

'Come on.' Pitt pulled the leash and led it away. 'You get fleas from hedgehogs.'

* * * *

Strand stood admiring the many paintings and sculptures in Stapleton's hall. The owner of Ebor Pharmaceuticals was obviously an art collector, although *this* art may not have been to everyone's taste. The pornographic Beardsley illustrations and Austin Spare pastels would make a Legionnaire gasp, and the tantric sex positions depicted in the Hindu carvings would be tricky for copulating eels, never mind humans. He strolled into the lounge and studied a garish Aleister Crowley painting. Three of the security team sat around the fireplace behind Strand. The fourth hurried through the door.

'I've been watching the grounds,' announced Hinds.

Strand moved to another picture. 'How interesting.'

'I thought you should know, Sir, there was a man looking through the gates.'

'I heard barking. It was probably a neighbour walking a dog.'

'You wouldn't like me to kill him?'

'No.' Strand glared at the bodyguard. 'I *wouldn't* like that.'

Sangster cleared his throat. 'Sir, why are we wasting time here? Shouldn't we go to the morgue tonight?'

'He's right,' said Browning. 'Tomorrow will be cutting things fine.'

'You could have a point.' Strand stroked his trim beard in mock thoughtfulness. 'But let me ask you a question. Why do you suppose Silva placed me in charge of this operation?'

The burly giants glanced at one another.

'Take your time. No need to blurt out the first thing that enters your heads.'

'Errr...' said Browning.

'No. I'm in charge, not because of *errr*, but because I'm better at this than you. I know what I'm doing.'

'But, Sir...'

'What did I tell you earlier? Do as you're told and don't question. I'm here to think and you're here for the muscle if it's needed. If I say we don't move until tomorrow, you can be certain there's good reason.' The lecture was interrupted by a trill in his pocket. He pressed the mobile to his ear. 'This call is private. If you'll excuse me?'

Four faces frowned quizzically.

'The hall,' he sighed.

'What about it?' queried Hinds.

'Get out - *now*.' Strand waited until the door closed behind the guards. 'Sorry about that,' he purred. 'Staff problems.'

* * * *

Chapter 29

For once the weather forecasters had been right. Quist arrived late at the office on Thursday morning and, switching on the radio for the nine-thirty local news, he peered through the window at the light covering of snow and the drifting fog. Thanks to smokeless fuels, inland fog was a rarity these days, but this icy mist was doubtless down to the frozen ground and warmer air. This would hamper today's investigation, but hopefully Rex Grant would be trapped at his uncle's moorland house and kept safely out of the picture.

Sinking into the leather chair behind the desk, the detective took out the Harley badges. 'Why were you left there?' he murmured. He fingered them meditatively and lit a cigarette as the newsreader told of Becca's death. 'Why did Selden lie to us?'

When Watson turned up, their first call would be Duggan's debt office for an enlightening chat with the skinhead. Quist narrowed his eyes as the next radio news story began. The Leeds manager of Brightshield Glazing, Carl Dreyer, was missing and his Maserati had been found abandoned near the Squinting Ferret in Acomb in the early hours. There was no sign of the owner, but his clothing had been draped across the bonnet and foul play was suspected.

'Brightshield,' said Quist. *So the Maserati that had been tailing them belonged to the seedy character who approached him outside the newsagent on Monday night.*

He noticed the flashing answerphone and, reaching over to play the messages, he stiffened as the next news story announced the Leeds murder of York resident Kevin Selden.

'*What?*' whispered Quist.

The detective gaped at the radio. *Selden had been murdered? He'd called here behaving in that peculiar manner, lied about Diane Woodall, and the following day someone had killed him?* So far, this bizarre mystery of planted badges and fictitious fiancés had been an intriguing diversion, but something far more serious than Quist had envisaged was going on here. Whoever wanted him involved in this could be behind the skinhead's death. *And why the hell was the Brightshield manager following him around? Come to that, where was he now, having left his clothes on the car bonnet? Was he dead like Selden?* Stubbing the cigarette, Quist clicked on the answerphone.

Beeep! 'Hullo, Guv. Sorry, but the Grimpen bus isn't running because of the snow and fog, so it looks like I'll be late. Bye.'

Beeep! 'Bernard?' The next voice was obviously scared. 'This is Amy Clarkson. About our talk last night - it's Doctor Gillette. He hasn't turned up at the lab and... well, I don't know, but I thought you and Rex might like to know. Er, ring me when you get this. Bye.'

Quist grabbed the telephone directory and rang Ebor Pharmaceuticals. A minute passed before he was transferred to the right department and Amy answered.

'I just heard your message,' he sighed. 'Are you alright?'

'I'm fine.' Amy checked to ensure no one was listening. 'I'm also very scared. I don't know why I called you.'

'I'm glad you did.' He laughed quietly. 'It must be the amazing sense of comfort and trust I instil in young ladies.'

'Yeah, that must be it.' Amy let out a nervous giggle. 'I've tried ringing Rex, but they said he's out. I'm not sure what to do any more.'

'Doctor Gillette still hasn't arrived?'

'No. The police are checking on him. We thought he was late with the weather, but he's not answering his phone. I know this sounds crazy, but if he's dead...'

'Then you're the only surviving member of the research team. Yes, I imagine that *would* be scary. Equally scary, I have to tell you the gentleman who lied about Diane being his fiancé was murdered last night too.'

'Jesus! You're joking?'

'It's just been on the news. Are the police there now?'

'Only the undercover men. They want to maintain a low visible presence as they term it.'

Quist thought hard. 'Amy, will you help me?'

'How?'

'I'm not sure why, but I believe these deaths could be connected with the products you worked on recently.' He took a deep breath. 'If Gillette hasn't shown up, then I assume his office is empty? I know it's asking a hell of a lot, but listen...'

* * * *

'Crazy!' croaked Amy. 'Absolutely crazy!'

Checking the corridor and closing Gillette's door behind her, she glanced fearfully around the director's empty office and at the computer on the desk, grappling with her conscience and wondering whether she was doing the right thing. *What on earth was she thinking of in agreeing to this?*

'You crazy bitch!' she hissed.

But what if Bernard Quist was right in his suspicions? What if South Lab's recent projects were somehow linked to the murders? The police had already searched through their work, hoping to find some connection or motive, so what harm could it do in letting this private detective see the data on the eye droplets and the sunblock? She couldn't imagine what he hoped to find, or even if he'd understand the chemistry, but he genuinely seemed to want to help.

Amy hurried to the terminal and punched at the keyboard, her stomach twisting into the sort of convoluted knots associated with boy scouts. *What would happen if Gillette or Doctor Keating, the assistant director, came in?* The doctor turned from the changing menus to apprehensively check over her shoulder. She knew exactly what would happen, and it involved a fan and excrement.

'Right,' she whispered, recognising the onscreen numbers. 'The project codes. Here we go.'

02239 was Calypso, the moisturiser. Amy clicked on the code and technical data filled the screen. Nodding, she exited back to the menu.

'Solstice. There you are - 02248.'

File Erased appeared. The code 02247 for the ultra-violet eye droplets was entered, but the result was the same. The girl sat back bemused, then out of curiosity keyed in the numbers for a mascara terminated three weeks earlier, and a lipstick two weeks before that. She shook her head at the pages of data.

'Still there,' she murmured. 'Yet the projects cancelled at the weekend are erased.' She checked the recycle bin and found it empty. 'You've been a busy boy, Will. So you cleaned South Lab and cleaned your computer too.'

* * * *

Chapter 30

To anyone weaned on the thrilling police stations of television cop shows, with their colourful hookers, loud-mouthed lawyers, and lunatics in holding pens, York Central on Fulford Road would be a boring disappointment. Constable Zoe Planer worked studiously by herself at a desk in the murder incident room.

'Who were they?' Katie Bradstreet marched in. 'I've just heard about Amy Clarkson visiting the Golden Fleece with three men, one of whom picked her up in a Ferrari?'

'That's right, Ma'am.' Zoe nodded. 'Rex Grant owns the Ferrari and he's the brother of Lisa Mirren's ex-fiancé Raoul. He lives in London, but Doctor Clarkson told her protection officer that he's here looking into Lisa's death. He has a sound alibi for Saturday – he was at the same London party as his brother. The Volkswagen Beetle belongs to Bernard Quist from Askham Richard. He has no police record, but we're running the usual checks on him.'

'Any luck locating Stapleton, or the owner of those fingerprints in the stolen Range Rover?'

'No luck with either. There are no records of Doctor Stapleton ever leaving the country.'

'Really?' Katie smiled. 'I'll be interested to hear how Gillette explains that when he turns up. I've been talking to the lab. Those black animal hairs the SOCO found on Becca Travis' legs were feline and match the ones on Lisa Mirren's body.'

'Leopard or lion, you mean? That's crazy. We've checked everyone connected to these girls and no one appears to have any link to zoos or big cats.'

'They still can't pin down the species and think the cat is possibly a hybrid.' Katie turned to see Gregson walking in. 'Has Mitchell taken over watching Amy?'

'Yes.' Gregson yawned and ran a weary hand through his hair. 'Plus we've got Sherman and Cromwell covering the lab. Her protection officer, WPC Farnon slept in her spare bed last night.'

'You'd better grab some sleep,' said Katie. 'Use the couch in my office. I've just been with forensics and there was no bag in the school furnace.'

'Jesus!' Gregson shook his head. 'Diane's bracelet, Lisa's binoculars and now Becca's bag. Could the Superintendent be right about sociopaths taking trophies?'

Katie turned back to Planer. 'So what's this about Gillette not showing up at the lab?'

'He isn't answering calls either,' said the Constable. 'Uniform are on their way to the house; that's probably them now.'

The Inspector snatched the ringing phone. 'Yes?'

'I've completed the autopsy,' said Jay Mortimer the Pathologist. 'Your Sergeant's on his way to you with the report.'

'You didn't start until nine. You don't mess about, do you?'

'Two half-burnt legs? It might have taken longer if there'd been arms too.' Mortimer hesitated. 'Longer still if there'd been any trace of blood in the legs.'

'No blood?' whispered Katie, her eyes widening. 'Just like Diane Woodall and Lisa Mirren.'

* * * *

Chapter 31

Quist turned his car into the Grimpen housing estate in Acomb and drove along the main street avoiding abandoned shopping trolleys, barking dogs and snowball-throwing kids. He grimaced at the depressing mess of steel shutters, graffiti and satellite dishes. Thanks to recessions and unemployment, Grimpen was no Beverley Hills. This situation was growing stranger and far more serious, and he debated whether it was right to further involve his young assistant. Watson was resilient and streetwise, but his safety would be the main concern.

The detective turned into one of the better crescents and pulled up outside number 22. Most of the estate gardens were littered with torn trampolines, dog mess and broken fridges, but not this one. On the occasions he'd accepted a lift home, Watson had insisted upon being dropped at the corner and this was Quist's first visit to the house. Climbing from the car, he peered over the fence at the multitude of figurines and saw why his assistant had been reluctant to speak of his mother's work.

Three military gnomes abseiled from the gable, a suicide in a noose dangled under a bush, and another with bloated features floated in the pond. Walking up the path, Quist passed tiny Jehovah's witnesses, a gnome injecting smack, another sodomising a squirrel, and an escaped prisoner with arrowed tunic and spade emerging from the snowy lawn. He rang the bell and studied the Yuletide gnome by the boot scraper - a drunken Santa urinating his name in a curl of brass wire. An attractive woman in T shirt and jeans answered.

'Mrs Watson?' He smiled. 'I'm your son's employer - Bernard Quist.'

'Ooh, hello. You'd better come in, luv.' Giggling, she pulled him into the tinsel-draped hall. 'The name's Jo.'

A fat ginger cat appeared from beneath the lounge Christmas tree. It spotted Quist, hissed and shot out through the kitchen.

'What's wrong with Hucknall,' she muttered. 'He normally

takes to strangers.'

'I have that effect,' confessed Quist. 'It must be my after-shave.'

'Mmmh!' She leant close. 'You smell okay to me, Bernard.'

He turned away uneasily. The shelves on his left held gnomes, identical to those outside, except these were wood. 'Your originals?' he asked, feigning interest.

'Yeah, I use these to make the resin moulds.' Jo picked up a wino with tiny bottle. '*Gnomes With a Twist*, I call them, but Johnny hates them. I sell them in garden centres and markets, but he gets embarrassed about me having them outside for advertising.'

'Really?' Quist glanced through the window at the rentboy gnomes. 'I can't imagine why.'

'I got a grant to start my own small business.'

'Amazing!' He motioned to a flasher, raincoat open and erection waving. 'And they say the government wastes money.'

'Glad you like them, Bernard. Hang on... I thought your name was Cyrano.'

'Did you indeed?'

'That's what Johnny calls you. I imagined you'd be Greek or something.' She pointed to the stairs. 'He's in his room; first on the right at the top. You might as well go up while I make coffee.'

Quist paused on the stairs. 'I'd love a coffee, but I don't suppose you have soya milk?'

'No chance, luv. It's the stuff from cows.'

'Then I'll take it black, please.'

'I see we've got similar tastes,' giggled Jo.

The detective pushed open Watson's bedroom door and gaped at the mess of clothing, comic books and music posters – the sort of devastation seen in crime movies where villains have searched an apartment. Magazines, CDs and computer games covered the carpet and drawers hung half-open with the linen contents spewing out.

'Gone back to sleep, have we?' Quist prodded the teenager-sized lump in the bed. 'Come on. Cyrano De Bergerac's here.' He shoved a hi-fi speaker under the motionless quilt, turned up the volume and switched on the CD player. The bed leapt and a terrified black face appeared.

'What the fuck...'

'Catchy little piece.' Quist killed the music. 'Who was it?'

'Er...' Watson rubbed his eyes. 'Rapping MC Jacker.'

'Not Mozart?'

'Obviously *you* won't like it.' The teenager rolled his head to clear the fuzziness of sleep. 'It's aimed at the under-thirties.'

'Years or IQs?'

'I feel like shit. Uurgh! What day is it?'

'Thursday. It usually arrives after Wednesday, unless you're an alcoholic, or an inventor with a time machine.'

'Yeah, yeah.' Watson yawned and sat up. 'Well, this is a surprise. You found the house then? What did you er, think of the gnomes?'

'They're... *different*.' Quist peered through the window at the misty garden and saw the white BMW parked near the Volkswagen. 'Very different.'

'I'll say. What with the busses not running, I decided to catch up on my beauty sleep after ringing the office.'

'Well your transport worries are over now.'

'You were brilliant yesterday, Guv' Watson pulled on a yellow sweater and rubbed his head to liven up the short curls. 'Talk about unexpected? You look like a librarian, yet you fight like a black guy in the ring. Those fast punches - wow!'

'Violence isn't something one should rejoice in. I told you, I hate aggression.'

'Good thing you didn't hate it last night; they'd have torn us apart. Speaking of fighting, have you seen anything of the SAS Captain?'

'I rang him before leaving the office, but the butler said he was exercising.' Quist jotted down the BMW number. Even if he could get close, identification of the driver was impossible due to the black glass. 'Apparently the snow and fog on the North York Moors is worse than here.'

'Butler?' Watson whistled. 'Cool.'

'I take it you don't have servants?'

'It's their day off. I expect you think the room's a shithole?'

'Nothing that four hours with a duster and bulldozer wouldn't sort out.' Quist turned from the window. 'I recall you once telling me about a friend of yours. Someone named Gareth Lestrade who could hack into any computer.'

'That's right - Gazza.'

'How do you think he'd cope with er, the police computer.'

Watson paused in tugging on a pair of jeans. 'The cops?' He raised a curious eyebrow. 'It *can* be done. Er, why would you want to get in there?'

'You'll soon see.'

'Shouldn't we ask that arsehole Selden a few questions first?'

'He'd have difficulty answering. He's dead.'

'*WHAT*?'

'Our favourite skinhead was killed in Leeds last night. Hacked to pieces by machetes.'

Watson shook his head. 'He lies about a phoney fiancé and the next day he's murdered?'

'It happened in Milverton. According to witnesses, from the way he was dressed in a swastika shirt, he was obviously looking for trouble.'

'I know about Milverton. Looking for trouble there? That's suicide.'

'Someone told him to lie to us. They must have either paid him or threatened him. I wonder...'

'I'm doing a little wondering too, Guv. Wondering why we don't drop this right now?'

'A gang from one of the illegal clubs there have been arrested for the murder.'

'So it isn't connected with the lab murders?'

Quist didn't answer. 'Don't you ever wear anything dark?' He gestured to the yellow sweater, blue jeans and red jacket.

'It clashes with my complexion.' Watson opened the bedroom door. 'A lift from the boss, eh? I'm honoured.'

'Your mother has made coffee,' said Quist. 'Hurry up and drink it, because we're going to Ebor Pharmaceuticals.'

* * * *

Chapter 32

Rupert Grant's newspaper read: *Ozone Hole Shock*, but the problem was somewhere over the third world. Rupert would only have taken an interest if a breach appeared above Yorkshire, and only then if it affected Sedgefield Grange. Sprawling on a Chesterfield couch, he turned to the international page and food riots in Africa.

'Hang the darkies,' he muttered. He'd never met the late Kevin Selden, which was a pity, for they'd probably have become good friends.

A petite girl walked into the morning room with a tea tray, a white robe accentuating her tanned legs.

'A mile in twelve minutes,' announced Marika. Three couches surrounded a large coffee table where she set the tray down. 'It's so invigorating. You ought to join me in the pool.'

Duck shooting and otter hunting were the only water sports that interested her husband. 'Have you read the paper?' he snarled. 'Greenpeace are moaning about another oil slick. When will the idiots learn that these problems are solved naturally? If you spill oil and cause a slick, Mother Nature simply soaks it up with birds.'

Sipping coffee, his wife stared through the French doors at the eerie beauty of the fog drifting over the terrace. The winters were mellower here than in the Carpathian mountains and Marika loved the crisp mornings of frosted cobwebs. The young girl was a believer in fate and destiny. Fate had certainly played a part in Rupert choosing Romania for his hunting break last May and booking the Bucharest hotel where she worked as receptionist. Toying with marriage for some time, he'd been considering a Thai wife, but he'd changed his mind on discovering East European girls. Marika weighed up his surprising proposal, decided in six seconds flat, and packed her bags for a new life as lady of the manor. The girl was jolted from her thoughts by her husband's hearty voice.

'How are we this morning?'

'There you are.' Marika beamed as Rex strolled in clad in a

black tracksuit. 'How nice to see you at last.'

'And you.' He grinned and kissed her. 'You were out on Tuesday when I arrived and again last night.'

'Are you staying until Christmas?'

'Just a few days, if that's okay? I have to see Dad on Christmas Eve.'

'I'm so sorry to hear about the Marines.' Marika's husky Romanian accent set the heart thumping and could make *condemned offal* sound sensual. 'Rupert tells me the recruitment officer was mentally ill. It's shocking, isn't it?'

'Er, quite.' Rex flopped onto a Chesterfield. 'I'll be sending a stiff letter to the relevant officials.'

'Have you been running?' Rupert eyed the tracksuit with the sort of revulsion evangelists reserve for anal sex.

'No, just going through a few katras on the lawn.'

'In the snow and fog?' Marika poured coffee. 'Which martial art do you practise?'

'Kung Fu. I have a private tutor in Tooting - a Tibetan monk.' He took Marika's offered mug. 'Training with Frank is expensive, but he says I've pretty much reached Bruce Lee's standard.'

'Barrymore took a call while you were out.' Rupert held up a sheet from the butler's notepad. 'Someone named Quist said it was a shame about the weather and best if you didn't try driving to the York party. He'll ring later and let you know if he's discovered anything.'

'Will he really?' said Rex, fuming. Like Quist, he knew about Selden's death from the news. He'd had to virtually beg this private eye to let him help with the investigation and now the big-nosed old fart was trying to dump him. Well he could forget that idea. 'Nice of him to be concerned,' he growled, 'but the snow isn't too bad and as soon as this icy fog thins out, I'll be heading over there.'

'How did yesterday go?' asked Rupert. 'What on earth did you do in the countryside without a gun?'

'This and that.' Rex sipped his coffee. 'I bumped into a girl actually.'

'Not a rambler?' Rupert wrinkled his nose. 'Those idiots who protest about keeping footpaths open? Waste of a good white skin.'

'No, I met her in York, not Lamberley.'

'Lamberley?' echoed Marika. 'Is that where you went? The place where Raoul's ex-fiancé was killed?'

Rex nodded. 'Did you ever meet Lisa?'

'Yes, a few times. I liked her, but she never really got on with Rupert.'

There's a surprise, reflected Rex, taking out a cigarette. He shuddered at the thought of Lisa discussing conservation with a man who complained in restaurants that the veal didn't taste young enough.

'So terrible,' muttered Marika. 'I rang Raoul to say how sorry we were. How's he taking it?'

Rex reached for the coffee table lighter. 'Well, you can imagine...' He froze as the girl gasped with horror and snatched his wrist to inspect his palm. 'What's wrong?' he demanded anxiously.

'Oh... nothing.' She released him. 'For a moment, I was sure I saw... I'm sorry. Forget it.'

'You scared the hell out of me,' chuckled Rupert. 'You leapt up like a hunt saboteur when they get a bullet in the leg. What was it?'

'Nothing.' She gave an embarrassed titter. 'Sorry, Rex; I'm seeing things. You must think I'm crazy.'

'Er, no.' Rex checked his palm. 'Not at all.'

'How about more coffee?' proposed Rupert. 'Come on, Darling. You're closest to the pot. Six sugars in mine.'

Rex studied Marika as she filled the cup. Her relaxed manner had disappeared. She looked paler and her smile seemed forced. *Hah - women*! He dismissed his thoughts. *It was probably that time of the month.*

* * * *

Chapter 33

Creeping out of Gillette's office, Amy gently closed the door. 'Are you okay?'

The doctor whipped around, sighing to see Nicole Patterson at the water dispenser. The secretary was only a temp and unacquainted with office protocol, especially the rules on never entering the research director's office in his absence. Thank God it wasn't Doctor Keating. The assistant director was the last person she wanted to run into here.

'I'm fine,' she lied, her heart-rate slowing. 'I was just dropping off some paperwork for Will. You scared the hell out of me. I've been jumpy ever since the police started this surveillance business.'

'I can't blame you.' Nicole sipped her water and pointed down the corridor. 'But you should be okay with the new *doctors* protecting you.'

Thirty feet away, a gorilla in a white coat pretended to use the photocopier whilst watching the girls. Thanks to his size, broken nose and 9mm armpit bulge, he looked more suited to snapping legs than handling test tubes.

'Yeah.' Amy headed the opposite way towards reception. 'Certainly blends in, doesn't he? The other undercover policeman is even bigger.'

'Where are you working today?' Nicole followed. 'I understand they've temporarily closed South Lab.'

'I've moved to East lab, along with *Doctor* Sherman back there and *Doctor* Cromwell.'

'I'm surprised you're here at all. If I was in your place, I'd be taking a month off with stress.'

'I know what you mean.' Amy reached the lobby and peered through the glass doors into the mist. 'But the police don't want me to change routines.' *Lynn Chandler wasn't behind the reception desk. This would be the ideal time to do this.*

'They think this murderer might go for you next?' The secretary shook her head in horror. 'That's awful. Hey, what are you looking for?'

'I'm just checking the police car is there.'

'Gary Mitchell? Don't worry. It's hard to see him in this fog, but his Honda is near the steps. Donna from the canteen keeps taking tea and biscuits to him, along with her number and obscene suggestions.'

Amy laughed. 'Listen, I'm keeping you from your work and...'

'Not at all. With Will not here, I don't have much to do.'

'Well, I'm afraid *I* do. I'll see you later, Nicole.'

'Take care.' The secretary headed back towards the administration area. 'You'll be okay, I'm sure.'

Amy set off for the labs, counted five seconds, and quickly retraced her steps to the lobby. The receptionist was still absent, and slipping through the door, she avoided Mitchell's unmarked police car and darted across the misty tarmac to a waiting Volkswagen.

'Hello again.' Watson leant through the passenger window. 'Hey, this is like a spy film, where agents meet and...'

'Yes,' broke in Quist, testily. 'I'm so glad to see you're okay. I really can't thank you enough for agreeing to this.'

'I still can't believe I *did* agree,' whispered Amy, 'but I'm afraid there isn't much to thank me for. I don't have any print-outs for you because the data on the Solstice and the eye droplets that you're suspicious about has been erased.'

'Really?' Quist raised an eyebrow. 'Intriguing.'

'Would you have understood what you were looking at?' asked Watson. 'You're no chemist, Guv.'

'I've dabbled in many things over the years.' The detective took a plastic bag from his pocket and shoved it in the glove compartment. 'That's a tub of the original Solstice sunblock. I bought it at a chemist this morning.'

'Ah!' Watson nodded. 'If Amy could have printed that data,

you were going to compare ingredients with the new experimental version?'

'Correct.' Quist shot the girl a warm, lopsided grin. 'I'm glad you trusted me.'

'Yes, I *do* trust you.' Amy studied him, chewing nervously at her lip. 'I don't know why, but I do. I can't tell you where they were sent for testing either. He's wiped all the information and shredded the paperwork from his desk.'

'Has he indeed?'

'The weird thing is, nothing else has been erased; all the other cancelled products are still on the computer.' She turned back to the lab. 'I have to hurry before they notice I'm missing. They'll wonder why I'm out here, supposedly under protection, yet alone in a foggy car park.'

'This mist is dissipating,' said Quist. 'They'll be able to see you soon. I'll ring you tonight when you get home to talk further.'

'Actually I'm leaving as soon as you've gone. They said to continue as normal, but after Will didn't show up, and then after accessing his computer…'

'You've had enough stress for one day.' Quist nodded. 'Yes, the best thing for you is to relax with your policewoman nanny.'

Amy glanced into the rear of his car, her eyes widening.

Quist turned, scowling at the figurine on the rear seat. 'A flashing garden gnome,' he muttered. 'What does your mother think I want with that?'

'You must have impressed her,' said Watson. 'She never gives them away. It's a wooden original, not mass-production resin, so make sure you paint it. You don't want it rotting, do you?'

'Heaven forbid!'

'I just wish this had been worth it,' said Amy, cringing. 'All that risk for nothing.'

'Hardly *nothing*,' corrected Quist. 'His erasing everything tells me a great deal.'

* * * *

142

Chapter 34

'The police are going,' said Strand, tapping his driver's broad shoulder..

'Okay.' Fisher waited until the patrol car left Gillette's house before pulling across the misty Fulford street and parking the Mercedes van outside. 'Do you want us to…'

'I want you to wait here.' Strand adjusted his sunglasses and opened the door. The fog was clearing, but icy patches remained and he checked that no one was watching. 'All of you stay here. There are a few more questions I need to ask.'

'But, Sir...' began Hinds.

'Wait here and don't move.'

Slipping down the side of the house, Strand found the drapes closed and the kitchen door locked. He rang the bell, waited a while, and then punched through the glazed panel to reach the key. 'Hello, Will?' The key was missing and, withdrawing his arm, he shouldered the door from the frame. 'Hello? Is there a doctor in the house?'

Gillette stood by the lounge fireplace clenching a glass. He trembled uncontrollably, eyes bulging behind his large spectacles.

'Ah, there you are,' said Strand, strolling in. 'I'm afraid that door will need a little attention. I *did* ring, but there was no reply.'

Gillette swallowed dryly. The ice in his whisky tinkled franticly.

'Tell me, Will, what were the police doing here?'

'They were checking on me.' The doctor's voice was a strangled croak. 'The laboratory staff were worried and called them when I didn't show this morning.'

'Oh dear! Are you sick? The curtains are drawn and that bottle on the bureau is almost empty. It was full last night; I notice little things like that. Why haven't you been to work?'

'*Why*? Can't you guess?' Gulping from his glass, Gillette laughed hysterically. 'I'm scared.'

'Scared? You look terrified. I'm somewhat familiar with the

look of terror.'

'Officially, I'm sick with stress and that isn't far from the truth. I told you the staff were suspicious over the chemicals, but it was nothing I couldn't handle. I take it those girls were murdered on your orders?'

'I'm afraid it was necessary.'

'But they knew nothing. Now we have police watching the place and asking questions. They're going through the records and searching for Stapleton. The only member of the research team you haven't killed has officers protecting her night and day.'

'Just as I hoped.'

'What the hell are you talking about?' Gillette crumpled into a chair. 'This project needs absolute secrecy and all you've achieved by these pointless murders is to fill the news with Ebor Pharmaceuticals and bring us all under police scrutiny.'

'Exactly, but I've achieved rather more than that. There's a little more to this operation than you suspect, Will. Believe me, everything is proceeding to plan.'

'*What*?' Gillette let out a staccato laugh. 'I don't know where I am. I have to tell you one thing, Silva another when he rings, and the police something else. Silva knows Stapleton has vanished, but he still believes I'm working on the eye droplets with no success.'

'Excellent!'

'*Excellent*?' He gulped again at the whisky. 'I don't know how I got through yesterday without cracking up - questions all afternoon, and then you turning up with those monsters. I'm sure the police know I'm lying about Stapleton being in Canada.'

'They know nothing about the… *project*?'

'Well of course not. If I told them anything, they'd put me in a madhouse. As soon as that money transfer goes through to the offshore bank, I'm out of the country and away from all this.' The doctor wiped a hand over his face and shook off the sweat. 'Everything has been destroyed apart from the data disc and Stapleton has that. I couldn't tell you anything last night; you said they were

Silva's guards.'

'Yes, part of his personal protection team. I left them outside today so we could talk.'

'So what now?' Gillette stood up unsteadily and reached for the whisky. 'The police think I'm ill and that Stapleton's skiing in Canada. Anyway, they're the least of my problems. I'm supposed to be working for Silva and he'll want to know what's going on.'

'The *least* of your problems?' Strand removed his sunglasses, his green eyes flaring. 'Actually you're problems are over. Face the fireplace.'

'What?'

'Do as you're told.' He locked his gaze upon Gillette. 'Turn around!'

The research director stiffened and shuffled to face the mantelpiece.

'No more problems, Will.' He reached over Gillette's shoulder to grip his chin. 'Silva won't bother you anymore.'

The doctor heard the snap and looked into Strand's blurred face - his head had been twisted around so sharply that his spectacles had flown across the room. Frowning, he raised a curious eyebrow and looked down at his own buttocks.

'Thanks.' Strand dropped the corpse and replaced his sunglasses. 'Working together was fun.'

Fisher revved the engine as his superior walked back down the drive.

'My suspicions were right.' Strand climbed into the van. 'Gillette *was* withholding something yesterday. He gave me two addresses where we might find Stapleton.'

Fisher eyed the dashboard clock and gave the other bodyguards an uneasy glance. 'What about the hospital, Sir?' he asked. 'Don't you think we should be heading for the hospital first?'

'Yes, we'll visit the hospital.' Strand checked his phone for messages. 'Mmmh, but not just yet.'

* * * *

Chapter 35

The light covering of snow had gone, leaving the Clifton streets wet and glistening. Quist had been right; you didn't need the house number to find a drunken gathering of bikers. You didn't really need the name of the street. The town would probably suffice. Watson heard the shouting, revving engines and rock music long before the Beetle entered Minster Avenue.

'Hey, there's a Harley.' The teenager pointed to an American bike amongst the cycles outside the house. 'Hello? Watson to Quist. Harley-Davidson dead ahead. Are you receiving? Over?'

'Yes, I heard you.' The detective stroked thoughtfully at his nose. 'Sorry, but I was thinking about the lab and that sunscreen.'

'I don't suppose you'd think about driving past this place?'

'I need to see these bikers and figure out where they fit into this.' He parked the car. 'Are you ready?'

'Oh absolutely.' People had shown more enthusiasm walking to the electric chair.

Watson had never been keen on hell's angels and gate-crashing one of their get-togethers wasn't his idea of sanity. He'd seen Quist handle himself, but there had been four opponents in the Squinting Ferret. With fifty, it might be different. The apprehension was justified. Six bikers were throwing Bowie knives at a treetop sex-doll in the garden and it wouldn't take them long to work out that screaming, running targets were more fun. They paused to glare at the Beetle in the same way the disciples might have glared, had Judas turned up drunk at a reunion asking if anyone fancied a kiss.

'Merry Christmas,' said Quist, climbing out. 'Eddie of the York Cannibals told us about your party.'

An enormous character cracked his knuckles and headed their way, his expression similar to that which police dogs adopt when trainers pull on padded arm-protectors. Watson groaned. This was probably the chapter's Sergeant-at-Arms. Chosen for their size and psychopathic natures, these gentlemen sort out trouble, or occasionally black kids and well-spoken strangers with big noses.

Quist raised his voice above the music. 'With it being the festive season, I thought a few bottles would be nice.' He opened the boot to reveal a case of Jack Daniels. 'I hope these will be okay.'

The biker eyed the box. 'Nice one,' he growled. 'Come on in.'

'Er, merry Christmas,' mumbled Watson, offering a bottle to an approaching mass of hair and denim.

The creature smashed the neck and emptied half the contents down its throat. *Satan's Heralds*, read the rear of its jacket, and *We Eat Our Own Dead*.

'Come on,' murmured Quist, picking up the box and gently pulling the youth. 'Don't make eye-contact.'

They moved through the garden, passing bourbon to anyone who scowled, and squeezed into the smoky, crowded passage. It ran to the rear kitchen, with stairs to the right and a large lounge to the left where raucous arm-wrestling bouts were taking place. Inhaling the fog of marijuana, Watson noticed the hi-fi and pile of CDs by the door. AC-DC, Shrapnel, Whitesnake, Iron Bastards, Def Leopard. He raised his eyebrows. There wasn't much point searching for *White Christmas* there.

'Hold this to blend in,' shouted Quist over the music. He gave him the last bottle. 'We don't want to stand out.'

'Oh sure.' Watson narrowed his eyes as a blonde-haired girl appeared from the kitchen. 'We look just like everyone else now.'

Most of the girls at the party were attractive, but this young woman was incredible. Watson preferred females with breasts larger than their own heads, but her small bosom was only a minor problem. A much larger problem was her left arm, or rather the way it was draped around a yeti in leather.

'How about that?' Watson grinned. 'Not bad, eh?'

'Extremely attractive,' agreed Quist. 'Have you spotted her friend's Harley badges?'

Realising she was being watched, the girl squeezed through the crush. 'Merry Christmas,' she yelled over the din. 'Are you two sure you're in the right house? You look a little out of place, to say the least.'

'Oh?' Watson glanced pointedly at Quist. 'We thought we were blending in really well.'

Quist gave one of his odd smiles. 'I hope your friend won't get annoyed over you talking to strange men?'

'Creeper?' She laughed. 'Don't worry, I can handle him.'

'Have you fed him recently?' asked Watson.

'Do you mind. That's the chapter President.'

'Sorry,' said Quist. 'My friend has a tendency to put his feet in his mouth. What's the occasion? Christmas party?'

'The first of many. Funny that you had to ask. You wouldn't be gate-crashers?'

'I'd rather you didn't advertise it.'

'If you've gate-crashed *this* place, you've more guts than I imagined. No, I won't tell.'

'Good!' said Watson. 'I'm hoping to leave with teeth.'

The teenager looked her over. Here was one of those fortunate women in their thirties with no need for make-up. Blonde hair curled loosely about the shoulders of a tan leather blouson, pert breasts filled her denim shirt, and her long legs were clad in tight black jeans and boots. He leant over to make himself heard above the music.

'You don't look like a hell's angel yourself, luv. I'd say you've had a shower and combed your hair recently.'

She giggled. 'Francesca's the name - Fran. Who are you?'

'Bernard Quist,' said the detective. 'This is Watson. I wonder if we could go outside where it's quieter?'

She gave him an inquisitive look, but led the way to the garden.

'Merry Christmas.' Watson flattened himself against the wall as more bikers crushed past into the passage. 'Bloody hell! They don't all live here, do they?'

'This is Creeper's place.' Fran pulled the teenager out of the writhing mass of denim. 'But he lets chapter members crash here. Six of us live here at the moment.'

Quist dodged a flying axe. 'You must have understanding neighbours.'

'We have terrified neighbours.'

'Who does the Harley belong to?' asked Watson.

'I shouldn't touch it,' warned Fran. 'It's Creeper's.'

Quist fingered the badges in his pocket. 'Expensive, aren't they?'

'He does contract work in Eastern Europe laying pipelines. The money is good. It paid for the bike and this place.'

'Where in Eastern Europe?' asked Quist. 'Has he been there recently?'

'Funny questions. You two don't fit in at all. What *are* you doing here?'

Quist smiled. 'Asking funny questions. I hear you were in Lamberley at the weekend?'

'Oh, you're cops? This is about the murder?'

'Actually it's a private investigation.'

'Private eyes?'

'*Consultant* detectives, apparently,' said Watson. 'We're quite big in seedy divorces, taking pictures of fraudulent cleaners, and complicated murders.'

'Divorce?' Fran pulled a face. 'My husband's a lunatic, but he won't come near while I'm with Creeper and the others. I've been trying to get divorced for months.'

'How about that, Guv?' Watson nudged Quist. 'Give her your card.'

'I imagine the police have questioned you?' said Quist. 'You were in Lamberley on Saturday.'

'Seven of us, yes, but we were in the pub at the time of the murder. The landlord gave us alibis. I can't really tell you anything about...'

Watson stiffened as a shadow fell over the trio. Creeper didn't look overly intelligent, but appearances can be deceptive. The tentacled aliens in late-night movies don't look clever either, but they still manage to build intergalactic saucers. A tattooed scarecrow stuffed with bricks instead of straw, the monster glared at Watson.

'What's goin' on, Fran?' he grunted. 'Why are you out here talkin' to wankers?'

'I'm on my way in,' she purred sweetly. 'This is…'

'I don't give a shit who *this* is.'

'I understand you own the Harley?' Quist ignored the tension and held out the badges. 'Would these belong to you?'

Creeper grabbed them. 'They're mine,' he rumbled, suspiciously. 'I lost them the other day. Where did you find them?'

'Over there.' Quist gestured to the gutter.

The biker fixed them back onto his leather waistcoat. 'I've never seen you before,' he hissed. 'What are you doing here?'

'Someone in the Squinting Ferret mentioned you were having a party and…'

'And who invited Sambo?'

'Come on, Guv,' said Watson. 'I think the party's definitely over.'

* * * *

Chapter 36

Amy walked through the refectory at Ebor Pharmaceuticals and sat next to Nicole Patterson at one of the window tables. 'Hi there,' she said. 'I'm looking for a big favour. A garage has been working on my car...'

'Yes, I heard you mention it to Will last night.' The secretary finished her coffee. 'That's why you've been using buses?'

She nodded. 'The thing is, it's fixed and ready to pick up. Now I know it's a little cheeky asking... I mean, I don't know you very well, but...'

'But you need a lift?' Nicole grinned. 'When do you finish?'

'I'm taking the rest of the day off, and as Will is sick...'

'And as I have very little to do if he isn't here...' The redhead laughed and stood up. 'No problem. Are you ready?'

'I certainly am.' Amy had been more than ready since checking Gillette's computer. She set off for the lobby. 'I didn't like asking. I owe you.'

'Forget it. How are you feeling, under the circumstances?'

'I've ignored police advice and I'm staying off work until after Christmas. A long break will do me good.' If Gillette discovered she'd been in his office, her break was likely to last longer than a weekend. 'I hear the police called on Will and he was okay?'

'Kind of okay. He says he's ill with stress.' Nicole rolled her sweater turtleneck higher as they reached reception. 'He's not returning until the new year either.'

'How do you find Will?' Amy pushed open the door and walked into the cold. 'Do you like working for him?'

'It's hard to decide in a week. As soon as his secretary returns, I'll be someplace else. A temp is never at the same place long enough to know anyone.' She unlocked a small Fiat. 'Where's the garage?'

'Micklegate, near my house.' Amy climbed in and glanced at the car by the steps. 'Do me another favour. Give the horn a toot when you pass the unmarked cop car.'

Nicole honked twice and DC Mitchell woke with a start, jerking himself upright in the Honda.

'It's nice to know the police are watching you,' laughed the secretary.

* * * *

Chapter 37

Archaic English land taxes meant that the smaller the footprint of a medieval construction, the less the owner had to pay to the crown. Many of York's older structures extend in lateral steps as they gain height, one of the best examples being the nine-hundred-year-old Shambles. Winding through the heart of the city, timber-framed Elizabethan buildings sprout on either side of the thoroughfare and overhang perilously into the centre, allowing people to reach from the upper storeys and shake hands. Watson's friend Lestrade lived on Saint Andrewgate at the end of here, and he and Quist hurried along the narrow cobbled street.

Now a place of enchanting, almost fairytale, beauty, the original appearance was horrifically different and something of a visceral nightmare for vegans like Quist. *Shambles* is an obsolete term for slaughterhouse meat market, and the raised pavements created a channel down which rivers of steaming blood, excrement and offal once gushed. The butcher's shops are now ornate tourist outlets, and in place of the dead animals, international holidaymakers fill the street, soaking up the almost tangible history.

'So this is where your computer boffin lives?' said Quist, nodding to the redbrick building ahead. 'York's answer to Bill Gates.'

Gareth Lestrade's apartment was in an old converted Granary. Renovated and imaginatively named *Granary Court*, every window in the building looked out onto the nearby Minster. Rent here wouldn't be cheap, but Quist knew that careers in computing were lucrative for teenagers who knew their stuff. He followed Watson into the yard, peering up at the enormous limestone cathedral beyond. With stained glass windows over fifty feet in height, and towers that soared above two-hundred, Quist never grew tired of gazing at this Gothic masterpiece.

Watson climbed the stairs to an upper apartment and rang the bell.

'Watty.' A bespectacled young man answered the door and

ushered them into the hallway. 'Hello? Who's this?'

'It's my boss, and we're after a big favour.' Watson grinned. 'We need some information.'

Lestrade eyed Quist warily. 'What sort of information?'

Watson sniggered. 'Okay, I know how he looks, but he's alright really.'

The detective stored this for future discussion.

'Well, if Watty vouches for you, that's good enough for me.' Lestrade headed for the lounge. 'He's told me a lot about you, Mister Punch.'

Quist glanced at his uncomfortable-looking assistant.

'Here we are.' Lestrade opened the door. 'Make yourself at home.'

Quist knew this would be tricky. With a multitude of posters, models and action figures filling the room, the place was a shrine to the television series *Star Trek*. Watson's friend walked over to a long table beneath the window, covered, as far as Quist could tell, with the sort of equipment they hook up to patients in intensive care.

'Welcome to the cyber-cave.' Lestrade sat at a large screen surrounded by computer banks and networked laptops. 'So what do you need?'

'Er...' Watson cleared his throat. 'Can you still get into the cop's computer?'

'The what?'

'Come on, Gazza. I've already told him you can hack in there.'

'I dunno.' Lestrade shuffled uncomfortably. 'It's illegal, you know?'

'You do surprise me.' Quist produced two twenty-pound notes. 'I wonder if these special vouchers would cover the electricity?'

Chuckling, Lestrade switched on the monitor and began typing, whilst the detective moved aside a Klingon sword and sat on a padded Borg cube to watch.

'I see you like *Star Trek*?' Quist held up a model of the

Starship Enterprise.

'Who doesn't?' said Watson. 'A Yorkshireman was the Captain of that ship. Boldly going where no one has gone before.'

'We're boldly going somewhere right now.' Quist gestured to the computer. 'How is it possible to break into the police and what made you do it?'

'It's a challenge for hackers like me,' said Lestrade. 'The Pentagon and the CIA have both been hacked, so the Fulford Road cop shop isn't exactly unthinkable. Plus, I was daft as a kid, nicking DVDs and things. I've learnt my lesson now though.'

'Gazza's also learnt how to wipe his record sheet clean,' added Watson.

Quist frowned. 'But surely they keep paper copies?'

'Yeah,' said Watson, 'but no one looks at them. It's easier to run checks by pushing buttons than spending hours searching through rooms of dusty files. Cops use the Internet so the different forces can access each other. They have shit-hot safeguards though. Top firewalls and advanced protective programmes.'

'I've no doubt.' Quist watched the complex screen. 'So how did you break in?'

'It's complicated.' Lestrade paused in his typing. 'How familiar are you with tech-jargon? Worms, Trojans and stuff?'

'About as familiar as Watson is with tasteful dress sense. Don't they have passwords?'

'You fool the computer into revealing them,' said Lestrade. 'When I broke in, I left a back door ajar. It won't take long.'

'You make it sound easy.'

'It is if you're a genius,' said Watson.

'Whoa!' Lestrade nodded to the screen. 'We're in.'

Quist shuffled his seat closer and watched the display change to the North Yorkshire Police crest above a menu.

'Okay, what do you want?' Looking Quist up and down, Lestrade winked. 'Points taking off your driving license? Your name removing from the sex-offender's register?'

Quist smiled sarcastically. 'I need to see what they have on the girl who was murdered on Saturday. The details that were left out of the media. Her name was Lisa Mirren.'

'Let's take a look.' Lestrade went through several menus, typed in the name, and text appeared. 'That's some report on her.' He indicated a key. 'Press that when you want to scroll the page.'

'Well done,' enthused Quist. 'The post mortem - amazing!'

Watson leant over. 'No blood in the cadaver, it says there. That's strange, isn't it, Guv?'

'Indeed,' murmured Quist. 'According to this, shock from major blood loss caused Lisa Mirren's death. The torn throat occurred afterwards.'

Watson frowned. 'Why would the killer tear her throat after she was dead?'

Quist turned to Lestrade. 'Could you find the post mortem for Diane Woodall?'

The young man cleared the screen, typed and sat back.

'Only enough blood in her to sustain life.' Watson read the data. 'It says even if she hadn't topped herself she wouldn't have lasted long.'

'Damn!' Quist narrowed his eyes. *This could be far worse than he'd envisaged.* 'And the file for Becca Travis, please.'

'The same,' whispered Watson, scanning the text as it appeared.

'Yes,' said Quist. 'Massive blood loss in all three girls before their death.' His eyes widened. 'Ah, and it says the forensic team found several feline hairs on Lisa Mirren and on what was left of Becca Travis. Panthera Pardus or Panthera Leo–the analysis is unable to determine which.'

'In English, Guv?'

'They've found cat hairs which they think belong to a leopard or a lion.'

'What?' Watson laughed. 'Are they serious?'

Quist ignored him. 'Mmmh, one victim was burnt, one

decapitated, and the lacerations on the other occurred *after* death.' Standing up, he walked slowly to the window and stared thoughtfully at the Minster for a while. 'According to those files, the bodies are stored in the hospital morgue.'

'You're looking into murders?' Lestrade turned curiously to his friend. 'I thought your work was all divorce papers and photographing wayward hubbies?'

'Up until to yesterday, it *was*.' Watson pointed to the screen. 'Don't you want to see if there's a suspect list or anything, Guv?'

'I don't think there'll be much point.' The detective returned to the computer. 'You joked about my driving license. Can you access such details?'

'Yes, DVLC is linked to the cops,' said Lestrade.

'I have two car registrations. Is it possible to find the owners?'

Watson sat upright. 'What cars?'

'You recall the Maserati by the railway?' Quist produced a paper with the numbers. 'It spent yesterday following us, along with a white BMW. I didn't want to worry you so I said nothing.'

'Cheers.' Watson laughed dryly. 'Really believe in keeping your assistants up-to-date, eh?'

'It won't take long.' Lestrade typed and waited.

'Why would anyone follow us?' quizzed Watson. 'Could it be anything to do with these murders?'

'There,' said Lestrade. 'Your BMW's from Lancashire.'

'Interesting,' said Quist. 'Owned by a Doctor Jordan Zucco, of Sunnyvale Hospital in Birchley, Ashton-Under-Lyne.'

'And that's your Maserati,' said Lestrade.

'As I expected.' Quist nodded. 'Carl Dreyer. The Old Forge, Bardsey.'

'*Expected*?' echoed Watson. 'Do we know him?'

'I met him the other evening. He was the Leeds manager of Brightshield Glazing.'

'Was?'

'This Maserati was on the news today,' pointed out Lestrade.

'That's right,' said Quist. 'It was abandoned in Acomb last night.'

'The code at the top of the screen means the cops have a special file.'

'Really?' Quist beamed. 'Could you find it for me?'

Watson regarded him inquisitively. *He'd smiled more over the last forty-eight hours than the past three weeks. Complicated puzzles obviously agreed with old Cyrano.*

'There.' Lestrade finished typing. 'But there's nothing new here. All this was reported on TV - the Maserati owner being missing and his clothes on the bonnet.'

Quist scrolled the text.

'Ah, *that* wasn't released,' said Lestrade. 'There was no mention of red powder being found at the scene.' He read the footnote. 'Substance currently undergoing analysis by Jay Mortimer M.D.'

'Well that rather confirms it,' whispered Quist. 'Ubasteri.'

'Confirms *what*?' asked Watson. 'Who bastard *what*? What's going on here? The Brightshield manager's been tailing us and he's vanished?'

'They won't find him either,' said Quist. 'Gazza, could you find me the number of Brightshield Glazing in Leeds and let me use your phone for a moment, please?'

'No problem.' Lestrade shrugged and busied himself with his mobile. 'That forty quid should cover it.'

'Red powder?' repeated Watson. 'Is this a drug thing? Raspberry-flavoured cocaine or something. Why was he tailing us?'

'I'm not sure,' said the detective, quietly. 'I need to check something.'

Lestrade passed Quist the phone. 'Press that to dial,' he said.

Like most sales offices, the phone was snatched on the first ring. 'Brightshield Windows,' chimed a syrupy voice. 'Luke here.'

'Lance Robson at the Yorkshire Post,' said Quist. 'We're preparing an article on the disappearance of your manager and...'

'Yeah, it's worrying,' admitted Luke. 'Have you heard about our Christmas offers, Lance? We pay your VAT if you purchase...'

'I understand Mister Dreyer is something of a recluse?'

'You could say that. I've seen him less than a dozen times.'

'So how does he run the business?'

'Phone, fax and video conferencing. He visits the office occasionally and attends evening branch meetings.'

'Does he do any selling himself?'

'He handles the bigger sales and visits clients personally if a rep experiences problems. Talking of sales, for a limited period, if you buy four windows you get a free door...'

'Does he have green eyes?'

'What?' Luke was taken aback. 'Er, yeah, as a matter of fact, he has quite noticeable green...'

Quist thumbed off the mobile. 'Of course,' he murmured. 'Ubasteri. I remember the green eyes now. He failed to persuade me to buy that night. It didn't work and that's why he looked so shocked.'

'What was all that?' demanded Watson. 'Why would you ask about his eyes, and how did you know Dreyer was a recluse?'

'Educated guesswork.' Quist consulted a scrap of paper and entered another phone number. 'Hello there,' he said. 'Is it possible to speak to Doctor Clarkson? Mmmh, I see. Thank you.'

'Amy's not at the lab?' Watson watched as he checked the paper again and hastily rang her home. 'She told us she was leaving early.'

'Yes, they say she left a while ago.' Quist sighed at the constant ringing. 'But she hasn't arrived home yet.'

'Don't look so worried. She'll be okay with the cops guarding her.'

'Let's hope so,' murmured Quist. 'Personally, I wouldn't be inclined to bet upon it.'

* * * *

Chapter 38

Quist knocked on the front door of Amy's house a third time before returning to the Beetle. 'She left work early,' he said. 'So where is she?'

'Hiding, if she's any sense.' Watson jumped back into the car. 'If it was me, I'd have left the country.'

'She only gave me her home number. I don't have her mobile.' The detective tugged off his leather overcoat and tossed it on the back seat. Climbing behind the wheel, he stared pensively at the youth.

'What's up?' Watson shuffled uncomfortably. 'What're you looking at?'

'As things are becoming clearer, I was debating whether to drop you at home before proceeding further. The thing is, I'll almost certainly require assistance and I fully believe you'll be okay with this.'

'Er, with what?'

'The situation ahead. You have a fast, open mind and you're stronger and much more resilient than you realise.'

'Er, right, Guv.' Watson gave a puzzled frown. 'Thanks for that... I think.'

'I need to warn Amy, and I was hoping she could tell us about Doctor Stapleton too. He owns the company and he should have all the answers I need.' Quist started the Beetle. 'We'll pay Will Gillette a visit and call back here later.'

'What do you want to see him for?'

'He's the director of research and he runs the lab for Stapleton.' The detective drove up Appleton Street and onto Micklegate. 'From what Amy told us about his secretive work routines, he'll know what's going on.'

'What *is* going on? Warn Amy? Warn her about *what*?' Watson shook his head. '*The situation ahead*, you said? *Things are becoming clearer*? What's going on, Guv?'

'I'm certain now that the three murders are connected with the secretive products that Gillette erased from the computer.'

'*Three* murders?'

'Diane was no suicide. Four counting Selden.'

'But he was killed by a bunch of nutters. It had to happen. A skinhead walking through Milverton alone dressed as a Nazi is like...'

'Like putting your head on a railway?'

'But how can suicide be murder?'

'Believe me, in certain circumstances it can.'

Watson pondered. 'When I asked earlier if Selden's death was connected with the murders, you never answered. But now you're sure?'

'Now I'm sure. Then there's Dreyer, the dead Brightshield manager.'

'Yeah, what's all that about? Why would he follow us, and what makes you think he's dead?'

'They found his clothes on the car bonnet with a quantity of red powder.'

'Meaning?'

'I'll explain shortly. Let me speak to Gillette first.'

'What about the biker, Creeper? Did he kill the girls? He admitted they were his badges.'

Quist shook his head. 'I don't know where he fits into this, but no, he isn't the killer.'

'How can you be sure? I don't understand.'

'I wouldn't expect you to yet, but you will soon.'

'Where does Gillette live?'

'Bell Lane in Fulford; it isn't far. I asked Amy for the address this morning in case we should need it.'

'Clever, aren't you?' Watson grinned. 'How come you gave me the job?'

'I'm sorry?'

'The assistant advert? Like I say, you're a clever bloke and I'm not exactly Einstein. There must've been other applicants, so why me?'

'Why?' Quist pondered for a moment. 'I liked you.'

'A shit-hot brain *and* excellent taste.' The teenager laughed. 'Personal question, Guv, but you don't have many mates, do you?'

'Personal and rather odd. Why do you ask?'

'Oh, I don't know – curiosity. I've worked with you for three weeks, but I don't know you, or anything about you.'

'There isn't much to know. I don't have any family and I live alone. If you want the sad truth, at the moment, my *only* friend is Larry Reynolds. We go back a long, long way.'

'Why did he leave York? Mum says the Reynolds Antiques shop has been there since she was a kid. I can't see why an old bloke would want to uproot himself and start again in another city at that age.'

'He must have reasons,' murmured Quist.

'Speaking of mum, she was quite taken with you. I reckon that's why she gave you the gnome.'

Quist glanced at the obscenity with the jutting penis in the rear seat. He'd been hoping some biker might have stolen it earlier in Clifton.

'She wondered if you ever went along to the seventies dance nights on Mondays at the Black Bull in Acomb?'

Quist shot him a cynical look before turning into Fulford.

'Er, no, dancing in a wig and kipper tie isn't exactly you, is it? So where *do* you go at night? She said I should ask.'

'Strange, actually,' said Quist. 'I can't imagine why, but she was surprised that I was called Bernard. For some reason she thought my name was Cyrano.'

'There's Bell Lane,' blurted the teenager.

'Ah, saved by the proverbial bell.'

The Volkswagen rolled to a halt outside number fourteen. Gillette's house stood silhouetted against the late afternoon sky.

'Nice place.' Watson whistled. 'Big, isn't it?'

Nodding slowly, Quist reached in the dash and pulled on a

162

pair of thin leather gloves before setting off up the drive. 'I have a bad feeling about this. Stay behind me and don't touch anything.'

'A bad feeling?' Watson zipped up his jacket and tagged on behind, a warning tingle prickling his spine. He reached the kitchen door and frowned uneasily at the hole in the glazed panel. 'Oh boy! That doesn't look like a letter box.'

'No, it doesn't.' Quist fingered the jagged edge and examined the red powder on his glove.

'What's that?'

'An indication that it's too late to ask Gillette anything.' He pushed the broken door, sighed as it collapsed inwards from the frame, and stepped over the mess. 'Far too late. Remember what I said. Don't touch anything.'

'Oh, shit! We shouldn't be doing this, Guv.' Watson looked around nervously and followed him through the kitchen passage into the lounge. 'Fuck!' he whimpered. 'He's... he's...'

'Yes, he is,' agreed Quist.

Will Gillette lay dead on the rug. His body had taken on the lifeless appearance, with pale blue face and glassy eyes, that even to untrained observers like Watson, denotes the difference between unconsciousness and a corpse. The head facing backwards clinched it.

Quist examined the twisted neck. 'The spine is severed at the skull base,' he murmured. 'From the finger-marks, it looks as if someone wrenched his head around from behind.'

'*Fingers* made those deep punctures? It looks like claws have been dug in.'

'Yes, to get a good grip, and whoever did this had great strength.'

'Fair enough. I'll be seeing you.'

'Where are you going?'

'Wales.'

'Come here and don't be silly.'

'Silly? That's a fuckin' dead guy you're messing around with. A murdered guy and you're telling *me* not to be silly? Oh hell, Guv, you must see that we can't get involved any deeper. For God's sake, leave it to the cops.'

'I wish I could.'

'What the fuck do you mean?' Watson laughed frantically. 'Make an anonymous call and then walk away from this. Tell them about those badges you found and this murder. Tell them they're looking for some twat with a gym membership and fingernails like Wolverine...'

'Calm down,' snapped Quist. 'Take some deep breaths. I can't leave this to the police. These murders aren't exactly routine police business. I may be the only one who can help.'

'I don't understand,' wailed the youth.

'Deep breaths! You'll understand shortly. I don't know why yet, but someone wants us involved in this. Selden was told what to say to interest me and get me to that railway line. I need to know who put him up to it, who planted those badges, and why?'

Watson shook his head jerkily. 'Why did they want us to go to the biker house?'

'Again, I'm not sure.' He looked around the room. 'Gillette was extremely worried. That bottle on the bureau is almost empty and the top has been left off. He was filling his glass so often, he didn't bother to replace it. Only one glass too. People who drink large amounts of whisky alone have serious problems.'

'You don't say. Watson gulped and tried the deep breathing.

'The curtains are drawn and the phone is unplugged. There are two ashtrays and both are full of cigar butts. He's been pacing the room too. Look closely and you'll see he dropped ash as he walked back and forth, especially by the windows where he stood watching around the curtains. Smokers who are stressed and deep in worried thought can flick ash without thinking.'

'Okay, he was worried. Now can we please get out of here?'

'I want to see if I can find Stapleton's address here first.' Quist checked his watch. 'Then we have to visit the hospital. It's five days since Lisa Mirren died.'

The Mercedes van stood in the central car park on Tower Street. Strand sat in the rear, gazing quietly at the striking remains of York Castle which topped a vast conical hill. Clifford's Tower reminded him of a huge white pork pie.

'I still don't understand,' said Sangster, finally voicing the worried thoughts of the other three bodyguards. 'Why are we just sitting here?'

'We're waiting for the right moment. Ah, speaking of which...' Strand snatched the buzzing mobile from his pocket and read the text message. 'Well, it's about time,' he muttered to himself. He leant forward and nudged Fisher's back. 'The hospital.'

The driver frowned. 'What about it?'

'It's time to go there.'

Fisher nodded and the van skidded out of the car park.

Squirming uncomfortably, Sangster looked up at the darkening sky. 'How far is it?'

'Oh, not too far,' said Strand. 'We'll be there in five minutes.'

'I really think we should have gone there sooner, Sir.'

'Do you know something?' Strand lit a cigarette and leered. 'For once, you're almost certainly right.'

Creeper sprawled in a beer-soaked chair rolling a marijuana joint. It wasn't easy. He was drunk, this was his tenth spliff, and his chisel-like fingers were better suited to forming fists than manufacturing cigarettes.

'Hey, you lot.' The biker focused on the spinning room and raised his voice above the heavy-metal din. 'How about some help here?'

It was a waste of time. The party was ending, less than a dozen remained, and everyone here in the lounge was in the same condition. Three lay comatose, one knelt vomiting over the hi-fi and, despite mild alcohol poisoning, two were attempting to copulate on the couch.

Creeper belched and turned back to the spliff as screams and brawling sounds came from the passage. Fighting was nothing new here; after the sixth scrap, he'd given up counting. The door crashed open and a biker's severed head landed in his lap. He blinked twice, peering at the blood through a swirling mist of intoxication. Creeper was used to having heads between his legs, but they were normally female and attached to a body.

'I hope your dental records are up-to-date,' said a voice from the doorway. 'Forensics are going to need them.'

* * * *

Chapter 39

'Bloody hell, Guv...' Watson followed Quist to York Hospital's main entrance on Wiggington Road. 'Do you really think this is a good idea?'

'Don't worry.' Quist glanced up as nasal screaming filled the air and starlings billowed over on their way to roost. A twilight chill had descended to freeze the city. 'Just act natural and stay close.'

'I'll rephrase that; is this a *sane* idea?' The teenager hung back at the doors. 'I'll wait outside and...'

'I've known slugs with more backbone. Come on.'

'Guv,' laughed Watson. 'First you find a murdered guy and you don't tell the cops. You search his house, trying to find Doctor Stapleton's address, and now you want to stroll into a morgue and look at a body. You can't do stuff like that.'

'Yes you can.' Quist took his arm. 'Now hurry up.'

He led the teenager through the hospital lobby and down a corridor to the right. The third door was marked *Mortuary* and *No Admittance*.

'Damn!' He tried the handle. 'It's locked.'

'Damn!' echoed Watson, with relief normally only provided by enemas. 'Ah, well, so much for that.'

'Check down there.' Quist pointed back to the lobby and pulled on his gloves. 'Make sure no one's coming.'

The youth set off, freezing as a metallic snap rang out. 'Jesus!' he hissed, running back to the open door. 'Are you crazy?'

'It was only a cheap lock.'

'How did you do that?' The steel tenon was broken inside the mortise. 'What did you use?'

Quist dragged him inside. It was an office, fortunately deserted, with filing cabinets and a desk covered in papers and books.

'I'll guard the exit,' proposed Watson.

'No need. We won't be long and I'm sure you're strong enough for this.'

'Strong enough to look at a dead girl?'

Quist opened the desk register at the last page. 'Lisa's in number eleven; it'll be through there.' He pointed to a door on their left.

'You make it sound like a hotel. Not only is this insane, it's incredibly illegal.'

The door led into a tiled ablutions area of cupboards, lockers, mop racks and steel sinks. Hosepipe hung on the far wall beside a further door.

'I just can't believe you're doing this,' said Watson.

Quist pushed open the door. The dark morgue lay silent, the crisp air thick with the smell of bleach, lemon, and something else. Something that had passed its sell-by date and, despite the detergent camouflage, left the youth feeling decidedly perturbed.

Watson zipped up his jacket. 'Cold, isn't it?' he whispered.

'Yes.' Quist flicked on the lights and buttoned his own overcoat. 'It has to be.'

His assistant shuddered. It was a cold reminiscent of supermarket chill areas, where milk and other perishable commodities are kept. He knew the commodities here were as perishable as you could possibly get, but decided not to dwell upon it.

'Listen,' he said, 'why don't we...'

'Get this over with quickly?' Quist pulled him down the three steps and nodded to the doors at the opposite end of the room. 'That's the way in for the ambulances. I'd better make sure it's locked.'

'Yeah, you do that.' Watson's panicky eyes only half-noticed the dissection tables and wheeled stretchers. Instead a morbid fascination drew him to the wall of metal hatches. 'Do you reckon they're all, er, occupied?'

Quist hurried back from checking the entrance. 'From the register, I'd say so.' He swung open number eleven. 'Remember not to touch anything.'

'Thanks. I needed that reminder.'

The detective slid out a steel drawer. 'Here she is.' A plastic

168

sheet covered a human shape and he pulled it from the face. 'Lisa Mirren.'

Watson had only seen one corpse in his life and that was Gillette. There was no way he wanted to see another, but a magnetism compelled him to gingerly peep from behind Quist.

'I'm sorry,' said the detective. 'You're not going to like this, but I'm afraid it's necessary.'

Watson recognised the dead girl from Grant's photos and the news. He had to admit, this stiff was nicer than Gillette. The skin was healthy pink, more like a sleeper than a cadaver, and her hair still held its golden lustre. He noticed the smoothness of her cheeks, her neck and...

'Hang about,' he gasped, heart pounding. 'Have you got the right bird? I know she looks the same, but I thought her throat...'

'Was torn out?'

Watson gulped. 'Maybe it's because I hang around with such a great sleuth, but I've started spotting details like that.'

'You also read the post mortem at Lestrade's.' Quist peeled away the sheet exposing a body free of autopsy scars.

The teenager's heart raced faster. 'But surely...' He halted as the girl's hand twitched. 'Guv, did you see...'

Lisa convulsed, eyes snapping open.

'Jesus!' Watson leapt back. 'She's alive.'

'No, I'm afraid not.' Quist dragged him away as the corpse flipped over onto hands and knees with incredible speed. 'Stay behind me.'

'*Fuck!*' His mind spinning, Watson stifled a scream. 'What the *fuck?*'

Lisa dropped her head, shrouding her features in a blonde curtain, a hiss escaping as arm and leg muscles flexed. Naked beauties stretching in the doggy position would normally excite Watson, but he much preferred them alive. This performance provided the same titillation as a bucket of ice water.

'Keep moving back,' murmured Quist. 'Do exactly what I

say.'

Lisa lifted her head and Watson froze in terror to see the golden hair fall from her scalp and turn to dust. Dark stubble replaced it, instantly sprouting into a growth of thick black fur.

'This is insane,' stammered the youth, his eyes bulging as the fur spread to cover her mutating face, torso and limbs. 'What the fuck is happening?'

'She's transforming,' said Quist, guiding him backwards.

Lisa's grey eyes were now an unearthly green which seemed to glow. Her nose and mouth had extended into a feline muzzle.

'No, this isn't happening.' Watson yelped as the creature sprang from the drawer and landed silently on the tiled floor, the swift and impossible transformation complete. He stared in sheer disbelief at a black panther. 'This is insane. This really *cannot* be happening.'

'It can smell the blood,' said Quist. 'It wants it.'

The teenager chanced a quick look around the room. 'What blood?'

'*Our* blood.'

'Oh fuck!'

'Keep backing away to the door, but don't make any sudden moves.' Quist stepped in front of him. 'You'll be okay. She's disorientated from waking and hasn't reached full strength.'

The huge cat paced slowly towards them, a deep growl rumbling in its throat and tongue lolling hungrily over razor teeth.

'Hullo, Lisa,' croaked Watson. 'We know Raoul's brother...'

'I wouldn't bother,' said Quist. 'What's left of Lisa is masked by hunger. You're no longer speaking to a human.'

'Why am I not surprised to hear...' He stiffened as the panther fixed him with a stare.

'She's trying to mesmerise you.' The detective backed up against one of the steel cadaver trolleys. 'Don't look into her eyes.'

Watson was too busy looking into her eyes to hear the warning. Cursing, Quist spun the wheeled stretcher around from behind in a wide arc, launching it at the cat. It sprang back, allowing him enough time to scoop the hypnotised youth over his shoulder, race through the exit and slam the door. The panther crashed against the woodwork, clawing frenziedly and shrieking in frustrated rage as he twisted the key.

'Are you okay?' demanded Quist.

Watson jiggled his head to clear the fogginess, and looked around in terror. 'Okay?' He sagged back against the door and laughed manically. 'No, I'm fuckin' well *not* okay. I couldn't move. I thought that thing was gonna get me.'

A black paw smashed through the wood, the claws fastening on his throat.

'It appears you were right,' said Quist.

* * * *

Alan Todd leant on a blanket trolley waiting for the elevator's arrival. The young man enjoyed meeting different people every day; it was one of the best parts of being a hospital porter. It was also fortunate, for they didn't come much different than the bearded character behind him.

'I wonder if you could help?'

Todd spun round. A moment ago the corridor had been empty. He hadn't heard them approach, but amazingly, five men stood less than a yard away.

'We're looking for the mortuary,' said Strand.

'Er, sorry.' The porter ran a wary eye over the black suits and sunglasses. 'The public aren't allowed down there.'

'Not allowed?' Most of Strand's people would have used *the glare* here; the effects left frozen victims devoid of will and open to orders. Strand occasionally indulged himself with blunter methods. His fingers locked on the man's throat like a tungsten clamp, his talons sprouting. 'I'll ask again.' He lifted the purple face effortlessly. 'Where will we find...'

'Through there,' croaked Todd. 'Down the stairs and left along the passage. The morgue's next to the blood bank.'

'Thank you.' Strand lowered him and retracted his claws.

171

Apart from occasions where recipients had weak necks, this technique generally gleaned fast results. 'You've been most helpful.'

He led the bodyguards to the stairs as the porter staggered to the nearest phone.

'Shouldn't we silence him, Sir?' asked Browning, looking back. He'll probably ring the police.'

'Forget him,' snapped Strand. *Probably* ring them? *He was counting on it.*

'Next to the blood bank, huh?' said Fisher.

'Feeling peckish, are we?' Strand glanced at him. 'Be a good boy and I'll see about letting you have a snack later.'

* * * *

'How do you feel about detective work now?' Quist peeled the talons from Watson's throat before they could puncture the skin. 'Still bored?'

'Fuck off!' The curse was a gargled stammer. The youth slid down the door and dropped to his knees coughing. 'What the fuck just happened in there?'

'Don't be obtuse. She turned herself into a panther.'

'I must be getting better at this deduction lark, because that's what I thought.' Watson crawled away and turned to watch the paw grope blindly through the hole, averting his face as it vanished and the cat's green eyes appeared. 'It's insane and totally fuckin' impossible, but yeah, that's what I thought.'

'We can't leave this thing,' said Quist. 'Some nurse or porter will meet it.'

'So what the hell are we going to do?' Massaging his throat, Watson backed up against the sinks. The door juddered and a hinge burst free. 'Shit! How strong is it?'

'Stronger than the door.'

'Come on, Guv, please. There's nothing we can do.'

The cat slammed into the wood a second time. Screws clattered on the floor.

'No.' Quist glanced around the ablutions room and grabbed a

mop from a bucket in the corner. He broke the head over his knee leaving four feet of shaft and a splintered point. 'I can't have this thing loose in a hospital.'

Watson gulped. 'What're you going to do with that?'

'Guess.' He flattened himself against the wall by the morgue door, brandished the makeshift weapon like a bayoneted rifle, and shooed his assistant away. 'Go up there to the end of the room.'

'I don't believe this.' Watson shuffled backwards towards the office, his entire body shaking. 'I don't believe...' The cat slammed the door again, this time crashing through. The green eyes locked onto him, its feline features contorting in glee. 'Oh my God!' The youth whimpered as realisation hit home - *he was bait to attract its attention.* 'Oh... my... God!'

Watson watched in paralysed horror as Quist lunged from his hiding place. The panther caught the movement, twisted and reared up, but the spike had been slammed between the front legs before any guard could be raised. Hissing and clawing at the pole, the cat twisted and spun, spraying blood and transforming the walls into something the Tate Modern would be overjoyed to exhibit. It collided with a closet and rolled onto its side, spewing gore onto the tiles. Quist kicked the spike hard, driving it through the ribcage and out between the shoulder blades. A dreadful chuckling erupted and then the cat juddered and lay still.

'It's over.' Quist tugged his overcoat straight. 'She's gone.'

Watson gaped at the blood; it was everywhere. He closed his eyes in the hope that, when they opened, things may be different or he may have woken. They weren't and he hadn't. 'I can't believe it,' he whispered, trembling uncontrollably.

'I know it's difficult to accept, but she was Ubasteri and...'

'No, you twat. I can't believe you set me up as bait.' He shook his head. 'She was *what*?'

'Ubasteri. We don't have time for me to explain here, but they're shapeshifters who live on human blood. They're like vampires, in that daylight is lethal to them...'

'What?' Watson ran a hand through his curly hair, his mind spinning. '*What?*'

'They're shapeshifters who…'

'I heard what you fuckin' said. It's going in my ears, but my brain is kicking it back out, okay?'

Lisa's fur had vanished and her body had reverted to human form. Watson's stomach lurched as her eyes fell into the skull and fluid poured from her ears with a stench like month-old fish.

'Oh, my God,' he croaked. 'What's *this*?'

'Complete molecular breakdown.'

The belly burst over the tiled floor, intestines and organs turning to a thick, gelatinous ooze.

'Complete *what*?' The teenager gagged. 'What the hell's happening to her?'

'In simple terms, Lisa had her blood drained by supernatural creatures which transformed her into one of them. The metamorphosis causes an entire change in cell structure and DNA. If the life spark is removed, the tissues decompose within seconds.'

'I'll try again. What the hell's happening to her?'

Quist thought for a moment. 'She's turning to gunge.'

The bubbling flesh had vanished and the bones were crumbling, the corpse becoming a putrid pool.

'Supernatural creatures,' whispered Watson. He leant against the wall dazed, the bizarre reality of what he'd just experienced finally beginning to sink in. 'Genuine shapeshifters? What did you call her? Ubasteri?'

'The Ubasteri were an Egyptian cult who worshipped Bast the cat god, but we have no time for this. We'll discuss it later when we…'

'We'll discuss it *now*. You knew what she was, but you took me in there unprepared and she tried to kill me.'

'How could I prepare you? If I'd tried to tell you about this, you'd have thought me crazy and never come.'

'Lisa was killed by vampire cats and you knew? How could

you know?'

'I've had a strange feeling about these deaths from the beginning. I was fairly sure when I found out about the feline hair, the missing blood in those murder victims, and Lisa's throat being torn after death.'

'The cat hair and missing blood I can understand, but...'

'They usually bite the carotid artery in the neck and drain the body. Camouflaging the feeding evidence with lacerations is common practise. When a victim is drained, it takes five days for the corpse to become Ubasteri and I knew Lisa would be waking tonight at dusk. That's why I insisted you came here. If I was to have your assistance, you had to see her for yourself. I'm sorry for putting you through that, but you'd never have believed me otherwise.'

'You can say that again.'

'And I was right. You *are* strong enough to cope with this. You did fine.'

'Oh absolutely! Apart from almost filling my trousers and having a heart-attack, everything was just fuckin' marvellous. That Diane bird on the railway was drained. Is she down here too?'

'She was decapitated,' said Quist. 'It's impossible for her to become a shapeshifter.'

'What about Becca Travis?'

'Charred legs? Was that a serious question?'

The gory transformation on the floor was almost complete, the mess drying and turning to scarlet powder. Quist brushed his blood-splattered leather overcoat and the stains fell away as dust.

'Hey,' said Watson. 'That's just like...'

'Gillette's door? Yes, whoever broke in cut himself. Their blood turns to dust on leaving the body. It confirmed my suspicions when I found it on the glass and I knew we had to visit the morgue.'

'Giant fuckin' cats murdered Gillette and you took me in there? They could still have been inside when...'

'I'm not an idiot. Sunlight is lethal to them and the afternoon sun was shining at the time. The killer must have called earlier in the fog.'

'Er, right.' Watson laughed weakly. 'Cats, Egyptian cults, sunlight? Whooo! I honestly can't get my head around this, Guv. I mean, if I hadn't seen it...'

Quist heard movement in the office next door, snatched Watson's lapels and dragged him swiftly and silently to the lockers. Strand and the bodyguards entered the ablutions room too late to see the broom closet close.

'Ah!' Sangster spotted the powder by the shattered door. 'Could that be the Mirren girl?'

'Either that or someone has spilt their paprika.' Strand bent to study the broken mop, then lowered his shades and peered into the morgue at the empty storage unit. 'Someone has done the job for us. Someone with a knowledge of the Elite.'

Two pairs of ears pricked up in the cramped blackness of the cupboard.

'The President won't like this,' said Hinds. 'We left it too late. We should have come last night, or earlier today.'

'He's right, Sir,' agreed Fisher. 'We were supposed to get rid of the evidence before she awoke. Why did you want to sit waiting in that car park? When the President finds out...'

'That's *my* problem, isn't it?' Strand frowned at Browning. 'What's the matter with you?'

'Blood!' The guard had stiffened. He sniffed the air, nose twitching and flattening into feline form.

'We're next to the blood bank,' said Strand. 'Come on. There's nothing for us to do here and we have another call to make.'

'It isn't the blood bank.' Browning sniffed again and turned to the cupboards lining the wall, his cat muzzle extending. 'This is fresh, live blood. Warm blood in motion.'

Sangster raised his head and tasted the air. 'He's right,' he said quietly. 'I think someone is in here.'

Watson tried swallowing, but his mouth was dry and his throat tight.

'Never mind.' Strand herded the team back into the office. 'We're leaving.'

'But, Sir...' Sangster's jaw fell. 'Whoever destroyed the girl obviously knows about the Elite. Hadn't we better find out what happened here? And this scent...'

'I said we're leaving. I want to get out before...' Opening the door to the corridor, he walked into a police officer. 'Before *this* happens.'

'Alright,' snapped the Constable. 'Hold it there.'

'Everything is fine.' Strand whipped off his shades and stared into his eyes. 'We're doctors.'

'Er yeah.' The policeman blinked. 'Sorry, doctor, but I'm looking for five men in sunglasses that are heading for the morgue. They assaulted a porter.'

'You don't want us. The ones you want are in there.'

'Right.' The Constable brushed by. 'Thanks.'

Quist waited until the footsteps passed through the ablutions room before opening the closet. 'Come on,' he whispered. 'Let's chance it.'

'What was that fee-fi-fo-fum shit?' stammered Watson. 'Could they really smell...'

'Move yourself.' Quist crept out and ran quietly through the office into the hospital corridor. 'Let's go.'

'Those footsteps belonged to a cop,' hissed Watson, following. 'He was in the morgue back there.'

'Yes, I saw him,' said Quist. 'I've also seen this one.'

'Don't move,' said the approaching police Sergeant.

Quist turned swiftly, dropping his voice. 'Keep your mouth shut. Don't mention shapeshifters. Tell them absolutely nothing, do you understand?'

'I'm a black youth,' said Watson. 'Being questioned by the impartial, non-racist cops isn't exactly a new experience.'

* * * *

177

Chapter 40

Rex brought the Ferrari to a halt on Minster Avenue, switched off the York map on his satnav and gazed over his shades at the motorcycles parked outside the suburban house. It was dark and lights shone behind the closed curtains. He wasn't sure how to go about this and he'd been hoping the private detective would be here. Quist was okay at questioning people and handy to have around if things turned nasty. He swallowed uncomfortably, then switched off the 007 soundtrack and climbed from the car.

'Oh, come on,' he muttered. 'You know Kung Fu. What are you scared of?'

Rex had never actually been in a fight, but he had plenty of cash. *If things got out of hand here, he could always pay them not to hurt him.*

This was obviously the place, but there was no sign of an all-day party. The front door was half-open, but no sound came from the house. The neighbours appeared to be out too, although if bikers had been partying next door, this went without saying. Sliding the Walther pistol down his waistband and taking a deep breath, Rex walked slowly up the path and reached for the bell. His finger hesitated and, instead of ringing, he pushed the door fully open and slipped inside.

Apart from party debris, the wide passage was empty. Judging from the silence, so was the house. *So where were the owners of the bikes parked outside?* Puzzled and apprehensive, Rex picked his way through the litter, his nose wrinkling at the weird metallic stench. He grimaced at the countless cigarette butts, bits of pizza, broken glass, severed hands, empty cans...

He slowly turned back. It lay in a pile of lager bottles, and no matter how much logic attempted to dissuade him, it certainly *looked* like a hand. It was hand-shaped, with fingers and ragged tendons, but a *human hand* on the passage carpet? He stared incredulously. It must have been quite a party for a biker to get this torn off and leave it behind. Nudging the grisly object with his toe, he backed away to the open door of the lounge.

The owner of the hand wouldn't have much use for it any more - that was obvious. He wouldn't need his legs either, which was just as well, for they lay by the fireplace. Apart from an autopsy, he wouldn't need anything, because like everyone else in the lounge, he was dead. Rex stood very still, his jaw falling. The metallic smell he'd noticed earlier wasn't garbage, but blood; a dark, sticky lake covered the carpet. He couldn't determine the number of claw-slashed bodies– limbs, heads and ragged corpses were everywhere. The logical part of his brain told him to simply count the heads. Another more basic part told him to soil himself and run.

He turned in a trance to the staircase. A disembowelled biker sprawled on the landing, his dripping entrails draped through the spindles like some horrific bead curtain. He shuffled numbly into the kitchen to find another corpse by the door.

'My God!' whispered a voice behind him.

Supressing a scream, Rex turned. A beautiful girl stood at the bottom of the stairs with wet blonde hair hanging over quaking shoulders. She clutched a shoulder bag and gaped at the body on the linoleum.

'Who are you?' he spluttered. 'What the fuck happened? I've heard things can get rowdy with bikers, but...'

'I was upstairs,' she whimpered. 'Some men came. I didn't see anything, but I heard screaming. It was horrible. I looked downstairs and saw Steve. He was lying in the passage and looked like that.' She jabbed a finger at the biker.

Rex flinched. Although the kitchen corpse still possessed a head, it had been twisted around to face backwards.

She screwed her eyes shut, short unsteady sentences tripping over one-another. 'I ran in a bedroom and the loft trap was open. Gary must have been to his dope stash. I climbed out of sight and waited. After a while it went quiet, but I didn't move. I... I didn't dare move. I waited and...'

'Hey, come on.' Rex snatched her as the tears rolled. 'You're in shock. Who are you?'

'Fran,' she sobbed.

'Er, are there any more bodies upstairs? Two friends of mine were supposed to be calling. A private eye and a young black...'

'I spoke to them. No they aren't here; they didn't stay long. You have to get me away from here, please. I really can't stand it any longer.'

'Okay, let's get you into the fresh air.' Taking Fran's arm, Rex led her down the passage and opened the door.

Matthew Strand stood on the step, blocking his path. 'I believe there's a party?' he said. 'Hope I'm not too late?'

Rex stiffened, frowning uneasily. 'Er, actually it's over and...' He fell quiet as a quartet of giants burst from a van parked behind the Ferrari.

Strand twisted angrily. 'You were ordered to stay in the vehicle,' he hissed.

'It's them,' shouted Fran. 'They're back!'

Rex didn't need it repeating. He slammed the door in Strand's face and pulled her down the passage towards the kitchen. The front door crashed from its hinges, and realising there was no time to move the corpse from the rear exit, he yanked Fran into the abattoir that had been a lounge.

'What a mess,' tutted Strand, the four bodyguards looming behind him. 'Parties, eh? Carpets are never the same afterwards.'

'Okay...' Eyes darting between the dismembered carcasses and the five killers in the doorway, Rex pushed the girl behind him and whipped out the Walther. 'Okay, freeze,' he shouted.

Fran gaped at the trembling pistol. Strand merely raised an eyebrow.

'We're leaving,' stammered Rex. 'Just get out of our way, okay? I don't want to use this, but I'm SAS and I will if...'

'That won't do any good,' said Fisher, brushing past Strand.

He thinks it's a replica, thought Rex, his mind racing. Aiming left, he fired at the wall to demonstrate the authenticity. A zing followed the loud crack as the ricocheting bullet tore through Fisher's throat.

'Fuck!' Rex watched in horror as the man stumbled back into the passage, a crimson carnation blossoming on his throat. 'Fuck! I didn't mean to...' He turned to Strand. 'You saw what happened. I fired to scare him...'

Fisher reappeared, wiping red dust from his vanishing wound, his leer revealing feline fangs.

'Oh Jesus!' moaned Rex, his spine turning to Vaseline.

'Hardly.' Strand stepped forward and the pistol exploded again with no effect. 'My people and Christ have as much in common as Herod and babysitting.'

Rex whimpered. The fact that someone was still alive after a bullet through the neck had yet to register fully. Logic had virtually departed, but what little remained said this second character wore a Kevlar vest. This was until the shirt puncture and hole in the door behind told a different story. He turned the pistol on Hinds and fired again. A bottle disintegrated on a shelf to his rear.

'I've no idea how much ammunition costs,' said Strand. 'But I'd say you were wasting money.'

Rex had to agree. The realisation finally sank in that the bullets were passing *through* these people. 'What are you?' he whispered. 'What the fuck *are* you?'

Sangster's face sprouted black fur, his eyes glowed green and his fanged mouth was extending. Fisher had dropped onto all fours, his face no longer human. The head of a huge panther now stretched the collar of his shirt.

Strand laughed, watching as Rex's face changed too, from shock to absolute terror.

There were only two ways out of here: through the window, or through these hissing cat creatures. It wasn't much of a contest. Rex snatched a chair, launched it through the curtains in the wide bay and grabbed Fran's arm. 'Run!' he yelled above the crash.

The pair leapt onto the couch and ducked through the hole, the drapes protecting them from the jagged glass. Browning and Sangster turned down the passage, but Strand barred the way. 'Let them go.'

'Let them go?' blurted Fisher, standing upright. 'But, Sir...'

'I don't understand,' yelled Sangster. 'He's seen what we are...'

'You don't need to understand,' snapped Strand. 'You just have to obey orders.'

* * * *

'Who the hell were they?' shouted Rex. Screeching tyres spewed smoke, rubber bit into tarmac and the Ferrari rocketed up the street. '*What* were they?'

'I don't know,' whimpered Fran. 'I think they were the same men who came before and killed...'

'*Men?*' Laughing crazily, Rex skidded onto the main road. 'Are we talking about the same bunch? Did you see them change? Their teeth? Their faces?'

'I saw them. Oh God!'

'They were turning into cats...' stammered Rex.

'I saw it. I don't believe it, but I saw it.'

'Did you see how the bullets went through them? Oh, Christ!'

'What are we going to do?'

'I don't know, but we were lucky to get out of there alive. Why didn't they chase us?'

Fran sobbed and shook her head.

Rex realised his voice was too high and his hands were trembling - not very macho, and it wouldn't inspire confidence in his terrified passenger.

'Do you smoke?' he asked.

'Yes.'

'Here, light two of those.' Passing Fran his cigarettes, he rammed in the dashboard lighter and pulled out his mobile. 'Calling the police is pointless. They'll already be on their way after that shooting, and those bodies will be found without any help from us. Besides, we couldn't possibly tell them what we just saw; that they were...'

'That they were changing into cats?' Fran passed him a shaky cigarette. 'I honestly can't believe what I saw.'

'Me neither. If they were the killers from earlier, why return?' Rex sucked hard on the tobacco and thumbed a number into the phone. 'Why murder a bunch of bikers and then come back?'

Fran wiped her eyes. 'Who are you ringing?'

'The private eye you met. I'll have to tell him about this, although he won't believe it. *I* don't believe it.'

'He mentioned Lamberley at the party. I think he's investigating the murder of that birdwatcher. Do you suppose what happened back there has anything to do with that?'

'I really don't know.' Rex tried another number. 'And he's actually helping *me* investigate.'

'I thought you said you were SAS?'

'This is a favour to my brother, Lisa's fiancé, and... damn!' He threw down the phone. 'I've been trying to reach Bernard Quist all day. There's still no reply from his home or office. Where *is* he?'

'Is that true? You're SAS?'

'*What*? Of course I am. Who the hell would think about lying at a time like this?' Rex wondered whether to book a few psychiatric sessions. 'Jesus, what on earth just happened back there?'

'You can ease off.' Still trembling, the girl glanced behind. 'Whatever they were, they don't seem to be following.'

'Thank God for that.' He brought the speed down. 'What did you say your name was?'

'Francesca... Fran.'

'Rex.' He smiled timidly, his head still spinning. 'Rex Grant. Okay, Fran, we seem to be clear. So what now?'

'I don't know.' She began to weep. 'I've been living back there since I found the courage to leave my husband. I don't really have anywhere to go.'

'Don't worry. You can stay at my uncle's place with me and we'll sort everything out in the morning. It'll be better than a hotel.'

'Will I be safe there?' sobbed Fran.

'From husbands, yes.' The crying made her small breasts jiggle and Rex couldn't believe he'd noticed after what had just taken place. 'I'm not so sure about giant cats.'

* * * *

Chapter 41

Tariq Aslam studied Quist across the police interview table, a recorder humming between them. 'A body has vanished,' he said.

'So you've mentioned.' Quist patted his pockets. 'I don't have it. For the last time, I don't know anything about this.'

'You were seen leaving the mortuary,' pointed out the Sergeant.

'I'm sorry, but it's approaching seven o'clock. Why are you holding me? Surely not body snatching?'

'Suspicion of burglary.'

'This is ludicrous.'

'So what were you doing in the mortuary?'

'I've told you.' Quist rubbed his eyes. 'We went in by mistake. We were looking for the A&E ward.'

'It says *Mortuary* on the door. The locked door.'

'I didn't notice and it wasn't locked.'

'Yes, we found it forced. We've fingerprinted, but you had gloves, didn't you? Why were you looking for A&E?'

'For the fifteenth time, my assistant hurt his arm.'

'On Wednesday you were seen with one of the employees of Ebor Pharmaceuticals where Lisa Mirren worked. Oh, that's our missing body in case you're wondering.'

'Amy Clarkson. Yes, she's a friend of mine.'

She was a friend in a huge amount of danger. Quist needed to get out of this police station and, difficult as it would doubtless be, somehow convince her of what he'd discovered. If he told the police the truth about the morgue or mentioned corpses transforming into panthers, he'd be locked up indefinitely.

'A gentleman named Rex Grant was also there. Is he a friend too?'

'He's the brother of Lisa's fiancé, which I'm sure you know. He wanted to talk to Amy about her. We went for a drink and...'

The door opened and an attractive middle-aged woman

dumped a bag on the table before sitting next to Aslam.

The Sergeant turned to the microphone. 'Eighteen-forty. Detective Inspector Katie Bradstreet has entered the interview.'

'What can you tell us about this?' Katie opened the bag and stood a flashing gnome on the table. This was unexpected, to say the least. 'It was in your car, Mister Quist. The police psychologist has suggested it may be a fertility idol worshipped by pagans.'

'Er, no,' said Quist. 'Actually my assistant's mother makes them.'

Aslam peered at the gnome as though it were something an incontinent dog had left in his kitchen.

'Really?' Katie held up a glass tube. 'Do you know anything about these sweepings from the morgue? Forensics have begun their analysis and believe this red powder is organic. What do you think to that?'

'Sounds intriguing,' said Quist.

'Doesn't it? You're fairly intriguing yourself, aren't you? I believe you knew someone named Kevin Selden?'

'I knew *of* him. He worked as a debt collector from my office building and I've seen him occasionally. I heard on the news that he was killed last night.'

'Yes,' said Katie. 'He worked next door to you; I've just discovered that. I've also discovered that Brightshield Glazing have a sales office in your building too. Carl Dreyer, our missing sales manager from Leeds was there on Monday evening.'

'That's a coincidence, isn't it?' Aslam grinned. 'People around Mister Quist keep dying. As he might say, it's *intriguing*.'

* * * *

Watson sat in the neighbouring interview room and handed Gregson a sheet of paper.

The Constable inspected the shakily-drawn cross. 'I see.' He massaged his weary eyes. 'You're saying that you can't read or write, huh?'

The teenager nodded. The moment the writing materials had

arrived, he'd used two pencils and a rubber band to fashion a crucifix and seemed loathe to let it go. The policeman had decided this was probably some black gang thing.

'Okay,' said Gregson. 'We've established that you're mute, and now we've found that you can't read or write?'

Watson shrugged apologetically.

Gregson motioned to a man in the corner. 'Raines, our signer, was a waste of time too, wasn't he? You don't understand sign language either, do you?'

He shook his head glumly.

'So any suggestions on how we *could* interview you?'

Watson sadly lifted his palms. *Keep your mouth shut*, Quist had told him.

'According to the statement given by your employer next door, you were trying to find A&E. It seems you hurt your arm?'

Watson nodded.

'Which one?'

He thought for a moment, then cradled the left, wincing in mock agony.

Gregson grabbed his lapels. 'Listen, you little shit, if you don't start answering...'

'Whoa!' The signer leapt up. 'The conversation's being recorded.'

'*What* conversation? Me talking to myself and this twat jerking me around? Well if he thinks...'

'Put him down.' Raines patted his shoulder. 'I think it'll be best.'

Gregson dumped the youth in the chair.

'Things are getting fraught.' The signer coughed uneasily. 'Why don't we all have a nice cup of tea?'

Watson twirled his wrist and held up two fingers.

'I see,' said Raines. 'Two sugars for you?'

'So you do know *some* sign language?' snarled Gregson.

* * * *

'What do you think?' Aslam followed the Inspector back to the incident room. 'Do you reckon they know anything?'

'They certainly know *something*,' sighed Katie, 'but they won't talk.'

'The kid definitely won't,' said the Sergeant. 'What do you want to do with them?'

'We can only hold them overnight, so get both sets of prints checked against the ones found in the Range Rover. Check if either has a connection to menageries or anywhere big cat hairs might be found.'

'I can't help wondering about what the Super' said earlier about murderers taking things from their victims.'

'Mmmh, the bag, binoculars and bracelet.'

Something else is missing in all three: their blood. How's the killer draining it and what's he doing with it?'

'I don't know, Tariq. The Pathologist is looking into that.'

Aslam let out a nervous laugh. 'If I didn't know better, I'd say we were dealing with a vampire.'

'Then don't.' Katie smiled tautly. 'Don't say it.'

* * * *

Chapter 42

The Ferrari sped through Pickering and onto the dark North York Moors. Rex didn't finish shaking until he reached the gatehouse of Sedgefield Grange. He also finished his story - Raoul's insistence that he investigate Lisa's murder, Quist and Watson, the chat with Amy and the badges that led to Creeper's house. Fran huddled in the passenger seat, listening and chewing nervously at her knuckles.

'That's about it,' he said. 'I found the dead bikers and you appeared. I still can't believe it.' He drove through the parkland as the gates opened, peering over his shades into the blackness on either side of the car. This morning he'd firmly believed the supernatural to be nonsense, but anything could be lurking out there. 'Any idea how your friend's badges came to be on the railway and at Lisa's murder scene?'

'I don't know.' Fran's eyes widened as the F50 cleared a wood and the manor appeared. '*This* is your uncle's? Just how rich is your family?'

Rex realised this would be a good time to defuse the tension and take her mind off the horror. 'Pretty rich. All the cash comes from Grant Homes, along with stock investments and...'

'Grant's? Your family owns the huge housing company?' Fran's amazement turned back to tears. 'How can we talk about houses after what happened? After what we saw?'

Rex shuddered. 'Yeah, it can't be much fun having your friends decapitated and disembowelled.' Empathic counselling had never been his greatest skill. 'Try not to think about the way they were clawed open and slaughtered. Come on. Falling apart won't help. You're going to be okay; I'll see to that.'

'Thanks, Rex.' Fran wiped her eyes. 'I can't believe it. You don't even know me and yet you're helping like this.'

'I'm a pretty amazing guy, aren't I?' Rex sped around the house and found lines of parked cars. Mercedes, Jaguar and BMW were the most numerous badges on show, with Porsche, Aston Martin and Bentley not far behind. There wouldn't be any point searching for second-hand Fords here. 'Damn, I forgot. Rupert's holding a hunt ball tonight. We could have done without this.'

Fran caught her breath as he braked hard and twisted the wheel, bringing the Ferrari to a sideways skidding halt. Stopping like this usually impressed female passengers, but Rex didn't realise it only worked if their IQ was as tiny as their skirt. Grabbing Fran's wrist as she climbed from the car, he glanced back at the dark parkland and hurried her up the steps to where Barrymore the butler held open the door. The sooner they were inside a bright house with other people, the better.

'Good evening.' Barrymore closed the door behind them. 'Merry Christmas, Miss.'

Rex peered over his sunglasses as a Dalek trundled out of the banquet room. 'What the hell...'

He led Fran towards the music. Napoleon stood near the door with his arm around Queen Victoria. Rex watched him groping her royal posterior and turned to see Elvis chatting to Nero, Mister Spock, and a debatable-looking vestal virgin. Hiawatha and the Frankenstein monster were eating at the buffet, and Gandhi gyrated with a nun on the dance floor to Wham's *Last Christmas*.

'I didn't know it was a costume ball.' Rex moved aside as Darth Vader and a guilty-faced Bo Peep brushed past on their way to a bedroom. 'Oh well! Come on.'

'We're going in?' said Fran. 'No, I can't face this.'

'After what happened, I don't fancy it either, but I need to see my aunt. I have to talk to someone about this to satisfy myself that I'm not crazy. Marika is open-minded and...'

'She'd better be *incredibly* open-minded if you're going to mention people changing into black panthers.'

'I know what you mean, but she comes from Transylvania. I've heard her talk about vampire mythology, so she may be able to help.'

'I feel so out-of-place.' Fran smiled feebly at his black

clothing and shades. 'You can say you're a hit-man or something, but what about me?'

Rex grinned. 'Let's say you've come as the most beautiful girl in the world.' Fran was mid-thirties, and like geriatric rock stars, he made a point of not touching any girl over twenty-nine. With this older woman he'd certainly make an exception. He led her through a group of Jack Sparrows at the buffet and poured two scotches. 'Here, drink this. It'll make us both feel better.'

'Thank you.' She looked around timidly. 'It's an amazing place.'

'Rupert believes if you've got it, rub their working-class noses in it.' He gulped the much-needed whisky and nodded to where his uncle stood with Calamity Jane, his spacehopper paunch shoehorned into a Santa outfit. 'That's him. I ought to warn you, he's a bit eccentric.'

'Eccentric?' Fran watched him scratching an arse that could be rented as advertising space. 'In what way?'

'He looks upon the common folk as if they were pubic hair in marmalade. His views on foxes and ethnic people are a little harsh too, but apart from that, he's not too bad. I'll introduce you.' Rex strolled across and clasped a hand on Rupert's shoulder. 'Evening Uncle.'

'You made it,' boomed Rupert. 'Good show!'

'Sorry to interrupt, but I'd like you to meet Fran.'

'Mmh! Nicely built.' Looking the girl over, Rupert drunkenly felt her muscle tone. 'A damn fine woman with firm rump and flanks. Is this the filly you mentioned this morning? The rambler?'

'Er, no. This is...'

'I see.' Winking, he brought his mouth to Rex's ear, his loud, boozy chuckle supposedly conspiratorial. 'Another of your empty-headed bed-warmers, eh? I expect the wife will want to look at her.' Rupert gave Fran's bottom a slap. 'She's over there chatting to Graham and Tania. Go on. I know you women like to chinwag about babies and cushion covers.'

'Er, right.' Rex jerked Fran away, his face crimson. 'Good

idea.'

'Please tell me the wife's nothing like that,' whispered Fran.

Marika wore a Marvel Comics costume–the skin-tight lycra suit of the Black Widow–and stood by the piano talking to Hitler and Eva Braun. Rex had seen Eva, or rather Tania Smythe, at Rupert's previous parties, a flamboyant woman, who constantly brushed back her hair and waved menthol cigarettes as if conducting an orchestra.

'It was hilarious,' said Tania. 'Andromeda and Kyle made the servants run around the courtyard whilst they threw stones at them. You should have seen their faces.'

'A picture,' laughed her husband, his Nazi moustache falling off. 'But they were whinging about bruises and sore feet.'

'It ruined the children's game,' said Tania. 'Until I pointed out that people get *very* sore feet in those unemployment queues.'

The pair collapsed into laughter, the sort heard from government benches when the raising of state pensions is suggested.

Rex leant close to Marika. 'We have to speak,' he whispered.

'Okay.' His aunt glanced at Fran. 'What's wrong?'

'Not here.'

'The blue room,' murmured Marika. 'I shan't be long.'

Nodding, Rex led Fran past Jesus at the buffet, opened the hall door, and almost fainted. A tall man in a cloak raised his arms and blocked the way, baring fangs and hissing theatrically.

'Look out!' Rex yanked the girl back and slammed a fist into the white face. 'He's changing into a cat.'

The man fell backwards and rolled under the hall Christmas tree. Whipping out the Walther PPK, Rex raced forward, trained the gun on his head, and then froze as plastic fangs were spat out.

'Ah.' Rex spirited away the pistol. 'You're Dracula, right?

'You bwoke my fuggin' nose,' spluttered the Count. 'You doopid fuggin' badard.'

'Er, sorry about that. I thought…' He dragged Fran quickly past. 'Hey, super costume, Count. Merry Christmas.'

Reaching the blue room and flopping gratefully onto one of

the blue couches inside, Rex pulled out his cigarettes. He flexed his knuckles and gave an embarrassed cough.

'That Hitler and his wife - ugh!' Fran knelt by the fire to warm herself. 'Talk about obnoxious.'

'Yeah.' Rex wiped his fist clean of blood, watching as the girl held outstretched palms to the flames. 'You look a lot better, Fran. How are you feeling now?'

'A hell of a lot safer and yes, a little better.' She gave a hesitant smile. 'This is a wonderful house, Rex. When we drove around the woodland and it came into view, I felt like the young wife in the film who saw Manderley for the first time.'

'Mandalay? In Burma? Well, maybe in a certain light...' He heard Fran laugh for the first time.

'*Manderley*. The house in the Hitchcock movie, *Rebecca*.'

'Never argue with a movie expert.' Rex drew on his cigarette. '*Rebecca* lives on Sunnybrook Farm.'

'A movie expert?' She attempted a lisp. 'Here's looking at you kid.'

'Sorry? Oh, I see. That's a line from a film, is it?'

Marika rushed in. 'It's hard to get away from Tania,' she said. 'And now some idiot has punched the village doctor out there. I'm glad to escape for a while.' She took a decanter of Glen Mhor from a cabinet and smiled at Fran. 'Nice to meet you. I'm Marika. Would you both like a drink?'

'Please,' said Rex. He waited until the malt was poured. 'This is Fran and we have a problem. This is crazy and I don't know how to begin.'

'Don't worry. You won't shock me.' Marika ran an eye over the girl. 'Does it involve violent pimps, drugs, pregnancy...'

'Panthers, said Rex. 'We've just been attacked by men who turned into panthers.'

* * * *

Chapter 43

The Mercedes van pulled up by the roadside and Sangster climbed out with the other three guards. 'Gillette gave you two addresses, Sir,' he said. 'One in Clifton and...'

'One in the village of Askham Richard,' confirmed Strand, taking out his phone. 'The forecast predicts fog again tomorrow, so we'll go there then. Wait with the others while I make this private call.'

'Tomorrow?' Sangster shook his head. 'Sir, nothing has gone right so far. We were too late at the mortuary. We let the hospital porter ring the police. We let them escape from the Clifton house. We really ought to...'

'Get out,' shouted Strand. He waited until the door closed before ringing Lucius Silva.

'Thursday,' said the Committee President in his exotic accent. 'You will have news.' It wasn't a question.

'Yes, you were correct.' Strand lit a cigarette. 'The Mirren girl *did* die the way you assumed and Stapleton has vanished.'

'Thank you for the bad news,' said Silva. 'I trust you are following it with good?'

'Indeed. I visited the morgue and that problem is resolved. The evidence was still dormant and has been destroyed.'

'No one is aware of what Stapleton created?'

'No one. Our anonymity hasn't been jeopardised.'

'I understand there has been a third murder? Another doctor from the York laboratory?'

'Yes, but her remains were burnt. All we need do now is locate Stapleton. Gillette is no use and there are no clues at the house, but I know Stapleton well. There are still a few places we haven't tried.'

'Don't disappoint me, Matthew,' said Silva. 'I want this over with as soon as possible.'

'Oh, I'm sure I won't disappoint you, Lucius.' Strand

thumbed off the phone, extended his feline talons and inspected them. 'And trust me, all of this will be over very soon.'

* * * *

'You believe us?' said Rex. 'You're not surprised?'

Marika shook her head. 'I'm very surprised, but yes I believe you. From your descriptions of the way their faces changed and how the bullets had no effect, I'd say they were definitely supernatural creatures.'

'Horrible!' Fran sipped her drink and huddled deep into the leather armchair. 'It was really horrible.'

'Supernatural?' Rex shivered. 'They could change into cats. Speaking in this normal setting, it seems crazy. Absolutely insane. If anyone had told me this yesterday, I'd have phoned a nuthouse.'

'I'm Transylvanian.' Marika shrugged. 'In my land, supernatural beings are an unpleasant fact. What exactly do you know about these things? Probably nothing?'

'Er...' Until today, his mother's copper rheumatism bracelet was the closest Rex had been to the occult. 'I once watched *Rosemary's Baby.*'

'Well, that's a work of fiction,' said Marika. 'It deals with Satanism, but it still illustrates how...'

'Hang on! It might have been *Ryan's Daughter.*'

'Transylvania?' said Fran, gulping her whisky. 'Did you ever meet anything supernatural there?'

'I knew someone who was killed by a vampire. I went to her funeral, where the village priest decapitated her.'

'Ugh!' Fran quaked.

'These cat creatures you describe,' said Marika, 'I've heard stories of an ancient cult who are able to shape shift. They're similar to vampires in that they live on human blood and can't tolerate daylight. I have many books on mythology in the library and I'll read up on them.'

'They drink our blood?' mumbled Fran. 'So you're sure? Those - *men* we met tonight were...'

'Supernatural?' Marika nodded. 'Yes, unfortunately I'm sure, but this is bizarre. Even in the wilds of Eastern Europe, such creatures are unbelievably secretive.'

'Why would they kill my friends?' asked Fran.

'The question is why would they leave clawed bodies with heads twisted around and limbs torn off? I've no doubt blood will be missing too. They'd never expose themselves by leaving corpses like that for the authorities. In civilised countries, their victims are never found. Why would they do this?'

'And why return?' demanded Rex. 'They didn't know Fran or I would be there.'

'Perhaps to dispose of the corpses; I really don't know. What on earth have you become mixed up in?' Marika pondered. 'Have you rung this private detective you met?'

'I've tried,' said Rex, 'but there's no reply. When I get through, I doubt he'll believe me. To be honest, I haven't the faintest idea how to handle this. That's why I wanted to speak to you. I had to talk to someone.'

'I suppose you've thought about the police, but...'

Rex laughed. 'You can imagine how they'd see it. A dozen people murdered and the only witnesses are ranting about monsters and firing a handgun.' He neglected to mention *illegal* handgun.

'Surely they'd believe the SAS?' said Fran.

'Huh?' Marika looked puzzled.

'That's enough for tonight,' said Rex, quickly. 'We both need rest, especially you, Fran. We'll sort this out tomorrow. Problems never seem so bad in the morning light.'

She smiled nervously. 'Even problems like *this*?'

'You did right to bring her here for safety,' said Marika. 'Do you have anywhere you can go, Fran? Friends or relatives?'

'Not around here. I have a brother in Manchester. I suppose I'd be okay there.'

'I'll take you in the morning,' said Rex. 'I assume it's alright for her to stay tonight?'

Marika smiled warmly. 'Lots of the party guests are staying, but there's a spare room between yours and Tania's.'

'Next door to me?' Rex sighed. 'Oh, well, if there's nowhere else...'

* * * *

Rex woke with a jolt and checked his Rolex. He always wore the luminous watch and black silk shorts in bed, but Marika's crucifix and the garland of garlic flowers from the kitchen were new. These cat people weren't vampires, but apparently they drank blood and he wasn't taking any chances. He snatched the cross. *Something had roused him, but what*? The Grange floodlights were switched off, leaving the room virtually black, but he made out a figure wrapped in white satin at the foot of the four-poster.

'Fran?' He hoped the answer would be a feminine affirmative, and not a feline hiss.

'I keep seeing those monsters,' whimpered Fran. She clutched the bedsheet closer, a sniffle betraying recent tears. 'Their cat faces! I'm scared, Rex. There must have been ten people left at that party and they're all dead. Horribly murdered.'

Throwing back the quilt, he leapt up and hugged her to him. Her hair was damp, and despite the garlic, he could smell her perfume; a musky fragrance named *Penetration*. 'Ssshh! Come on.' He took off the garlic wreath, ruining the Hawaiian tourist look, and stroked her shoulders. 'It's okay now. Uncle Rex is here.'

The room was warm, but Fran trembled. She sobbed and squeezed closer.

'There, there.' Rex basked in the feeling of male power that comes from a girl crying on the shoulder. 'Uncle Rex will make those nasty pussy cats go away and everything will be okay.' Walking her to the windows, he gazed at the frozen parkland. 'I've always adored frosty nights. Just look at the stars up there. Aren't they beautiful?' He stroked her waist and gestured to the Plough. 'Look, there's Pegasus.'

'That's sweet.' Fran sniffed. 'No one has ever shown me the stars.'

'*Romantic* is my middle name.' He pointed to another constellation. 'That one is Orion. The line of three stars across the middle is Orion's belt, and do you see the cluster under his belt? That's Orion's dick.'

Fran pouted, her eyes moving down his chest to the shorts with the embroidered SAS dagger. Smiling and raising her hand, Rex kissed the slender fingers as she caressed his cheek. It felt alien and very nice. Foreplay usually amounted to jingling the Ferrari key ring.

'Come here,' he growled, drawing her mouth to his.

She responded hungrily, moulding to his body, running her hands through his hair and clawing at his back. Their mouths locked, her tongue snaking in to lap greedily at his tonsils and her nipples pressing hard. Amy Clarkson unexpectedly flashed into Rex's mind, until the sheet fell away exposing Fran's nakedness and the doctor instantly vanished. His hand travelled south to discover, not the bald smoothness favoured by the models he usually dated, but a triangle of golden fur.

'I want you, Rex,' she whispered, panting. 'I want you now.'

'Well...' He pulled her to the bed. 'I can't say I blame you.'

He reached to remove the crucifix and decided against it. This morning he'd have laughed at the idea of shapeshifters, but it seemed there truly *were* such supernatural creatures creeping about in the night. Rex left the cross alone, electing to go with all the health recommendations and make love wearing protection.

* * * *

Chapter 44

The Custody Officer chewed a sandwich and peered through the police station window. It would be nine o'clock before the sun rose above York, but no one would see it this Friday morning thanks to another bank of icy fog. Sighing, he marched along the detention corridor, opened cell four and froze. He'd seen many sights here over the years: crazed students yelling about Jesus, drunks head-butting walls, and prior to the hasty removal of spaghetti from the canteen menu, a man who managed to hang himself. Never before, however, had he seen anyone in an Upright Tortoise Asana, balanced on their hands with both legs knotted behind the neck.

'What the fuck are you doing?' he asked.

'Yoga.' Quist disentangled himself. 'It tones the muscles, aids the glands and settles the mind. You ought to try it.'

'Come on. You're being released.'

Quist stretched and strolled out, the aroma of coffee, burnt bread and bacon greeting his nostrils.

'You're entitled to breakfast.' The officer escorted him down the passage. 'Fancy anything?'

Quist eyed the policeman's sandwich. The toast resembled cork mats and the contents were thankfully unidentifiable. 'I don't suppose you have muesli or tofu?'

The sarcastic grin suggested not.

Katie Bradstreet stood with Watson in the detention lobby, the latter signing for the return of his laces, chewing gum and other property with which he might have killed himself. The Inspector's yolk-splattered coat and the half-eaten sandwich on the table told Quist that his assistant hadn't been so fussy over the breakfast offer.

'Inspector Bradstreet.' Quist smiled curtly. 'I understand you're letting us go?'

'We've nothing to hold you on,' said Katie, clearly frustrated. The lab had returned a negative match on the fingerprints found in the stolen Range Rover. 'Besides, while you were helping with our enquiries, developments occurred that suggest you aren't directly implicated in the investigation.'

'Developments? Not another murder?'

'I'm not at liberty to say. I said you weren't *directly* implicated. That doesn't mean we're finished with you. By the way, how well do you know Doctor Stapleton?'

'Not at all.' Quist pulled on his leather overcoat. 'Why should I know him?'

The Inspector raised an eyebrow. 'Just thought I'd ask. I don't suppose you called on Will Gillette in Fulford yesterday, or attended a biker's party in Clifton?'

'No. Sorry.' Quist nudged Watson. 'Morning,' he muttered. 'Any bruising from the interview?'

'He can't answer, can he?' growled Katie. 'Or didn't you know that your employee was a mute?'

'Come on.' Grabbing his few belongings, Quist signed the acceptance and took the youth's arm. 'Let's go.'

'Hey,' snapped Katie. 'You need to take *all* your personal effects.'

Quist turned to the flashing gnome on the desk. 'I don't suppose you want to keep that for your garden?'

'You signed for him.' She jerked a thumb at the phallus. 'He's all yours.'

Snatching the wooden statuette, Quist pushed Watson into the elevator as Gregson entered the lobby.

'We just took a call in the incident room,' said the Constable. 'Sounds like another girl is missing.'

'What?' Katie's mouth fell open. 'Who the hell is it this time?'

* * * *

'Cat people?' stammered Watson, his eyes wide. 'Fuckin' cat people? People who turn into fuckin' cats?'

'Yes,' said Quist, closing the station door behind them. 'I must say, you've summed it up quite eloquently there.'

200

'Am I glad we're out, Guv.' Watson zipped up his jacket against the icy fog and glanced about warily as they left the police grounds. Cars crawled past on Fulford Road, their lights reflecting eerily on the billowing whiteness. 'I haven't said a word all night.'

'I hope nothing has happened to Amy Clarkson,' said Quist. 'I didn't like what Bradstreet said about *developments*.'

'I don't like *any* of it. I've got to admit, I prefer the boredom of divorce cases to shitting myself in terror. That cat thing in the morgue - I saw it, but I still can't accept it.' Watson laughed nervously. 'Supernatural shapeshifters in York? Here in the daylight it feels unreal, doesn't it?'

'Unfortunately it's all *too* real. I need to speak to Amy. Could I borrow that mobile of yours?'

'Oh, right!' Watson waved the phone. 'Not making crap jokes about texting now that you actually need a mobile, eh?'

'When you're quite ready.' The detective held out a hand. 'This *is* rather important.'

'Yeah, they're pretty useful when you need to warn someone about vampire cats, aren't they?' Watson thumbed the button. 'Oh! It needs charging.'

'Outstanding!' Quist set off, looking for the nearest taxi rank. 'Let's get back to the hospital for the car.'

'Cat people?' Watson stuck close, looking back over his shoulder. Somewhere in the mist, a ghostly church bell tolled. 'Genuine shapeshifters, like in the movies? What was it you called them?'

'The Ubasteri. We're in a hurry so I'll condense this. According to mythology, they originated in Egypt during the Eighteenth Dynasty. The Pharaoh Akenhaten worshipped Aten, the sun, and moved from Thebes to build a city at Amarna in the desert. A small group of renegade priests formed a cult there, the Ubasteri, who renounced the sun god and secretly worshipped the cat god Bast. Their aims were immortality and power, and they performed dark rites with human sacrifice and blood drinking to achieve this.'

'Ubasteri,' said Watson. 'You're sure you don't mean *batshit crazy*? As in this all sounds totally batshit crazy.'

'As it turned out, their vile practices angered both Aten and Bast. The two gods cursed them, granting immortality, but at a huge price. The Ubasteri were transformed into night creatures. Because they consumed human blood, they were forced to exist exclusively upon it. They had shunned the sun and so daylight became lethal to them. Aten declared they would never again stand in the warmth of his golden disc.'

Watson stared at Quist. 'You believe this crap?'

'It's mythology, but here they are in York, so who knows? As you saw with Lisa Mirren, the Ubasteri create others with their bite. They spread in Amarna like a plague, until the citizens rose against the expanding cult, killed them with fire and abandoned the cursed city to the desert. The people returned to Thebes believing they'd wiped them out, but they were wrong.'

'So that bunch at the hospital were Egyptians?'

'No, there are no original Ubasteri left. Their cult continues because being drained of blood transforms you into one of them.'

'How do you know all this shit?'

'I've studied mythology and anthropology. There are these things called *libraries* where you can learn about shit.'

'Yeah, yeah.' Watson smirked at the sarcasm. 'So how do you get rid of them? Stakes and crosses and all that?'

'Religious items have no effect,' said Quist. 'Wooden stakes in the heart will kill them, as you've seen, as will silver, decapitation and fire. Sunlight destroys them instantly. Normally, they don't emerge by day, but if it's overcast, they can tolerate the light for a few minutes.'

'Oh boy!' Watson peered into the fog. 'I'd feel safer with a few silver bullets. Er, and maybe a gun to put them in. Do they have a reflection?'

'They drink blood, but they aren't vampires.' Quist quickened his step. 'They show up in photographs and cast shadows too.'

'You seem to know everything and last night was no big shock to you. Okay, you've read about them, but am I right in thinking you've run into them before?'

'I'll explain later. The thing is, I told you these murders weren't routine police business. I expect you can see now what I meant?'

'They're not exactly consultant detective business either. What the hell can *we* do about this?'

'We did fine last night. We stopped that panther from harming anyone in the hospital.'

Watson flinched at the memory. 'Poor old Lisa. What a way to go.'

'Lisa died on Saturday,' said Quist. 'The thing we destroyed was Ubasteri.'

The youth walked faster as they reached the city wall. Today, the medieval stonework reminded him of a Hammer horror film set. 'So those girls from the lab were killed by these cats?'

'They were indeed, but there's far more to this.'

'Yeah, and more than one cat. There was a whole bunch at the morgue, sniffing the air like I was a bowl of milk.'

'Yes, so we'd better exercise caution and ensure you come to no harm. With the Harpo Marx routine at the police station, I don't suppose you rang your mother? We don't have much time, but do you want to call home to quickly freshen up and allay any worries?'

'I'm a big boy. Staying out's not unusual for me.' Watson noticed Quist's stubble-free chin. 'Talking of freshening up, how come the cops let you have a razor?'

'Never mind about shaving. We have to find Amy and let her know what we're dealing with. I only hope I can convince her.'

'What about Rex? Are you going to ring him too?'

'Er, no.' The last thing Quist wanted was the ultimate silent killing machine running around with a gun full of silver bullets. 'No, we'll call him later, but we do need to see Creeper again. Our involvement in this has been engineered by someone who left those badges to draw me to that Clifton house. I have to know why. Now that you know about the Ubasteri, can I rely on your help?'

Watson laughed and nodded nervously. 'You know what? After last night, bikers don't seem quite so scary.'

* * * *

'Doctor Gillette's secretary?' said Katie Bradstreet, hurrying into the police incident room. 'Gregson tells me his temp Nicole Patterson is possibly missing? Who let us know?'

'Her landlady rang,' said Constable Planer. 'Mitchell's been watching Amy Clarkson since last night. Gregson has gone to take over the next surveillance shift and Mitchell's going to call at Nicole's address and look into it.' He held up an envelope. 'By the way, you wanted a picture of Doctor Stapleton. I finally managed to get one.'

'About time,' said the Inspector.

'I asked at the lab, but there simply aren't any.'

Katie opened the envelope. 'So where's this from?'

'An advertising firm took this for a trade mag. It's a shot of the lab, but if you look carefully, you'll see the doctor climbing from a Porsche on the far left.'

Katie sighed at the microscopic figure in the rain. 'This is no good. You can't see...'

'Er, no, so I had the section enhanced. The blow-up's in the envelope too.'

She took out the picture, her colour draining. 'You're telling me this is Stapleton?'

'Yeah.' Planer shrugged. 'I know it's blurred, but...'

'You're absolutely sure? *This* is Stapleton?'

'Doctor Keating at the lab confirmed it. What is it, Ma'am? Does the face ring a bell?'

'It certainly does.' Katie shook her head. 'What the hell is going on here?'

* * * *

Chapter 45

The mewing of peacocks mixed with the sharp calls of jackdaws as Fran peered at the tethered falcons on the rear terrace of Sedgefield Grange. Patchy fog still shrouded the moors, but the view from the dining room was reasonable. Moulded latex transformed the falcon hoods into human heads and gave Rupert's birds the creepy appearance of mythical harpies. A peregrine sported Enoch Powell's head, a goshawk wore the cigar-sucking face of Churchill, and a gyrfalcon displayed the crowned head of Thatcher.

Fran turned from the bizarre birds as Rex hurried into the busy dining room pocketing his mobile. 'Did you speak to Bernard Quist?' she asked.

'No. God knows where he is.' Rex pushed through the crowd of hung-over guests at the buffet. 'He doesn't carry a mobile and I don't have Watson's number, so I left messages on his home and office answerphones. I told him everything that happened last night.' He kissed her cheek. 'Not *quite* everything.'

She lowered her voice. 'Attacked by shapeshifters. It's unreal in the morning light.'

'I still can't believe it. I let Quist know that we were heading to Manchester too. Your brother lives at this side of the city, you say? It's about seventy miles, so we'll grab something to eat and leave now. Depending on the fog, it shouldn't take long to drop you off and get back along the M62.'

Fran pouted. 'You're coming straight back?'

'I have to. Quist couldn't cope before, but now with these cat things involved, he'd be lost without me. I said in the message that I'd meet him before dusk. He needs me, you see?'

'What if I was to say *I* need you?'

'Don't worry. I'll keep in touch and as soon as I've sorted this out, I'll be straight back to see you. That's a promise, okay?'

Fran nodded glumly.

'Hey!' He lifted her chin. 'Here's looking at you kid.'

'Okay,' she smiled. 'Help yourself to breakfast. I still don't have any appetite.'

'Er, just one thing…' Rex headed for the buffet tureens. 'It's probably best if you don't mention the SAS. We need to keep a low profile, you know?'

Grabbing some scrambled eggs, he sat with Fran at the giant dining table next to a crumpled Graham Smythe. Still dressed as Hitler, the man nursed a pounding head. Rex turned from gulping down the eggs as his nervous-looking aunt appeared.

'Are you okay?' he asked.

'Not really,' murmured Marika. 'Would you come to the library when you're finished here?'

'Er, sure.' Rex glanced down the table at the broken-nosed Dracula. *Shit - perhaps he was pressing charges.* 'What's wrong?'

'Probably nothing. Wait until we're alone.'

'Have you seen Tania?' broke in Smythe's drunken voice. 'She started arguing and flounced out after you left the ball. I can't find the silly bitch.'

'She probably stormed home,' said Marika. 'You know what she's like.'

Rex pushed his plate aside, anxious to get away before the awful woman appeared. 'Ready when you are,' he whispered.

Marika led them into the oak-panelled library. 'I hardly slept,' she said, opening a bookcase and taking out a small casket. 'After the party, I was reading into the early hours. The creatures you encountered sound like the Ubasteri, an Egyptian cult who worshipped the cat god Bast. They're feline shapeshifters who drink human blood, and dying that way transforms you into their kind. Sunlight destroys them, as does silver, fire, decapitation and piercing their heart with wood or silver. Think of them as vampires, but far more lethal.'

'Incredible,' whispered Fran.

'Lovely,' muttered Rex. *Far more lethal* didn't sound good. 'Thanks for the lesson, but I'm hoping never to meet them again.'

'I had terrible dreams too,' said Marika. 'All concerning you,

Rex. You'll think I'm silly, but I want to try something.'

Intrigued, he sat on a couch by the fire with the girls either side, Marika opening the box on the table before them. 'You want to play cards?' he asked, confused.

'They're tarot cards,' said Fran.

'I know that.' He gave an embarrassed cough. 'It was a joke.'

'It's not often I have such vivid dreams.' Marika spread the pack. 'I need to make sense of them and I want to see if the cards can help.'

'You're psychic?' asked Fran.

'Yes. I have dreams and get fleeting visions, like yesterday when I saw...' Marika glanced at Rex and thought better of it.

'You're going to read my fortune?' Rex laughed quietly. 'I didn't think you'd be the type for this stuff.'

Marika smiled faintly. 'You don't believe the tarot can be used to see the future?'

'Maybe by Santa Claus.'

'Transylvania has many superstitions and customs. These cards belonged to an old gypsy lady who recognised my gift and taught me. In my land gypsies don't burn tyres and steal electrical cable. They play violins, and dance around fires with tambourines. Many have the second sight. Believe me, I've found these cards really work.'

'Yeah.' Rex smirked. 'If you say so.'

Fran watched Marika shuffle. 'What does he have to do?'

'Pick five.' Placing the deck facedown, she swept the cards into a circle. 'Lay them in a cross with your last choice central.'

'Sounds easy.' He slid five from the ring and arranged them.

'Alright. Turn them one at a time. Start at the top and work anti-clockwise.'

Lighting a cigarette, Rex flipped the first. It was like an Asian film poster with lightning crackling onto a crumbling building. 'Nice.' His face lit up. 'That looks exciting.'

'The worst card in the pack.' Marika squirmed. 'The Tower

signifies death, destruction and violence.'

'It could have been better then?' said Fran.

Rex needed no help identifying the scythe-wielding skeleton on the next card. 'Hey,' he drawled. 'Things are looking up.'

'It isn't as bad as it seems,' said Marika, unconvincingly. 'The Death card has many complex meanings. It can symbolise change and resurrection.'

The next was the Moon.

Marika looked puzzled. 'Keep going,' she said.

The fourth was the Star.

'And the last. This is the most important.'

Rex hesitated, then turned over an innocent-looking Five of Pentacles. Marika sat back, grim and confused.

'What do these last three mean?' asked Fran.

'Each has its own meanings, but together like this...' Marika gathered the cards and shuffled. 'Pick three more. Don't lay them in a cross. Just pick them and show me.'

Rex pondered, and chose the Tower, the Five of Pentacles and Death.

Marika turned ashen.

'This is bad, isn't it?' gasped Fran. 'What does it mean?'

'Surely you're not taking this seriously?' said Rex, chuckling.

'I need to consult my books,' said Marika. 'But I'm certain this is connected to my dreams and to something I saw on Rex's hand.'

'So come on,' he prompted. 'What *were* these dreams and what did you see that caused that fuss yesterday?'

'Not yet.' Marika hesitated. 'Not until I'm sure. It would only have you thinking me crazy. Let me read through my reference works first. I'll tell you everything when you return this afternoon.'

Rex looked at his hand. His limited dealings with the supernatural amounted to a magazine feature on palmistry he'd once read. The basics he'd picked up entertained a certain type of girl, and it was easy explaining how the lines on a giggling model's hand meant imminent sex with a playboy in sunglasses. What he saw now wasn't so simple to explain.

'This is wrong,' he said. 'My left hand's different.'

'Let me see.' Marika grabbed his wrist.

'This life line has changed; it's shrunk!' Rex laughed timidly. 'It's shorter than a blind test pilot.'

Marika checked his right palm, but the life line there had vanished completely. Rex searched his arm, on the chance it had ignored rational science and somehow migrated north. There was no sign of it.

'*Shit*!' he said.

* * * *

Chapter 46

Amy Clarkson still wasn't home. The neighbours hadn't seen her since the previous day when she left for work, but the lack of police presence informed a relieved Quist that her absence wasn't Inspector Bradstreet's *development*. Instead of waiting, he'd set off for Creeper's house in Clifton, but the freezing fog made the car journey excruciatingly slow. The windscreen wipers thrashed back and forth fighting the ice particles.

'So they're supernatural cat people?' said Watson, still trying to come to terms with the Ubasteri.

'*Supernatural* is a term we use when we don't understand.' Quist stared into the fog, driving steadily. 'Mirages, hypnotism, and acupuncture were all supernatural before science dissected them.'

'So how come science says there are no shapeshifters?'

'Scientists aren't infallible, and they're terrified to study the paranormal for fear of being branded cranks. Read the historical literature of other civilisations and you'll find they've hardly gone unnoticed. Look into Aztec and Mayan folklore. Read up on the Mesopotamians, Romans, Chinese and Abyssinians. They all had their shapeshifters and monsters long before Europe discovered them in medieval times.'

'It's still hard to believe. You say the Egyptians didn't manage to wipe the Ubasteri out, but why haven't we got shut of them since? I know what the church was like with witches. Why didn't it hunt down these furry bastards too?'

'It *did*, but few were destroyed. We're speaking of a resourceful and cunning species with great speed, strength, and hypnotic powers. Mesmerised people can be ordered to do anything, and it's hard to slay such a creature when the slayers are ordered to kill each other. They've always viewed themselves as superior to us; they refer to themselves as *the Elite*.'

Watson nodded. 'Okay, let's get this right. These panthers drink your blood and that turns you into one of them?'

'When they bite, feline enzymes attack the chromosomes, altering the cell structure. A DNA transformation begins, and from the moment of the bite, the victim is controlled by the cat. Blood is drained over a period and more enzymes are introduced each time they feed. With the final blood removed, the victim falls into a brief coma where they metamorphose fully to awake as Ubasteri. However, as with Lisa Mirren, if *all* the blood is removed, the nervous system shuts down. The victim dies, but the enzymes still work on the cells. Because these are *dead* cells, it takes longer; five full days before they transform.'

'That's why you went to the morgue yesterday; Lisa died on Saturday. Hey, what are you looking for?'

'We're close to Minster Avenue.' Quist squinted into the fog and spotted a newsagent's shop on the left. 'Ah, this is the junction where... Damn!' He stamped the brake as flashing blue lights and police cones materialized ahead. 'I think we may be too late.'

Watson watched the officers diverting traffic. 'They've cordoned off the biker's street. What the hell is this?'

'I've an awful feeling this is Bradstreet's *development*.' Quist reversed the car and parked by the newsagent. 'I'm going to buy some cigarettes. If ever you need information, Watson, call in a local shop.'

The youth watched him enter the store and emerge minutes later. 'Well?'

'It isn't good news.' Quist jumped back into the Beetle and paused to light a cigarette. 'According to the locals in there, our biker friends are dead.'

'*What*? All of them?'

'Ten of them, apparently, including Creeper.'

'Dead, as in murdered?'

'As in clawed limb from limb. The police found them last night and they're tying these deaths with the lab murders. What could they have discovered to make them do that?'

'Ten wiped out,' croaked Watson, trembling. 'What am I mixed up in here?'

'So much for questioning Creeper.' Quist started the car. 'Let's try Amy's place again. We really have to find her.'

'Shit! Do you think the cats did this, Guv?'

'From the terrible way they died, undoubtedly.' Quist gave a lopsided smile. 'Don't worry. I'll ensure no harm comes to you.'

'Don't worry?' Watson burst out laughing, a release of tension. 'Yeah, right. I feel about as confident as the lady-in-waiting when Anne Boleyn said: *the fat bastard's bluffing*.'

* * * *

Detective Constable Mitchell drove slowly along the alley behind Amy Clarkson's terraced street. 'Christ alive!' he muttered. Straining to keep the doctor's taillights in view, he parked his Honda as she drew up by the back door. 'This bloody fog.'

He heard Amy enter the house, flicked the wipers to clear the screen, and tried orientating himself. This alleyway ran between the terraces of Appleton Street and George Street. Thanks to the icy conditions and still air, the fog had collected between the two rows of houses, bringing visibility down to a few feet.

He took out his mobile. 'It's Gary again,' he said. 'Everything okay, Doctor Clarkson? How long will you be?'

'Not long,' said Amy. 'About five minutes. I'm just picking up a change of clothes and a few necessities.'

Mitchell climbed out as headlamps lit up the Honda's rear window. Martin Gregson was taking the next surveillance and protection shift.

'Sorry I'm late,' said Gregson, pulling up and leaning out of the car. 'It's the fog.'

'I've only just arrived myself,' said Mitchell. 'There isn't much to report. Amy picked up her car from the garage yesterday and spent the night at her sister's in Heslington with WPC Farnon. She's going back there once she's grabbed a few things.' He squat beside the window. 'Hey, that biker house sounded like a real bloodbath from what Farnon said. Some of them had their heads twisted around like Will Gillette, didn't they?'

212

'That's right. The Inspector is surmising that Gillette's murderer could have killed the bikers too.' Gregson sighed. 'Listen, another girl could be missing.'

Mitchell's jaw dropped. 'Another?'

'It's Gillette's temporary secretary, Nicole Patterson.'

'She gave Amy a lift from work to the garage yesterday.'

'Her landlady rang the incident room.' Gregson handed him an address. 'She lives near here, so they want you to speak to her.'

'I'll head there now.' Mitchell nodded to the invisible house. 'Like I say, Amy will be out soon.'

'See you later,' said Gregson, raising the window.

Jumping back into the car, Mitchell revved the engine and slowly vanished into the rolling fog. Gregson settled down to wait, oblivious to the white BMW approaching along the alley without lights and pulling up behind. Muffled footsteps arrived at his driver's door and his visitor tapped on the side window. Half expecting his colleague to have forgotten something, the policeman glanced up at the luminous eyes and razor fangs.

'What the fu...'

Talons exploded through the glass. Gregson dived over the seats, booted open the passenger door and tumbled screeching onto the cobblestones. *What in God's name was this thing? Could this be their serial killer?* Never, not even in his most bowel-churning nightmares, had he expected the murderer to look anything like *this*.

Amy heard the shrieking and opened the back door.

'Get inside!' screamed Gregson, bursting from the fog some twenty feet away, his face petrified. 'Get inside now!'

Something dark loomed behind and the policeman was yanked back. Drifting whiteness enveloped him and the noises reminded Amy of an eager child ripping wrapping paper from a present.

'Oh, no!' She stepped back inside as a steaming red splurge squirted from the fog to splatter at her feet. 'Oh Jesus, no!'

The milky wall billowed and, for a second, the doctor could

see. Her mind registered two things before the air currents changed and the nightmare vanished: a dismembered body in a pool of gore and the glowing eyes and fangs of the furry creature squatting over it. Rooted to the spot, she tried screaming, but couldn't. Something broke the silence with a chuckle and footsteps began to approach. It was a safe bet they didn't belong to Constable Gregson.

The laugh came again. 'Code red,' growled an inhuman voice. 'Officer down.'

Amy slammed the door and rammed home the bolt. She raced to the front as something huge crashed into the wood, firing splinters and a hinge across the kitchen.

What was happening? What in Christ's name was it?

Whimpering, she fumbled with the front door key, limbs shaking and mind racing. *Thank God she lived in a terrace. If she escaped through the front, whatever that hideous thing was, it would be stuck in the rear alley. It couldn't reach her without going around the row or literally smashing its way through.* Unfortunately it had figured this out and settled upon the latter option. Moaning, to hear the kitchen door explode inwards, the doctor fled into the fog, raincoat flapping like a cloak, and ran blindly up Appleton Street. Something burst snarling from the house behind her, something that sounded decidedly unfriendly and none too pleased with its breakfast running away.

Two ghostly orbs suddenly glared in the fog and Amy rolled over the sloping bonnet of a Volkswagen Beetle. Most people are shocked when hit by a car, but she'd never felt so grateful.

'Are you okay?' Watson opened the door. 'Good thing he was driving slow because of the fog...'

'Move,' screamed Amy, leaping onto his lap. 'Get away from here now.'

Quist didn't wait for explanations. Slamming into reverse, he stamped the accelerator, hurled the car around, and screeched out of Appleton Street.

'Jesus!' said Watson. 'What the hell were you running from?'

'Believe me,' she panted. 'You don't want to know.'

'Yes we do,' said Quist.

Watson saw her terrified face. 'No we don't.'

* * * *

Chapter 47

Hazard signs flashed above the M62 ordering motorists not to exceed fifty, but the electricity could have been put to better use. Like most of the cars racing along the misty motorway, Rex's Ferrari hurtled west at eighty.

'We're over half-way,' said Rex, passing signs for Dewsbury. 'We'd have made better time if it hadn't been for those idiots on the A64 crawling along because of the fog.'

'You don't seem worried.' Fran regarded him curiously. 'You're very brave, aren't you? I'm still scared after last night, and I'd be terrified by those tarot cards.'

Rex winked at her over the shades. 'My training doesn't allow me the luxury of fear. Anyway, the tarot thing is nonsense. If I listened to Marika's daft prophesies, I'd stop looking at the calendar and start checking my watch.'

'But what about the way your life lines have changed?'

He looked at his blank palm, coughed nervously and changed the subject. 'There's a service area coming up,' he said. 'I need petrol and cigarettes. If you fancy blowing twenty pounds on a sandwich, now's your chance.'

Fran shook her head. 'With all this, I don't feel the least bit hungry, but I'll phone my brother to let him know I'm coming. I lost my mobile back at Creeper's.'

'You can use mine.' Rex fished the phone from his jacket. 'I'll try Quist again first. He may have discovered something about Lisa Mirren, even *without* my help. I wonder if he's checked the answerphone yet. Lord knows what he thought about my blood-drinking cat message.'

'He probably thought about straitjackets.'

The same message still played on Quist's office machine. Fuming, Rex tried the home number. 'Still no one there.' He passed Fran the mobile. 'I can't believe I'm letting that idiot help me investigate.'

'This investigation of yours…' she said, keying digits into the phone. 'You told me all about it, but you never mentioned who owns Ebor Pharmaceuticals.'

Rex shrugged. 'Amy never said.'

'But whoever owns the lab may have answers…'

'I know you're only trying to help,' he laughed, 'but why not leave the detective work to men, okay?'

'Okay, I suppose you're the expert. By the way, this phone of yours isn't working.'

'It's fully charged. You're obviously not doing it right.' Rex tore up the slip road into the Hartshead Moor Services and braked outside the complex. He took the mobile and stabbed the menu. The back fell off and a spaghetti of micro-circuitry landed in his lap.

'Really?' Fran raised her eyebrows. 'Perhaps you could give me a lesson.'

* * * *

Quist arrived at Briar Cottage seconds after Rex's failed phone call. A dazed Amy Clarkson shuffled in behind him followed by Watson.

The teenager clicked on the lounge light. 'You almost left your gift in the car,' he said, standing the wooden gnome on a table.

'Thank you, Watson.' Quist glared at the obscene figurine with its pointy hat and jutting penis. 'Yes, don't forget that thing at a time like this.'

'Nice place, Guv.' The youth gazed around at the antiques, bookcases, and paintings. 'How do you afford all this?'

'Pour Amy a drink,' said Quist, watching as the frightened girl sank into a chair, her frame visibly trembling. He headed back to the passage telephone. 'It's in the cabinet there.'

Watson found a bottle of Askaig malt and glasses. He handed one to the doctor and half-filled it.

'Thanks,' whispered Amy. She gulped the whisky and held the shaking tumbler for a refill.

Quist listened to the answerphone and rang Rex. A digital

217

voice informed him that the mobile was unavailable. Understandable, as it lay scattered across a services car park where it had been thrown in temper.

'Grant left a message.' The detective turned up the heating to warm the shivering doctor and joined them in the lounge. 'He called at the biker party after we left, discovered the bodies and found that girl we met. They left for Manchester and he's returning before dark. It's odd that he's turned off his phone. His sort can't exist without one.'

Watson woefully fingered the dead mobile in his pocket.

Shrugging off his coat, Quist poured a drink and ran a concerned eye over Amy. She already knew of Gillette's murder, courtesy of her protection officer, but had only just heard about their horrific encounter with Lisa Mirren. 'Grant ran into five of the Ubasteri at Clifton,' he said. 'He managed to escape. They were probably the same group we heard at the hospital.'

'*Shapeshifters*?' Amy gaped at him. 'A policeman has just been murdered in front of me and you talk about people changing into panthers?'

'But you saw one yourself,' said Watson.

'I thank God you arrived when you did,' she stammered. 'But what I saw... You can't honestly believe it was some supernatural cat thing?'

Quist nodded. 'From what you've told me, yes.'

'All I remember seeing in the fog were the huge fangs and the eyes. The eyes seemed to glow.'

'Yeah,' said Watson. 'That sounds like one of our pals.'

'You saw more, but blocked it,' said Quist. 'The human mind has many defence systems.'

'This is crazy.' Amy swallowed more whisky, slipping off her raincoat as the room began to warm. 'I saw *something*, but all this you told me in the car about feline shapeshifters coexisting alongside humanity? Come on, Bernard. This is the twenty-first century.'

'Yes,' said Quist. 'People invariably view this kind of thing as myth, or if they realise there may be truth in the legends, as something from the murky past. This makes things easy for creatures like the Ubasteri. Centuries ago, everyone believed in ghosts, vampires and shapeshifters. Towns were insular and the population retired at sunset. If someone had strange habits and only appeared by night, people became suspicious. Nowadays no one notices.'

'The thing I saw had to be some lunatic in a furry mask,' muttered Amy. 'I can't accept this nonsense. You should have taken me to the police.'

'I saw Lisa change,' said Watson, 'and I still find it hard to believe. Cat people living among us doesn't make sense. Someone would have found out.'

Quist walked to a bookcase and tossed them a volume. 'Find me a picture of a vampire,' he challenged, lighting a cigarette.

'*Horror Movies*?' read Amy, her scepticism soaring higher.

Watson handed it back at a photograph. 'There you go.'

'How do you know this is a vampire?'

'He's got a cloak and pointy teeth. What's your point?'

'Hollywood has much to answer for,' said Quist. 'Vampires don't wear cloaks. Nor do they come scratching at windows after the funeral. If they did, even morons would recognize them for what they were. It's the same with the Ubasteri. Despite certain eccentricities and their reclusive natures, they blend into society perfectly. Some have had centuries of practise.'

'Come on, Guv.' Watson laughed. 'Running around covered in fur...'

'The creature in the morgue had woken from metamorphosis and was ravenous. You saw an Ubasteri in its predatory form, as did Amy in the fog. They can shapeshift at will and all have green eyes, but most of the time they look perfectly normal. They're sometimes spotted, of course; have you never wondered about the occasional big cat sightings in Britain?'

'So where are they all?' demanded Watson. 'If all their suppers turn to moggies, how come we aren't crowded with them?'

'A few victims will be selected for their society–the Elite, as they call themselves–but the majority will be destroyed. Becca and Diane for example. One burnt and the other mesmerised into decapitating herself.'

'Oh right.' Amy shook her head in anger. *This twaddle was beyond belief.* 'Of course.'

Watson nodded. 'They drank most of Diane's blood, hypnotised her, and sent her to the railway. So that's what you meant by *suicide can be murder.*'

'You actually believe that?' said Amy. 'Someone could tell you to commit suicide and you'd *do* it?'

'I was paralysed last night,' said Watson. 'She stared at me and I couldn't move.'

'Lisa stared at you?' Amy laughed dryly. 'You really want me to accept that poor dead Lisa turned into a fucking cat and chased you around a morgue? Why wasn't she destroyed like the other two? Why did they leave her to become a monster?'

'That's been puzzling me,' admitted Quist.

'I bet it has.' Amy laughed again. 'So how do you know so much about this claptrap? This secret *Elite* society?'

'I know this is hard for you.' Quist sat down and drew on his cigarette. 'I once wrote books on shapeshifter mythology. Certain supernatural mysteries fascinated me. Why, for example, is almost identical folklore common to every civilisation? There had to be something behind the legends. I travelled in remote areas of Europe, compiling research for two years, and found solid evidence of supernatural creatures like the Ubasteri, firstly in Germany, and later in Romania, Hungary...'

'And now you're saying they're in Britain?' broke in Amy.

'They've always been here. Like I told you, a tiny clandestine society existing alongside ours.'

'You've known this for a while?' snapped Watson. 'Why the hell didn't you tell anyone?'

'Who? The authorities and the police? No official body would take me seriously and I'd end up in an asylum. I published my research, but the books were long ago dismissed as rubbish.'

'Surely you could make *someone* believe you, Guv.'

Quist shrugged. 'You two find it hard to accept and you've both *seen* a shapeshifter. Modern man simply doesn't believe such things, and unless the Ubasteri emerge from their shadowy cat flap and advertise themselves, he never will.'

The irate teenager shook his head. 'So panthers are out there killing people and you turn a blind eye?'

'Things are more…' Quist squirmed uncomfortably, '*complex* than that. I'm not exactly proud of the fact, but you can't lead much of a crusade from a padded cell.'

'Yeah, right,' said Amy. 'So why the change of heart now?'

'My involvement has been engineered. I now know that the man who approached me to investigate Diane's death was hypnotised, told what to say and then made to kill himself before I could question him. Later, when I saw the autopsy reports on your colleagues, and read of the big cat hair and the dust in Dreyer's car, I came to realise that Ubasteri were behind everything. These creatures are normally invisible, but they're up to something at the moment - something to do with this.' Quist reached into his coat pocket. 'Solstice.'

'Where did you get that?' gasped Amy.

Quist tossed the tub of sunscreen to her.

'Ah!' She saw the label. 'This is the one you bought from the chemist. For a moment, I thought it was from our experimental batches. It's the same four-hundred millilitre white pot.' She handed it back. 'Well whether I believe this rubbish or not, something unusual was definitely going on with Will Gillette's strange work routines and the data he erased. He cleared out his desk too and shredded the papers.'

'What sort of papers?' asked Quist.

'I don't know. Invoices for chemicals, I think. One was called Merlax.'

'*Merlax*?' Quist frowned. 'Merlax was used in certain dubious pesticides until it was banned. It's a rather nasty organic mercury compound.'

'Why would Will have ordered that?'

The detective smiled grimly. 'I've a damn good idea.'

'Grandier Laboratories,' said Amy. 'I don't recall the other substance, but the name on the invoice was Grandier.'

'Really?' Quist headed for the telephone.

Watson followed him into the passage, listening as he spoke to an operator and jotted down a number. 'You've found the place?' he asked.

'It's in France,' said Quist, dialling.

'Do you honestly think they'll give private client information to anyone who just...'

'Hello.' A Parisian accent coloured Quist's perfect French. 'This is Ebor Pharmaceuticals in York, England. I need to speak to someone who can locate a missing order.'

The teenager stared in amazement.

'Delon here,' said a voice, eventually. 'Is that Doctor Gillette?'

'Doctor Soames, his research assistant.'

'Ah! I'm sorry, but I can only deal with Doctor Gillette. He gave specific instructions.'

'So Will told me, but he asked me to look into this. Our latest consignment hasn't arrived.'

'But according to my secretary, the orders were cancelled on Tuesday.'

'Cancelled?' shouted Quist. 'He told the girl to double them.'

'But...'

'What strength will it be?'

'Strength?' Delon sounded puzzled. 'Porphyrene only has one strength.'

'Yes.' Quist hung up. 'I imagine it does.'

'Well?' queried Watson.

The detective returned to Amy in the lounge. 'Does Porphyrene ring any bells?'

'*That* was the name on the invoice,' she said. 'I remember now you've said it.'

'Experimental retinols indeed. Organic mercury compounds and Porphyrene. Incredible!'

'You know what Porphyrene is?' asked Amy.

'I read about it a few years ago. You've heard of the rare metabolic disease Porphyria, where defective haemoglobin absorbs light at a different wavelength to normal? Sunlight is painful and burns. Porphyrene was manufactured by a French company to combat it, but it didn't work. Grandier was probably the lab in question.'

'So it's a photochemical filtering agent?' said Amy.

'Yes, but a dangerous prototype. French scientists have been experimenting with it on unusual blood diseases, but only in terminal cases.'

'Whooo!' Watson whistled. 'Is there anything you don't know?'

Quist held up the sunscreen. 'The last batch of Solstice was sent for testing a week ago?'

Amy nodded. 'A week ago yesterday. That's right.'

'So that's it!' Quist nodded. 'Solstice wasn't terminated due to lack of results. The results of that last batch must have come back positive. It actually worked. I don't believe it.'

'Don't believe what?' demanded Amy and Watson in unison.

'Haven't you guessed yet?' The detective smiled grimly. 'You've been producing sunscreen for the Ubasteri.'

* * * *

223

Chapter 48

Gary Mitchell switched on a sympathetic smile as the door of the house swung open. 'Mrs Hepworth?' He flipped open his police warrant card in the time-honoured way. 'I'm Detective Constable Mitchell. You rang us concerning your tenant? Nicole Patterson?'

The woman nodded. 'Actually, I feel a bit silly. I phoned to report a possible missing person and they put me through to your murder incident room.'

'Understandable under the circumstances.' Mitchell walked into the hallway. 'I'd like to see her room, please.'

'Yes, of course.'

Mrs Hepworth led him up two flights of stairs and unlocked a door with a master key. The bedsit belonged to a girl; Mitchell didn't need his detective training to tell that. The pink quilt had a feminine look and the tables were littered with cuddly toys.

'How long has Nicole been lodging here?' he asked.

'Just under a year.'

'And when did you last see her? Yesterday morning?'

'I haven't seen her all week. That's why I rang you.'

'A week?' He frowned. 'When I heard she'd gone missing, I assumed she didn't arrive home last night. She gave one of her colleagues a lift into town when she left the lab yesterday.'

'You know her?' The landlady looked puzzled. 'Did you say lab?'

'Ebor Pharmaceuticals.'

'The place where those murdered girls worked?'

'Yes. That's why her disappearance was naturally passed to the murder squad.'

'What was she doing there?'

'She was the research director's secretary.'

'Are you sure we're speaking about the same girl? The Nicole who rents my room works for a temping firm called the Mazarin Agency.'

'That's right. The director's secretary had an accident and Nicole is filling in. She's been working there all week.'

'She never said.' Mrs Hepworth shrugged. 'Oh well, if you saw her yesterday, she's obviously fine. I wonder where she's been staying over the past week?'

Mitchell glanced around the bedsit. A photo of two young women stood on a bookshelf, their cheerful faces filling the frame. 'Who are the girls?' he queried.

Mrs Hepworth frowned curiously. 'Nicole and her sister.'

The policeman stiffened. 'Er... which is Nicole?'

'The blonde on the right. I thought you knew her?'

'Yes.' Mitchell stared at the stranger. 'Until now I believed I did.'

* * * *

Chapter 49

Fisher brought the van to a halt on the lane outside Askham Richard village. Quist's cottage and the surrounding meadows were smothered by the same fluffy shroud that choked York; the kind of fog usually only seen in movies of Dickensian London. If this unusual weather continued, Yorkshire would be guaranteed a white Christmas, albeit not in the accepted sense.

'This is the other address that Gillette gave you?' asked Browning.

'Yes.' Strand dropped the window and saw the Volkswagen Beetle in the drive.

'Doesn't Stapleton drive a Porsche?' said Hinds. 'I don't think that's a Porsche.'

'Porsche or not, someone is home.' Strand turned to Browning and Sangster. 'Go in there and kill everyone you find.'

'Go in and kill everyone?' said Sangster.

'If I wanted repetition, I'd invest in a parrot. Kill Stapleton. If Stapleton isn't there, kill everyone that *is* there. Are we clear?'

Clambering out, the two guards vanished into the fog and made for opposite sides of the cottage. Fisher opened his mouth to speak, and seeing Strand's expression, closed it. It had finally sunk in, that lapdancers in the Vatican were likelier than Strand explaining his bizarre decisions on *this* field trip.

* * * *

'You're serious?' said Watson.

'I can't accept these creatures exist.' Amy swallowed uncomfortably. 'And now you're saying I've been making sunscreen for them?' Her heart beat faster. 'Take me to the police station, Bernard.'

'Think about it,' snapped Quist. 'Will Gillette had you producing eye protection and advanced sunscreen with mercury and dangerous experimental substances. He had a compartmentalised work system, where no one was allowed to see the end results, and

226

afterwards he destroyed all the evidence.'

'I know Will ordered them.' The doctor laughed, a staccato release of stress. 'But why on earth would he use Porphyrene and Merlax in the Solstice. The police station, Bernard; I want to go there *now*. I can't believe I let you bring me here after that Constable was killed. I was crazy not to go straight there.'

'Vampire cat sunscreen?' Watson whistled. 'We must be talking factor ten-thousand.'

'For God's sake, think about what you're saying,' snapped Amy. 'If these cat people are so protective of their secrecy, as you claim, the finished projects would simply have been cancelled. Any suspicions over bizarre ingredients, odd work routines, or anything else would have been forgotten. By murdering the research director and his team, they've drawn the police and media to the lab. This is utter nonsense.'

'I'm sorry,' said Quist softly, 'but I'm afraid it's all real.'

'So where do the bikers and Selden's fake story fit in?' quizzed Watson. 'And that Maserati...'

Two sounds terminated his questions: the lock breaking on the French windows and the kitchen door bursting open. Sangster stepped inside from the garden and Browning appeared at the opposite end of the lounge.

'Can we help you?' asked Quist.

Browning's green eyes glowed and Sangster hissed, his muzzle extending and lips peeling back from elongating fangs.

'Shapeshifters,' moaned Amy. 'They're fucking cat people.'

'Well spotted.' Quist grabbed the girl and tossed her over the couch. 'Stay behind there.'

Watson leapt beside her as Quist ducked and darted at Sangster. The charge was too swift to dodge and he toppled backwards into the garden as the detective's head rammed his midriff. Powerful arms locked around Quist from behind and furry lips snuffled at his throat. A lapping tongue might have been pleasant were it Amy, but this feline mouth was seeking an artery. Quist slammed an elbow into Browning's groin, a squeal verifying the existence of Ubasteri testicles, and he crouched sharply to shoulder-pitch him onto the floor by the open staircase. Hissing and thrashing, pinned down by a foot across the neck, the transforming creature screeched as Quist snapped off a banister spindle and plunged the makeshift stake into its ribcage.

'Look out,' shouted Watson. 'Behind you.'

A huge black cat dived through the French doors, slamming into the detective and throwing him like a rag doll. Sangster had transformed fully, his suit hanging in tatters where the feline form had burst from the material. Crashing into a table and struggling on his back, Quist grunted as the panther pounced on him. He rammed a hand under the jaw to keep the snarling mouth from his throat, and searched desperately for a weapon, all too aware that the talons were about to start clawing and disembowelling. Something had fallen from the wrecked table to his right.

Sangster hadn't anticipated Quist's strength. Looking down at the wooden legs sticking out from his furry chest, he gurgled blood and rolled over in a dead heap. There wasn't much else he could do with a garden gnome buried waist-deep in his heart.

* * * *

Strand turned to the two bodyguards in the rear of the van. 'Go and see what's keeping them.'

Hinds frowned. 'They've only been gone a few moments.'

'I'm aware of that. Now do as you're told.' He watched them clamber out into the fog and waited until they reached the cottage gate. 'Oh, by the way...'

Turning, Fisher saw Strand's sneer and the silencer levelled on his torso. 'Er...' he began.

By the time he'd registered that the gun was firing, two bullets had ripped into his chest, and the four had hit Hinds.

'It's been fun, boys,' said Strand. 'But I'm afraid you're now surplus to requirements.'

* * * *

228

Chapter 50

'Unbelievable!' Watson emerged from behind the couch. 'Absolutely unbelievable!'

'Thanks for the help,' spluttered Quist. He leant against the fireplace massaging aching ribs through a blood-drenched shirt.

'Didn't look like you needed help, Guv. I thought these twats were dangerous? You handled that pair okay and look at the size of them.'

'I was lucky,' said Quist. 'They didn't expect me to attack.'

'They probably didn't expect you to snap that off either.' Trembling uncontrollably, Watson checked the spindle used on Browning. 'Solid oak and two inches thick.'

'The staircase is old.' Quist shrugged. 'Full of woodworm.'

'What the hell...' Amy tottered to her feet in shock, the Ubasteri no longer sharing a pigeonhole with leprechauns in her scientific mind. 'They were going to kill us, but *you* killed them.' She gaped at the legs protruding from Sangster's chest. 'You killed them with a spindle and *that*?' The wooden flashing gnome had been rammed in to the jutting penis.

'Nice work!' Watson laughed nervously. 'In up to the bollocks, as they say.'

The corpse by the stairs squelched sickeningly. Amy turned away as Sangster's abdomen burst and the contents bubbled.

'Ugh!' Watson retched. 'Are they going to change to pizza topping like Lisa?'

'They'll decompose faster.' Quist dusted his shirt. The blood had powdered and was easily brushed away. 'They're older.'

'They were shapeshifters,' stuttered Amy, her head in worse turmoil than her stomach. All vestiges of scepticism were gone. 'It's all real. Everything you said about these cat people is true. The thing that chased me - was it one of these two?'

'Possibly,' sad Quist. 'They were certainly at the morgue last night. I recognised their voices.'

229

'I'm sorry, Bernard.' She watched Browning's remains crumble to dust. 'These things have tried to kill me twice now, and both times you've saved my life. I'm so sorry for ever doubting you.'

'How did they know Amy was here?' demanded Watson. 'Maybe we were followed?'

Quist nodded. 'There were five of these creatures at the morgue.' Lifting the gnome from Sangster and gripping it like a rifle, pointed hat out front, he stepped through the French doors. 'The others may be waiting.'

'You're not seriously looking for giant cats in the fog?' The terrified youth followed him down the cottage gable with Amy tagging on. 'Armed with a fuckin' garden gnome?'

'Wait here by the corner,' murmured Quist. 'If I'm attacked, run. Don't try anything heroic, alright?'

Watson nodded briskly. 'If you insist.'

The detective moved cautiously to the silent lane beyond the gate, fanning left and right with the gnome. He stood motionless, listening and gazing into the billowing veil, then lowered his eyes. 'Ah, our friends weren't alone.' He crouched by two crumpled suits on the tarmac. 'Come take a look.'

'What happened here?' whispered the doctor.

Quist searched the jackets. 'Bullets.' He picked six jagged stars from the dust inside and flinched. 'Or what's left of them.'

'They were shot?' said Amy. 'But we heard nothing. Someone must have used a silencer. Are the bullets...'

'Silver?' He tossed them down. 'Yes, they are. From the spread, they're hollow-point rounds.'

Amy gulped. 'Silver dumdum bullets?'

'They don't look so *elite* now, do they?' said Watson. 'Who killed them?'

'Hello, what's this?' Quist took a card from one of the pockets. 'Sunnyvale Clinic. Birchley, Ashton-Under-Lyne. A peaceful oasis for troubled minds.'

'Sounds like a loony bin.' Watson narrowed his eyes. 'Isn't

that where the BMW is from?'

'BMW?' echoed Amy.

'Yes,' said Quist. 'It's been following us for the past few days, conveniently allowing me to see the number. It's registered to this address. Speaking of addresses, how did they know mine. I'm certain we weren't followed here. Unless…' He turned slowly to the Beetle. 'No, surely not.'

Watson followed him to the car. 'Surely not *what*?'

Dropping into a press-up position, Quist checked under the car and quickly shuffled around to the rear bumper.

'Bernard?' Amy watched in disbelief as he brought out a small black box. 'Is that what I think it is?'

'You've got to be joking,' croaked Watson.

'A magnetised transponder on the chassis.' Quist climbed to his feet. 'They had a tracker on my car?' He strode back up the path and into the lounge. 'What the hell is going on?'

Watson gazed at the powdered remains of the intruders in the disarray of furniture, the gravity of the attack sinking in. 'So what do we do now, Guv?'

'Sunnyvale.' Quist examined the tracker, then placed it in the fireplace and smashed it with a poker. 'The Lancashire mental hospital on the planted card. That's where the answers lie.'

'*Planted* card?' gasped Amy.

'Of course it was planted - just like those badges.'

Watson laughed uneasily. 'Someone shoots a pair of cats and leaves them for us with a handy address card? This is getting weirder by the minute.'

'This has all been planned,' said Quist. 'The badges to get us to the biker house, a tracker under the car to follow our movements, and now the card pointing us to this institution near Manchester. Ebor Pharmaceuticals manufactured a sunscreen for the Ubasteri and for some reason the research team were murdered. Who on earth would want us involved in that?'

Bewildered, Watson ran a hand through his hair. 'We still

don't know why they wanted us to go to the biker's place. Hang on. If these four Ubasteri have been driving the BMW, how come we were tailed in the daytime?'

'The windows will be sunlight-protected; I noticed they were dark.' Quist stroked his nose. 'But if they *did* travel here in it, where is it, and where's the fifth member of their group? Perhaps he shot them, but why?'

'When are you setting off for Lancashire?' asked Watson. 'Tomorrow morning?'

The detective shook his head. 'The sooner the better. We'll go now.'

'*We?*' Watson's pent-up tension erupted in a hysterical laugh. 'I was hoping for the latest mobile phone this Christmas, not a label tied to my toe. Two things, Guv. One - you said I was strong enough to take all this. You're wrong. Two - if someone is tracking us and the card was planted, this is probably a trap.'

'Almost certainly a trap, but I only want to see the place, and I may need your help. Don't worry; I'll ensure you come to no harm.'

Amy took a deep breath. 'I'm coming too.'

'I thought doctors were clever?' said Watson. 'You're already on their pussy hit-list.'

'No,' said Quist. 'It would be far better if...'

'These cat things know where I live and they've tried to kill me twice. I can't go to the police with this, I can't go home, and I definitely won't put my sister and her kids at risk by going to stay there again. No, I'm coming with you.'

'A hotel?' angled Quist. 'We could drop you on the way and...'

'I saw how you handled those giant panthers and I'll feel safer with you.' Amy linked arms with Watson. 'If it's safe enough to take him, it's safe enough for me. I'm coming.'

* * * *

'At last.' Strand watched the Beetle crawl along the lane and past the foggy farm track where he waited in the van. 'I thought you'd never leave.'

He chuckled as Quist vanished around the bend, then pulled out of his hiding place and drove back to the empty Briar Cottage. Five minutes ticked by before a white BMW drew up in front.

'Not late, am I?' The driver opened the boot.

'No problem.' Strand climbed from the van. 'They've only just left.'

'I hope this is okay. It's a bit messy.'

'Ah, that'll do nicely.' Strand inspected the plastic-wrapped corpse. 'Let's get it inside.'

'Where do you want it?'

'I see you've ripped his guts out.' Strand ran a finger down what was left of Constable Gregson's blood-soaked face and licked it. 'Better make it the bathroom.'

* * * *

Chapter 51

The fog had cleared after Tadcaster, and Quist's soft-top Beetle tore south along the M1 motorway at seventy. The sky resembled a heap of soggy blankets - grey, but tinged with an eerie lavender that threatened snow.

'Leeds.' The detective realised he wouldn't reach Lancashire before dusk and nodded to an approaching sign. 'Don't you think a hotel...'

'Bernard,' snapped Amy, 'will you please stop trying to dump me at every town we pass.'

'I'm only thinking of your safety.'

'So am I. Speaking of which, I hope Rex is okay. He said in his answerphone message that he'd bumped into some of those creatures last night. If they tracked me to your cottage, they may be following him and that biker girl.'

'I shouldn't worry.' Watson laughed in the rear seat. 'The SAS are well-trained.'

'Trained to handle shapeshifters?' said Amy.

'Yeah, and aliens and stuff. The training will be secret at somewhere like Area 51, so the public doesn't realise such things exist and get panicky.'

Quist had bitten his tongue long enough. 'I'm sorry,' he sighed, 'but Grant is no more SAS than I'm a ballet dancer. He isn't the military type. Can you honestly picture him living off his wits behind enemy lines and abseiling through windows to rescue hostages?'

Watson glanced at Amy. Thinking about it seriously, it was easier to picture Mister Bean performing heart transplants.

The doctor shook her head. 'Why would he lie?'

'People with boring lives have exciting dreams and fantasies they wish were reality.'

'But his family are loaded,' said Amy. 'He certainly isn't lying about that. He's one of the heirs to the Grant housing company.'

'Millionaires get bored too,' said Quist. 'Why do you think they experiment with drugs, and religious cults? When fantasists meet strangers, they get a chance to briefly live their dreams. An unemployed girl on holiday may say she's a model. A road sweeper a pilot.'

'And you think Rex is the same with the SAS?' asked Watson.

Quist shrugged. 'Despite his wealth, he's still basically unemployed. It sounds more thrilling to tell strangers he's a Captain than a privileged wastrel.'

Watson turned to Amy. 'That *does* explain a few things.'

'Exactly,' said Quist. 'That's why I didn't contact him when I realised what we were dealing with. I didn't want him around before, but now... well, it's safer for everyone with him out of the picture. Taking this girl to her brother's should keep him out of the way.'

'So he lied to me.' Amy pulled a face. 'I hate it when men do that.'

'He means no harm,' said Quist. 'I'm guessing he's recently been turned down by the military and he feels rejected. Acting out the macho fantasy probably makes him feel better.'

'I suppose you could be right,' agreed Amy. 'I imagine most people have things they keep covered.'

'Not me,' said Watson. 'No secrets in *my* closet. How about you, Guv?'

'My closet isn't exactly empty.'

'Oh? What's this then?'

'If I told you, it wouldn't be secret, would it?'

'Whatever.' Watson grinned. 'Here's hoping it doesn't involve choirboys.'

Quist shot him a withering glance in the rear-view mirror. 'Speaking of secrets, Amy, I've been hoping to talk about the secretive owner of your company. Now that we have time, perhaps you can tell us about this elusive Doctor Stapleton?'

'Elusive is the right word,' said Amy. 'Like I told you, Will

Gillette ran everything. We were lucky to see Doctor Stapleton once a week. She's a real recluse.'

'*She*? Stapleton is a woman?'

'Doctor Francesca Stapleton. Didn't you know?'

'Fran,' whispered Quist.

'Nice going,' said Watson, eyes wide. 'Fuck all out of ten for deduction there.'

* * * *

Marika sat in the library at Sedgefield Grange. Blowing dust from the old leather book, she opened Richard Quayle's *Creatures Of Darkness* and found the design: the red inverted pentagram in a circle. Spreading the tarot again, she randomly picked three cards, but knew they'd be the same: the Moon, the Tower, and the Five of Pentacles. Ominous, foreboding and sinister–fancy words were fine, but drawing the same cards ten times was downright bloody ridiculous!

She was certain now. Everything tied in with her psychic nightmares and that brief vision: that mark on Rex's hand. His life would shortly end, sometime tonight, and she knew the terrible shape his death would take. Marika took out her phone. This would be better face-to-face, but waiting for his return was futile. She'd have to ring and somehow try to convince him of this new horror. She began keying in Rex's number as a scream sounded above. Racing from the library, she ran up the stairs to find a maid sobbing hysterically in the west corridor.

'Julie,' gasped Marika. 'What is it?'

The ashen servant pointed to a bedroom.

Marika walked into the room where her party guests Graham and Tania Smythe spent the night, or more precisely, where Graham slept after his wife stormed home. Everything appeared normal; dusters and polish lay on the dresser and the blanket chest stood open. Julie must have been taking out fresh linen, an assumption confirmed by the sheet on the floor. She looked again, stiffened to see blood on the cotton, and peered in.

A clawed corpse had been crammed inside, the head torn off

and legs broken and twisted to ensure a snug fit. Numb and dazed, Marika stared at the head between the ankles. The white face stared back at her, terror filling the glassy eyes and jaw hanging wide in a silent scream.

Rupert arrived, still dressed in his Santa outfit. 'What's up?' he slurred, drunkenly. 'Barrymore tells me a maid is screaming like a stag with its stomach out. What's the matter with her? What's the matter with you?'

'She didn't go home,' stammered Marika. 'She was here all along.'

'*Who* was here? The maid?' He rolled his head to clear the alcoholic fog. 'What are you blabbering about, woman?'

His wife burst into tears and waved a trembling finger at the blanket box.

Rupert gazed in at the headless corpse of Tania Smythe and belched. 'Damn them!' he hissed. 'Those bastard foxes.'

* * * *

Chapter 52

Birchley lay to the east of Ashton-under-Lyne, an isolated hamlet on the rugged Pennine moorland. The black Ferrari cruised to a halt at the end of Forest Lane, a rural cul-de-sac flanked by high walls on the outskirts of the village.

'*This* place?' Rex stared over his shades. 'Your brother lives *here?*'

'There's no place like home,' said Fran, jumping from the car. She spoke into the gatepost intercom and returned as the wrought-iron gates electronically parted.

Built in Victorian Gothic style, with towers, shuttered windows and security bars, the Sunnyvale mental hospital stood in private parkland encircled by high railings and cameras. Moors flanked three sides with an area of dark woodland to the south.

'Your brother actually owns an asylum?' asked Rex.

'He owns the property.' Fran laughed at his stunned expression. 'He also heads the governing medical board and runs things here.'

'Wow!' Rex took the F50 up the drive to a marble porch. 'There we go - a lift to the door. It was fun being your chauffeur, but it's time I was heading back. Hey, there's no need for tears.'

'I'm not crying.' Fran rubbed her eyes. 'It's dust.'

'Oh.' His disappointment was obvious. 'Listen, you'd better give me your number if I'm to keep in touch.'

She stroked his leg. 'Why not stay the night?'

'It's tempting, but I told Quist I'd be back before dark.'

'Okay, have a quick coffee and meet my brother before you go. You'll only be ten minutes and I'll give you my number and addresses where you can reach me.'

'Oh alright.' Rex kissed her cheek. 'Ten minutes then.'

He climbed from the car and noticed the gates had closed. Someone had anticipated his decision.

* * * *

Amy stabbed Rex's number into her phone and passed it to Quist as he drove.

'Damn it!' He cancelled the digital apology. 'Why is his phone still switched off?' Keying in the number of his cottage, he waited until the answerphone kicked in, then deleted the message and recorded a new one. Amy and Watson listened, their eyes wide.

'Doctor Stapleton?' said Watson. 'So you reckon this blonde he's taken to Manchester, the one we met at Creeper's, is the owner of Ebor Pharmaceuticals? More to the point, you think she's one of the Ubasteri?'

'From your description, it sounds like her,' said Amy.

'It's Stapleton,' snarled Quist. 'Rex has to be warned. Let's hope he rings me.'

Watson shook his head in amazement. *So that sexy girl was some supernatural creature who could change into a cat?* He briefly pondered how she might look licking her own arse. 'They're supposed to be going to her brother's,' he said. 'We haven't a clue where that is. Why was the multi-millionaire owner of a dermatology lab living with those bikers? What's going on?'

'I don't know,' said Quist. 'But I believe we'll be finding out shortly.'

* * * *

The cat's head knocker on the door of Sunnyvale scowled at Rex.

'Smile,' said Fran. 'You're being watched.' Shielding her eyes from the afternoon light, she motioned to the cameras in the porch roof. 'Security is tight. Some of the inmates are dangerous.'

Electronic locks whirred and a bald character in a hospital coat opened the door. 'Ah, Francesca,' he said. 'Your brother informed me you'd be calling.'

'Hello, Don.' She kissed his cheek. 'Is Jordan about?'

'Doctor Zucco is busy with the patients.' Staying out of the daylight, he waved them into a hall with stairs sweeping up to the right and a modern reception desk. 'I doubt he'll be long.'

Rex was surprised after seeing the eerie gothic exterior. Everything was as it should be in a mental hospital–clean and clinical, with antiseptic on the air, and ceiling cameras focused on the entrance, reception, and staircase. Having never visited one of these places before, he was frustrated to find no one dressed as Sitting Bull or Napoleon.

'Rex Grant.' Fran wiped her eyes. 'Meet Donald Houghton, my brother's chief of security here.'

Rex noticed Houghton had the eyes of a ferret, a green-eyed ferret that would probably sell heroin outside schools.

Houghton's mouth wrinkled in a lousy imitation of a greeting. 'Nice to meet you.' The voice belonged to a refrigerator. 'Francesca's friends are always welcome.'

'Er, right.' Rex pushed the shades up his nose, unsure of how to feel over being welcome in an asylum.

'We'll be in Jordan's quarters.' Fran walked to a steel door by the staircase. 'You'll let him know?'

'Are you a policeman?' asked an elderly woman at the bottom of the stairs. Tousled white hair and a peculiar smile that belonged on a Jehovah's Witness told Rex this wasn't a doctor.

He shook his head. 'SAS, actually.'

'Oh, I need a policeman. They're monsters and the police have to be told.'

'Come on, Maureen.' Houghton hurried over with two orderlies. 'Let's get you back to your room.'

'You're one of them,' she said. 'I need a policeman.'

'But you don't like policemen, do you?' Houghton turned to Rex. 'Maureen has problems with authority. She strangled two police officers.'

'No, I don't like them.' Maureen tittered. 'Their faces turn black when you squeeze their necks.'

'Er, yes.' Rex's own face turned a different colour. 'Merry Christmas.'

Fran punched keypad digits and the metal door slid open.

'This keeps people like Maureen safely outside,' she said. 'Jordan's quarters are completely sealed.'

'Very wise!' Rex hurried through into a separate hallway, with several rooms leading off and a barred window looking onto woodland. He patted his pockets. 'Damn, I'm lost without a mobile. Can I try Quist again?'

'Help yourself.' Fran nodded to the phone on the hall table and headed for the kitchen. 'I'll make some coffee.'

'Black, no sugar,' shouted Rex, tapping a number he was now familiar with.

The detective's office machine clicked on with the usual apology. *Where was he? Didn't this private eye ever check the answerphones?* He stabbed in the private number, but this time Quist's message had changed.

'Rex? If that's you, I'm whispering in case she's with you. Fran is Francesca Stapleton, the owner of Ebor Pharmaceuticals, and she is extremely dangerous. I know this must be hard to believe, but you must trust me. I'm certain she killed Lisa Mirren and others, including those bikers you found. I Know she looks human, but she's one of those cat creatures you met last night. You must get away from her, Rex. Get away as soon as possible.'

'Was that no sugar?' said Fran, behind him.

⁂ ⁂ ⁂ ⁂

Chapter 53

Lucius Silva stood with hands clasped behind his silk suit, gazing through one of the giant windows in his Salford Quays penthouse. The final rays of sunlight twinkled on the Manchester Ship Canal below.

'Not a good report, is it?' he said.

'Er, not really.' Galeen, the head of the Presidential security team, tried to prevent his voice quaking. Normally it would be difficult to imagine *anything* quaking on his muscular frame, except for the stitching where the suit jacket stretched over his huge shoulders. 'Your computer expert Polanski has finally managed to access the police files. He called with this information a moment ago.'

'I wonder if you'd run those main points by me again?'

Galeen gulped. 'Doctor Stapleton's research director Will Gillette was found dead last night, and a fourth girl from Stapleton's laboratory vanished this morning, along with the officer detailed to protect her. We're ringing Strand's mobile, but there's no answer...'

'The main points,' Silva reminded him.

'Stapleton appears to have been living with a group of motorcyclists in the York suburb of Clifton. Ten of them were killed there yesterday. The police have Stapleton's fingerprints and photograph, along with feline hairs, presumably shed by her. They also have the Mirren girl's powdered remains from the hospital. A fracas took place there and an employee gave a good description of Strand and his team.'

'No, not a good report.' The President studied the Salford docklands, the modern glass buildings reflecting the crimson sunset.

'Carl Dreyer, one of Tayman's people from Leeds, is also probably dead. The police found clothes and red dust in his car. Er, that's more or less it.'

'Not good at all.'

'Er, what would you like me to do, Sir?'

Galeen regretted the question the moment it left his lips. This giant steroid advertisement was head of security, but the position afforded little protection from the President's wrath. Silva once existed in an age where leaders killed the bearers of ill tidings, and the response here might easily be: 'Throw yourself in the cellar furnace'.

Silva nodded slowly. 'Strand told me Mirren's corpse had been destroyed along with all evidence. He lied to me; I never thought he could be so stupid.'

Galeen snatched the trilling telephone. 'It's Tayman, Sir,' he announced. 'He needs to speak to you urgently before the meeting.'

Silva took the phone and closed a hand over it. 'I'm expecting a visitor,' he said. 'She should have arrived by now, so show her up.' The President waited until the bodyguard exited before speaking to Tayman. 'Frederick, I understand this is urgent?' He listened, inspecting his nails. 'How interesting! I'll see you here at six-thirty.'

A young woman was ushered into the penthouse, Galeen closing the door behind her.

'There you are, my dear.' Silva replaced the telephone, his lips curling back from sprouting cat fangs. 'Come here and make an old man very happy.'

* * * *

Frederick Tayman poured a celebratory cognac and looked down onto the streets of Christmas bustle from the upper windows of the Brightshield Glazing office tower. The York problem had been a real worry. The Leeds branch manager's disappearance had to be explained to Silva, but from what he'd discovered this afternoon, Strand was in the shit and things didn't seem so bad after all.

Chuckling, he turned to watch the sun sink beneath the Liverpool rooftops. Being Elite, Tayman wasn't a fan of sunsets. Whilst most spectators found them breathtaking, he found them fatal. A beautiful sunset would take away more than his breath. It would take away his very existence.

He sipped his drink and ran a finger down the dark office window. The new filtration process was complete and solar radiation would soon be blocked by transparent glass instead of this mirrored

243

shielding. The Elite would drive vehicles with clear windows and wear eye protection resembling ordinary spectacles. Strand was as good as dead and Tayman had a revolutionary breakthrough for the society. If this didn't bring about his promotion to Vice-President, nothing would. He twitched excitedly, spilling brandy.

Ah, what a wonderful evening this would be.

* * * *

Chapter 54

'Could I er, use the bathroom?' stammered Rex.

'Call me over-sensitive,' said Fran. She reclined on the couch in Doctor Zucco's private lounge, watching as Rex headed for the hall. 'But you seem nervous. Did you get through to your friend?'

'No, I got Quist's answerphone again.' He edged through the door. 'Shan't be long.'

'Haven't you forgotten something?'

'Er, a goodbye kiss?'

'Directions.' Fran laughed. 'Down the corridor. Third on the right.'

Rex closed the door, raced across the hall to the security door and scowled at the coded keypad. Trying to leave through reception was stupid anyway. It would be locked and if Quist was right, the staff might be Stapleton's people. *Francesca Stapleton? Could Quist's insane message actually be right? Could that lovely girl really be the laboratory owner, not to mention a fucking overgrown cat?* Surely not–he'd seen her in daylight–but he'd no intention of waiting to find out. This wouldn't be the first time he'd sneaked through a window to escape a woman, and if it all turned out to be some horrible mistake, he could turn on the Grant charm and apologise later.

Bars covered the hall window, and sprinting down the passage, Rex groaned to see more in the bathroom. He glanced about desperately and eyed the ceiling CCTV cameras, praying that no one was watching. If he didn't get out in the next few minutes, he'd be missed. *How long did a toilet visit normally take? He'd never timed himself?*

A door stood ajar at the end of the passage, the steps behind leading down into darkness.

'Yes,' he whispered. 'A cellar.'

This was more like it. Maybe there would be a hatch, or a coal chute he could crawl up. Rex flicked on the light and ran down, halting on the last step. Eight prison cells lined one wall of the white-tiled basement, facing a surgical complex and laboratory. Steps led up to a delivery hatch in a recess at the far end. He noticed the shackles fixed below, as if someone had been chained there, and to his dismay, the padlock securing the hatch. Tiptoeing by three empty cages, Rex peered at the naked inmates in the next five–a young Chinese girl and four disfigured men sleeping on the floor. Wincing at their blackened burns, he made for what looked like an external door to the left of the hatch.

'Help me.' The girl was awake, her body pressed against the bars and arms reaching out. 'You're not one of them, are you?'

'What's going on?' He tried the handle and found it locked. 'Who are you?'

'The keys,' she whimpered. 'Please! They keep them in the drawer there.'

Rex ran to the desk. 'I reckon that door leads outside,' he said, snatching a key ring. 'Do you know if any of these open it?'

'Yes, the shiny key fits every cell.'

'Okay, don't worry.' He unlocked her cage. 'Everything is going to be...' The Chinese girl slammed him to the floor. 'What the fuck...' he spluttered, then noticing her green eyes and fangs, decided not to bother.

She straddled him, hissing and pinning his arms, as black fur covered her nakedness and a cat muzzle sprouted in a crackle of bone. Her strength was unreal, and struggling for Marika's crucifix beneath his sweater was useless.

'Listen,' croaked Rex. 'I've lots of money and I'm sure we could come to some arrangement without...'

Fully transformed now, the huge panther chuckled, spraying his face with saliva. The feline grin descended to his throat and he moaned in horrified resignation to feel her tongue lapping the flesh as it sought a pulse. Rex knew the Chinese would eat practically anything, but he'd never envisaged himself on their menu. He closed his eyes, whimpering in petrified anticipation of the inevitable as the drooling lips fastened on the skin. And then she was gone. Another huge cat had slammed into her ribs, knocking her off Rex and rolling her against the wall. The Chinese panther sprang up and two men stepped forward, one half-emptying a silenced machine pistol into it.

Rex watched in open-mouthed terror, as the tattered feline corpse slid down the tiles leaving a smear of scarlet slime. Guns had always been a turn-on for him, but he noticed the smoking weapon was now trained on his chest, and felt sure he could look at the Uzi from this angle all night without any stirring in his jeans. The panther that had freed Rex rose on its rear legs and shed its black fur, crackling as the bone structure changed. Golden hair sprouted on the head and the cat swiftly transformed into the naked form of Fran.

'You have no sense of direction.' She lifted Rex from the floor, her voice heavy with mock sympathy. 'I told you the bathroom was third on the right. I assume you got through to Quist and he warned you? Is he on his way here?'

'One....' Rex found his voice and gestured to the two men. 'One of these is your brother?'

'I don't have any brothers. Meet Doctor Jordan Zucco and Doctor Leo Atwill.'

Roused by the skirmish, the disfigured prisoners hissed at Rex, their eyes fixed not on his face, but his throat. Part of his mind assured him this was a nightmare. The remainder joined forces with his bowels to outvote it. He turned back to the girl.

'You're Doctor Stapleton?' he whispered.

'Oh, I think you know me well enough to call me Fran.' She strolled to a cell and stood out of reach as a claw shot through the bars. 'They're insane, but that's why they're here in the caring hands of Doctor Zucco.'

Rex's eyes darted from cell to cell. '*Ca...*' he stuttered.

'Cats?' prompted Fran. 'We're known as Ubasteri, but we much prefer *Elite*. You'll find that's a more appropriate description. I'm Elite, as you've just seen. Jordan and Leo too, and Donald who you met upstairs.'

He closed his eyes, guts lurching at the memory of their night together.

'I'll ask again,' said Fran. 'Is Quist on his way here?'

'I didn't speak to him. It was an answerphone message.'

'I see. After you phoned, it was obvious from your behaviour...'

'Drop the gun!' Rex pulled out Marika's crucifix, gripped the cross in both hands and backed away from Zucco. 'Drop it, you cat bastard. I'm not afraid to use this thing.'

Fran shook her head. 'Although your aunt has knowledge of the supernatural, she's never met the Elite.' She plucked the cross from Rex's trembling hands. 'If she had, she'd know this religious rubbish is useless. You wore this in bed, remember. I didn't scream, did I?'

He sagged against the wall. 'You moaned quite a bit.'

'Turn out your pockets,' snapped Zucco. 'Everything on the desk.'

Rex emptied his jacket, glaring at the redundant garlic and holy water bottle he'd gathered before setting off.

'I assume your gun's in the car.' Fran ran her hands over him, rubbing her nakedness against his leg. 'The bullets aren't silver like Jordan's, but without a silencer it would be awfully loud. We're remote here, but we wouldn't want any walkers phoning the police, would we?'

Rex pulled back. 'Why don't you put your fur coat back on?'

'Ooh, and you told me you loved my body. Speaking of phones, sorry about your mobile, but I couldn't let you keep it.'

'You mean *you* broke it?'

'I'm afraid I squeezed too hard. I don't know my own strength, do I?'

Rex recalled her intimate caresses, and his testicles shrivelled and vanished. 'I don't understand. You were living for weeks with those bikers and...'

'Only five days.' Fran sat on the desk. 'I spotted the bikes at Lamberley after I killed Lisa. Certain people would soon be searching for me and a biker chapter was the ideal hiding place; much better than the hotel I'd picked. I left my stolen car and thumbed a lift when they left the village. Attractive women are always welcome and they never ask questions. I called in the village pub first and spoke with the landlord. As far as he's now concerned, I was there with them all the time.'

'Hypnotism?' whispered Rex. 'Did you kill them? Did you kill ten bikers?'

'Was it ten?' She giggled. 'I'm afraid I didn't count.'

'But the place was a slaughterhouse and you were clean.'

'I usually feed naked. I'd just showered when you arrived.'

'I thought at the time your hair felt damp.' Rex was jolted by an uneasy memory. 'Your hair felt damp last night too.'

'Yes, I had to shower before coming to you. Tania's husband searched everywhere for her after the party, but he never tried their bedroom blanket box.'

'Oh shit!' groaned Rex. 'But this is crazy. You can walk about in sunlight.'

Fran nodded to his personal effects on the desk. 'Why don't you light two cigarettes and I'll explain?'

He lit one and grudgingly passed it with a shaking hand.

'Sunlight is lethal to the Elite.' Fran drew on the smoke. 'Being wealthy, we can explain our daytime absence as an eccentricity, but even eccentric recluses need to be seen occasionally.'

'True,' said Zucco. 'We emerge briefly on dull days with specialised optics, but prolonged exposure is fatal. The rainy northern climates are best. There are over eighty Elite in the north of Britain.'

'Yeah, Florida would be shit,' said Rex sarcastically. He lit another cigarette and pocketed the pack and lighter. 'And I know how much cats love to lie around in the sun. You bloodsuckers certainly have your problems.'

'Sunlight is no longer a problem,' said Fran. 'My laboratory has been working on two special projects. We started with an eye solution, to filter daylight and free us from wearing protective shades, but I realised it was possible to use a similar process and create a barrier cream for our skin.'

Rex recalled his talk with Amy. 'Solstice?'

'The research team were only allowed to work on single parts of the formula, but the ingredients were rather bizarre. The director told them it was an advanced version of Solstice, specialised and different to combat the failing ozone, but it certainly shouldn't have been *that* different.'

Rex sucked on his cigarette. 'So you murdered them to prevent them talking?'

Fran shook her head. 'Actually, they knew very little.'

The more she spoke, the worse he felt. Rex had seen enough movies to know that explanations like this were only given to captives prior to killing them. The captives, however, always escaped with clever trickery to foil the villains and save the day. Unfortunately this wasn't a movie.

'These are the last guinea pigs.' Fran gestured to the cells. 'Expendable patients with no relatives and all traces of their existence wiped from the records.'

'You mean...'

'Jordan transformed them into Ubasteri and used the sunscreen and eye droplets.' She pointed to the shackles under the cellar delivery hatch. 'The sun rises over there.'

'They were all fried,' broke in Zucco. 'Until two weeks ago, when these four only experienced burns and slight blinding. Francesca modified the next batches and you witnessed the results.'

'The Chinese girl.' Fran smiled. 'Jordan tested the final batch on her. I kept a tub from each test shipment, and when he rang with our success last Friday, I used the cream and droplets myself. I've been exposed to daylight all week. We perfected the Solstice, Rex, and I'm the final proof.'

Rex laughed harshly. 'So you can take holidays in the sun at last. They think the British and German tourists behave badly. Fuck me! Wait until they meet you lot.' He looked from Fran to Zucco.

'*The Elite*? That was the least egotistical name you could come up with, was it?'

She laughed with him. 'One obstacle remains, however, and it's a major one.'

'Oh, how I wish I could help you.'

'That's exactly why you're here.' Fran kissed his white cheek. 'Here's looking at you, kid.'

* * * *

Chapter 55

Quist brought the car to a halt fifty yards from the moorland psychiatric hospital and looked around the dark cul-de-sac. Ivy-covered walls loomed on either side of the lane and an owl called in the skeletal branches overhead.

'Sunnyvale,' said Watson, closing the road atlas. 'Yeah, nice and isolated. No neighbours to complain about cats crapping in their garden flower borders. Now we know where it is, let's grab a hotel and come back in the morning.'

'Morning will probably be too late.' Quist pointed through the wrought iron gates. Freezing ground fog had rolled in from the Pennine Moors to gather knee-deep in the gardens and drift around a black Ferrari by the porch. 'Rex is in there. I had a feeling that Sunnyvale would turn out to be the home of Stapleton's *brother*.'

Watson nodded. 'Yeah, but I've watched enough horror films to know that you never piss around with monsters until daylight.'

'Don't worry. You two are waiting in the car.'

'You mean you're going in?' Amy glanced apprehensively at Watson as the howl of a distant village dog caused several others to strike up in a mournful choir. 'Why, for God's sake? I know Rex is in there, but...'

'I don't want to sound negative, Guv,' said Watson, 'but by now, the poor bastard probably looks like a butcher's dustbin.'

'I'm going in.' Quist executed a three-point turn. 'There. In case you need to make a quick getaway, you're facing the right way out of this cul-de-sac. You'd better jump in the driving seat, Amy.'

'I'm your assistant.' Watson looked hurt. 'What about letting *me* drive?'

'Amy has a license.' Quist passed the youth a card. 'This is my friend Larry's new Oxford address. If anything happens to me, I'd like you to contact him.'

'Hey, Guv, don't talk like that.'

The detective turned to Amy. 'You have your phone and

there's a Manchester street map in the atlas. The city is around ten miles to the west. If we're separated, go there and get a hotel. Don't try following me in there, okay?'

Amy shook her head in disbelief. 'It's probably a trap, but you're still going in? You don't even seem scared.'

'I hide it well,' said Quist. 'Yes, I'm going in.'

'Good luck, Bernard. Be careful.'

'He'll need more than luck,' said Watson. 'Remember that howling we just heard, Guv. Watch out for guard dogs.'

'Cats with guard dogs? Are you being serious?' Quist shook his head. 'No, dogs would die of terror. They're dim-witted, but susceptible to supernatural vibrations.' He shot Watson a lopsided grin. 'Still, you fit the bill, but you seem unaffected.'

'Yeah, yeah, it's been fun working with you.'

Amy kissed his cheek. 'Be careful,' she repeated.

'Keep the doors locked and stay alert.' Quist climbed quietly out. 'You'll be safe enough.'

'Wow!' Amy watched him melt into the shadows. 'That's what I call brave.'

Watson punched down the door locks. 'That's what I call insanity.'

The walls flanking the moorland lane ended before the gates and a path ran alongside the hospital perimeter railings. Quist headed left to the corner of the grounds where the track led off into a misty wood. Bending two railings, he squeezed through and crouched behind a shrub, looking up at the small oblong shapes in the trees. CCTV units were positioned at intervals covering the grounds, although none appeared to be focused on the bushy corner where he'd entered.

Tasting tobacco on the night air, he crouched lower, studying the wood beyond the railings. Seconds ticked by before he pinned down the scent, spotted a cigarette glow in the trees, and the two figures watching him. He stared at the secretive pair. No, not watching *him*. Like the detective, they were watching the hospital. Whoever they were, it wasn't a problem, and neither were the cameras provided he stayed below the mist. Quist turned away, dropped into a press-up position and disappeared beneath the layer of ground fog.

The detective crawled to the building, following the wall to the first window where an evergreen shrub supplied cover. He climbed to his feet behind the foliage, dusted off dead leaves, and peered through the security bars into the dark lounge. Luck definitely favoured him tonight. The bottom sash was open, and bending the bars, he clambered in and gazed around in the blackness.

On a couch to his right lay a shoulder bag. There was enough light from the window to find a purse and see that the credit cards belonged to Francesca Stapleton. Digging deeper into the bag, he smiled grimly to find a tub of Solstice cream and the laboratory label confirmed his suspicions–the prototype sunblock had been perfected. This Solstice had obviously been used when Stapleton murdered Lisa Mirren in daylight.

Hearing movement outside the lounge door, he ducked behind the couch as the click of the light switch suggested his luck had ended. The click of the gun being cocked confirmed it.

'I assume the traffic was bad,' said Doctor Zucco, chuckling. 'We expected you earlier.'

'Heavens, a trap,' said Quist, standing up. 'Well what a surprise!'

* * * *

The car temperature had plummeted and Watson's breath clouded as it escaped chattering teeth. Blowing heat into his hands, he eyed the building behind the Beetle in the same way a perceptive duck might eye a pan of orange sauce. *What was Cyrano thinking of going in there? Did he really imagine he had any chance of rescuing someone from a high security hospital run by giant cat monsters?*

Watson was no expert, but he'd gleaned plenty of supernatural knowledge from television. He knew not to mess with monkey paws and Chinese puzzle boxes. He knew, when you saw hooded arseholes chanting in the woods, you didn't hang about to watch. He knew not to read from Egyptian scrolls when mummies were within earshot, and he knew never to upset brats with 666 on their scalps. Above all, though, he knew that entering a place like this after sunset was as sensible as getting the daughter of a Mafia boss pregnant and ditching her.

'What do you call a cat with no legs?' he murmured.

Amy turned to him. 'What?'

'I've thought of a joke. What do you call a cat with no legs?'

The girl's stare was colder than the car.

Watson sighed. 'Just trying to relieve the tension.'

The minutes passed like a tortoise crossing wet cement. Watson glanced up as a white speck landed on the screen.

'Ooh, look,' he whispered. 'It's snowing.'

'Never mind snow,' snapped Amy, checking her watch. 'Where's Bernard? I'm starting to get scared.'

'Starting? I've been scared shitless for the past two days.'

'It's about time he...' Bright headlights turned into the lane. 'Hey, watch out!'

They ducked as a vehicle approached. Watson peeped through the side window as the engine grew louder and a Mercedes van cruised past.

'Look,' he hissed. 'It's going to the nuthouse.'

'Yes.' Amy tilted the mirror to watch. The van waited for the gates to part and continued to the porch, where a bearded man climbed out and let himself in. 'I wonder who that was?'

'Maybe a doctor.' Watson giggled nervously. 'I don't reckon it was an inmate; he wasn't in a straitjacket.'

'They'd have to get up pretty early to catch you out, wouldn't they? No wonder Bernard has you working for him.'

'Yeah. After kicking around with Cyrano, I'm getting good at this deduction lark and...' He turned from the hospital and noticed a saloon parked twenty yards away. 'Hang about...'

Amy turned and stiffened. 'Where did that car come from? It wasn't there when we ducked down.'

'It must've arrived with the van. Oh Jesus, it's a white BMW too.'

'You think...'

'I fuckin' well *do* think. It's got to be the one that's been following us.'

'Why is it parked there?' Amy fumbled for the ignition, her heart pounding. 'Is the driver still inside?'

'I can't tell.' Dread flooded Watson's stomach. 'The windows are too dark.'

Ivy rustled on the high wall by the Beetle. He looked up and choked back a terrified squeal to see a figure moving stealthily along the stonework.

'Drive!' he shrieked in the girl's ear. 'Now!'

The pair screamed as someone landed on the bonnet and tore off the canvas roof.

* * * *

Chapter 56

Quist emerged from behind the couch. 'Doctor Stapleton, I presume?'

'Full marks,' said Fran, grinning. Zucco stood beside her, his Uzi pistol pointing at the detective. 'Nice to see you again.'

'I understand your biker party went downhill dramatically after I left.'

Fran moved behind him, searching from neck to ankles, as a bearded man entered: a good-looking character in a blue suit.

'Matthew Strand.' He held out a hand. 'Pleased to meet you, Bernard.'

'I almost met you in the mortuary.' Quist stared at the hand as if it were anthrax. 'I heard your voice when you found Lisa Mirren.'

'Yes. Nice work with that broken pole.'

Quist glared at Fran. 'I take it you were the one who made her Ubasteri?'

She smiled sweetly. 'It was necessary.'

'Was it really?' He turned back to Strand. 'You'll be the driver of a certain white BMW, I imagine?'

'I'm afraid not,' he said. 'Your deductive powers have failed you for once. Why don't you sit and I'll pour us both a drink? I know you enjoy Hebridean malts.'

Quist settled himself on the couch and watched him at the drinks cabinet. Zucco and Fran sat in armchairs opposite, their guns still pointing.

'Crawling under the ground mist was smart,' said Fran. 'Unfortunately, some of the CCTV cameras are infra-red.'

'Ah, Bowmore from Jura,' said Quist, taking Strand's offered glass and sipping the whisky. 'One of my favourites, along with Askaig.'

Strand held out a cedar box. 'And these are your favourite Cuban cigars.'

'So you're all Ubasteri?' Quist waved the Cohibas away and

stared at Strand. 'I take it you're the *brains* behind this strangely convoluted scheme to get me here?'

Fran giggled. 'I noticed you didn't seem surprised to find Jordan and I waiting.'

'I wasn't,' said Quist. 'The clues you left were as subtle as an old *Carry On* movie.'

'You knew?' Strand shook his head. 'You knew we were Elite, you realised this was a trap, and you walked into it? Why?'

'The question *I* was about to ask. Why did you want me here, and why go to all this trouble?'

'The original plan,' said Strand, 'was to have the terrified Doctor Stapleton come to your office seeking help. Her research staff were being murdered, she was hiding at a hotel, and she'd made a dreadful discovery: Gillette was using her lab to produce sunscreen for monsters. After you'd seen Lisa Mirren and realised Fran was telling the truth, she'd get you to bring her here to her *brother's* for protection.'

'Then I saw the bikers in Lamberley,' said Fran. 'My idea was more, as you put it, convoluted. Rather than seek you out, I let you involve yourself. I sent the mesmerised Kevin Selden to you. Then I left the badges to have your inquisitiveness bring you to me at Creeper's house. I decided to use your insatiable curiosity.'

'So I'll ask again,' said Quist, quietly. 'Why?'

'We need your help, Bernard.' Strand sipped his whisky. 'Help with a rather tricky problem.'

'I *am* a consultant detective. What sort of help? Maybe help in finding a lost bag of cat litter?'

Strand chuckled. 'We both know you're more than a detective. Those window bars you bent are slender, but they're steel. You also killed two of my people today. You're very powerful, aren't you?'

'I take lots of exercise, and much as I hate to upset your schemes, I don't help murderers.'

'Oh, you will,' said Fran. 'You'll do whatever we ask.'

'How to persuade you?' said Strand. 'That was our problem. You're such a loner with no friends or loved ones. We couldn't mesmerise you, could we? Dreyer soon found that out.'

Quist nodded. 'Brightshield Glazing must have a successful sales record. I realised later that he'd been trying to hypnotically force me to buy. Why did you kill him?'

'He was following you,' said Strand. 'When the mesmerism had no effect, Dryer's superior would have ordered him to discover why, but I couldn't have him spoiling things.' He knocked back his drink. 'You called Fran's scheme *convoluted*. As she says, it was supposed to be; it was meant to intrigue you. Not only did it draw you to us, but along the way you made acquaintances. People whom I imagine you've grown to care about.'

'Well you seem to know quite a bit about me,' hissed the detective. 'You certainly appear to have done your homework.'

Strand shrugged. 'I was never a lover of homework, Bernard. *Acquaintance* is a nice word, but I prefer the term, *hostage*. We have Grant in the cellar and if you'd like more persuasion...' He turned to the door as Amy and Watson were pushed in. 'How about this?'

'Hullo, Guv,' said Watson, trembling with terror.

An old man walked in behind Amy.

'Who needs homework when one can cheat.' Strand laughed loudly. 'Take them down to the cells, Larry.'

'Okay,' said Larry Reynolds.

* * * *

Chapter 57

Katie Bradstreet looked up from the papers on the incident room desk. 'Still no sign of Constable Gregson or Doctor Clarkson?' she asked.

Sergeant Aslam shook his head. 'We found Gregson's car where Mitchell left him in the alley behind Amy's. The window is broken and there's blood in the street. Both doors are smashed on Amy's house and we found more black animal hairs. It doesn't look good.'

'That's the understatement of the fucking year. Even if Gregson's been hurt, where could he be?'

'Who do you suppose the girl was who claimed to be Nicole Patterson?'

The Inspector shook her head. 'And where's the *real* Nicole Patterson?' She held up the papers she'd been reading. 'Have you seen this report on the morgue sweepings? That powder is all that's left of Mirren's corpse.'

'What?' Aslam blinked. '*What?*'

'Which brings us to the missing manager of Brightshield Glazing,' continued Katie. 'You recall Dreyer's car was found in Acomb?'

'Yes, with his clothes on the bonnet and some...'

'Powder. Yes, I've checked with forensics and it's the same.'

'You mean the dust was Dreyer?' The Sergeant gaped at her. 'His corpse was powdered? What could you possibly use to turn people into dust?'

'I don't know, Tariq.' Katie shook her head. 'What the hell are these feline hairs doing at the crime scenes? The lab still can't identify the hairs found on Lisa Mirren and Becca Travis. Does our killer have some weird hybrid pet?'

'Could the *weird hybrid pet* be responsible?' Aslam laughed uneasily. 'Most of our victims seem to have been savaged by an animal like a big cat.' He held up the file he carried. 'I have a forensic report of my own. You were right about Doctor Stapleton. Her prints are all over the biker's house in Clifton. They match the ones taken from the lab and her home on Linden Mount.'

'Yes, they would.' Katie nodded to the picture on the case noticeboard. 'The blow-up might be grainy, but the girl in the photograph is definitely the one I met at Clifton. What was the owner of a laboratory doing pretending to be a biker and living there with them? And why would Will Gillette tell us she was out of the country skiing?'

'That's not all.' Aslam handed her the report. 'Those were Stapleton's fingerprints on the stolen Range Rover found at the farm outside Lamberley.'

Katie's eyes widened. 'Now that *is* interesting.'

'Absolutely,' said Aslam. 'If Stapleton drove a stolen vehicle to Lamberley that day, she was almost certainly involved in her employee Lisa Mirren's death. But the landlord at the Hound told us she was in his pub with those bikers at the time.'

'What is it, Zoe?' The Inspector turned as Constable Planer slammed down her phone and approached the desk.

'Rex Grant,' said Planer. 'You know he's been staying at Sedgefield Grange on the North York Moors?'

'Don't tell me he's dead?' Katie let out a short laugh. 'Everyone else is.'

'That call was the Pickering police. They have uniform at Sedgefield attending reports of a death. It turns out a woman has been decapitated and she's very pale. It looks like her blood was drained.'

'*What?*'

'Grant took someone named Fran there yesterday and the description fits Francesca Stapleton.'

The Inspector leapt up. 'Are they still there?'

'No one knows where they are,' said Planer. 'They set off for Manchester this morning, but Grant's not answering his mobile. Do you want me to...'

'Yes, I do,' snapped Katie. 'Alert the Manchester police. Alert everyone. I want them found.'

Mitchell entered the incident room with a sheet of paper.

'Don't tell me...' She held out a hand. 'Another corpse?'

'Bernard Quist,' he said. 'I finished the checks you wanted, but there isn't much.'

'You're not joking.' Katie read the few lines of type. 'This is it?'

'He's lived alone outside Askham Richard for the past two years and operated as a private investigator in York for just six weeks. Beyond that there's very little.'

'What about his records, credit cards and...'

'The car and a telephone are registered to his address, and he owns a TV license, but that's it. He has no criminal record and I can't find any trace of him historically. Prior to the last two years, it's as if he didn't exist. I asked around his office building to see if anyone knew him, but it didn't help.'

'How about the kid who works for him?'

'John Watson lives on the Grimpen estate in Acomb with his mother, Joanne. According to her, he started at the detective agency three weeks ago, but she knows nothing about his employer. He left with Quist yesterday and she hasn't seen him since. She didn't know he'd been here overnight. Didn't know he was mute either.'

'Where do you reckon those two fit into this?' asked Aslam.

'God knows.' Katie scowled. 'But I wish I had them here now.'

* * * *

Chapter 58

Watson peered miserably at the laboratory paraphernalia on the desk opposite the basement cell and wondered who'd be dissected first. Sullen resignation had overtaken terror. He knew how cats kept dismembered prey alive for hours, playing agonising games with it. He'd have much preferred a Christmas game of naked Twister with Suzy Baines back on the estate in York.

'Cat got your tongue, Guv?' He nudged Quist. 'You haven't spoken since they locked us in here.'

'I don't know what to say.' The detective stood motionless at the cell door, brow resting on the bars. 'I can't believe Larry is involved with the Ubasteri.'

A hiss from the adjoining cage told them the burnt creatures were still hungrily watching them.

'I can't get over his strength.' Watson ran a hand through his wiry hair. 'How old is he? He jumped off a wall, ripped the canvas top off your car, and dragged us out. We tried fighting him, but it was a waste of time.'

Amy sobbed at the memory and Rex held her. 'Are you okay?' he mumbled.

'*I'm* not okay,' snapped Watson. 'So much for keeping us out of danger. I was hoping to spend Christmas in one piece this year. Not ripped apart with bits of me coughed up in a fuckin' furball.'

'I'm sorry.' Quist turned. 'I shouldn't have brought you or Amy. I should have insisted on a hotel for you both. I honestly thought you'd be safe if...'

'Never mind *sorry*. What are we going to do?'

'Do?' Rex took out his cigarettes with a shaky hand. 'What *can* we do?'

'Oh, I don't know,' snarled Watson. 'How about using some of that SAS training to get us out of this?'

Rex gulped. 'Er, well...'

'Just forget it,' said Amy. 'We know you've been lying.'

'Lying?' Rex sagged. 'Er…'

'What was all that crap?' Watson glared angrily. 'Shot in the leg? Missions in Iraqi jungles? What the hell are you?'

Rex shrugged dejectedly and lit the cigarette. 'Nothing,' he whispered. 'I'm nothing. A failure.'

'We don't have time for self-pity.' Quist narrowed his eyes. 'That lighter of yours is silver, isn't it?'

'Yeah.' Rex clicked the Zippo shut. 'Why?'

'They haven't realised, otherwise they'd have taken it. Silver is lethal to the Ubasteri. It might come in handy.'

'Absolutely,' scoffed Watson. 'We might get a chance to melt it and make a few bullets.'

'Hang on to it, Rex.' Quist glanced up the staircase as the door opened. 'Hide it away quickly.'

Strand descended the steps with Fran and Doctor Zucco. 'So how are we all settling in?' He laughed. 'No problems with the room, I hope?'

'Where's Larry?' asked Quist.

'He'll be along presently,' said Fran. She'd changed into a short Italian dress and jacket, both cut from black silk. 'Apparently he feels uncomfortable about facing you. I can't imagine why.'

Amy held tightly onto Rex as the shapeshifters approached the bars.

'Captain Grant.' Strand smirked at their closeness. 'I've always considered Doctor Stapleton to be my girl, and now she tells me about your night together. I'm speechless.'

'You didn't?' Amy backed away from Rex. 'On top of all that shit you told us, you screwed a cat?'

'No. Er, well, yes.' The cigarette quivered in the man's mouth like a demented metronome. 'I didn't know she…'

'What do you want?' demanded Quist. 'Why don't you tell us what's going on?'

Strand took out a cigarette and lit it. 'As I mentioned earlier, I need your help, Bernard. I want you to kill someone for me tonight.'

Watson, Rex and Amy peered at Quist, before slowly turning back to Strand.

Strand fished a tub and a small plastic bottle from his jacket. 'I think Doctor Clarkson can tell us what these are?'

'Solstice sunscreen and UV eye drops,' muttered Amy.

Quist gestured to the cellar hatch. 'Looking at those shackles and the creatures down here, I'd say this is where the products were sent for testing?'

'Correct,' said Strand. 'Fran's been using them since Friday and felt no ill effects until this afternoon. We've both applied a new layer of cream.' He stroked a hand down his cheek. 'Tomorrow I'll walk in sunlight for the first time in two centuries.'

'Let's hope it turns out nice,' grunted Watson. 'We've had crap weather recently.'

Strand laughed and produced a CD. 'Everything we need to begin manufacturing is here in Gillette's research. Can you imagine what this means? A new dawn. No more glasses and time limits on dull days. The Elite can live amongst you in direct sunlight.'

Zucco chuckled. 'The future looks bright, if you'll excuse the pun. It always made sense to live in dull climates, but there are such wonderful pickings in Bangkok, Rio, Montevideo...' The doctor recited the cities the way a gourmet would list spices.

'Great,' said Watson. 'You'll be able to shit on an exotic beach and bury it in the sand.'

'Get to the point,' said Quist. 'You want someone killed? From your recent track record, I wouldn't think you'd need any help.'

Fran strolled close to the cell. 'It's time you understood about the Elite and our organization in Britain. We began forming groups to assist one another long ago; developing practises to safeguard our secrecy. We select superfluous prey that won't be missed - prostitutes, homeless and other dregs - but they're never allowed to transform and we don't leave drained corpses with wounds. Prey is disposed of in furnaces. The smaller the society, the easier the anonymity.'

'Humans join occasionally,' said Strand. 'Wealthy individuals are chosen and those whose skills can assist the Elite. A nice system, wouldn't you agree? We keep a low profile, regulate our numbers, and hardly ever bother the normal people.'

'No, just the *dregs*,' said Quist, contemptuously. 'Why are you telling us this?'

Strand drew on his cigarette. 'Someone named Lucius Silva arrived in Manchester after the war and wormed his way into our society.'

'He's ancient,' said Zucco. 'Older and supposedly wiser than any other Elite. Everyone listened to him like a guru.'

'He began shaping our people and creating a hierarchy,' continued Strand. 'Silva is now President, controlling a committee of twenty leaders from around the north of Britain who, in turn, control the members in their regions. Laws were introduced to theoretically protect us, the changes occurring over years as his power intensified. The rules suffocate, but deviation is punishable by execution.'

'In the old days we could hunt any time,' said Fran, angrily. 'We used common sense when choosing prey. Now applications have to be sanctioned by area controllers, who take responsibility for blunders. If anyone is spotted–a British big cat sighting–they're executed. It's ridiculous!'

'Red tape.' Quist tutted. 'Who needs it?'

'*We* don't.' Fran gave a curt smile. 'Unfortunately, because he rules by terror, most of the Elite are loyal to our President.'

'Most? Ah, I see. We're talking revolution.'

Strand nodded. 'Fran was told to research eye protection, but she experimented further. Silva knows nothing of the Solstice and our daylight abilities. It's time to rid ourselves of his ludicrous regulations and begin afresh.'

'So this is who you want killed?'

'At tonight's Winter Solstice meeting,' said Strand. 'Solstice– appropriate, don't you think? When the Committee see the sunscreen, we'll be hailed as the greatest benefactors of all time.'

'And then you'll slaughter Silva,' said Fran. 'It should be a night to remember.'

'What the fuck?' gasped Watson. 'Am I thicker than pigshit, or am I missing something?' He jerked a thumb at Quist. 'You want *this* bloke to assassinate your President, the most powerful big cat in Britain?'

'That's right.' Strand winked at the detective. 'He's one of the few *blokes* who can carry it off.'

'And here you are, Bernard,' said Fran. 'Right on time for the assassination, as we planned. I mesmerised that debt collector and gave him the fiancé story to arouse your interest. I chose him because he worked in the same building; Larry mentioned him. He also told us of your curiosity.'

'Did he indeed?' said Quist. 'Then you ordered Selden to commit suicide and the badges were planted to draw me to Creeper's address.'

'My address.' The girl nodded. 'It was a better hideout for me than the hotel we'd originally chosen. I left one of his badges on the railway, knowing you'd go there after listening to Selden, and Larry left one by the Wolds river. We knew you'd speak to the Lamberley pub landlord and trace the bikers. I also *spoke* to the landlord after Lisa's death and looked lovingly into his eyes. He now swears that I was there with them at the time she died.'

'Who was she hiding from?' asked a bemused Rex.

'Their President,' said Quist. 'I don't think he'd be pleased with Lisa's bloodless corpse being left to become Ubasteri.'

'That's right,' said Strand. 'We knew Silva would send a security team to dispose of the corpse and deal with Fran. I took charge to leave him with less protection. I sent two of his guards into your cottage knowing what would happen to them...'

'And shot the others and planted the Sunnyvale card,' broke in Quist.

'Correct. We left Lisa Mirren's corpse to reduce Silva's security, but also to let you see her. Larry told us you keep a low profile, but if you discovered Ubasteri were involved in the murders, your sense of responsibility would take over. After you read the police reports, I knew you'd go to the morgue. I delayed my visit and allowed you to find her first.'

'How could you know I'd read...'

'Larry never took that Oxford train, as you've doubtless guessed. He bugged your car and followed you in Doctor Zucco's BMW listening on the receiver. We knew you'd traced its registration. We knew you were going to the railway, to Lamberley, to the Clifton party, and the morgue. We always knew what you were up to.'

'I found the transponder,' said Quist. 'It never occurred to me to look for listening devices too.'

'After you met Fran at Creeper's house,' continued Strand, 'she was to kill the bikers and rush to you for protection. This *damsel in distress* would convince you she'd escaped an Ubasteri attack and persuade you to bring her here to her *brother*.'

'But Rex found me first,' said Fran.

'You turned up with those cat things.' Rex peered at Strand. 'How did you know I'd be there with her?'

'I didn't,' said Strand. 'I had to speak with Fran before she left and I told the bodyguards Gillette had given me the address as one of her possible hideouts. I was surprised to see your Ferrari outside. I knew who you were, of course. We checked your registration when Larry saw you in Lamberley.'

'But you attacked us,' said Rex.

'Improvisation. Silva's guards spotted Fran and rushed to help me. I turned it to my advantage. When she had you believe we killed the bikers, I played along and allowed your escape. You were acquainted with Bernard and I knew you'd make a good hostage.'

'You thought you were taking *me* to Manchester,' said Fran. 'In reality *I* was taking *you*. We saw that Amy also had hostage potential. You didn't save her today, Bernard. She was chased to frighten her and bring you closer together.'

'All this to get me here and provide you with hostages?' Quist shook his head. 'Why do you want an outsider to kill this President?'

'We can't get near him,' said Strand. 'Silva knows assassination is possible and seals himself in a fortress on Salford Quays surrounded by guards. Metal detectors make it impossible to get weapons inside, and every hi-tech device is incorporated into the building's defences. Automatic gun pods with silver bullets cover the corridors and stairways. They operate when they sense movement and heat...'

Quist glanced up as Larry trudged resignedly down the steps. 'Why?' he gasped. 'Why have you been helping them, for God's sake?'

'I'm so sorry, Bernie.' The old man grimaced apologetically. 'But they're the ones helping me.'

'Silva can sense other Elite,' said Zucco. 'Your eyes aren't green like ours and he'll allow you close. He wears Kevlar armour under his clothing, so I suggest you go for his head...'

'Forget it,' snarled Quist, his eyes still on the miserable-looking Larry. 'I won't help your schemes.'

'You're forgetting our hostages,' said Fran. 'And you still don't know why my research staff were killed. We needed a few murders to get the police searching for a crazed killer.'

'That's *you*,' said Strand. 'When you left this afternoon, Larry and I planted a few things in your house: Lisa's binoculars, Diane's bracelet, Becca's bag, Gillette's wristwatch and some motorcycle badges.'

'I might have alibis.' Quist glared at Larry. 'I was in a cell when the bikers were killed.'

Strand walked close to the bars. 'I roughed up a hospital porter last night, knowing he'd call the police. I was responsible for your arrest. I knew they couldn't hold you, but I wanted to get the police interested in you. They're not interested enough to search your cottage, but a phone call would remedy that. Even if my planted evidence doesn't stick, they'll still investigate and that wouldn't do at all, would it?' Strand reached in his pocket and held out a wallet. 'Believe me, it will be a thorough investigation.'

Quist read the warrant card inside. 'Detective Constable Gregson.'

'Dead police officers are far more provocative than binoculars and bracelets. Larry killed Gregson outside Doctor Clarkson's and what's left of him is in your bathtub.'

'That was you?' stammered Amy, staring at Larry. 'But what I saw...'

'Silva has no idea who you are,' said Strand. 'You'll be allowed close at the meeting. It will be simple.'

Quist visibly wilted. 'Why, Larry?' he whispered. 'You told them everything about me. Why?'

'I'm sorry, Bernie.' The old man turned away, unable to meet his eyes. 'Just do what they ask and it'll soon be over. Killing Silva will be easy for you.'

Rex sucked hard on his trembling cigarette. As far as Strand was aware, the man next to Quist was an SAS killer and ideal for such a dangerous mission. He decided not to point this out.

'We bumped into your friend Larry in October.' Fran draped an arm around the old man's waist and kissed his cheek. He squirmed, uncomfortable with the embrace. 'When I found it was possible to produce a sunscreen, Matthew and I visited another member of our group who despises the President, Bob Quarry in Glasgow. We spent days planning how to kill Silva, before fate stepped in. Matthew and I were hunting junkies one evening in the old part of town.'

'Talk about luck,' said Strand. 'Larry was stalking the same addict.'

'*What*?' Watson turned to Quist, confused. 'But he can't be Ubasteri, Guv. His eyes are brown and I've seen him in daylight before they invented that cream.'

Strand ignored him. 'We wanted Larry for the assassination, but he's too old and slow.'

'So he suggested me instead,' muttered Quist.

'That's right. We met again last week in Glasgow to finalise plans and supply the tracking and bugging devices.'

Watson looked Quist up and down. 'I've asked if I'm missing something,' he said, gaping at the shapeshifters. 'You're staking everything on Cyrano killing the top cat in a fortress with armed guards? First you pick a geriatric and now *him*. Do you cat people use psychiatrists? Some practise in the evenings, you know?'

Strand grinned. 'He doesn't have much confidence, does he, Bernard?' He checked his watch. 'The meeting begins at seven, so Fran and I will leave now with Doctor Clarkson and Captain Grant. I need time to show the sunscreen to the Committee. Doctor Zucco will follow in thirty minutes with you. He'll explain on the way what you're to do.'

'You're taking these two.' Quist glanced at the teenager. 'What about Watson?'

'Never put all your hostages in one basket.' Strand unlocked the cell. 'No, he stays here.'

'Get to the wall,' snapped Zucco. He trained his gun on Quist and nodded to Rex and Amy. 'You two, out!'

'Cheerio for now, Bernard.' Fran ushered them up the stairs. 'Make sure you guard him, Jordan.'

Larry shook his head. 'Bernie can't get out.' He turned uneasily from the detective's icy stare and watched Zucco lock the cage. 'I tried the bars earlier and I couldn't move them.'

'Fuck me! There's a surprise,' murmured Watson. 'Seventy-odd and he can't bend steel.'

Quist smiled tightly as Larry shot him a rueful glance.

* * * *

Chapter 59

Silva stood at one of his penthouse windows. He held a small terrier in his arms, stroking the terrified animal and watching the blizzard swirl above the converted warehouses on Salford Quays. He turned from the snowstorm to see his bodyguard Galeen admitting Tayman into the lower level of the enormous lounge. The Committee Executive wore a charcoal suit, his bald head gleaming as he glanced around, searching for the President amongst the vegetation and rocks.

'Frederick.' Silva tossed the dog into the snake pit. 'Punctual as ever.'

'Of course, Sir.' Tayman rushed past the lily pond and up the steps to the elevated control level. 'I'm never late for meetings, especially if it concerns something as important as...' The words faltered as he reached the pit where the king cobras Kali and Shiva wrestled with their supper.

'Important *as*?' prompted Silva.

'As I mentioned on the phone, I believe the Vice-President's loyalty is in serious question.'

'Perhaps you'd like to tell me about it?'

Like to? Tayman stopped himself laughing out loud. 'Strand and Stapleton have been spending time at Zucco's asylum and with Quarry in Glasgow. Something is going on between them.'

'Yes I know.'

'You do?' Tayman sagged. 'I suspected they were planning something, and for the past month, I've had the hospital and Quarry's house watched around the clock. Strand has...'

'Around the clock? How was that possible?'

'I used a private agency. They watched Sunnyvale from a nearby wood and...'

'Humans?'

'It was the only way during daylight and they can be disposed of afterwards.' Tayman smiled. 'They rang this afternoon when Stapleton turned up at the asylum in a Ferrari. That's when I called you. They rang again later to let me know Strand had arrived too.'

Silva fixed Tayman with his cold green stare. 'How did your investigators recognise the visitors?'

'Er, pictures.'

'Not only have you had humans watching the Elite, but you supplied photographs for identification? All this was without authorisation, wasn't it?'

'It was for the good of the society.' Tayman gave a nervous twitch. 'If my methods displease you, I beg forgiveness, but they worked. Strand was ordered to kill Stapleton and he failed. He obviously knows where she is, but he's done nothing. They're plotting something and I think we'd better look into it fast.'

Silva turned to stare through the window. 'How old do you suppose I am, Frederick?'

'Er…' Tayman plumped for an enigmatic answer. 'Older than any of us, Sir.'

'Older than you could possibly imagine. Just as this snow covers Raven's Wharf, a deadly ash once covered Pompeii. I watched as it spewed from Vesuvius.'

'Ah! Getting on quite a bit then?'

'And tell me...' Silva strolled to a control panel. 'How do you suppose I've managed to exist for so long?'

Tayman looked blank. *It probably had little to do with monitoring feline cholesterol and drinking low-fat blood.*

'By anticipation and constantly being several steps ahead.' The President spoke into an intercom. 'Send her in, Galeen, then bring the item I requested.'

A girl entered the lower lounge, the golden light from the fire flickering on her red hair, white sweater, and leather mini skirt.

'Frederick, I'd like you to meet Sarah Aldridge.' Silva watched her stroll by the cat statue of Bast to mount the steps. 'Or Nicole Patterson, as she's been known for the past week. Sarah has been working at Stapleton's laboratory since the research director's secretary met with an accident.'

'Aldridge?' Tayman twitched as Sarah sat on an ornamental boulder and crossed her legs. 'She's one of those missing Scottish secretaries; I recognise her from the photos.'

Silva nodded. 'I was aware Sharp was killing without permission, and my security staff were watching him long before you became suspicious. I had them bring me an office girl from Glasgow while they were observing his movements.'

'You knew about Sharp?'

'I've known about every item of information you've ever brought to me. Stapleton was taking too long with her experiments and she and Strand were spending too much time with Zucco and Quarry. I knew there was a conspiracy. Gillette, the Research Director at Stapleton's company, was conducting the work for her, so I knew he'd have answers.'

'So you had this girl abducted to place in there?'

'That's right. I saw to it that Gillette's secretary met with an accident and when the agency sent Nicole Patterson, she was intercepted and replaced.'

Tayman shook his head. 'How could you know who'd be sent?'

'Ah, the wonders of modern technology. Accessing Gillette's personal terminal was impossible, but it was simple enough to hack the company computer to discover which secretarial agency they used. The agency computer was then accessed, the real Nicole was disposed of and Sarah went in her place.'

'Is she Elite?'

'I am now.' Sarah's green eyes sparkled and she pulled down her neckline. The cat bite, covered by the turtleneck sweater over the past week, had vanished. 'Lucius saw to it a short while ago.'

'Transforming her fully was impossible earlier.' Silva stroked Sarah's hair. 'I needed her to watch Gillette by day and report what he and Stapleton were up to. Gillette told her everything after she mesmerised him and my suspicions were correct. Plotting *has* been going on, Frederick. Rather subversive plotting.'

'Really?' Tayman brightened.

Silva smiled. 'According to her reports, Stapleton was making no progress, but that was a lie. Not only has she completed the eye droplets, but a barrier sunscreen has been developed and apparently it works. Stapleton is able to walk in sunlight.'

'What?' Tayman twitched. 'Are you joking?'

'Me? Joking?' Silva peered curiously at him. 'Was that a serious question?'

The stunned Executive pulled his thoughts together. 'You say they're plotting against you?'

'Gillette didn't know much about that. Apparently they mean to replace me with Strand, although I can't imagine how they hope to accomplish it. That's why I let him talk me into his heading the York operation; I wanted to see where his schemes would lead. They'll probably attempt their coup at tonight's meeting. Quarry and Zucco are in this too, and I expect they'll try to sway the rest with this sunscreen.' Silva's eyes cut into Tayman like emerald lasers. 'Speaking of withholding information, I believe one of your people has disappeared: your Leeds manager, Dreyer?'

'He'll turn up. That's why I didn't trouble you, Sir.'

'He's dead. His ashes were found by the police. Why didn't you report his disappearance?'

'*Dead*?' Tayman twitched. 'I didn't know. Actually, er, I was going to mention it tonight. Like I say, I didn't want to bother...' The words faltered and the twitching increased. This wasn't going quite how he'd expected and things needed an upward turn. 'I almost forgot. The new glass filtration system is ready.'

'Now that Doctor Stapleton has developed a sunscreen, I don't think that matters. Such a pity she chose to side against me.' Silva looked over the Executive's shoulder. 'Ah, there you are at last.'

Tayman hadn't heard anyone enter, but three security personnel were silently climbing the steps from the lower level. On the intercom, Galeen had been told to bring something. It was a chainsaw.

275

Silva signalled to Sarah, who slipped down from the boulder. 'In light of this subversive activity, I've decided upon a purge,' he said. 'Time to restructure our society and dispose of the undesirables and dead wood.'

'Er, right,' said Tayman. 'Er, why has he got that chainsaw?'

'It's the ideal tool for removing dead wood.'

The two empty-handed guards snatched Tayman and bent him facedown over the boulder. Galeen revved the saw, drowning the shapeshifter's scuffling and whimpering.

'Time for a society cleanse.' The President raised his voice over the mechanical roar. 'You've been bending the rules, Frederick, and you'd stop at nothing to climb the hierarchical ladder. The position of Vice-President has always been your ambition, hasn't it?'

'Er, with respect...' stammered Tayman, 'I think this is a bad idea. If you let me...'

'You already had that annoying twitch when you became Elite.' Silva slipped an arm around Sarah and nodded to the bodyguard. 'Galeen has a cure for it.'

The saw hovered over Tayman's neck before ripping agonisingly into his spine and slicing through the flesh to spark on the rock below. Galeen killed the motor, thuds filling the silence as the bald head bounced down the steps.

Silva smiled with satisfaction. 'You were always too pushy for my liking, Frederick. Even with promotion, you still wouldn't have been content, would you?'

Galeen didn't know whether the President expected an answer, but if so, he was disappointed. He snapped to attention as Silva turned to him.

'Go to Zucco's hospital and bring Strand and Stapleton here. I don't wish to see Zucco, Atwill, or Houghton again. Do I make myself clear?'

'Yes, Sir.' The bodyguard watched as Tayman's head melted to sludge like raspberry ice-cream in a frying pan. 'Absolutely, Sir.'

* * * *

Chapter 60

Rex sat in the front of the van between Atwill and Strand, staring miserably at the snow as they motored through Manchester. The blizzard had little effect on the weekend crowds. The pavements and bars were bright and alive with Christmas revellers and the streets were filled with traffic. The *exciting detective stuff* had turned out different to what Rex had originally envisaged in Wiltshire. The meeting with his brother seemed a lifetime ago, and although he couldn't recall his expectations, he was pretty sure they didn't include being the hostage of bloodsucking cats. This had to rate as his shittiest Christmas ever.

Amy sat in the rear of the van and gave a sullen nod as he twisted to check on her. Fran sat beside her and blew him a kiss. He glowered and turned away.

Strand twiddled at the radio, smiling with approval as Slade's *Merry Christmas Everybody* poured from the speakers. 'Lovely, isn't it?' He leant forward, peering up at the snowfall. 'Shall we take a toboggan up on the moors when this is over?'

Rex didn't answer.

'Another couple of miles to Salford Quays and the fun begins.' Strand turned up the music and tugged a curtain across the back of the seat to conceal Amy. 'For once I'm looking forward to the meeting. These gatherings are usually so tedious.' He grinned at his silent prisoner. 'I can tell you the good news now. I didn't say anything earlier. I didn't want Clarkson or the black kid getting jealous.'

'Good news?'

'Your future, Captain Grant. We've chosen you to be Elite. Fran will see to it after tonight's takeover.'

Rex's jaw fell into the footwell. '*What?*'

'You'll be an ideal addition. Wealthy and a special forces background. Just the kind of…'

'Hang on, please. If it's money you want, you can have it

without...'

'We want your money *and* you.'

'But, Jesus...' Rex laughed manically. 'I don't want to be a fucking cat.'

'You'd turn down immortality? Then perhaps it's just as well that I'm not giving you a choice.'

'Look, I don't know why, but I made up that SAS stuff to impress people. Yes, my family are rich, but I'm no Captain. After Christmas, I'll be supervising some shitty building site.'

'The housing company is another reason we chose you. A few family accidents and you'll be the sole owner. Fran told me all about you, so it's pointless lying. You're exactly what we need, so get used to it.'

'But...'

'I said get used to it!'

'And what about Amy?'

'Doctor Clarkson has nothing to offer. It's too late for dinner, so we'll have to call her supper.'

'You bastard!'

'You've formed an attachment?' Strand sneered. 'Those human feelings won't last and soon you'll be able to have any woman you want. With our feline powers you can...'

'I don't do so badly now, pal.' Rex cringed, realising that he was bragging about his sexual expertise to a supernatural cat. 'You don't have to kill Amy.'

'Of course we do. She knows everything, just like that mouthy brat back there.'

'You're going to kill Watson too? After Quist assassinates Silva...'

'Ah, Bernard is somewhat different. Anyhow, don't worry about Amy. You can have Fran.'

'I thought she was your... *girlfriend*.'

Strand chuckled. 'Emotional relationships don't rank highly with the Elite. Once you're with us, you can screw her any time. She's

278

very good, as you already know.'

'Thanks,' croaked Rex, a mental picture forming of Fran feeding on a torn corpse, her furry cat body plastered in crimson slime. 'Yeah, thanks a lot.'

* * * *

Chapter 61

Watson watched, horrified, as Zucco jammed the Uzi silencer through the bars of the next cell. He blasted the inmate and the stench of putrefaction filled the cellar.

'Sorry about the smell,' mocked the doctor. 'We no longer need our guinea pigs.'

Whenever Zucco looked at him, Watson got the distinct impression he wasn't seeing a cool, black youth, but a mouse. 'It stank pretty bad in here before you started shooting,' he muttered. 'Maybe your litter tray's full.'

'Shut it!' snarled Zucco. 'Two hostages are quite sufficient and I have an excellent cure for negro insolence. An agonising remedy I discovered in the old days with my slaves.'

'Leave him alone.' Larry turned hesitantly to the teenager. 'Look, I know how you must be feeling and I'm sorry, but it had to be this way.'

'Thanks for the concern.' Watson flopped against the rear of the cell in a miserable heap. 'And bollocks!'

'So what's the story?' said Quist. 'I thought we were friends.'

'We *are* friends, Bernie.' Larry averted his eyes, his expression the sort of thing seen on dogs that have chewed slippers. 'If there'd been any other option...' He ran a weary hand through his hair. 'I had to tell them about you. They wanted me to kill Silva, but I knew I couldn't.'

'The manager of Brightshield Glazing was no problem for you. He was younger than their President too.'

'Silva is powerful and he has a fortress with guards. His whole environment is set up to thwart assassinations. I know my limitations, Bernie. I'm too old and slow for that. You're the only one I know who's capable. I hate this hostage business, but it had to be this way. I knew you wouldn't help them willingly.'

'But why are *you* helping them?'

'We have a deal.' Larry took a deep breath. 'Strand will soon be the new President and I have refuge within his society.'

'What?' Quist's face fell. 'Are you mad?'

'I told you the other night that I was tired of it all. I'm not like you; I never have been. I don't fit in with this modern world. I'll be better off with the Ubasteri.'

'*I* fit. In the past, you've managed too. You can't give in now. You told me the urges had passed.'

'I lied. You've always been better at it; younger and more adaptable.' Larry shook his head sadly. 'No, I've made up my mind.'

'But you can't join Strand. You've tried before. The yoga, the vegan diet and...'

'And they all failed. Oh, they worked for a while, but the urges always returned. I knew how you felt, so I told you I didn't need to bother with special diets due to my age. That's why I made the regular trips to Scotland.'

'For the deer. Yes, I suspected.'

'Not just deer. There are plenty of junkies in Glasgow and Edinburgh.'

'Oh, Larry.'

Doctor Zucco laughed. 'Why do *you* care about junkies? They're just...'

'Because I'm human,' shouted Quist. 'That's why I care.'

'But that's the thing,' said Larry, quietly. 'You're *not*, are you, Bernie?'

'Yes I am. Inside I always will be.'

Larry closed his eyes. 'Please try to understand, I've had enough of the secrecy and upheavals every time we disappear. With Strand it'll be different. In his society I can kill whenever I feel like it.'

Quist lashed the bars. 'You don't have to kill people.'

'Yes I do,' said Larry quietly. 'We were meant to kill.'

'No! You can...'

'Bury my instincts like you? I've tried and it doesn't work for me. Don't you see, Bernie? We're not the same. I *want* to kill people.'

'Er, I wonder if I could butt in?' questioned a voice behind Quist.

The detective turned to Watson.

'Thanks. Now would you please tell me just what the *fuck* you're talking about?'

Zucco leered, his green eyes twinkling. 'He doesn't know, does he?'

'Guv?' The youth climbed warily to his feet. 'What does he mean?'

Red lights flashed on the desk control panel. Zucco leapt to the CCTV switches and brought up the lobby reception on the monitor screen. Houghton the head of hospital security was speaking to a large visitor.

'Damn!' hissed Zucco. 'Why is Galeen here?'

'What's happening?' demanded Larry. 'Why did your man press the silent alarm?'

'Galeen is in charge of Silva's bodyguards. Let's turn up the volume and hear what they're saying.'

He didn't get chance. The pair froze as Galeen drew a silenced gun and fired twice into Houghton's heart.

'Silva knows!' Zucco snatched the Uzi and headed for the stairs. 'He must know something. Come on.'

'What about Bernie?' Larry turned anxiously to the cell. 'We can't leave these two here.'

'Never mind them. We have to get rid of Galeen and warn Strand.'

'But if anything happens to us, these two will be...'

'Move yourself,' rasped Zucco. 'We don't have time for this. You made a choice and you're with us now.'

Larry hesitated, then followed, pausing briefly to give the cell inmates an apprehensive look from the top of the steps.

Quist darted to the front of the cage as the cellar door closed. 'Move!' He pushed his assistant aside and grabbed the bars.

'I don't believe it.' Watson's eyes widened as Quist pulled.

'For a moment, it looked like they were moving.'

'They were.' Quist stepped back panting. 'But I don't have the strength to break them.'

'Er, right.' This didn't exactly stun Watson.

'Okay, there's no other way.' Smiling uneasily, Quist slipped off his coat and dropped his wristwatch and signet ring into a pocket. 'I'm going to get us out, but I should warn you, you won't like this.'

'Shit!' The youth gaped at the CCTV screen on the desk, oblivious to the acute drop in temperature. 'There's another big bloke arrived in the lobby with a machine gun.'

The sound of tearing cloth behind Watson accompanied the horrific crackle of twisting bones. The teenager turned to find that Quist had vanished. The gigantic black wolf that stood in his place shrugged apologetically and gave a guilty, lopsided grin.

* * * *

Chapter 62

Larry hurried behind Zucco, following him to the security door that separated the doctor's private quarters from the hospital. 'You must know how your President's bodyguards operate,' he said. Tugging off his jacket, he glanced back towards the cellar. *What the hell was he thinking of, leaving Bernie and Watson down there?* 'Do you suppose Galeen's alone?'

'I doubt it.' Zucco checked his gun and listened with his ear to the metal door. 'Silva will have sent at least two. This will be risky, but his security are pretty dumb and we have the advantage of surprise.'

The room grew icy as Larry's face extended noisily into a bushy lupine muzzle, the teeth falling from his mouth and turning to dust, forced out by sprouting yellow fangs. He grew in height, shoulders widening and shirt bursting, to reveal an expanding torso of tatty white fur. The pale creature looked ancient. It wasn't often that a wolf appeared to need a Zimmer frame, and if Larry had been in a zoo, the RSPCA would have sadly insisted he be put to sleep.

'Okay.' Zucco pressed his ear to the door again, his breath clouding on the air. 'Are you ready?'

The monster nodded, red eyes glinting.

'Right, we rush out together and take Galeen off-guard. I shoot him and you pounce on any other Elite who may be there.'

The wolf looked again at the cellar.

'Forget your friends,' snarled Zucco. 'Get your mind on this.' He tapped in the code, raising his pistol as the door slid open. 'Ready?'

As plans went, this could have been better. The doctor realised it the moment silenced gunfire tore through his side to liquefy his heart and blow the scarlet mess out through his armpit. A silver bullet smashed Larry's shoulder. Shrieking, he hit the emergency door-close button and leapt back behind the falling corpse. Whoever shot Zucco had been waiting to the right of the door and Larry had glimpsed a second gunman near the reception desk. White-hot silver pain fried the wounded arm, sizzling in agonising ripples across his shaggy back.

This was insanity. How could he possibly have left Bernie and Watson trapped in the basement? He had to get them out of that cage right now.

Turning back to the cellar, Larry stiffened to see the large figure at the hall window and the gun levelled on his face. Silva had sent *three* guards.

'I'm so sorry, Bernie,' he whispered.

The window shattered and silver smashed into his skull to replace the remorse.

* * * *

'Will you come down,' begged Quist, impatiently. 'I won't hurt you.'

'Fuck off!' Watson clung to the bars in a shaking ball at ceiling height.

'I look unusual, but it's still me. Come on, we don't have much time.'

The teenager gaped at the huge black monster below. The wolves he'd seen in the past, on TV and in zoos, reminded him of big husky dogs, but this thing wasn't like that at all. This vicious-looking bastard should have been wearing a nightcap and sitting in the bed of Little Red Riding Hood's granny. If Quist's nose had seemed large before, it was enormous now, his face resembling a furry alligator. Pointed ears sprouted either side and smouldering amber eyes gazed up at Watson.

'We have to get out,' said Quist. 'Zucco or those gunmen could appear at any moment.'

'What's happened?' whined Watson. Something was moving behind Quist and he realised it was a tail. 'What the fuckin' hell have you done?'

'I've turned myself into a wolf.'

'Oh... my... God!'

The youth lost his grip and fell. Hairy paws caught him and gently set him down, where he backed away jerkily, glued his spine to the wall and stared up. He had to stare up; Quist had grown six inches.

'I knew how you'd react,' said the wolf, 'but it was the only way.' Paws crackled as taloned fingers sprouted. 'In this form, I have greater strength. Larry couldn't move these bars, but I'm younger and stronger.' He grabbed the metal and heaved.

'Yeah,' droned Watson in monotone. 'Younger and stronger.'

Quist strained, forming an opening at waist height. 'Come on,' he grunted, squeezing through. 'And don't forget my coat. I'm naked, so I'll need it when I change back.'

Watson gawped as if in a dream.

'Pick up the coat and get out here - now.'

Slowly lifting the leather overcoat, Watson slipped a leg through the gap.

'You have to snap out of this.' Quist grabbed his arm to help, saw the petrified reaction and let go. 'I don't want to slap your face; in this form I'd take your head off.' He wagged his tail and grinned to show it was a joke. The glowing yellow eyes and razor fangs didn't help.

'You're a werewolf!' whispered Watson.

'There's just no fooling you today.'

'You're a genuine, real-life fuckin' werewolf!' He gulped; unwise and painful when the mouth feels desiccated. 'That's why Strand wanted you? They picked you to kill their President because you're a werewolf?'

'Yes, but we have to get out. That door at the end of the cellar looks like it leads into the grounds. Where are my car keys?'

'I've been working for a werewolf?' Watson poked gingerly at his furry chest and snatched his hand away. 'That's what you were talking about with Larry? He's a werewolf too? That's what Amy saw in the fog–the glowing eyes and fangs. It wasn't a panther. It was Larry.'

'The keys? Where are they?'

'Incredible!' Watson stared for several seconds and shook his head. 'Yeah, whatever. After people turning into fuckin' cats, I don't know why this shit should surprise me one bit. Your so-called mate took the car keys when he brought us in.'

'Damn!' Quist turned to the CCTV screen on the desk and flicked through the camera controls with a clawed finger. 'We'd better see what's happening upstairs before we run for it. Those visitors could be anywhere and they looked pretty dangerous.'

'You should take a look at *yourself.*' Trembling, Watson tore his eyes from the creature to watch the changing screens. Rooms and corridors appeared and disappeared. 'Why do you think they shot the guy on reception?'

'I presume this Silva character has found out about the takeover bid and intends to stamp it out. Zucco said the first caller was head of Silva's security.' Galeen appeared onscreen in the lounge. 'Ah, there he is. I imagine the second one is a bodyguard too. And look, there's a third outside.' Quist found the lobby camera and gestured to a decomposing puddle. 'Mmmh! Speaking of Zucco...'

'Yeah, I recognise the suit.' Watson turned away queasily and spotted Amy's mobile and the small pile of items where Rex had emptied his pockets on the desk. 'Hey, talk about luck!' Grabbing the phone, he jingled the Ferrari keys under the wolf's snout.

'Excellent!' growled Quist. 'If we leave by this cellar door...' Larry appeared onscreen, his naked corpse lying in the hall. 'Oh...'

'Ah!' Watson saw the hole in the old man's head. 'Is he dead?'

'Was that some attempt at a joke?'

'Hey, it's only been two minutes since I found out that werewolves actually exist. I don't know anything about them or what kills them.'

'Silver. According to Strand, the security squad use silver bullets in their...'

Not only did Quist possess increased strength in his lupine form, but every sense was augmented. He heard the door handle turning at the top of the cellar staircase, snatched a silenced pistol from the desk and fired. Seeing a giant wolf on two legs was the bodyguard's first surprise. A silver bullet in the heart was the second. He rolled down the steps, his Uzi clattering at Watson's feet.

'Pick it up,' said Quist.

'*Fuck*! You killed him, Guv.'

'Well spotted. Take his gun.'

'I don't want anything to do with machine guns. I don't intend...'

The wolf bared its teeth. 'Pick it up!'

Watson picked it up.

'And grab my coat. We need to move fast before anyone else comes.' Frisking the dead bodyguard, Quist found three UZI magazines. He glanced at the CCTV screen before following the youth to the door by the cellar hatch. 'Goodbye, Larry,' he mumbled.

'I've tried it,' said Watson, his spinning mind still attempting to come to terms with the furry monster. 'It's locked.'

'Take these and I'll try.' Handing him the spare ammunition, the huge wolf rammed its talons into the jamb and tore the door from its frame.

'Ah! Watson nodded. 'It looks like you have a knack.'

Quist snatched the UZI, checked the silencer and safety catch, then bounded up the steps into the blizzard. He crouched low, eyes darting around the snowy gardens. The driveway gates had been left open by the hit squad, and beckoning Watson, he moved cautiously towards the corner of the hospital. The youth scurried out, sheltered behind Quist's shaggy back and followed through the trees, gulping uncomfortably to see the bizarre paw-marks in the snow and the furry testicles beneath the creature's tail. The wolf halted abruptly, dragged him behind a large tree, and lifted its snout to sniff. Watson had seen dogs act this way when they picked up a scent.

'Keep still,' growled the wolf. 'I can smell a cat around this corner.'

Springing into the tree branches, Quist climbed onto a

horizontal bough that extended beyond the hospital frontage, moving silently along until the patrolling bodyguard came into view. Not the most intelligent individuals, Silva's security expected targets to be at ground level, and even when the scent of blood told him to look up, Quist had time to fire and leap down beside the Ferrari before the dead creature hit the snow.

'Nice shot,' whispered Watson, running from the bushes.

'Get behind the wheel,' hissed Quist.

'What about me having no driving license?'

'Get in and don't be sarcastic.'

Watson threw Quist's coat into the footwell, gunned the engine, and watched fearfully as the monster clambered awkwardly in, its furry bulk filling the car.

'Why are we waiting?' The wolf squeezed its head under the low roof. 'The engine will have alerted the gunman in the house. Hanging about is a bad idea.'

Kicking open the front door, Galeen raced out levelling a pistol.

'Now would be a good time,' pointed out Quist.

Whimpering, Watson stamped the accelerator, covering the bodyguard in snow and gravel as the Ferrari screeched away.

* * * *

Chapter 63

Doctor Atwill brought the van to a halt at the front of the SSS building on Salford Quays. Rex grunted as Strand dragged him out with a grip that rivalled a bench vice.

'Here we are,' said Strand. 'Silver Security Systems.'

The other offices in this deserted business park had closed for the evening. Rex waited until his captor turned to the huge warehouse, before glancing along the snow-covered street. The brightly-lit modern waterfront they'd just driven through, with its busy theatres and restaurants, lay just around the corner.

'You're stupid even to think of running.' Strand gestured to Atwill. 'You wouldn't get twenty feet before he changed to feline form and caught you.'

Atwill nodded. 'Then I'd bite off a kneecap to prevent you trying again.'

Gulping, Rex watched Fran climb out with Amy. 'Are you okay?'

'Oh yeah,' muttered Amy. 'Just wonderful!'

Fran smoothed out her short dress and eyed the doctor. Amy was petrified, but hid it well. Fear before slaughter tainted the meat of most creatures, but humans were different. The greater the terror, the better the taste. Perhaps it was the adrenaline, but fright left the blood so much sweeter.

'For goodness sake, smile,' said Fran, giggling. 'Cheer up, Amy. It might never happen.'

'Oh, I think it probably will,' said Strand. He clasped a pair of shiny handcuffs on Fran's wrists. 'Those should pass for silver and you'll certainly pass for my prisoner.' He took her arm and pushed Rex across the snowy lawn to the entrance porch. 'Come along now. Let's not keep Lucius waiting.'

'Good evening, Sir.' Costigan, one of the security team, admitted them into the lobby. 'I wasn't informed you'd be bringing Doctor Stapleton.' He ran an eye over Amy and Rex. 'And who are they?'

'They're here to be questioned by the President.' Strand brushed snowflakes from his suit. 'Doctor Zucco will be arriving soon with a third human.'

'Yes, Sir.' The guard watched as they walked into the lift, waiting until the doors had closed before lifting the phone.

Silva had just finished speaking to Galeen on the external line when the lobby light flashed. 'Yes?' he said.

'Strand and Atwill are here,' said Costigan. 'With Stapleton and two humans.'

'Yes, Galeen said they must have left the asylum before he arrived.'

'Strand says Zucco will be following.'

'He's mistaken,' said the President.

* * * *

The lift arrived at the fourth floor, opening onto a wide passage where Holland and Boam, two of Silva's security squad, waited by the conference room. Rex looked around. The black-suited guards with their Uzis, the ceiling hi-tech robo-sentries and the steel elevator all combined to give him a feeling of Deja Vu. This could be a scene from a Bond movie, a series of films he'd studied in preparation for his Marines training. Silva's guards turned, eyes blazing green and smiles exposing cat fangs, and the 007 illusion instantly vanished.

'After you.' Strand pushed Rex and lowered his voice to speak with Atwill. 'Wait out here. You know what to do when Zucco and Quist arrive.'

Atwill hung back as the guards opened the chamber. Rex glanced at their silenced Uzis–obviously standard pussy issue–and shuddered to see the congregation of shapeshifters staring malevolently from the circular table.

'Ah, Doctor Stapleton.' The President eyed her handcuffs with unguarded amusement. 'Are you aware that your progress report on the eye droplets is overdue?'

Fran and Strand exchanged looks. *He was supposed to be surprised at her appearance.*

'You've brought friends, Matthew.' Silva smiled courteously at Amy and Rex. 'Well no need to stand. Three chairs are spare, although they require dusting.'

Strand turned to the seats where Tayman, Quarry and Peel always sat, and the piles of crimson ash on the leather.

* * * *

Holland and Boam watched quietly as Atwill paced the corridor and reached in his jacket for a cigar.

'Not out here.' Boam pointed to the ceiling. 'The smoke detectors.'

'Oh!' he frowned. 'Then where can I...'

'Please...' Holland opened the room where Sharp died three nights ago and waved him inside. 'Through here.'

The doctor frowned suspiciously at the plastic sheet covering the floor, and stiffened as something pressed against his spine. He heard the splutter and saw the scarlet explosion beneath his chin. Atwill's medical specialisation was psychiatry and anatomy classes were a vague memory from the distant past. Had his heart and lungs been surgically removed and laid out, he'd have recognised them, but shredded and blown through his chest like this, there was no chance.

Holland changed magazines on the machine pistol as Atwill crumpled onto the plastic, then closed the door on the stench.

* * * *

Chapter 64

The Ferrari flew along the moorland lane. Braking hard at a junction, Watson threw the black car into a sickening spin, bounced it off the verge, and regained control to squeal down the road towards Birchley village.

'Be careful!' The wolf opened its eyes. 'These Pennine roads are covered in snow. Go right at the village and...'

'Listen, Fido,' stammered Watson. 'When I want safety advice and directions from a fuckin' overgrown Doberman, I'll ask, okay?'

The wolf shrugged. 'Okay.'

The car skidded to a halt at the hamlet. 'Er...' Watson peered around. 'So which way?'

'Right,' said Quist, patiently. 'Head towards Stalybridge and central Manchester.'

'You're going to follow them?'

'Rex and Amy will soon be dead, or worse, and I'm entirely to blame. I can't possibly abandon them. I can't leave Strand and Stapleton either. Remember the things they know and the items they planted in my cottage?'

'So what are you going to do? Kill them?' Watson accelerated. 'This is crazy, Guv. We've no idea where they're going.'

'Silver Security Systems is on the waterfront.' The wolf held out a paw. 'Amy's mobile, please.'

Watson handed him the phone and watched deadpan as he clumsily began searching Google Earth with furry taloned fingers.

* * * *

The saloons on the A635 garage forecourt provided excellent camouflage. Speeding vehicles never noticed Tony and Derek in their parked police car.

'Whooo!' said Tony, sitting up behind the wheel. 'Check this out.'

'Nice one.' A Ferrari shot by and Derek turned off the boxing match on his phone radio. 'Let's do it.'

Tony hit the siren and tore off the forecourt, cursing to see the F50 pull over down the road.

'I thought he'd put his foot down,' snapped Derek.

'What's he playing at?' Tony cruised past to park the patrol car in front. 'I was hoping for a good chase.'

Lowering the glass, Watson took a deep breath as the officers swaggered through the snowstorm.

Tony had only been with the force two years, but his nasal drawl already contained the condescending superiority and sarcasm perfected by traffic police the world over. 'Evening, Sir. With respect, have you heard of speed limits?' He bit his tongue. He'd used *respect* and *sir* before noticing it was a black teenager.

Derek *had* noticed, and his tone was professionally tailored to suit. 'What's your game, Sooty? I know it's a stupid question, but is this Ferrari yours?'

'Not really,' admitted Watson. 'Sorry about the speed, but it's an emergency.'

'Emergency?' Tony chuckled. 'Run out of ganja, have you?'

'It's my dog. He's hurt his leg and I'm taking him to a vet.'

The monster in the passenger seat leant across and held up a paw for inspection. The policemen gaped at the glowing eyes, then slowly turned to the gun in the footwell. Wagging its tail, the wolf grinned and gave a pained whimper.

'*Get...*' coughed Tony 'Get out of that fuckin' car right now.'

Slamming into reverse, Watson threw the F50 backwards, span the wheel and screeched around the patrol car.

'Shit!' Derek scrabbled for his radio. 'Shit, shit, shit!'

Tony tore it from him. 'You won't believe this,' he babbled, 'but we've got a black kid with a fuckin' pet wolf. He's driving a Ferrari west towards the city centre.'

Derek snatched it back. 'And he's got a fuckin' machine gun.'

* * * *

Police sirens wailed as the Ferrari took a roundabout anti-clockwise sending the Manchester traffic into the kind of chaos normally only seen on stock car circuits. The wolf winced as Watson launched them into yet another heart-stopping skid.

'I thought you could drive?' he growled.

'I *can* drive.' The youth glanced at the police cars in the mirror. 'What the fuck do you call *this*? Knitting?'

'Just out of interest, who taught you?'

'Mates let me have a go in their cars, but I picked up most of what I know from computer games.'

'Ah!' Quist raised what passed for eyebrows and turned back to the satnav map on Amy's mobile.

'I'm doing better than usual. On the computer, I've normally killed myself by now.'

Slamming into third, he took a corner on two wheels to turn onto Chorlton Road, then dropped to second and stamped the accelerator. With a Ferrari, this was like pulling the trigger of a gun.

'Your driving is certainly *different*.' Flattened by G-force, Quist watched the bright shops strobe past. 'They'd queue all day for this at Disneyworld.'

'You're the problem,' shouted Watson. 'You're shitting me up. Why the hell don't you change back to normal?'

'Call me pessimistic, but there's a teensy chance you'll crash and we'll end up on foot. I run faster on four legs and I'm naked.'

Flashing blue light filled the road ahead. Watson checked the mirror. 'Shit! We're sandwiched and they're parking across the street.' He mounted the pavement. 'Hang on.'

'Ah!' said Quist. 'The Computer College of Motoring obviously covers roadblocks. Damn! The lights are red.'

'What lights?' Horns drowned the youth's question as the F50 shot over the busy crossroads. 'Oops! I don't reckon we had the right-of-way there.'

'I couldn't say. My eyes were shut.'

'Well, not to worry.' Watson checked the mirror again. 'The cops are having problems getting through the traffic stream.'

'Okay, slow down so we don't attract attention.' Quist consulted the map. 'Turn left, then take the second right.'

Watson pulled into a quiet street lined with businesses closed for the evening.

'Reverse down there.' The wolf nodded to a dark, narrow alley leading to one of the empty office car parks. 'Hopefully the police will assume we raced off.'

Braking and spinning in the tail, the teenager killed the lights and inky shadow shrouded the car. Prising his soaking fingers from the wheel, he slumped back onto the headrest with a practically orgasmic sigh, finally able, for the first time since escaping the cell, to slacken the taut mass of intestinal knots. Luminous yellow eyes blinked in the darkness, the realisation of what he was sitting beside hit home and the abdominal boy scouts went back to work with a vengeance. Several seconds passed before Watson cleared his throat.

'So, er, don't you think it's time you explained?'

'Explained what?'

'*What?*' Manic laughter escaped. 'How come you're a fuckin' werewolf?'

'Oh, yes, that,' said Quist.

* * * *

Chapter 65

The plan was simple. Strand would explain how he'd exposed a plot: Stapleton had perfected a sunscreen with which she hoped to sway the Committee into dumping Silva in favour of her. She'd been aided by Quarry and three human doctors–Amy, Rex, and Quist–who were promised feline immortality for their services. While the President reeled in shock and the Committee were captivated by the Solstice, Quist would be brought in by Zucco. Silva had nothing to fear from a defenceless human and the werewolf would get close. Close enough to tear off his head while Atwill kept the guards busy outside. Strand would take command, and thanks to the cream and the droplets, he'd be hailed as the saviour of the Elite and the new President.

The Committee shuffled uncomfortably at the conference table. Rex, Amy and Fran stood in silence, the latter staring at the red dust. *Silva knew something! From his suave manner and the unhealthy condition of Quarry, that was obvious.*

'Forgive my tardiness.' Strand sprawled in the chair opposite the President and unbuttoned his jacket. 'But I think you'll find this was worth the wait.' Despite his coolness, he felt as relaxed as a tightrope walker with hiccups, but the only option now was to bluff it out until Quist showed.

'Correct me if I'm wrong, Matthew.' Silva gave a sham look of puzzlement. 'But didn't I say I had no wish to see Doctor Stapleton?'

'You did, but I uncovered some disturbing facts in York and I knew you'd want to question her. She's been plotting against you. These two helped her, along with another human who'll be arriving shortly with Zucco.'

Rex wrapped his arm around Amy, holding her close, as the white-haired shapeshifter ran an indifferent eye over them. *So this was the character who Quist was supposed to kill? He didn't look strong, but the aura of evil power was so intense, you'd have felt it behind lead shielding.*

'How interesting.' Silva nodded politely to Rex and waved them towards the empty seats. 'Please, young man, brush away that dusty mess and sit down.'

Rex didn't move and held tightly onto Amy. The terrified girl eyed the Ubasteri and the huge Egyptian statue of Bast beside the door, clamping her teeth to prevent them chattering.

'You're clearly aware of this treachery.' Strand motioned to the dust. 'Tayman, Quarry, and Peel were involved too and...'

'Yes, I'm aware,' said Silva. 'I'm aware of Quarry's part in this conspiracy. I'm aware that Peel was Stapleton's Yorkshire Controller and guilty of incompetence. Tayman was guilty of... well, being Tayman. I've decided to purge our society, Matthew. To rid it of disloyal elements. I explained this to Tayman earlier. So as not to miss the meeting, he was brought on a shovel.' He gestured to the cat creature's ashes and pressed the intercom.

'Yes, Sir?' Boam's voice barked from the speaker.

Silva's eyes stayed on Strand. 'Is Doctor Atwill still out there?'

'No, Sir. We've vacuumed him up.'

Strand and Fran exchanged fleeting glances. He *knew*, but how could he? And how *much* did he know? It was time to begin wooing the Committee.

'I have something you all must see.' Strand produced a tub and a bottle from his pocket. 'Something which...'

'Ah, the eye protection I ordered,' enthused Silva. 'And the Solstice too.'

'*How*?' Strand couldn't have looked more astounded had the President broken into song. 'How could you possibly...'

Holland and Boam entered carrying guns. They were followed by a red-haired girl.

'Nicole?' gasped Amy. 'Nicole, what are *you* doing here? I don't understand.'

Sarah smiled and the light glinted on her cat fangs.

Silva watched as Amy's legs buckled and she sat at the circular table with Rex. 'You must be Doctor Clarkson,' said the President. 'Sarah here told me all about you.'

'Sarah?' Amy gave Gillette's secretary a bewildered look. 'So you're not called Nicole Patterson?'

Silva stroked the redhead's arm. 'No, Sarah replaced the real Miss Patterson at your laboratory when I became suspicious of Doctor Stapleton.' He ran a quizzical eye over Rex. 'I'm sorry, young man, but I'm afraid I don't know you.'

'Rex Grant.' He sullenly dusted dried cat from his jeans. 'Your *friends* here murdered my brother's fiancé.'

'How terrible.' Silva turned to Strand. 'But not as terrible as betrayal, Matthew. My security have just had an educational chat with Quarry.' He pointed to a cooling poker in a bucket by the wall. 'He was most enlightening after the insertion of white-hot metal. Will Gillette was also informative after Sarah mesmerised him. He told her all about Stapleton's covert research and their amazing success. I assume you have the Solstice data disc with you?'

Strand turned to the door where Holland and Boam stood, his eyes drifting over their guns. 'So I assume you know everything?'

'Virtually. I'm afraid Holland was overenthusiastic with his anal probing. The heated poker burnt into Quarry's heart before he could explain how you intended to kill me.'

'*Kill* you?' Strand feigned astonishment as he spotted his chance - *keep him talking until Quist arrived*. 'It's pointless now denying my ambitions to take over the Presidency, but assassination was never part of the plan.'

'Oh?' Sitting back, Silva crossed his legs. 'Perhaps you should explain why you'd want to depose me.'

Strand dropped his eyes, furtively checking his watch. 'I felt new leadership would be advantageous to our people.'

'Ah, for the good of the Elite?' Silva pointed to Fran's handcuffs. 'We've established that you're not Matthew's prisoner, so why don't you remove those silly things and sit down, my dear? We both know they're not silver.'

Pulling a derisive face, Fran flicked open the fake manacles and flopped into the vacant chair beside Strand.

'So apparently you're unhappy?' Silva raised his eyebrows. 'Unhappy with everything I've achieved? The way I've streamlined, protected and governed our people? The security I've introduced?'

Strand shrugged. 'The early days were excellent, Lucius, and I can't argue with the benefits you brought, but seven decades is a long time and things need to change. *Everything* needs to change eventually. Salford Quays–this entire area outside–was one of the busiest British ports, but they closed it down and turned it into what we have now. That move generated countless billions and gave birth to thousands of businesses, including this one. Things that don't progress stagnate and we're all beginning to feel stifled.'

'All?'

'I'm not the only one who wants change. Everyone feels the same.'

'Really?' Silva ran his green eyes over the Committee. 'Why don't we ask?'

Shuffling feet filled the silence. Checking the time again, Strand realised he had to prolong things. If just one of the sixteen remaining members spoke, the rest might follow. Knowing Willman's secret views, he caught the funeral director's eye across the table. 'How do *you* feel?'

'I er, have no complaints.' The elderly shapeshifter cleared his throat. 'I confess I preferred the old days, but of course, they're long gone. The time when European peasants feared the shadow of the cat.'

'Wonderful days,' agreed Silva. 'But you forget the torch-carrying mobs with their wooden stakes and silver bullets.'

'But that was centuries ago, Sir,' broke in Sarandon, the nightclub owner sitting by Fran. 'The planet has advanced...'

'Indeed it has,' snapped Silva. 'If our existence became known today, it would no longer be peasants pursuing the Elite, but specialised SWAT teams.'

'Willman has a point about the old days,' piped up Polanski, the computer expert. 'I once hunted beautiful Scandinavian girls. All I feed upon now are junkies and beggars.'

Strand smiled to himself as everyone nodded in tentative agreement.

'Excitement,' said Fran. 'Everyone remembers the excitement and spontaneity of the hunt before all the regulations.'

'Security regulations are essential,' hissed Silva. 'If the authorities knew of our existence, modern technology would wipe us out. The Elite would be exterminated and dissected on laboratory tables. Is that what you want?'

Strand shook his head. 'I merely advocate a leadership change to prevent stagnation and the relaxing of rules to give our people more power and freedom. I've no intention of jeopardising security.'

'Yes, power,' echoed Willman. 'All this power and yet we're unable to use it. We've always been the stronger species–the Elite species–but now we hide from our food.' He let out a nervous laugh. 'The Elite hides from humans and we need permission to take them.'

'Permission even to take beggars and other scum,' added another disgruntled voice. 'All we're allowed to feed upon is human garbage. Yes, we do need more freedom.'

Several heads nodded in agreement.

'I see,' said Silva. 'So do you believe Matthew would make a better President?'

'You've done wonders, Sir.' Sarandon squirmed. 'But perhaps Strand's right and change is needed. Perhaps it's time to step down.'

'You see how they feel, Lucius?' Strand held up the sunscreen. 'And what better day could there be for change? With this Solstice we can now...'

'Yes,' frowned Polanski. 'What *is* that?'

'What is it?' Strand reclined in the chair. 'Allow me to enlighten you.'

* * * *

Strand came to the end of explaining the cream and droplets in detail, purposely taking his time and pressing home every point.

The President sprawled in his chair, listening in silence as gasps of awe drifted around the table. 'Well...' he said finally. 'My leadership would obviously appear to be unpopular.'

'Not exactly unpopular...' began Polanski.

He raised a hand to silence him. 'No one, however, can accuse me of despotism. If everyone feels the same and agrees, I'll step down and hand the Presidency to Matthew.'

Strand sat upright in genuine shock. 'Well, if you say so, then...'

'Feline democracy, gentlemen.' Straightening his suit and leaning forward, Silva steepled his fingers. 'Why don't we take a vote?'

* * * *

Chapter 66

'It's a long story, but I could condense it.' The wolf sat back in the Ferrari and crossed its shaggy legs. 'You recall I told you how I was once a student of the supernatural and mythology? It was years ago, but I became something of an authority and wrote several books...'

'Very interesting,' said Watson. 'You said you were condensing this.'

'I researched many aspects, but I was especially interested in the existence of mythological creatures: vampires, Ubasteri, werewolves and suchlike.'

Sirens sounded close by and the pair relaxed again as they faded.

Taking one of Grant's cigarettes from a pack by the gearstick, Quist awkwardly pushed home the dashboard lighter with his paw. 'I was compiling a work on lycanthropy - *Creatures of Darkness*. There were plenty of ancient references, Pliny and Plato, but nothing modern. In any case, speaking to people is always the best research, and I travelled to Eastern Europe, hoping to gather folklore first-hand and maybe find evidence of an actual werewolf.' The lighter popped and he lit the cigarette.

'And?'

'And I bloody well found one, didn't I?'

'Wow! You got bitten?'

'I was attacked and left for dead. You watch horror films; I imagine you know how it works.'

Watson spluttered as smoke swirled through fangs.

Quist looked as sheepish as possible for a wolf. 'Sorry.'

'So you were right - cigarettes can't hurt you.'

'They're hardly silver bullets.' He lowered the window, reached out a paw and tapped ash. Sirens could still be heard several streets away. 'Fire and silver are the only things harmful to me.'

'Those bullets outside your cottage.' Watson narrowed his

303

eyes. 'And that dickhead's SAS lighter…'

'The touch actually hurts,' said the wolf. 'The bullets were painful to pick up; it's similar to a jellyfish sting.'

'Unbelievable! So you *did* get your face cut in that bar fight the other night, but it healed. Can you catch diseases and viruses and stuff? Cholera and Malaria?'

'Not even the common cold.'

'Hardpad, worms and mange?'

'Don't be facetious.' The wolf gave a lopsided smile. 'Every so often I have to change identities. I never grow older, you see? My hair doesn't lengthen and I don't shave. The years roll by and I remain exactly as I was on the night of the attack. I had to become a loner, altering names and moving around to prevent acquaintances becoming suspicious. Larry was pretty much the only friend I had.'

'So what's your real name?'

'I was born Richard Quist. I rotate names – Quayle, Quist, Quinn. Sometimes I've masqueraded as my own grandson.'

Watson recalled the signet ring. 'RQ? I thought that ring must've belonged to your dad.'

'No. I've had goldsmiths thicken the band from time to time as it wore thin, but it's done pretty well for its age.'

'It's age? When did it happen?'

'1790.'

'Er, right.' Watson sat quietly for a moment while it sank in. 'Anyway, some mate Larry turned out to be.'

The wolf drew on the cigarette. 'Like me, he never asked for this and he was much older. He always found it difficult to suppress the urges we feel. The urges to kill. I met him in San Francisco after the 1906 earthquake where he was using the chaos to his, er, *advantage*. I tried to change him, to help him adapt, and for a long while it worked. It appears, ultimately, I failed.'

Watson checked the sky between the buildings. 'The moon isn't full. How come you've changed?'

'I can shapeshift any time during the hours of darkness. Most evenings I change and go running in the woods.'

'A jogging werewolf?' Shaking his head, Watson took a deep breath and switched on the radio. 'I'll see if there's a local news station reporting on possible road blocks.' Duran Duran's song *Hungry Like the Wolf* blared from the speakers and he quickly switched it off. 'Er, yeah…' He cleared his throat and started the car. 'Let's forget the radio. I reckon the cops must be gone by now. We should be okay.'

'They'll still be looking for us.' Quist picked up the phone and examined the map. 'We're not far from Salford Quays. This time stay clear of the main roads and I wonder if you could stick to the speed limit?'

'I'm wondering something myself. These urges you mentioned? I'm not complaining, of course, but er, why aren't you eating me?'

'Ah.' The wolf grinned. Watson really hoped it was a grin. 'What colour are my eyes?'

The youth glanced apprehensively at the enormous furry head jammed under the roof. 'A sort of yellowy orange glow.'

'Amber! If they were red, you'd have problems.'

'You're saying it's like cowboy movies, where goodies wear white hats and baddies wear black? Nice werewolves have amber eyes and nasty ones have red?'

'There's a dangerous beast within me, Watson, but I've managed to control it. Mainly because I've never taken a life.'

'You've already wasted four today.'

'I mean killing a human with tooth or claw. When a werewolf kills, or if it consumes flesh, the bloodlust grows as it did with Larry. The urges are always stronger at the full moon. I keep it restrained with yoga meditation and a vegan diet. If I consume animal products, the dark monster begins to rise.'

'Well, whatever you do, you carry on restraining it, Guv.' Watson pulled out of the alleyway, giggling uneasily as he recalled the beef crisps and other meaty snacks he'd offered Quist over the past few weeks. 'Make sure you stick to those fuckin' apples and nut cutlets whenever I'm around.'

* * * *

Completing a cautious circuit of Silver Security Systems without headlights, Watson drew up on the Salford street some fifty yards away facing the brightly-lit entrance porch. The Ferrari engine ticked over, the wipers fighting the blizzard.

'Well done!' said the wolf. 'Somehow you managed to get us here alive.' He gestured to the van by the front doors. 'That will be the vehicle Strand used to transport Amy and Rex.'

'Hey, nice deduction, Guv; it's the only other *vehicle* in this business park. With everything closed, this place is like a ghost town.' Watson glanced around Raven's Wharf. Converted warehouse office blocks loomed darkly on either side and he gazed at the huge building ahead. 'There are no windows on those lower levels and the back doors onto the quay were steel.'

'Yes, the front door there is the only option.'

'It's not *much* of an option, what with their meeting in full swing and the place filled with big cats. Look at the size of Tiddles in there.'

'Yes, he obviously drinks plenty of bowls of milk.' Quist watched the burly Costigan in reception. 'That's why I'm going alone. You know I've no choice.'

'If what they said about it being like a fortress is right, that porch will be armoured glass and locked. There's no way to break in.'

'Mmmh, Strand also mentioned the defences: robo-sentries, alarms and suchlike.'

'Exactly. You'll last as long in there as a snowman in the Sahara.'

'Hello!' murmured Quist. Another Mercedes van sped along the deserted street and pulled up behind Strand's. 'Someone is late for the meeting.'

'It's the cat guy from the loony bin.' Watson watched as Galeen jumped out and rushed through the snow to be admitted by the guard. 'The one who ran out after us.'

'Yes.' The wolf deliberated. 'How wide would you say those double doors were into the porch and lobby?'

'Dunno,' said Watson. 'About eight feet. Why?'

'So wider than the car?'

'*What*? You're thinking of driving through both sets of glass doors?'

'No. I'm staying in this form and letting you drive. As soon as we're in the lobby, I'll leap out while you reverse and vanish.'

'You're kidding?'

'Afraid not.'

'This sounds about as clever as a tissue paper condom. Listen, Guv, you er, you're going to be okay...' Watson gave an uncomfortable grin. 'Aren't you?'

'Well, I'm not planning on jumping in front of any silver bullets, but to be honest, this isn't going to be easy. Even if I get Rex and Amy out, there's still Strand and Stapleton. If they escape and carry out their threats, I'll have to disappear.'

'Yeah, that's a pretty neat frame-up job those pussy bastards have done on you.' The youth took a deep breath. 'So this could easily be goodbye? I'm just starting to realise how cool being mates with a real-life werewolf could be, and now... well, now you...'

'Good Lord!' Quist eyed him speculatively. 'For an awful moment, I thought you were actually going to pat me. Come on now. Weepy sentimentality doesn't suit your cool, streetwise image.' He smiled as affectionately as possible for a wolf and turned back to the building. 'Let's do it. Don't use the headlights.'

'*What*?' gasped Watson. 'You want to go *now*? There are two guards in the lobby.'

'The longer we wait, the less chance Amy and Rex have.' Quist held the door ajar and picked up the Uzi. 'Let's go, while they're talking with their backs to us.'

'Okay, Guv. I'll wait for you outside that marina we passed back there.' Watson gunned the engine and shifted into first. 'I'm not staying in there long, so are you ready to jump?'

The wolf stuck up a shaggy thumb.

'Here we go.' Bracing himself, the youth tore along the street. 'Get ready.'

The Ferrari hit the porch hard, the glazed doors exploding over the bonnet, and ploughed into the reception beyond, sending the guards diving for cover. Watson stamped on the brakes, the screech of rubber on marble joining with the ear-splitting cascade of glass as he slammed into reverse. Glass wasn't all that fell. Triggered by vibration, a steel sheet dropped from the ceiling behind them to seal the lobby.

'Shit!' He rammed it hard, writing off the rear end. 'Oh shit!'

'Ah, some sort of security shutter,' growled the wolf. 'I must admit, I never expected that.'

* * * *

Chapter 67

'Oh dear!' Strand hid his smirk at the lack of votes for Silva. 'And now, despite all the wonderful things Lucius has accomplished, who believes it's time for a new ruler? Who'd like to see me as leader and major changes within the society? Less restrictions and laws, greater freedom and power, not to mention the unbelievable boon of daylight existence.'

Silva sat motionless as, with the exception of Rex and Amy, everyone slowly and fearfully raised a hand. 'I see.' He scrutinised his nails. 'Unanimous.'

'Yes.' Strand lost the battle to restrain his sneer. 'No hard feelings, I hope?'

'Not at all. This has been constructive and informative. I had suspicions that you all felt this way, but I was never certain.'

Strand nodded in sham regret and checked his watch. Zucco should have been here with Quist by now.

'I'm afraid Doctor Zucco won't be coming,' said Silva, seemingly reading his thoughts. 'As a matter of fact, he won't be going anywhere anymore.'

Rex glanced at Amy. *Zucco was dead? Did that mean Quist and Watson were also dead?*

Silva smiled at Strand's confused expression. 'My security people called at the asylum shortly after you left. Killing me was never your intention, you claimed.' The emerald eyes locked onto him. 'That was a lie. You intended to eliminate me using your lupine assassin.'

Strand stared aghast.

'Your secret weapon was slaughtered with Zucco and Houghton. Speaking of slaughter...' Silva turned to the guards by the door. 'Please try not to damage the table. It's quite old and valuable.'

Strand's jaw fell as the meaning registered. The Committee understood too, but the faster members only had time to lift their buttocks from the seats before Holland and Boam opened fire.

309

Several seconds ticked by before the silenced splutter of gunfire ended. Strand opened his eyes and gaped through an acrid cordite haze at the shredded carcasses around the table. Arterial splatters and scarlet puddles expanded to cover the polished surface. He turned from Fran's bewildered frown to the petrified Rex and Amy, realisation dawning that, incredibly, their bodies were still intact. How long that would continue was debatable. Metallic snapping behind signified that Holland and Boam had reloaded.

Rex cautiously uncoiled from the shivering ball he'd contracted into, marvelling at his self-control. Sixteen cat people had been blown apart around him and his pants were bone-dry.

'Don't look so astounded, Matthew.' Silva chuckled softly. 'How could I have you shot when the bullets might have damaged Gillette's research. Now, if you'd care to hand the disc over?'

Strand felt the hot silencer of Holland's gun by his ear. Silva had meant what he said about a society purge; this mass execution was premeditated. The guards had evidently been briefed earlier and Strand had been used to expose the genuine feelings of the members. With the temporary exception of himself, the Committee were dead, and the chances of achieving a coup now were slim, to say the least. He took out the data disc and slid it across the table between the blood pools.

'Thank you,' said Silva. 'And thank you for prompting them into disclosing their disloyalty.'

'Don't mention it,' rasped Strand.

'You need me.' Fran eyed the smoking machine pistols. 'Only a chemist could interpret the data on that.'

'I *have* a chemist.' Silva pointed to Amy. 'And a lab upstairs equipped with Merlax and Porphyrene. Gillette was very helpful after Sarah mesmerised him. He even gave her these.' He produced two containers identical to Strand's. 'Doctor Clarkson can analyse them and interpret the disc formulas. She's less likely to try anything stupid.'

Amy gagged at the stench of the decomposing Committee.

'Only if you let Rex live,' she stammered.

'Yes,' croaked Rex. 'I think killing me would be a bad idea.'

'If you insist,' lied Silva. As soon as this situation was under control and he had Amy in the penthouse, he would bite her and use hypnosis. Grant was superfluous, but the guards would be peckish and the young man was full of healthy blood. 'He can help you set up a production base for the cream and droplets.'

Strand wrinkled his nose as one of the bodies burst open in a gush of intestines. 'I assume we don't have time for the traditional last cigarette?'

'You assume wrong.' The President signalled and Holland secured Fran's wrists behind her back. The handcuffs were SSS Elite issue, the rims razor-sharp. 'As you can doubtless sense, my dear, those manacles really *are* silver.'

Fran winced at the sizzling pain, watching as the guard cuffed Strand and yanked him upright. 'You aren't going to kill us?'

'Of course I am, but not yet.' Silva strolled to his private penthouse door and keyed in the combination. It opened onto a staircase. 'You've probably realised by now that I'm no fool. If Doctor Clarkson encounters problems she may need your help. You'll be held until she completes her work and until I form a new Committee from our more loyal people. The leisurely dissection of your living bodies will be their first warning against future thoughts of treachery.'

'We'll be happy to help out,' snarled Strand.

Boam pulled Rex out of his chair, rammed an Uzi into the small of Strand's back, and nodded to the corridor.

'Come, Doctor Clarkson.' Standing courteously aside, the President gestured to the stairs as Sarah dragged Amy from her seat. 'To the penthouse, before you faint from the stench in here.'

* * * *

311

Chapter 68

Kicking the car door wide, Quist wrenched Watson from the Ferrari and dived behind the closest of the gigantic statues that decorated the lobby. A second later and Galeen's machine-gun fire would have cut them in half. Watson pressed his face into the marble, screaming as bullets ricocheted inches from his head. He opened a terrified eye and noticed the plaque by his nose.

SPANISH WOMAN IN BATH. HENRY MOORE

Another burst shattered the senorita's head, or perhaps her elbow; it was difficult to tell with Moore's artwork. Watson knew this was Sod's Law, or some bastard's law. A fortress filled with supernatural cats, the very last place he wanted to be, but the moment he saw it, he just knew he'd end up inside.

'Stay down,' snarled the wolf, shouldering his Uzi.

'Don't worry,' gibbered Watson.

Quist jammed the silencer between the statue's legs and fired. Costigan flew backwards over the reception desk, chest bursting open in a grisly explosion. Galeen was faster and dived behind a sculpture on the opposite side of the foyer to return the shots. Quist rolled left and fired again over the statue's three breasts.

'I killed the lobby guard.' The wolf ducked as another volley smashed the bosom. He reached into the teenager's jacket for a spare magazine. 'The other guard is pinned down like us.'

'So what do we do?' moaned Watson. 'There's gonna be more here soon.'

'I know.' Pushing him flat to the floor, the wolf used his furry body as a shield. He aimed low on the Ferrari, turned his head and fired. 'That's why this is our only option.'

'*Shit*!' Watson's profanity was masked by the explosion of the petrol tank.

Blazing fuel rushed across the lobby to the corner statue where Galeen had half-changed into cat form. Slapping at his flaming fur and screeching, he leapt out shooting wildly. Quist knew it must be difficult to hit anything when your crotch is on fire, and emptied his gun into the guard's chest.

'Look out!' The wolf dragged Watson through the smoke to the nearest door as the burning torrent washed towards them. The lobby water sprinkler kicked in with negligible effect. 'Move! You won't be able to breathe soon.'

Quist slammed the door on the raging fire and peered around the vast room they'd entered. This had to be the workshop where the company produced their hardware. Technical equipment, computers, and machinery filled rows of tables. Grabbing the gun in his teeth, he bounded down the central aisle on all-fours to the loading doors.

'Damn!' he hissed. 'I wanted to get you out of here before looking for Amy and Rex. This is the only other exit and you need an electronic combination.'

'Ah!' Watson sagged. 'Can't you bust it?'

'These doors are solid steel. Come on, we have to go back. That sprinkler is holding the fire down, but it's designed for waste-paper bins, not burning cars.'

'What about the porch shutter that came down? Can we get it open somehow?'

'Mmmh, this might work.' Passing Watson the gun, the wolf trundled a trolley of welding cylinders up the aisle to the reception door. 'I'll go first. Hold your breath, keep your head low and follow me. Run by the desk to the door on the other side. Are you ready?'

Quist burst back into the blazing lobby pushing the gas tanks. Gasping at the intense heat blast, Watson darted out behind him through the smoke, kicking open the door into a wide stairwell.

'That should do it.' Quist joined him and handed him his smouldering coat. 'I wedged the cylinders between the shutter and the car.'

'Oh, lovely. You saved your coat,' said Watson. 'Those tanks won't do the Ferrari any favours. Or *us*, if we hang around.'

'I imagine it's insured,' said Quist.

Chapter 69

Boam pushed Strand and Fran out of the conference room. Holland followed, dragging their trembling human captive into the corridor and shutting the door on the decomposing Committee.

Rex silently groaned. *Once Amy completed her work, there was more chance of Captain Ahab joining Greenpeace than him leaving this place alive.*

'You don't have to do this,' said Strand. 'You can't like these stifling rules any more than I do. If you release us and help…'

Rex flinched at the piercing crack. Holland's headbutt spoke far more eloquently than any argument on loyalty.

'I see.' Strand spat blood, which turned to powder in the air. 'I'll take that as a polite refusal.'

Rex glanced back along the corridor as they reached the elevator. Boam and Holland were ignoring him, concentrating instead on their silver-manacled prisoners. Guarding a terrified, harmless mortal was evidently pointless. Locked in a cell, he was as good as dead, and if escape was at all possible, now would be the only time to try. *Surely those months of training for the special forces could be put to some use?* Holland was closest, and Rex summoned the miniscule dregs of courage that remained. Knowing he'd hesitate and fail if he considered the insanity of this, he prepared to sprint and slammed an elbow down into the guard's groin, following with a vicious windpipe chop. He may as well have hit the wall. Not only did Holland look like an Easter Island statue, he felt like it. The green-eyed monster didn't move, except to give a psychopathic glower of surprise.

'Er, sorry about that.' Rex grinned idiotically. 'It was an accident. I have this nervous spasm.'

Holland's backhand slap launched him fifteen feet down the passage.

Strand eyed Fran as the elevator opened. One guard was busy with Grant, his back turned, the other was watching the unexpected fracas.

'No.' Boam guessed his thoughts and pressed the gun to Strand's ribs. 'Don't be stupid.'

Groaning and crawling to his knees, Rex saw two cigarette lighters had fallen from his jacket. He shook his head to clear the grogginess and double vision. He realised it was just one lighter, and it was silver.

'Up!' Shouldering the Uzi strap, the shapeshifter kicked him. 'Get up now.'

Rex palmed the lighter as talons dragged him vertical.

'I said *up*.' Holland pushed him towards the waiting trio. 'Get in that lift.'

'Okay, okay.' Squeezing the silver case, Rex mentally recited feverish prayers.

'Try anything again and I'll claw your ears off.'

Rex whimpered. If this lunacy failed, his days of wearing sunglasses were over. He hurled the lighter at Strand's guard like a crazed bowler, smacking him hard in the face. The feline screech was deafening, the blinded cat creature dropping the gun, clasping an eye, and collapsing against the wall. Holland frantically unslung his weapon, but too late. Strand had already crouched to snatch Boam's Uzi in his cuffed hands, and glaring over his shoulder, sprayed bullets down the passage.

Rex dived low as Holland's torso exploded in the hail of silver. 'Watch it,' he gibbered. 'You almost hit *me*.'

Strand blew Boam's head apart. 'Yes, almost.' He ran close and jammed the gun to the cowering man's head. 'You wouldn't believe how difficult it is to aim with your hands behind your back.' He pulled the trigger and tutted to find the clip was empty.

'Come on,' shouted Fran. 'We're helpless in these cuffs and the silver pain is unbearable.' She shoulder-pushed Strand into the elevator as the fire alarm wailed. 'Leave him and come on.'

Rex watched the door shut, and felt his sweat-soaked brow where the hot silencer had pressed. He juggled with the options of fainting or vomiting, and settled on the latter.

315

* * * *

Silva climbed to the penthouse upper level as the klaxon screamed.

Sarah followed, dragging Amy up the steps. 'What is it?' she quizzed.

'The fire alarm.' The President checked the control panel and silenced it. 'From the reception lobby.'

'Trouble?'

He scanned the CCTV monitors and switched to the lobby cameras only to find static. 'The security shutter is down,' he murmured, noticing the indicator light. 'According to this, the lobby sprinkler is operating.'

A dull boom jolted the building.

'Lucius?' whispered Sarah, gripping Amy tighter.

Descending the steps, Silva pressed a window control and the armoured glazing slid up, snowflakes drifting in as he leant out. The glass porch below had vanished and the mangled steel shutter lay across the street. Ruptured water mains gushed onto the lawns and flame spewed from the lobby.

'Yes.' He returned to the controls and activated the robo-sentries. 'I believe you could refer to that as *trouble*.'

* * * *

Chapter 70

Rex snatched the gun from Holland's decomposing corpse, grateful that he hadn't eaten since breakfast. Gagging, he searched the bubbling mess for magazines, found a spare, and stuffed it in his jacket with the silver lighter. Exhilaration briefly wrestled with terror and nausea as he weighed the Uzi in one hand. His choices were limited: follow Strand and probably meet more guards, or follow Silva and try to help Amy; an almost certain death versus an almost definite death. Swallowing hard and clutching the gun, he ran under a dormant robo-sentry and headed for the penthouse.

Returning to the conference room was pointless, as the exit Silva used was locked by a code. Fortunately the fourth passage door opened into a stairwell, and moving warily beneath another mechanical sentry, he bounded up. A thump shook the building, deeper and more juddering than the hi-fi bass in a teenager's car. *What the hell was happening below? Were the guards preventing Strand's escape with heavy artillery?*

Rex raced around a landing, reached the top of the steps, and threw open the door to a rooftop garden of potted shrubs and ancient Egyptian statues. Realising he'd climbed too far and descending a flight, he opened the corridor door.

'*Shit!*' He dived back into the stairwell as the robo-sentry rotated and, for the second time in two minutes, a volley of silver bullets narrowly missed.

Someone must have activated the damn things after the explosion he'd heard. The penthouse passage was covered, the sentry on the landing below meant he couldn't go down the stairs and the only route was back up. Rex returned to the rooftop garden snowstorm, where the neighbouring warehouses in the empty business park had begun to reflect a flickering red glow.

'Oh, *wonderful!*' He peered over the parapet handrail at the fire raging through the lower floors. Even if he *did* manage to get by the cats and automated guns down to ground level, a nice cremation awaited. 'Well that's just fucking brilliant!'

He noticed the open penthouse window some ten feet below him and the coil of garden hose by his feet.

'Are you crazy?' he stammered, tugging at it and half-hoping it would snap so he could drop the insane idea that was forming. 'You're a sexy playboy, not a hero.'

The hose was the reinforced, heavy-duty type, and quickly knotting one end tightly around the handrail, he threw the remainder over the edge. This was madness, but apart from waiting here to burn or have his blood drained, it was the only option. Shaking and sweating, Rex secured the Uzi sling around his neck, climbed the parapet, and gingerly lowered himself backwards.

'Oh, what are you doing?' He scuffled down the wall until level with the window, kicked off into space, and swung towards the opening, whimpering at a sudden memory of tarot cards. 'What the hell are you doing?'

* * * *

Amy stared at the changing screens, praying for a glimpse of Rex, as Silva flicked through the CCTV controls. The burning technical lab appeared, smoke parting to reveal Fran clumsily using bolt croppers behind her back to free Strand from his manacles.

'What happened to the guards?' said Sarah. She watched Strand release Fran, key in the door combination and escape onto the wharf. An inrush of air nourished the flames, the inferno killing the camera. 'And where's the human?'

'Matthew knew the exit code,' hissed Silva. 'I should have changed it more frequently.'

'If you'd activated your robo-sentries earlier, they wouldn't have got away.'

'My dear girl...' Silva began working through the cameras again. 'You haven't known me long enough to realise that only a suicide would speak to me in that manner.' The conference room corridor appeared onscreen, red dust and dark suits covering the floor by the elevator. 'Ah! Holland and Boam - I wonder how Matthew overpowered them? And where is Grant?'

Amy shuddered. The chances of him being alive were slimmer than an anorexic whippet, but so far there had been no sign of his corpse.

'The ground floor is ablaze.' Sarah eyed the changing monitors nervously. 'Why aren't the sprinklers working?'

'The water main that supplies the system runs beneath the lobby. According to these pressure readings, it was destroyed by the blast. This place will burn like tinder.' Silva adjusted controls. 'The corridor robo-sentries are still operational, but I've now deactivated those on the stairs to allow you down. Costigan and Galeen should have been in reception. Go find them and bring them up here if they're still alive. Don't be long.'

'What about Rex?' said Amy, trembling.

Silva chuckled. 'I really don't think we need him.'

Amy watched Sarah leave. 'Your guards are probably dead,' she said. 'The police and the fire brigade will be here soon and we're trapped until then. It's over. Your building, your plans–it's all finished.'

'Hardly.' Dragging her around the snake pit, Silva stabbed a keypad to open the private elevator. 'I have the disc, I have samples of the cream and droplets, I have you to work on them, and as you can see, I have an escape route past the fire.'

'I won't help if you leave Rex to burn.'

'As you can imagine, Sarah was also frightened and uncooperative when she was abducted.' He pulled the petrified girl close and gripped her upper arms, feline muzzle extending. 'Allow me to show you how I remedied that.'

Furry lips brushed Amy's throat; *apparently the remedy wouldn't involve balanced reasoning.* A tongue caressed the flesh, locating the racing artery, and sharp fangs replaced the softness. Something large splashed into the pond in the lower section of the lounge, and Silva twisted away.

'Ah, Mister Grant.' The shapeshifter noticed the hose and

realised that Rex had swung in through the open window. He laughed at the drenched figure. 'We wondered where *you* were.'

'Amy, get away from him.' Rex swatted a lily pad from his head, moaned to see Silva's cat features and pointed the dripping Uzi. 'Get back!'

'He's wearing body armour,' screamed Amy. Unable to break the taloned grip, she jerked away to arm's length, offering a clear shot. 'I just felt it.'

'Put that gun down, you fool,' said Silva. 'We both know you don't have the courage to fire. Put it down now and I may not open your torso and force you to eat your own intestines.'

'Let Amy go,' shouted Rex, shocked and astonished by his new-found courage. 'Get your paws off her.'

'I *said* put it down.'

Rex whimpered as he pulled the trigger, and Amy leapt from the penthouse control area into the lower level shrubbery. Staring incredulously at the smashed arm that had held her, the shapeshifter screeched and turned back to the pond, its green eyes glowing.

'Oh no!' Rex fired another two bursts and missed. 'No, no, no!'

Silva descended the steps, head and neck changing to that of a white panther. The contorted features reminded Rex of a furious gargoyle, but if *this* face were ever to adorn a cathedral roof, no pigeon would dare crap on it. Silver bullets ricocheted off concealed armour and his frantic brain tried coordinating shaking hands to train the Uzi on the cat's unprotected head.

Snack!

Rex croaked in horror. The sound told him the gun was empty. Releasing the clip and scrabbling in his jacket, he managed to ram in the spare, before a claw snatched the Uzi and flung it across the room. Now fully transformed, the wounded panther had burst from the Kevlar and leapt to the lily pond. Dragged from the water by his sweater, Rex punched the cat's flank, almost shattering his hand on the ribs.

'Sorry about shooting you.' He grunted as the snarling white cat slammed him against the wall. Silva was older than Rex, probably a few hundred years older, and only had the use of one claw now, but terror outweighed any feelings of macho humiliation. 'Why don't we talk about this?'

Rex ducked as the talons released his sweater, slashed out and gouged through the brickwork. The time for reasoned discussion was definitely past. Darting away, he made it up the steps, then fell by the elevator as claws ripped his leg and snapped the shin bone. Battling nausea and searing agony, he pulled out the silver lighter, screaming as his arm was torn and broken. He rolled, gasping and moaning, by the large hole in the floor. Something undulated at the bottom, but tears blurred his vision.

'You caused me to feel pain,' growled the white panther, seething with fury. Standing on rear legs and closing the talons of his good arm around Rex's neck, Silva dragged the man upright and slowly crushed his windpipe. 'No one has done that for a very long time.'

'Leave him,' shouted Amy. The panther twisted and hissed to see her taking aim with the discarded gun. 'Let him go or...'

'Fuck that!' squawked Rex, his face blue. 'Blow his fucking head off. Now!'

Silva thrust him backwards and dived into the open elevator. The door closed, bullets ricocheting off the steel, but Rex didn't see it. He was face-down in the snake pit.

* * * *

Chapter 71

Clutching Quist's overcoat, Watson ran up the stairs behind the bounding wolf and paused to catch his breath on the final landing. 'I have to ask,' he said. 'Why do you keep ripping the doors off every time we reach a new level?'

Quist spat the Uzi from his mouth and stood upright. 'They're fire doors.' Peering through the panel to ensure the corridor was empty, he tore it from the hinges. 'I'm allowing the hot smoke from downstairs to get through.'

'Oh, right.' Watson watched as the swirling black cloud above him rushed out over the ceiling of the passage. 'Er... why?'

'To confuse the robo-sentries. They operate on movement and heat. Smoke masks movement and hot gas masks our warmth.'

'Will it work?'

'We've passed beneath three already.'

'Shit! I never saw them.'

'And they never saw us; that's the idea.'

Watson backed across the landing, watching in horror as the temperature plummeted and the monster transformed. Wolf fur and fangs fell out and crumbled to dust, expelled by sprouting human teeth and hair, the crackling lupine form twisting and shrinking back into a naked, middle-aged man.

'Whooo!' The trembling youth tossed him the overcoat. 'That's one hell of a party trick, Guv. What's with the cold when you do that?'

'If you really want to talk esoteric metaphysics at a time like this, the transformation leeches energy from the atmosphere.' Quist slipped on his coat and picked up the Uzi. 'These silver bullets should hopefully eliminate any problems we encounter. I'll change back if absolutely necessary, but I don't want Amy or Rex to see me.' He stepped over the broken door. 'One person knowing my secret is more than enough for...' A robo-sentry swivelled, powdering the wall as he leapt back. 'Damn! There isn't enough smoke up here to fool its sensors. That was close.'

'Yeah,' agreed Watson. 'But not as close as *this*.'

'Drop your gun,' said Sarah. She stood on the stairs pointing a pistol. 'Drop it now.'

'Oh, hello.' Quist casually threw down the gun. 'We're looking for two friends, Amy and Rex. I don't suppose you've seen them?'

Sarah chuckled. 'I should forget them. The female is with Lucius in the penthouse and the other will be dead by now.' She turned to Watson, the teenager freezing as their eyes locked. Quist stiffened too as she turned the hypnotic glare on him. 'I could have shot you when your backs were turned.' She lowered her pistol. 'But this is more fun. Pick your gun up and put it to your friend's head.'

Quist bent slowly, lifted the weapon and pressed the silencer against his assistant's temple. Watson whimpered like a puppy.

'Turn and face him,' ordered Sarah.

Shaking and moaning louder, the youth shuffled around until the muzzle touched his sweat-soaked nose.

'Very good. Now pull the trigger.'

Quist twisted and fired, blowing the gun and three fingers from the girl's hand. She clutched the smashed stump and doubled over in agony, her feline shriek jolting Watson from the trance.

'Shit!' he spluttered. 'Hey, nice bluff.'

'Sorry,' said Quist, 'but your hypnosis doesn't work on me. You're going to take us to Amy and...'

Sarah attacked with unbelievable speed, face changing to cat form and eyes blazing green. Sidestepping, Quist caught an arm and used the momentum to launch her into the passage where the robo-sentry greeted her with a blizzard of silver.

'Fuck me!' Watson watched her corpse disintegrate in a crimson splatter dance. 'You say we've walked under three of those?'

Quist nodded grimly as the gunfire ceased. 'And the penthouse must be along there, past that lethal contraption.' He grabbed the youth's sweatshirt and ripped a strip of cloth from his midriff.

'What the…' Watson gaped in disbelief.

'I need something hot.' Igniting the fabric with his cigarette lighter, Quist tossed it high into the corridor. 'Something hotter than me.'

Already confused by the increasing smoke, the sentry locked onto the flames, allowing him time to shoot the small device beneath the unit.

'There,' said Quist. 'That was almost certainly the sensor.'

'*Almost* certainly?' stammered Watson.

'Come on. We'll soon find out.'

* * * *

Groaning, Rex felt his head to ensure it was still there. His left arm and lower right leg were lacerated and broken, but a scorching numbness had set in which temporarily killed most of the pain. Anyway, he was alive. The cat's claws seemed to have missed his arteries and things could certainly have been much worse. He turned and saw that things *were* much worse.

'Oh fuck!'

Two king cobras reared in the gravel four feet away, facial hoods flaring and black eyes staring spitefully. It's tricky for snakes to look cute, but Kali and Shiva weren't even trying.

Amy arrived at the pit edge. 'Snakes,' she croaked. 'Cobras.'

'Well spotted.' Rex blinked away streaming perspiration. 'Er, I'd rather not move, so why don't you shoot them and we'll talk natural history later?'

The girl took careful aim and pulled the trigger.

Snack!

'Oh no!' whined Rex. 'Please, not again.'

'I must have emptied the gun when I shot at Silva.' She knelt trembling by the pit. 'Oh God, what do we do?'

'I don't have many options.'

The sides were only five feet high. Even with fractures, Rex could make that, and especially with his scaly incentive. Wiping the sweat from his eyes, he eased himself back from the snakes and clambered slowly and painfully onto his good leg.

'Hey, this is going to be okay,' he whispered, taking Amy's hands. 'They won't attack provided I take it nice and easy like...'

The first strike hit him in the thigh and the second in the buttock. After the third he stopped counting. Amy heaved the screaming man out of the pit as Quist burst through the door with gun raised.

'There's only Rex and Amy in here,' shouted the detective. He raced across the penthouse to the upper level. 'Close the doors behind you to keep out the smoke.'

Watson followed him up the steps and saw Silva's pets. 'Rex has been bitten,' he gasped. 'Do something, Guv!'

'Do something?' Quist shot him a disbelieving look. 'Like what?'

'I dunno. Suck out the poison or something.'

'Watson, those are cobras, he has multiple bites, and this isn't an old cowboy movie.' He quickly examined the groaning man. 'Oh! He's been bitten in the femoral artery.'

'Is that bad?' Watson glanced at the sobbing Amy, pretty sure of the answer.

'Strand and Stapleton?' Quist gripped Amy's shoulders. 'Where are they? There was supposed to be a meeting of the Ubasteri?'

'They're all dead or gone,' she stammered, pointing. 'That door is a lift. Silva used it to escape. He said it goes down past the fire.'

'It's like tequila,' said Rex, grinning weakly at her. 'I can't feel my legs.'

Quist ran to the elevator. 'Does this keypad operate it?'

'Yes.' Wiping her eyes, Amy pushed him aside and stabbed four numbers. 'I watched him code it in.'

'I can't see,' whimpered Rex. He groped for Amy, found Watson's hand and squeezed. 'I know this sounds stupid, but I'm glad *you're* here.'

'Er, right.' Watson returned the squeeze. 'Don't mention it, mate.'

Rex wailed at the pain as the detective lifted his armpits and dragged him into the lift.

'Get in, Watson,' said Quist. 'I don't know where it goes, but let's find out before the fire kills the electrics.'

Amy hit the button and the elevator descended fast.

'Oh shit! Look at this, Guv.' Watson cringed as Rex's gurgling face began to blacken, his body going into spasm. 'Is there an antidote for cobra venom?'

The detective raised an eyebrow.

Amy sobbed again. 'Even if there is, we don't have time to find a hospital.' She knelt, supporting his head. 'We don't have time for anything.'

The lift opened into a basement with several tunnels running off.

Quist made up his mind. 'There is *one* antidote,' he muttered. 'The only one under the circumstances.'

Amy heard crackling bone, felt the freezing drop in temperature and felt fur brush her face. She turned from the dying man, gaped at the huge wolf crouching beside her and fainted as it buried its teeth in Rex's arm.

'Nice going, Guv,' said Watson. 'Now we have two to carry.'

* * * *

326

Chapter 72

Strand's Lamborghini sped north up the M6, weaving through the morning traffic. 'So you don't need the data disc?' he asked. 'The samples will suffice?'

'Of course.' Fran held up the Solstice tub. 'We can produce the cream and droplets as soon as we find a chemist with lab equipment.'

'Excellent.' Killing the lights, Strand lowered the black glass and smiled at the pink blush of dawn on the eastern snow clouds. 'A beautiful morning.' He sucked in the crisp rush of air. 'The best I've seen in centuries. All things considered, it didn't turn out too badly, did it?'

'Silva is still alive,' said Fran. 'We might have been better leaving the country than heading to your Scottish place.'

'Why? The Committee and his security team are all dead and his fortress will be rubble by now. With the Solstice, we can take over and reshape the Elite.'

'I now know never to underestimate him.' She heard the siren behind and turned to see blue lights. 'How fast are we travelling?'

Chuckling, Strand pulled onto the shoulder at the Kendal turn-off. By the time the police car had stopped and the two officers had marched to the Lamborghini, he was leaning on the bonnet lighting a cigarette. 'Is there a problem?' he asked.

'Problem?' snarled the Sergeant. 'Do you have any idea how fast you were going?'

'Yes.' Strand stared at them both. 'A hundred-and-twenty. I wasn't speeding.'

'No.' The Constable's eyes glazed. 'No, you weren't.'

'I don't know why we... ' The Sergeant blinked. 'For some reason we thought...'

'You're wasting our time,' said Strand. 'We're in a hurry.'

'They need a lesson,' said Fran, climbing out. She kissed the Constable's cheek, took his cap and set it on her head. 'How about driving the wrong way along the carriageway and ramming into the first truck they meet after reaching eighty?'

'Why not?' Strand tapped his cigarette ash on the Sergeant's tunic. 'Return to your car and...' The words ended as his outstretched hand took on the scarlet appearance of tandoori chicken. Turning incredulously, he peered at the clouds where the morning sun had begun to burn through. 'What the hell...' His eyes widened in terror as smoking fingers agonisingly shrivelled. 'No. How can...'

'The sunblock isn't working.' Fran dived back into the Lamborghini, hissing as solar rays blistered her face. Blackened flesh fell sizzling from her jaw. 'Get inside behind the glass.'

Scrabbling for the door handle with the dripping mess that had been a hand, Strand collapsed whining into the seat, face liquefying and eyes bursting to spill down bubbling cheeks. His feline screech jolted the police from their trance. The Sergeant grabbed the door to prevent it closing and sunlight flooded the car interior. The driver melted to a thick sludge, and beside him, impossibly, a huge black cat writhed and screeched as it too dissolved.

The Constable had just recovered from one form of mesmerism, but this was another. He was unable to wrench his eyes from the nightmare, not even to glance at his shoes, as his superior covered them in a gush of half-digested breakfast.

* * * *

The Saab raced up the M6 shoulder to the front of the tailback and drew up behind a line of police cars. Katie Bradstreet and Tariq Aslam jumped out and were met by a uniformed Inspector.

'I'm told you have two bodies?' snapped Katie. 'One is a Doctor Francesca Stapleton?'

'According to the lads who stopped the car, there were two.' The ashen officer pointed to a large tent and handed over a woman's bag. 'We er, think it's two bodies.'

'You *think*? Is the car burnt?'

'You'd better take a look.'

'Yes, this is Stapleton's.' Aslam searched the bag as he

followed his superior. 'The credit cards and other identification belong to her.'

Lifting the flap of the shelter, Katie walked around the Lamborghini to the open door and pulled on latex gloves. Crimson ash covered the leather and filled the footwells. A blue silk suit lay mixed with the dust on the driver's seat, and lifting the jacket arm, she gulped as a Cartier watch and more ash gushed from the cuff. The woman turned vacantly to her Sergeant.

'Just like Lisa Mirren and Carl Dreyer,' whispered Aslam.

Gingerly searching, Katie found a wallet. 'Matthew Strand,' she read. 'Who's that?' She lifted a plastic tub from the coat pocket, and gently blew red dust from the label.

SOLSTICE - BATCH 0043

Katie turned from the powdered corpses and leant against the car, dazed. Clichés have always littered police dialogue: the D.A's been on my back all morning. It's all there; count it. He knows too much. I asked you all here because I'm ready to name the killer. Although unaware, the bewildered woman muttered one of the top twenty.

'Fuck me, Tariq,' said Katie. 'How do I put *this* in my report?'

* * * *

329

Chapter 73

'When exactly?' Speaking softly, Amy leant across the pub table, although it was unlikely that anyone would overhear. *I Believe In Father Christmas* tinkled from the inn speakers, mingling with the boisterous chatter of Sunday lunchtime clientele. 'When did you swap Stapleton's sunblock for the normal cream you bought at the chemist?'

'When I broke into the Sunnyvale clinic and found her bag,' said Quist. 'I just had time to quickly change the label before they caught me. I ducked behind a couch and hid her prototype tub underneath before they searched me.'

Quist and Watson sat opposite Rex and Amy in the King's Arms. An attractive building of timber and stone, the powdering of snow transformed the York riverside tavern into a chocolate box scene. All four were exhausted after a night spent scouring and bleaching the detective's cottage. Constable Gregson's body now lay in Stapleton's Bishopthorpe house, along with the other incriminating evidence. A semi-credible story had also been agreed upon for the authorities that didn't involve the supernatural.

Watson slurped his lager. 'So Strand and Stapleton are dead, but Silva's still alive.' He turned to Rex. 'Speaking of being alive, *you're* very quiet.'

'I still can't believe it.' Rex massaged his tired eyes. 'I had no say in the matter. You just did it.'

'You were in no state to say *anything*,' said Quist.

'You'd be dead, if not for Bernard,' pointed out Amy. 'I know his snakebite antidote was rather extreme, but...'

'He turned me into a monster.' Rex glanced about irately, ensuring no one was listening. 'Some creature from a late-night movie.'

'Is that such a bad thing?' Watson shook his head, bemused. 'You don't think it's kind of cool?'

Rex hit him with the sort of look Saint Peter would have

received at the Pearly Gates, had he asked: *Yes, Mister Kennedy, but apart from that, how did you enjoy your Dallas trip*? 'I've been turned into some paranormal Rottweiler.' His eyes widened at a sudden realisation. 'Some overgrown, supernatural dog and my name's *Rex*.'

'Well, how about that?' said Watson. 'Strand was going to turn you into a supernatural cat and the boss turned you into a supernatural dog.'

Quist's mouth curled into a lopsided grin. 'The police station is on Fulford Road. One more drink and then I suggest we get it over with. Everything should be fine provided we stick to the agreed stories.'

'We'll be interviewed for hours,' said Amy. 'Especially you, Rex, after you took Stapleton to Sedgefield and she killed that woman.'

Rex had decided to play stupid and claim he'd no idea who Fran was. At the time of Tania's murder in the Grange, this was true. Quist guessed that, after meeting him, the police would have little problem believing the *stupid* part. The detective stared thoughtfully, once again wondering if he'd done the right thing.

'Ah, speaking of dogs, watch this,' said Quist, gesturing to a spaniel that strolled across the stone-flagged floor. Homing in on the smell of Watson's crisps, it bolted as a different scent took over. 'You'll find animals are terrified of you, Rex, apart from the nastier types who are often quite friendly. Selden's Rottweiler, for instance. I imagine they see us as kindred spirits.'

'Lovely!' snarled Rex.

'Lycanthropy,' said Amy. 'Werewolves and Ubasteri. I'm still trying to get my scientific mind around shapeshifting, but I think I've finally come to terms with it.'

'*I* bloody well haven't,' said Rex. 'I tried changing in your bathroom mirror last night and scared myself to death.'

Watson smirked. 'I thought nothing scared SAS heroes.'

Rex pulled a face. 'I've already apologised for those lies.'

Amy squeezed his hand. 'Lies or not,' she said, 'you were

wonderful when you swung in to rescue me. As far as I'm concerned, you're a *real* hero, and you wouldn't believe how much better you look without sunglasses indoors.'

'My psychic aunt couldn't believe it when I rang this morning,' muttered Rex. 'She's been having premonitions about me and she saw a pentagram appear on my hand. She claims it signifies a werewolf victim and she was convinced I'd be killed by one last night. Marika can't understand why I'm still alive.'

'Er, that's because you *aren't*.' Quist smiled sheepishly. 'Technically, you *did* die.'

'*What*?'

'You're different now; a supernatural creature and no longer actually human.'

'You're joking?' whispered Rex. '*Aren't* you?'

'Whooo!' Watson sniggered. 'Cursed.'

'Curse or gift,' said Quist. 'It's up to you, Rex. There was no time for deliberation, but I wouldn't have bitten you, if I thought you'd be dangerous.' The detective covered his unease with a smile. *Such things were impossible to predict and he'd certainly been wrong about Larry.*

Amy clasped Rex's arm. 'But look how you recovered and how quickly your bones healed. You also said this morning how stronger and faster you felt.'

'And you won't age,' added Watson. 'What about that Marines course you told us about? You won't be too old to re-apply next year. If you balls it up again, you can take it the year after, and the year after that.'

'The SAS fantasy is over.' Rex sighed. 'I rang my father this morning and I start with Grant Homes in January. How the hell do I work that with this?'

'You adapt,' said Quist. 'As I had to.'

'It's okay for you,' said Rex. 'With no photos and records. No one notices when a friendless nobody vanishes every few years. I'm the heir to Grant's and my picture is always in the gossip columns.'

'You'd be the dead heir,' snapped Amy. 'It may be difficult, but you survived.' She turned back to Quist. 'You managed, didn't you? Adapting old birth certificates, changing names and moving around. I take it you never married?'

Quist shook his head.

Watson laughed. 'I've heard how women carry on when they discover their hubby's a secret cross-dresser. Imagine what they'd be like to find he was a wolf.'

Amy ran an eye over Rex. 'Modern women have modern outlooks. I'm with Watson on this; I think it's kind of cool.' She smiled sexily. 'A little exciting.'

'Definitely cool,' said Watson. 'Centuries ago, they'd have burnt you at the stake. These days, you'd probably become a TV celebrity.'

'Yeah, yeah.' Rex grimaced. 'You say I can't eat meat?'

'Any animal product,' corrected Quist. 'Yoga meditation keeps the dark side in check too. Don't worry. I'll give you a few lessons.'

'Whoopee! I'll try to find a window in my diary.'

'Dark side?' Grinning, Watson stood up and headed for the bar. 'Hey, Obi Wan, let's drink to future investigations not being as hairy as the last one, eh?'

'I can't guarantee it,' said Quist. 'Come along. I'll give you a hand with the drinks.'

'*Hairy.*' Watson chuckled. 'Did you see what I did there? I should be on stage with stuff like that.'

Rex watched as they vanished into the crowd. 'Were you serious?' he asked. 'Do you really think it's, er, exciting?'

Amy nodded. 'As a scientist, I certainly find it astounding and fascinating.' She blushed slightly. 'Yes, exciting too.'

'Providing the police don't lock me up, I've decided to spend Christmas at Sedgefield and I thought we might see more of each other. I need to talk to someone about this. How do you feel about dinner?'

'Dinner would be wonderful, Rex.'

'Great!' He cheered up at last. 'I know this romantic restaurant where...'

'Just one thing. If this should lead to, er... How shall I put this? How passionate are you during sex?'

'I'm sorry?' said Rex.

Amy took a deep breath. 'Do you bite?'

* * * *

Most people would find Trudeau's expensive, but not the regular clientele of stockbrokers, bankers and celebrities. Lucius Silva sat in the London restaurant eyeing one particular celebrity with open interest this Christmas Eve lunchtime. She sat two tables away with Jake Lyle of Wash-Day Sinners, the music world flavour-of-the-month. Despite being illiterate and looking like any other anorexic teenager, Flaxen Taylor was paid obscene amounts to remain extremely thin and walk in straight lines wearing silly clothes.

The supermodel felt his stare and grew confused. Her street education told her to squawk 'fack off!', but he looked rich, certainly richer than Jake and by next month no one would have heard of Wash-Day Sinners. What was a girl to do?

Silva had a covert London address near here, and on the occasions he indulged himself with human food, it was normally in establishments like this. He'd never dined during daylight hours before. The ancient cat creature turned from the girl to the papers on the table and gazed at the data again. Persuading a chemist to work on the samples and Stapleton's disc had been simple. Before he died, the gentleman had kindly laboured through the night to supply a batch of Solstice and these formula notes. Silva held his hand in the window sunlight, laughed quietly and snapped his fingers.

'This claret is delectable,' he said, as a waiter appeared by his side. 'Pour me another glass.'

'Of course, Sir.' *At a grand a bottle, it ought to be.* The waiter couldn't say why, but something about this customer made him want to be elsewhere, preferably another city. 'Chateau Lafite 45. I must compliment you on your choice of wines, Sir. You're clearly celebrating Christmas in style.'

'Celebrating?' He smiled thinly. 'Yes, I suppose I am. This is the first sunny day I've enjoyed in a very long time.'

'I hope you enjoy many more, Sir,' lied the waiter, anxious to be away.

'Thank you. I'm sure I will.' Silva peered at the model's throat. 'Yes, I'll drink to that.'

End

Also from MX Publishing

MX Publishing is the world's largest specialist Sherlock Holmes publisher, with over a hundred titles and fifty authors creating the latest in Sherlock Holmes fiction and non-fiction.

From traditional short stories and novels to travel guides and quiz books, MX Publishing cater for all Holmes fans.

In addition to Tim Symonds' novels, the collection includes leading titles such as *Benedict Cumberbatch In Transition* and *The Norwood Author* which won the 2011 Howlett Award (Sherlock Holmes Book of the Year).

MX Publishing also has one of the largest communities of Holmes fans on Facebook with regular contributions from dozens of authors.

'Sherlock Holmes and The Adventure of The Grinning Cat'
'Sherlock Holmes and The Nautilus Adventure'
'Sherlock Holmes and The Round Table Adventure'

"Joseph Svec is brilliant in entwining two endearing and enduring classics of literature, blending the factual with the fantastical; the playful with the pensive; and the mischievous with the mysterious. We shall, all of us young and old, benefit with a cup of tea, a tranquil afternoon, and a copy of 'Sherlock Holmes, The Adventure of the Grinning Cat'."
Amador County Holmes Hounds Sherlockian Society

www.mxpublishing.com

'The Final Page of Baker Street'
'The Baron of Brede Place'
'Seventeen Minutes To Baker Street'

"The really amazing thing about this book is the author's ability to call up the 'essence' of both the Baker Street 'digs' of Holmes and Watson as well as that of the 'mean streets' of Marlowe's Los Angeles. Although none of the action takes place in either place, Holmes and Watson share a sense of camaraderie and self-confidence in facing threats and problems that also pervades many of the later tales in the Canon. Following their conversations and banter is a return to Edwardian England and its certainties and hope for the future. This is definitely the world before The Great War."
Philip K Jones

www.mxpublishing.com

The Detective and The Woman Series

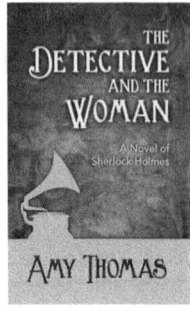  

'The Detective and The Woman'
'The Detective, The Woman and The Winking Tree'
'The Detective, The Woman and The Silent Hive'

"The book is entertaining, puzzling and a lot of fun. I believe the author has hit on the only type of long-term relationship possible for Sherlock Holmes and Irene Adler. The details of the narrative only add force to the romantic defects we expect in both of them and their growth and development are truly marvellous to watch. This is not a love story. Instead, it is a coming-of-age tale starring two of our favourite characters."
Philip K Jones

www.mxpublishing.com

Also from MX Publishing

Our bestselling books are our short story collections;

'Lost Stories of Sherlock Holmes' , 'The Outstanding Mysteries of Sherlock Holmes', The Papers of Sherlock Holmes Volume 1 and 2, 'Untold Adventures of Sherlock Holmes' (and the sequel 'Studies in Legacy) and 'Sherlock Holmes in Pursuit', 'The Cotswold Werewolf and Other Stories of Sherlock Holmes' – and many more……

Also from MX Publishing

"Phil Growick's, 'The Secret Journal of Dr Watson', is an adventure which takes place in the latter part of Holmes and Watson's lives. They are entrusted by HM Government (although not officially) and the King no less to undertake a rescue mission to save the Romanovs, Russia's Royal family from a grisly end at the hand of the Bolsheviks. There is a wealth of detail in the story but not so much as would detract us from the enjoyment of the story. Espionage, counter-espionage, the ace of spies himself, double-agents, double-crossers...all these flit across the pages in a realistic and exciting way. All the characters are extremely well-drawn and Mr Growick, most importantly, does not falter with a very good ear for Holmesian dialogue indeed. Highly recommended. A five-star effort."
The Baker Street Society

www.mxpublishing.com

Also from MX Publishing

The Sherlock Holmes and Enoch Hale Series

The Amateur Executioner
The Poisoned Penman
The Egyptian Curse

"The Amateur Executioner: Enoch Hale Meets Sherlock Holmes", the first collaboration between Dan Andriacco and Kieran McMullen, concerns the possibility of a Fenian attack in London. Hale, a native Bostonian, is a reporter for London's Central News Syndicate - where, in 1920, Horace Harker is still a familiar figure, though far from revered. "The Amateur Executioner" takes us into an ambiguous and murky world where right and wrong aren't always distinguishable. I look forward to reading more about Enoch Hale."
Sherlock Holmes Society of London

www.mxpublishing.com

www.ingramcontent.com/pod-product-compliance
Lightning Source LLC
Chambersburg PA
CBHW072318020726
47501CB00002B/558